THE MASON KEY

Volume One

Also by David Folz

The Mason Key II—Aloft and Alow
The Mason Key III—The Return

The Mason Key
Volume One

A Novel

DAVID FOLZ

Lively House Publishing
Depoe Bay, Oregon

Copyright © 2007, 2012, 2018 by David Folz

All rights reserved. No part of this book may be used or reproduced in any manner whatsoever without written permission except in the case of brief quotations embodied in critical articles or reviews.

Folz, David.
The Mason Key—Volume One: A John Mason Adventure

ISBN: 978-1-4243-4050-7

1. Mason, John (Fictitious Character) Fiction. 2. Great Britain—History. 3. 18th Century—Fiction.

The Mason Key—Volume One is published by:
Lively House Publishing
Depoe Bay, Oregon

For information please direct emails to:
david@dfolz.com or visit our website:
www.themasonkey.com

Cover design: Teri Rider
Cover art based on an engraving from *Illustrated Home Book of The World's Great Nations*, People's Publishing Company, Chicago, IL, 1888.
Book design: Teri Rider

New Edition: 2018
First Edition: June 2007
Author's limited edition re-released, 2012
Previously published by A Word with You Press, 2012
Printed in the United States of America

10 9 8 7 6 5 4 3 2 1   18 19 20 21 22 23 24 25 26 27

Acknowledgments

First and foremost, I want to thank my soulmate, best friend, and wife, Kathleen Craig without whose astute editing observations this work would be sadly lacking. Next, I give thanks to my sister-in-law, Robin Craig for her insight into the Masonic/Templar connection, as well as allowing me use of her library of related material, my sister Paulette Hartding who painstakingly poured over every syllable in a valiant effort to root out typographical errors, my sister-in-law Ronda Hipshman for bringing forth several points to be examined and lastly, my sister Nordeka English whose editing skills were invaluable in making this work complete.

*"The lips of wisdom are closed, except
to the ears of Understanding."*

The Kybalion

PART ONE
THE HERITAGE

FOREWORD

To the person who happens upon these pages, be forewarned. These stories encompass events of my life and, in doing so, divulge secrets that have been guarded through the ages by the followers of Hermes Trismegistus, the great sage of old Egypt.

The knowledge of which I write has been woven into my life after being passed from the Knights Templar to my father, John Elkins, Grand Master of London's Old Dundee Masonic Lodge and, finally, to me.

— John Mason, Keeper of the Key

CHAPTER ONE

The following took place at the Old Bailey Courthouse, London, England on the 27th day of May in the year 1778 when I was but fourteen years of age.

Like an insect under a microscope, I stood beneath a large suspended mirror so that the sunlight would be reflected into my face. Whilst I wrung the pungent vinegar from my ragged shirttails, a concoction devised to prevent the spread of gaol fever, the magistrate sniffed his nosegay and eyed me for the more obvious symptoms of livid pustules, purple spots, or twitching.

The magistrate's oversized eyes, made even more so by his thick spectacles, glanced up from the pages before him to make contact with the jury. After a deep draw from the nosegay, he said, "As the defendant refuses to divulge his full name, this court has no recourse other than to refer to him as Robert the Thief."

His pale, wrinkled claw of a hand protruded from the sleeve of the black silken robe and clutched the gavel as he continued, "Robert the Thief, this court, having found you guilty of the felony of housebreaking along with the theft of private property whose value has been found to be in excess of £500..." Cutting his proclamation short, he paused to take another breath through the nosegay while layers of powdered curls rose and fell about his shoulders as he craned his neck to read the document before him.

He rose up from his great black leather chair and leaned over the desk to peer down at me while raising his voice to such a level as to reverberate off the stone walls of the courtroom, "and your stubborn refusal to divulge the location of the items remaining at large and the identity of your accomplices, this court has no recourse but to sentence you to the maximum punishable by law. Therefore, it is hereby ordered that you be taken to Tiburn Tree where you will be hanged by your neck until you are dead. The date of your execution is set for Sunday noon, nine days hence."

The gavel slammed down, emitting a sound not unlike the closing of the iron door to my prison cell. His eyes were hooded as they looked away with disgust and I was forgotten within the space of time it took his puppet's mouth to drop open and exhale, "Next case!"

My shackles dug into my wrists and ankles from the strain as the pug-nosed turnkey pulled me from the courtroom. Forced to walk ape-like due to my heavy iron constraints, I was taken in tow back down the passageway to the cold stone prison. After the doors of the Old Bailey had closed behind me, silencing the hoots and laughter from the courtroom, the magistrate's words were still echoing in my ears, "Hanged by your neck until you are dead." The jury had been an eerie lot, sitting in their chairs with the expectant leer of vultures, hardly able to restrain themselves in anticipation of the next carcass to pick over. It seemed there was no one among them who didn't thirst for blood. I was only a thief. I had never harmed anyone, yet there was not a sympathetic face among the lot.

The air tasted fresh and I took it in greedily, for I knew it wouldn't be long before the heavy ironclad door would open and I would be forced to breathe the filthy age-old stench of the prison. Reflecting on my sentence, I took consolation in the fact that I now had a set date. I must endure this hellhole for little more than one week. With a sigh, I told myself that this hell was, at last, nearly at end. The day will soon come when I shall be breathing fresh air all the way across town to Tiburn Tree. And I will be passing my old manor for one last time, as few as three streets from my home on Green Street.

Tiburn Tree. I had seen many a man, woman, and child carted down Oxford Road on their way to that dreadful place. I oft' times wondered why they called it a tree, for it resembles nothing of the like. An odd piece of construction, the gallows consisted of three vertical posts forming a triangle. The posts are connected to one another at the top by cross beams for supporting the nooses, while the structure stands high enough to allow the cart with its condemned to pass beneath. It would be from the cart that I should make my final statement.

I had no idea what to say. What can be said to an audience of onlookers who are simply there for sake of entertainment? Should I care what a crowd of sods are thinking as they sit expectantly in their rows of elevated wooden seats, their so-called Marble Arch? Then there would be those looking on from their carriages, as well as those who mill about the cart at a convenient distance to either throw rotten fruit and vegetables, or to applaud, depending on my popularity. I was sure they would be expecting a lengthy air-dance; however, I did hope to disappoint.

Though I was never allowed to watch these events, for my father forbade it, I had been told of them in intricate detail by my friend, Pike. Pike had described the hanging of his own father down to the eye-popping, turnip-faced, tongue bulging, twitching and jerking that went on for minutes before he finally succumbed. Pike said the only escape from the slow strangulation was to give the executioner two shillings to pull on your legs so that the noose could tighten sufficiently to cut off all blood flow to the brain. Or, if you were really fortunate, the pull might snap your neck, making the whole affair quick and painless. Perhaps, he might do the same for me if only I had the two shillings. If only I hadn't given all my meager funds to the turnkeys and prisoners as garnishment for the privilege of keeping my clothes. Now my only option was to perform a Turpin; that is, jump high into the air past the end of the cart in the hope that when I reach the end of my rope, the force will snap my neck. The performance is named after the famous highwayman Dick Turpin who had escaped prison on several occasions only to be recaptured and, ultimately, hanged at Tiburn. He surprised his audience by making the leap, cheating the executioner of his two shillings and the mob of witnessing a cruel and painfully slow death. Perhaps I should have thanked my father for forbidding me to be present at executions, for had he not done so, I might find it even more difficult to be the one at centre stage.

Envisioning myself standing on the cart before the crowd, it occurred that I might have a view of the elm trees In Hyde Park, as they are just across the road from the gallows. I believed it would give me great comfort to be in sight of the very trees that hold such fond memories. How I loved climbing those trees.

After the last iron gate clanged shut behind me, I stood in my prison cell with its slimy black walls filled with men and boys who, like me, were too poor to pay for better lodging and decent food. It was one of three sections of the prison, this being called the men's Common Ward. Though difficult to imagine, I have heard that the women's side of the Common Ward is even worse than this stink pit. Our only break from this eight-by-twelve foot room is during the four hours we are let out into an open courtyard which, though lined with cold stone floor and walls, is just as filthy as this cell. The air is thick with the stench of filth, vomit, rancid body odor, and molding rags that had once passed for clothing. My manacles consisted of three sets of heavy iron ankle and wrist shackles, two of which had been removed for my trial but quickly reinstalled upon my return to the prison.

Three sets of iron is my punishment for having no money with which to pay the turnkeys in order to reduce them to the minimum requirement of one set. The only advantage was that I had become so thin that they now fit loosely enough to slide off. This enabled me to discard them as soon as the turnkey left my cell, as well as slide them quickly back on the instant I heard the telltale jingling of his keys down the corridor.

If it weren't for Pike and Laura, I should have starved by now. Though they couldn't visit me without risking arrest, they did send money by way of a messenger. To be sure, their intentions were heartfelt, yet the relief they had in mind had been reduced to a mere pittance by the time it made its way to those in charge of supplying my food. I suspect the messenger took a hefty share, only leaving me enough to stay alive. Not that I mean in any way to discount their intentions, but I felt I might have been in better stead had I starved to death a month past. As it was, nine more days could not pass quickly enough.

Lying in the dim light that filtered down from two barred windows high on the wall, I felt the unforgiving wooden planks press against my fleshless bones. Our sleeping accommodations were no more than a wooden platform standing six inches above the blackened stone floor while our privy was a long wooden trough at the foot of the platform. The privy was an ever-present fixture in our nostrils which, no doubt, was cause for my repeated dreams of swimming through rivers of filth.

I have spent a great deal of time reflecting upon how my short life of only fourteen years had come to this wretched state. No doubt, it was a sad way of passing the time, yet reflecting was the only thing remaining for one to do while in this miserable hole. There were few, if any, distractions to take one's mind from his predicament as we were daily subjected to the pounding and wailing of a man gone mad who, two cells down, reminded everyone that we were all going to die.

Then there was Rodger, three doors in the other direction, whose whimpering could be heard throughout the night while he periodically cried out from dreams that rats were eating his penis. Though I don't doubt the possibility of it, for rats were here in great supply, his penis would have had to have grown back each night in order for it to be eaten again.

We were fortunate, however, for Tom McVane who, at the far end of the narrow corridor, sang Irish lullabies throughout the day or night until someone in his room would shut him up. Of his singing I never tired, for it provided a pleasant background for the stories we would tell of our lives. These stories were our only escape from this miserable existence and I owe McVane many thanks for the comfort of his haunting voice which helped the days pass into weeks.

Sometimes the monotony was broken by the occasional carrying away of someone who had succumbed to gaol fever. I had not thought it possible to smell something more foul than the air in this prison but was proven wrong when the first victim of the fever was brought past our cell. We called it the 'dead breath,' for the body exhaled an air so horrible that it cut through one's nasal passages and entered his stomach, causing it to retch. Most would turn away and bury their faces in their clothes for a good hour after the dead person had been taken out so as to avoid the nausea.

It was not unusual for the death sentence to arrive well ahead of the condemned, courtesy of the turnkeys. The customary hour of silence being observed by the other prisoners as a form of courtesy gave me no solace whatsoever. In fact, it had the opposite effect, for I welcomed any distraction that might serve to take my thoughts from the rope that was soon to be tightening around my neck.

I heard the shuffle of my friend Peter's padded feet. When excited, he could make a good deal of noise due to his being a rat of exceptional size. He often did this when waiting for the turnkey to bring my gruel. He knew that as soon as the dirty wooden bowl slid beneath the rusted iron plate of the door, I would give him his share, just as I had every day of my imprisonment. This daily sustenance gave him his great size and strength while my reduced portion had withered me to a mere skeleton of my former self.

The loss of weight was a price I couldn't afford to pay, for it was an unspoken arrangement agreed upon by the two of us, an agreement that allowed me to lie in the huddled mass while he stood watch and, when necessary, do battle with the other rats who wished to sink their hungry teeth into my sleeping flesh.

The iron plate slid up and the bowl of gruel slid in. Scooping up the bowl, I found the gruel in its usual tepid state and downed the sludge while holding my nose to deaden the noxious taste. Peter jumped and squealed and when, with a nibble at my breeches, he threatened to sink his teeth into me, I set the bowl back onto the floor. I could hear the bowl tip as he sank his snout into its contents to slurp up the remaining lumps of the tart liquid.

As I sat in the corner staring blindly into the cold, musty darkness, I could hear the steady drip of condensation from the thick floor planking above my head as it fell into an unseen puddle near the rust-encrusted iron door of my cell. Strange as it may seem, that sound gave me one of the few comforts I enjoyed in this hole, for if I focused on it long enough, I would soon be brought in mind of the patter of rain as it fell from the copper roof panels above the second floor window of my home in London's West End.

My bedchamber was adequately furnished with bed, night stand, and a small desk and roundabout chair which sat next to the window. The window faced the street, making my room the grandest place to live. There was always something going on that afforded me hours of entertainment while I sat unobserved above it all. On evenings after supper, Father would be in the parlor with Mother and my little sister, Lilly, resting in his high-backed leather chair, puffing on his ivory-stemmed pipe and reading the Gentleman's Magazine. I, however, preferred the privacy of my room where I could read Smollett or DeFoe by candlelight or watch the passing traffic on the street below.

Horses trotted by, pulling their passenger coaches or loaded wagons on their way to unknown destinations while neighbors conversed or argued over the latest news of those ungrateful American colonists. Musicians and street vendors would go from door to window while the iron wheel rims of the wagons and coaches grated on the flat granite stones of the street. Upon the whole, the noise was most irksome to the other residents while quite pleasant to me.

One might think that my parents would have taken that room for their own but they preferred quiet and chose to have their bedchamber at the rear of the house.

"It is both quiet and peaceful," my father would say, "and I should appreciate it if you and your sister were to stay out. It is the one place that Mother and I may have our privacy."

My memory of their room is quite limited due to the few times I had ever been allowed into it, one being the day of my sister's birth. Another time was one of which I have no memory at all as it was the day that I was born. Mother oft' times told me that while she gave birth to me, the rain beat so hard upon the roof that she felt as though we were beneath a thousand drums. She said that the storm had been so powerful that Father was out all the next morning repairing the shutters, all but two having been torn from the house. She often smiled as she reminisced telling me that the wind howled so that the midwife couldn't hear my cries, resulting in my receiving two extra smacks upon my bottom. That was on the tenth of October in the year 1763.

My early childhood was composed of a combination of both chores and school, with the exception of a few other activities such as Sunday picnics in the park or playing with my sister in the backyard. And there was the occasional running about in the streets with other children, which I generally experienced at a time when I was supposed to be doing my chores.

As I saw it, the other children were the fortunate ones, for most of them didn't have to go to school, thereby affording them time to complete their chores during the day.

Unlike them, however, my work began early. Before I went off to school each morning, my first chore was to sweep the night's rubbish from the street in front of the house and dump it into a large barrel in the passageway next to the stoop. After mother's inspection of my work, I was allowed in for a hearty breakfast and, once it was consumed, I set off on a lengthy fast-paced walk to arrive at the day school by 9 o'clock. The remainder of my chores would be waiting for me upon my return, which was close upon half six o'clock. It was at that time that the other children on my street would be in the midst of having their fun and, upon seeing me, would attempt to coerce me into joining them. The daily temptation of fun was only increased by the certain knowledge that my chores would commence the second I stepped through our front door.

On one of those days, I was returning home from school and I remember the warm glow of the sun which brought out the brilliant indigo of my new calico shirt. I had just turned the corner onto my street and was dutifully headed towards home, which was situated midway between the streets of Norfolk and Park. There was an open field between two houses that the children used for playing football. A game of heavy combat was well underway as a goal had just been scored by the largest of them.

Amidst the discussion of who was to give the initial toss, one of the boys, whose name was Butch, sauntered over to me and handed me the ball.

"Let Bobby have a go." A few faces of protest turned toward me but were quickly turned away when Butch clenched his fists and stared them down.

"I says it's Bobby's turn!" Butch was the oldest and largest boy in the manor and, if so disposed, could beat any of the other boys on our street to a bloody pulp. There was no doubt amongst anyone that he held the title of manor bully, yet he was my friend. He had started out quite young instilling fear of the bloody nose into all the other children including some much his senior. It was not much later that he could find no challenger to oppose his title, that is, until he locked horns with me. Although I could not beat him, I would get in a good punch that had enough force to bloody his nose or, perhaps, fatten his lip before he had me down. This process repeated each time he challenged me and I never failed to accept. Though I would end up the worse for it, bloody nose and lip, bruised ribs and stomach, it was due to my perseverance that he finally tired of beating me. And I want to think that the bloody nose and lip he received from me had something to do with his reluctance to continue, for he could never manage to beat me without paying a price.

I'll never forget that glorious day when I held my ground after he had chased the others away with threats of, "Who's gonna be the next one to get it," before approaching me with clenched fists. We stared each other down for two full minutes, our eyes fixed with unblinking determination. I had prepared myself for another pounding, my fist ready to go for the bridge of his wide nose the second he shifted his weight. I was caught completely off guard when he relaxed his fingers, arched his brows and offered his hand saying, "Bugger if I ain't getting tired of givin' you beatins', Bobby. Suppose we may as well be mates, then. What d'ya say?"

And now the great and powerful Butch stood before me with outstretched hand offering me the ball. How could I refuse such privilege? Within a second, I had the ball singing over the heads of the opposing team and into Butch's awaiting hands. He then took three steps and tripped over one of our smaller teammates. The ball tore from his grip, struck Jimmy, one of members of our team, in the back, and arced high in the direction of the goal marker. Leaping upward, I struck with a downward stroke sending it bouncing off the head of one of the boys from the other team before shooting past the goal guard. Having scored a point within the first few seconds was sheer luck on my part but I was now fully committed.

There was no way I could leave the game. It was when we were in full struggle with my shirt torn, the knees of my trousers black from mud, and my elbows bloody that two hours had passed and Mother's call made the screams and laughter of the street shrink into nothingness. I had had a great deal of pleasure and knew for certain that I was in for an even greater deal of pain. Once inside the door, Mother said nothing, but only pointed to the back door and I went directly to my chores.

Our backyard was covered by intricate patterns of paving stones in the shape of triangles, the result of my father's hard work and professional pride. Before the stones were set in place, Father had painstakingly dug a cistern to a depth of twenty feet and finished the bottom and sides with stone and mortar. The cistern was covered by a heavy copper plate above which sat a table with a pump attached. Above the table stood a copper circular structure with a pitched copper roof that captured rain while channeling it via a gutter that dropped through a pipe to the cistern below. If the water was high, we used it not only for drinking but for cooking and washing. If it was low, however, we used it only for drinking. Most people did not have this innovation and, for their water, had to rely upon the water furnished through a copper pipe that tapped into the River Thames upstream of the city and, after sitting in the Chelsea Reservoir in Hyde Park, channeled through a series of wooden pipes and valves that ran under the streets of Grosvenor District. Twice each week, the water flowed and each home could access it by turning a valve which dispensed the water into a copper tank in their cellar. Though the water from the water works reservoir was not polluted as badly as the water in East London, Father thought his toil well spent each time we drank from our cistern, as we were of the precious few who drank water. Most, if not all, would drink only ale.

I was busy sweeping around the covering to the cistern when I heard the unmistakable slamming of the front door. Father was home from work and it wouldn't be long now. I kept sweeping. Minutes passed with only the sound of my broom scraping on the stones. I was in the process of scooping up the accumulated dirt with the dust pan when, "ROBERT!"

"Yes, Father." I heard the unmistakable sound of leather smacking the palm of his calloused hand.

"Inside, boy!"

Here it comes, I thought; pain, much pain.

"Do you think I pay for your schooling because I like to work extra hours each day?"

SMACK, went the razor strop. The sting sent fire across my buttocks and down my leg.

"My friends don't have to go to school. Why must I?"

"Your friends will grow up with no education and you wish to do the same, do you? No, you will learn a thing or two just as I am teaching you now!" The strop came down with a sharp rendering SMACK and I could feel my skin hot and beginning to swell as the pain spread and burned deeper. Before it was over, I experienced a degree of pain well beyond what I thought I could stand. After which, I did much standing and lying on my stomach where Mother took pity and applied a poultice to the affected area. This never failed to bring about a welcome relief.

Mother always cared for me after a turn with the razor strop and I wondered that if she felt so bad for me, why then couldn't she simply not tell Father that I had misbehaved? I would not have been punished and she would not have to see to my blistered arse. Upon reflection, even though the pain of the strop was severe, the memories of the fun I had had that day in the street with my friends was worth every stroke. And in spite of the occasional punishment I received, I must maintain that the Elkins household was, for the most part, a happy one.

My mother, with her golden hair cascading to her waist was, in addition to being the handsomest woman my father attested to having ever set eyes upon, was incredibly strong, for I had known her to lift great bundles of tallow without a strain. When in public, she always carried herself with pride, her shoulders held back, her chin pointing out the way with purpose. Never afraid of hard work, she exuded the will and strength of her German heritage, yet embodied all the tender warmth and love a child could hope for.

My father stood a powerfully built six feet-two inches with straight black hair tied back to the top of his collar. He received other men with both a tight-lipped smile and a crushing handshake generally testified to by the groan uttered from those subjected to it. Father was a hardworking man who supported the family by putting in eleven hours a day, six days a week as a bricklayer. He didn't make a great deal of money, yet it was sufficient to pay for our food and clothing and to send me to school.

My mother earned additional income by making candles during the day and selling them to my aunt and uncle who leased a shop in Covent Garden Market.

When I wasn't in school, I would often be found in the cellar helping Mother with the making of those candles.

My sister, Lilly, of four years carried a mane of golden hair. Both her hair and marine-blue eyes conspired to make her a miniature copy of Mother. Although still quite small, she would do her best to help with the few chores Mother would allow. That is to say, chores that would keep her from close proximity to the fires or hot wax. Although the making of candles was physically difficult, it was also tedious in that it required exact timing and with Lilly underfoot, Mother and I worked even harder to prevent her from injury. And there was the heavy odor of melted tallow wafting from the pots hanging in the kitchen fireplace that gave us all headaches and nausea if we didn't take periodic breathers in the backyard. To be sure, candle making required a great deal of the day yet there were many other chores to be done within that time.

It was escape from work, however, that most occupied my thoughts. And my imagination bore fruit on occasion where I found ways in which to sneak out to play with the other children of the manor. In order to accomplish this, I would ask to play in the backyard with my little sister. We would start out by playing with her dolls but soon I would have her proving to me how high she could jump and, when she had thoroughly convinced me of it, I would then wish to know how fast she could run in circles. After perhaps half an hour, this activity would give way to her wishing to go into the house for a nap.

It was then that I would search out my friends in the street. Mother didn't approve of my running about in the street so I was forced to do it behind her back by sneaking out of the backyard. Our backyard, like most other backyards in northwest Grosvenor, was surrounded by red brick walls. In order to escape the confines of the yard, I had to utilize an old wooden egg crate to scale the wall, which landed me in my neighbor's yard. Then, if the coast was clear, I would sneak through the two-foot separation between the next two houses. It was through that opening that I would make my escape to the street, meet my friends, and take part in the usual pranks. By the usual pranks, I mean to say throwing things at passing coaches, spitting contests, a few rounds of tag in summer, or a snowball fight in winter after which I would duck back into my yard in time for Mother to check up on me. Oddly, I was never caught, though I suspect she turned a blind eye to my little escapades so long as I returned home within a respectful time. In retrospect, had she informed Father of all my misbehaviors, I might not have survived childhood without a good deal of scarring on my backside.

For all appearances, our house was no different from all the other homes on our street. So much so, that it was not uncommon for one to walk to someone else's door thinking it was their own. Yet our home did have two major distinctions not visible to the eye, in that it had been built by my father's own hands, after which he had paid off the house in full. To own your home was a great accomplishment, indeed, for in our manor few to none had managed it. But then, my father was quite different from our neighbors. He put in an eleven-hour day, much the same as most men, but that was after he had paid off the house. Before then, he had taken on a side job under the employ of the local coal shoveler. The work was extremely laborious, requiring him to unload his cargo from the colliers docked at Billingsgate before hauling it by wagon to the Grosvenor District where he would then distribute it to the neighboring houses. This he did in the late hours of the evening. And this he did for ten years.

"My children will not be born into a tenement," he would say to my mother in reply to the many times she had begged him to stop before he killed himself.

To her surprise, as well as all of our neighbors, he did not work himself to death. In fact, he paid off the mortgage in full the day before I was born. Mother has often stated that the reason for my late birth was due to her not wishing to make my father the liar.

Upon the whole, the early years of my childhood were the happiest years of my life for I was blessed with loving parents, an education, and a little sister who worshiped me to the point of following me everywhere. Oft' times in summer on a Sunday after church service, Mother would prepare a light meal of sliced beef or mutton between slices of toasted bread and, along with some cheese and a bottle of claret, pack it into her basket. We would then walk the few streets to Hyde Park and, after a leisurely stroll, Father and Mother would choose a suitable patch of grass and spread out our olive green woolen blanket. Once we had finished our meal, Father and Mother would recline on the blanket and discuss events of the previous week while I would pick out the most prospective tree to climb. Lilly would attempt to follow though she could never manage to reach the lower branches. After my disappearance into the brush of the tree, Lilly would lose interest in my endeavour and return to lie down next to Mother and Father. Lilly didn't know that, had she been able to reach the branches, Mother would not have let her climb into the tree. And it was only through my father's assurances that she allowed me do it. Before I could start up any tree, it would have to pass Father's inspection. And once he was satisfied with the sturdiness of trunk and branches, he would take me to the side, out of earshot of Lilly and Mother and whisper in my ear,

"Bobby, you will not fall and make me the liar, will you son? Take a strong grip of those branches—a strong grip." Then he would give me a squeeze with his powerful hands as a reminder. Not enough to hurt but enough that I could feel his conviction.

Mother's lips would pull tight against her teeth while I climbed, though I remarked repeatedly, "I am truly taking care, Mum. See, I'm taking hold with both hands. See!" Although I would grip the branches hard, it did nothing to alleviate the bite mark left upon her bottom lip.

Once above the lower branches, the lush foliage of the great elms shielded me from the scrutiny of Mother's eyes. In this place I was free to explore the ridged spreading arms reaching out and filling the air, defying gravity, as no brick or post was needed to support them. Climbing high into the maze of endless foliage, I became both explorer and discoverer in a world occupied solely by myself and the tree. I enjoyed being alone up there where everyone appeared small while walking beneath me, none ever knowing, save my family, that I sat birdlike on a branch far above them. The wind would gust causing the limbs to rise and sway while I leaned back into a fork in the branch watching the miracle of nature swirl about me.

It was on one such occasion, when at the age of seven, I had climbed up high into one of the great elms, picked out a prospective fork in a limb and lay back with my hands clasped behind my neck. Taking notice of the swaying world about me, I couldn't seem to attain that 'alone feeling' I had expected and it puzzled me a good deal. Still, I let my eyes roam lazily from leaf to leaf observing the various scarlet-hued leaves that testified to the oncoming winter. As my gaze passed from a group of branches above I fixed upon a set of eyes peering back.

CHAPTER TWO

Instantly springing up, I took hold of a nearby branch for security and scanned the foliage above. Then I saw the partial silhouette of a boy intruding into my private world. Actually, it was I who had intruded upon his private world for he had sat motionless for some time while observing me. His clothes, if they had once been clothes, were reduced to soot-embedded rags. The bones in his face protruded close to the surface of his skin and his blackened bare feet hung beneath him. His eyes were like dark iron, never blinking in his stare as he sat in emaciated silence while I made my way up to him. His hair was a dark, dirty brown and his nose runny and dusted with a layer of coal soot. At first he did not speak but only continued his stare.

I decided to break the ice and said, "Hello. My name is Bobby. What's yours?"

After looking me over for a minute, he spat and I watched as the glob fell to the ground.

"Me name's Pike," he said, a dimple on each of his cheeks appeared, giving him the appearance of smiling, though I knew he wasn't.

"That's an odd name. What does Pike mean?" I said as I spat.

His eyes followed my spit to the ground before he spoke, "It's what me friends calls me. On account I stole a pike off the London Bridge."

"Why did you steal it? What would you wish with a pike?"

"Oh, I suppose it's on account of the 'ead what was on it."

"A head was on the pike?"

"O'course, that's what pikes is for. They puts 'eads on 'em when they wants to make a point."

"But doesn't the pike already have a point?" I asked.

"O'course, but I'm talking about the sod what got 'ung. It's 'im they wants to make a point about. Like, say an ex—ex—somethin' or other."

"Example?" I said.

"Yeah, that's what I was sayin'. Putting his 'ead on the pike is like a sign what says you better not do what 'e did else this'll be you."

"Do they do that to everyone that's executed?" I asked.

"No, just the ones what's famous. The others just get buried or given over to the medicos for dissection."

"Dissection? Why would they wish to dissection them?" I said, confused at the meaning of the word.

"I don't know. I suppose it's a sort of punishment for those that's kin to 'em what's gotten 'ung."

"That's a nasty way to treat someone that hasn't committed any crime other than being related." I said. "Why did you wish the pike with a head on it?"

"Cause it was me pop's 'ead and I wanted to bury it with the rest of 'im."

"And did you? Bury it, I mean?"

"Yes I did. Do you want to see it?"

"You would show me? I've never seen a dead head. But then, your father would not wish you to dig him up."

"Well, it weren't me pop after all, just some other thief what looked like 'im. I never really found me pop. I know they 'ung 'im though. Everybody said they did and I ain't seen 'im since the constables took 'im away. You want to see the 'ead?"

"Bobby! Come down now, son." Father's deep, resonating voice commanded.

"I have to go now. Perhaps I can see it some other time. Where do you live?" I said as I climbed down.

"In St. Giles," he said solemnly.

"I don't know where that is but I shall look for it after school tomorrow. Perhaps I shall see you there. Good day, Pike!"

"Good day, Bobby!"

On the walk back home, I asked my father where a place called St. Giles might be found. "St. Giles!" he said, oddly perturbed, "How did you come to hear of that place?

"I met a boy up in that tree I climbed and he said that he lived there," I replied.

Before he could answer, Mother said, "You'll not need to know where that place is, Bobby!"

"But Mum, I told him I should like to visit him there after school tomorrow."

"No son, I cannot allow it," Father said. "You see, St. Giles is a very dangerous place. It is not safe for even a grown man to venture there unless he had a constable with him."

"But why, Mother? Why is it so dangerous? If Pike lives there, can it be so dangerous?

"Is that his name? Pike? What an odd name it is. I wonder how he came to have such a name."

I started to explain but stopped myself, realizing that to do so would only be confirming her feelings about St. Giles.

"He said it was something to do with making a point," I said.

"A point? A point indeed," Father chuckled.

Lilly held my hand while looking upon her outstretched finger saying, "Point, point, point," and Mother and Father laughed aloud.

The following day I asked several of my classmates where I might find St. Giles yet received only blank stares in return. Though I didn't pursue the matter further, I never forgot Pike. Every Sunday when we went to the park, I would look into all the trees in hopes of finding him, yet, always to no avail. Over time, I seemed to have made him into some sort of dirty fairy, envisioning him flitting about the treetops of the park in his rags, filthy hair and, with runny nose, spitting on people as they passed beneath him.

St. Giles often came to mind as well. I conjured up all sorts of images of dangerous thieves and cutthroats lurking about and feared for Pike's safety. Yet I harbored a hope that he would someday find his father. Thief or no, at least if he had a father, he had a family. Perhaps his father would give him a bath and new clothes. Perhaps…

It wasn't until two years later when I had reached the age of nine that I heard of him again. We had come across town to bring our latest batch of candles to my Aunt Beatrice and Uncle Rupert's shop in Covent Garden Market when we found Aunt Beatrice in a most uneasy state.

Aunt Beatrice was a small woman of ivory complexion; sunshine seemed to radiate from her eyes. Her smile was one of love that carried a deep-felt cheer which beamed joy into anyone who stood upon the receiving end of it. It was, however, the expectation of receiving that smile that made it so distressing to find her cross. In fact, I had believed her incapable of such an emotion till that day. With her forehead drawn up into coarse ridges, she shook her head, sending her golden curled locks into unraveling springs as she spoke.

"Ingrahm's Produce is being picked clean by that villainous Lord Pike and his gang of urchins. Thanks to him, we shall soon be in ruins!"

"Oh, it's not all that dire, Bea," Rupert said in a consoling tone, "a few missing apples and pears will surely not put us in ruins."

Uncle Rupert was a large man with deep-set eyes and tanned complexion. Uncommonly tanned, for I had seen no one in London with much colour in their skin save the blacks, East Indians, and seaman returning from the southern climes. Yet Uncle Rupert was none of these and although he had a most cordial nature, he was not one to be made game of, for he could produce a strop within a second if I or my cousins misbehaved. To be sure, he would never take the strop to me. No, he would leave that to my father. Yet he would give you the look and you did not dare risk his wrath.

"They are just hungry boys trying to get a bite to eat. They won't be back for a while, Bea. I am certain of it."

Aunt Bea's face flushed as she shook a pointed finger at Rupert.

"Hungry or no, they are eating up our profits and soon we'll be the ones going hungry. I just finished our ledger and we are scraping by. If business does not improve soon, Rupert, we shall be undone within two months. Oh, I know those boys are hungry but we cannot afford to feed them all. If only we hadn't leased a shop so close to that awful parish of St. Giles."

Uncle Rupert reflected for a moment before replying, "Well, I suppose I could set up a chair on the street and keep a closer eye on the merchandise if need be while you deal with the purchases."

"Mark my words, sooner or later that Lord Pike will be caught by Fielding's men and that will be the end of him, as well as his gang of guttersnipes. Tiburn Tree will see to that."

"Bea, surely you don't wish for that?" Mother frowned.

Aunt Bea pressed her fingers to her temples and sighed.

"No, I suppose I don't." Looking up to the ceiling, she said, "May the Dear forgive me for that." Then, turning to Mother, "I take it you didn't come all the way across town to receive an earful of our troubles."

Mother smiled and said, "Think nothing of our trip, dear. It is always such a pleasure to see my little sister and brother-in-law that it is well worth the coming. I am so sorry to hear of your having a rough go of it. To be sure, owning a business is no easy matter. ...Where might you be off to, young man?"

"Just outside, Mother," I said, standing in the doorway to the street.

"Don't go running off now. We won't be staying long. We need be starting back home before dark."

"I won't go far, Mother, I promise," I said, while surreptitiously scanning the other shops for signs of Pike.

The street was crowded with throngs of well dressed shoppers while the air carried the mixed odors of perfume and spices wafting out from the various haberdasheries. Then there were the ragged beggars contrasting with the dandies who, clad in feathered tricorn hats and floral embroidered waistcoats, accompanied ladies wearing vibrantly coloured bodices above multilayered, space-hoarding hoop skirts. The shop owners, with their goods displayed outside their doorways, looked about for prospective customers while horses hauled loaded wagons up and down the street to replenish the market. It wasn't long before I heard a ruckus down the way just as a scattering of boys (for I could only make out their rags flying in the air behind them) ran across the square and disappeared around the next corner of a church as an angry shop owner gave the hail and cry: "Stop! You filthy little thieves."

Shortly thereafter, I saw a man with a long club running in their direction shouting, "PIKE, YOU LITTLE SNEAK, I'LL GET YOU THIS TIME!"

My first thought was to go after them, but that would not do for I certainly wouldn't wish Pike and his friends to think me the enemy. Still, I was somewhat relieved to discover that he was still alive after all that time. I only wished I had gotten a glimpse of him to be sure for, though unlikely, it was possible that someone else might have had the same name. He had seemed so hungry that day in the park and I had often feared that he had long since starved. If it were my old acquaintance, Pike, then his survival was likely due to my uncle, as well as others like him, who might turn the other way long enough to give him the opportunity to grab a morsel now and again.

How fortunate I was, I thought, not to be in that sorry state of affairs; how fortunate to have Father and Mother to care for Lilly and me.

After that day, I fancied a new image for Pike. Instead of the dirty fairy jumping about in the treetops and spitting on people, he became the dirty leader of a dozen street urchin followers, hauling stolen fruit and bread to eat on the floor of some rat-infested hovel in St. Giles. I felt pity for him and wondered what it would be like to be forced to live off of odd morsels you might glean as a lowly street thief.

The spring of '72 was in full swing and Easter gave us ten days free from school followed by ten more at Whitsuntide. I had been taking full advantage of my time with the manor boys for we had since formed our own club and went by the title of, The Hell and Death Gang. The idea of the name came from the cries of our victims. The club's leader, Butch, was elected unanimously by way of outright threats of severe physical pain. Immediately after the election, I had been appointed Butch's second in command. Butch's job was to keep the members in obedience to his leadership by various means, such as punching, throwing, or kicking down anyone who challenged him. My job was to keep them all entertained. I managed this by creating missions.

The various missions required resources such as rocks for throwing at windows of passing coaches or dead rats for throwing from the rooftops onto the heads or backs of coach drivers. And, if left unattended, a pail of paint was taken from behind the sign shop on Oxford Road and used for dipping the dead rat while taking care to leave the tail clean so that one might throw it at the head of the coach driver without getting the incriminating paint on one's fingers.

Mrs. St. Clair, an elderly woman, resided in the three storey house directly across from my home, and was generally sitting in a rocking chair on her stoop when I arrived at our front door. And, as was often the case, I gave the customary wave which she returned with a wizened and heavily creased smile upon her paper-thin lips. Though Mother knew little of my daily shenanigans, Mrs. St. Clair seemed to know everything. I had, for some time, noticed her surreptitious observance of my comings and goings and took her silence to mean that she sympathized with my boredom and was willing to let it be our little secret. She was an adult, however, and, as such, had limits to her tolerance.

Later, as I sat in my upstairs window, she had words with Father upon his approach and it was only a quick piercing glance from those ancient eyes that told me she was telling all. Once Father reasoned the razor strop would not coerce me to relinquish my position as second in command, to say nothing of disassociating myself from the gang, he decided it was time to take me out of school and put me to work in the trade as his apprentice.

I thought this a grand privilege and was thoroughly excited when, the next morning, we walked together to his work site, a house located on Brooke Street, only six streets from home. It was during our daily walks to and from the project, carrying our tools in our canvas bags, that I came to know my father in a different light.

CHAPTER THREE

The house was a two storey with a basement like our own and the other men were now setting up on the second floor level. The tenders were building a scaffold and my assignment was to haul sand, cement, water, and lime from the wagon in the street to where the mortar was to be mixed.

Fred Lapeer, one of the real mason tenders (for I was, as yet, not worthy of any title), counted out the required measurements of sand, cement, and lime with a shovel.

I would have the job of turning the mixing drum. Once the water was added and mortar was thoroughly mixed, it exuded a wet earthy odor that eventually permeated the air throughout the work site.

Taking up a mortarboard and setting it down on a plank supported by stacks of brick on either end, Fred would shovel the fresh mortar onto the board where it became my duty to convey it up to the masons.

Billy Hanssel, another tender and son of Father's foreman who, heavily built and adequately muscled for the task, had the responsibility of carrying bundled bricks in a specially made carrier shaped to the contour of his shoulder. Once loaded, he would carefully make his way up the scaffold ladders to stack the bricks beside each mason. This process continued throughout the entire eleven-hour day.

There was, however, within the eleven-hour day a time of respite consisting of a ninety-minute break for dinner where Father and I would hurry home to get a bite of one of Mother's sandwiches. The sandwiches were a recent invention of Lord Sandwich, First Lord of the Admiralty who, when placing meat between two slices of bread in order to make a quick meal so as not to impair his wagering time at one of the gambling houses, coined the word, 'Sandwich'. Mother's sandwiches were usually prepared with a bit of broccoli or cabbage between a layer of beef tongue and cheese, a modification of her own design which gave much added flavor to the original invention. Once finished with our meal, we would relax for a time before returning to work.

To be sure, the work was extremely toilsome and taxed my young body dearly. Upon the whole, the trade proved to be an exciting affair for this was the first time in my life I had done men's work. And it was through this work that I gained an appreciation for what Father did to provide for his family. As the days passed, I listened and observed with great intensity in order to better my ability in performing my tasks. And it was by doing so that I became aware of just how revered Father was by the other masons. Not that I hadn't had the utmost respect for the man, but witnessing this admiration from others brought me to realize his innate power and strength conveyed well beyond the circle of my family.

My father was, by trade, a bricklayer and stone mason. Yet, to say that his craft was simply laying bricks or stone would be an immense understatement. He was foremost a Freemason, which is to say that he was a member of an organization whose roots sprouted from the days of ancient Egypt. It was during our walks to and from the work site that Father would explain the history of the Freemasons and how it pertained to us, as well as how it affected our daily lives.

"It is a way of living, Son. The foundations and structures you are building are also the foundations of your life. Each stroke of mortar placed by the trowel, each measurement of the square, each brick or stone set in the mortar bed will be the measure of your way in this world. Someday you shall take my place in the lodge and, with time, you will grow to bear the responsibility of being a man of truth."

At the time, I remember thinking, what is so difficult about telling the truth? How could it be such a great responsibility? I had no idea that taking such a responsibility was well beyond the ability of most men.

The weeks passed quickly once I had gotten used to the pace of the work and it seemed like no time at all had elapsed before the walls were complete. This meant that we would turn our work away from laying brick and concentrate upon setting the floors, interior walls, door frames and windows, whereupon the plasterers would soon arrive. At this time the majority of the mason crew would be split, one remaining to do the finish work while another crew began work on new project. And as soon as the house reached completion, I was allowed the privilege of attending the customary topping-off celebration.

The celebration was held at the finished house shortly before its occupation by the new owner and involved drinking of much ale and spirits accompanied by various contests. One of these contests involved journeyman masons who were required to lay up a short wall of brick while their tenders supplied them with mortar. The first to complete four layers, or courses, was deemed the winner and his prize, as well as all prizes, was a percentage of the money that had been wagered against him. Another was a brick tossing contest performed by tenders. For this contest, the tenders would compete in pairs. One man on the ground would toss bricks to his partner who waited at the top tier of a thirty-foot-high scaffold. The first two-man group to stack thirty bricks in place on the scaffold planking became the winners.

The contest I most remember was the one my father invented and had appropriately named, 'The Crusher'. What made this contest most exceptional was the fact that it required the use of extraordinary strength. And as very few men possessed, or aspired to possess this power, even fewer would entertain the idea of entering. It was at some time prior to the contest that contestants for 'The Crusher' had already been decided upon. From what I had been told by the other men, it always came down to my father, for he possessed the title of 'Unbeaten' while never having more than one challenger.

As the men arrived, I was surprised to discover that, not only were the men who had worked on this particular project in attendance, but a large group from Father's Masonic lodge had arrived to join in the festivities, each calling out to Father by name, saying such as, "I got my money on you, John," or "Go easy on 'im, John!"

His hand held high above his head, Mr. Skinner shouted, "Are you ready?"

The other masons crowding around my father and his competition, Mr. Simmons, were seated facing each other before a makeshift table composed of wooden planks supported at each end by a stack of bricks. On the table before each man sat a brick of hard baked red clay. The faces of the surrounding crowd wore a mixture of tense excitement while their calloused hands displayed the accumulation of many years of hard work in the trade. The air between each man carried the heavy odor of sweat, while everyone waited in silent anticipation. The journeymen occupying the front rows gripped their vouchers tightly.

I sat on the floor at the feet of these men and could smell the fresh mortar clinging to their trousers.

Father placed his heavy hand onto the brick before him.

Mr. Simmons, a man of equal weight and stature, sat tall in his seat, his fingers on his brick, yet not covering the surface quite as well as the thick heavy fingers of my father. After a threatening glance from the no-nonsense foreman, Mr. Jack Hanssel, the shouting subsided. While waiting, I watched the droplets of perspiration tracing runnels down his cement-powdered arm. Suddenly, the silence was broken as Hanssel dropped his fist like a hammer onto the table while shouting, "GO!"

What immediately followed was the sound of a low murmuring, not unlike a tribal chant, the steady repetition of the word, "GO!" that increased in intensity until it grew into a roar.

Gripping their bricks with one hand while holding their wrists with the other, the two men began squeezing. In seconds, the brick in my father's hand began to crackle as small fissures formed on the surface. Simmons' features seemed to swell, turning a cherry red, as though at any second his whole head might explode. As his sweat fell in a continuous drip from his face onto his brick, a groan escaped his throat. The crowd, realizing Simmons' strength was waning, roared with a combination of cheers and boos while reluctant hands released their coins.

"Father, I know you can do it! I know you can!" I cried as I rose from the floor to get a better view of my father's powerful hand tightening its grip.

I was intently watching the cracks that continued taking shape across the surface of the brick testifying to the intense compression of my father's hand when I heard a voice nearby whisper to someone, "He's the Keeper, ya know."

Then the other man who, due to the density of the crowd, I also could not see, replied in a low tone, "He is, is he?"

Keeper? What was that about, I wondered before losing my train of thought as a powdery cloud of red dust formed in Father's hand and the brick slowly gave way. Soon the sides of the brick fractured and quickly crumbled into tiny jagged pieces

Father's share was twenty percent of the winnings, a full £6 and we walked home that day in great spirits. Mother would soon be wearing a new 'Victory Bonnet', a name she had long since given them, for Father purchased one of those wide-brimmed flowery coloured hats for every Crusher contest he had won.

At the end of each day, Father and I would carry our tools back home and, as we turned the corner onto our street, pass many of my old friends playing in the street. Some waved while others, with blank expressions, would only stare.

Butch would always have a smile for me and I knew he desired with every fiber to have what I had. His father was not skilled in any trade but made his money as a stock jobber, a position which kept him forever worried and if not at work, he could always be found in a highly intoxicated state at the local tavern. The only contact Butch ever had with his father was when he felt his father's fist.

As for the other children, I didn't know whether they were jealous that I worked with Father, or that they felt themselves fortunate that they did not have to work. Nor did I care, for I had lost all desire for playing and pulling pranks.

"Bobby, you are a good lad; not above mischief although you are at the least learning the value of hard work."

"I promise to keep out of mischief, sir," I said. "May I continue working with you? Must I go back to school?"

"I have given orders to your teacher to give you steady instruction in mathematics. Upon this subject, I find you lacking and, in future, it will be necessary for you to know it well. And until you have a better footing, I shall not bring you back to the trade. It is of great importance that you learn all that you can, Robert, for some day you shall become a Master Mason such as me."

Turning to face him, I could see pride in his hardened features.

After a pause, he said, "It is your heritage, Son. Your grandfather and your great grandfather have passed it down from generations before them."

"How many generations, Father?" I asked.

Placing his heavy hand upon my shoulder, he stopped and turned me to face him. With a stern expression, he said, "As far back as the Templars."

Uncertain of his meaning, I paused before daring to ask, "Who were the Templars, Father?"

"The noblest group of knights there ever was," he said.

"Knights! Will you tell me of them, Father?" I begged.

With a smile, he resumed his pace and said, "I believe it was in the year 1118 during the time of the great Crusades to the Holy Land. A French nobleman named Hughes de Payen left his homeland along with eight other knights and journeyed to Jerusalem. Their objective was to assist in protecting the Pilgrims who traveled the roads to the City."

"Who were the Pilgrims, sir?" I asked.

"They were people in search of the ancient origins of Christianity, such as the places where Christ frequented during his life.

Once in Jerusalem, Hughes obtained permission from King Baldwin, the Patriarch of the city, for his men to camp on the Temple Mount, a place that had, one thousand years earlier, been the site of King Herod's temple. They then proceeded to secretly excavate beneath the temple. After nine years of hard, backbreaking toil, they found what they had been looking for."

"What was that, Father?" I asked. "What were they looking for?"

"The Temple of Herod had been built directly atop King Solomon's old temple. He was a very wealthy king, that Solomon, and his treasure was legendary. You see, it was rumored that he had hidden a good deal of it, telling no one of its location. Hughes had heard of this treasure and decided to look for it within Solomon's Temple itself. Their objective was to find an interior room known to the ancients as the 'Holy of Holies'."

"What kind of treasure, Father?" I prodded.

"A treasure of great wealth! It was suspected that there was gold and many precious stones hidden away."

"Did they find it? Did they find the gold?" I asked, my excitement growing.

"Oh, they found many things, but the things they found were not what they had expected to find."

"There was no gold, Father?" I said with a breath of disappointment.

"Yes, they found gold, but they also found something worth much more than any gold or jewels. You see, it was a treasure of a different kind, for back in the final days of the Judeo-Roman War, a war which spanned the years of AD 66 to 70, a treasure had been buried in various chambers or secret pockets within this very room."

"Where is the treasure now, Father?"

"It has been safely hidden away in a secret place. The location is only known by a few selected descendants of Hughes De Payen and of his wife, Catherine St. Clair."

"Who might those descendents be today, Father?" I asked.

"That is a closely guarded secret, son."

As we approached our home, he stopped again and motioned toward the house.

"It is ours and no else may make claim to it. I built it with my own hands from the foundation up. It is your foundation as well, for your heritage lies within the cornerstone."

"What do you mean by cornerstone? How could our heritage be in a cornerstone?" I asked.

"I shall explain the cornerstone later."

"But…"

"Enough. Let us see who lives within this handsome structure."

But before he took another step, I asked, "Father, what is a Keeper?"

"Where did you hear that?" he snapped.

"During the contest, someone said you were the Keeper."

"Who was it?" he said sharply.

"I don't know, I couldn't see him through the crowd."

"Well, then, think no more of it, Son."

"But Father, what is a Keeper?" I asked.

"Do not speak of it again; not to anyone. Do you understand? Not to anyone!"

"Yes Father," I said, although I didn't understand at all. I wanted to prod him further but knew full well the futility of it, for no one ever coaxed anything from Father, other than his wrath.

As we came through the door all was forgotten when we were struck by the aroma of Mother's delicious meat pie, plum cake, and smoking joint of mutton with stewed cabbage. These smells could be quite maddening while waiting for Father to finish saying grace and it took the utmost restraint not to dig into the food like a starved savage.

Once we had filled our bellies, we would discuss the day's events. Father and I generally spoke of our progress at work while never failing to mention the upcoming completion of the house we were currently constructing. The sale was due to bring in profits well above the salary of £31 per month he paid his men. Then Mother would comment on her and Lilly's progress in learning a new kind of stitch or producing the latest batch of candles.

On one occasion, Father brought up a discussion which had taken place during a recent meeting at the Old Dundee Masonic Lodge. The discourse concerned the recent burning of the Royal Naval Ship, *GASPEE*, by the American colonists of Rhode Island. Apparently this subject nearly succeeded in bringing about a great deal of political division amongst the members.

"Politics is not what the lodge is about. It is a violation of our rules to discuss politics, and that is exactly what Bill Sedgewick did when he started ranting about the colonists' rights and how they deserve to have a seat in Parliament. He knew full well that to do so is against the lodge rules yet he did it anyway. As far as I am concerned, burning a government ship is treason and they should hang every last man that had any part in it," Father said, slapping the table with the palm of his hand.

"I quite agree but why would they do such a thing in the first place?" Mother asked.

"Dear, I don't know why and I really don't care what happens to them. A man gets from this world what he puts into it. If you destroy things then you may very well be destroyed in return. But that is not my point."

"Why is it such a terrible thing to discuss recent events?" Mother asked, with her eyes transfixed on Father's face.

"Because some of our members happen to be members of Parliament, while others have relatives over in America, which in due course could give rise to opinions that would, if expressed, bring each side to give serious offense. And if that should occur, well, we would soon lose sight of the Masonic Code that brought us all together in the first place."

"Why didn't someone try to stop Bill from continuing with this discourse?" Mother asked.

"Oh, we did one better. After three warnings we took him for a walk down the Pelican Stairs and onto the dock, rigged a line off the yard of a boat which happened to be tied alongside and made use of it by means of a hoist and proceeded to give him a good dunking."

"My word, you actually dipped him into the Thames?" Mother said, pressing her fingertips to her lips.

"Three times before he sobered enough to realize we weren't going to let him free until he shut his mouth."

"What happened then?" Mother asked with a wide-eyed gaze. I couldn't discern whether it was from disapprobation or thrilled anticipation.

"We hauled him out and someone got him a blanket. It was then that the Grand Master expressed his disapproval and said, 'Sedgewick, if ever you speak on the subject, you will be banned from the Lodge.' When Sedgewick started to protest, the Grand Master said, 'No! Not another word, make no mistake, you will be banned.'"

Father shook his head and sighed, "Those colonists are such ungrateful fools! Why would anyone do such a thing? After all the Crown has done for them, what more could they desire?"

"My cousin, Gerta, wrote to me last year from Charleston," Mother said in a somber tone. "In her letter she mentioned that Parliament is taxing sugar and molasses of all things, the very thing they rely upon for rum exports."

"And why shouldn't they be taxed? Everybody has to pay taxes," Father said, sending the plates bouncing as his heavy fist dropped onto the table.

Mother smiled and, stroking his cheek said, "Dear, you are going to spoil your supper. Is that worth getting upset over?"

Perhaps it was the tone in her voice, or the way she looked at him, but she always knew how to defuse Father's temper. For within a second his whole countenance changed to one of mirth, as though the whole conversation had never taken place.

Upon the first week of my return to school, I happily welcomed the break from hard work. Yet, as time passed, I became aware of an ever-increasing desire to return to physical labor. The trade had conditioned me well for I had gained the ability to do physical things of which I had not thought myself capable. My legs and arms had become muscular and the idleness of the classroom caused them to twitch uneasily while I felt the growing desire to take hold of a shovel or sack of lime. To compensate for this, I would periodically rise and lift my desk while pretending to adjust its position. This irritated the teacher to the point of threatening me with the belt. However, strange as it may seem, he refrained from carrying out his threats. I say *strange* because he had never spared the belt in all my years of schooling. Could it be that I showed no fear? Could it be that he feared I might retaliate? I suspect the former as well as the latter were the true reasons for this restraint.

As the days passed into weeks, I applied myself wholeheartedly to the subject of mathematics. Gradually, though, I felt the inactivity of the classroom weaken me.

I was to have no relief until shortly after my tenth birthday.

Father had begun work on a new church only a few streets distant from our home. To be sure, the work on the church had nothing to do with his day job, for that lay primarily in the building of houses. This work, however, was to be done purely for God. Therefore, it was decided amongst him, as well as several other masons, that they would volunteer their services on Wednesdays and Fridays for four hours in the evening after their eleven-hour day had ended.

My argument for helping him at the church was that I owed thanks to God as well. It was, however, for selfish reasons alone and had nothing to do with thanking God. I simply wished to condition myself for the following summer when my mathematical studies would be completed and I would be allowed to return to my apprenticeship.

On the days of working at the church, I would hurry home from school so that I might get a quick bite of dinner before Father and I left. As we walked to the church, I could not help but notice the deepening lines beneath Father's eyes. The smell of mortar, still fresh from his regular work, clung to him as a reminder that his day's work was not finished. The labor seemed to be taxing his patience, as well as his tolerance, for our conversations became short and, as the days passed, words between us grew to be few. To alleviate his fatigue, I did my best to make his work as easy as possible. This I did by keeping him continuously supplied with freshly mixed mortar, as well as seeing to his supply of brick, a task that had grown easy for me prior to returning to school but now required the utmost of my strength.

Although I had been used to working on houses of up to three stories in height, the church was to be built to a height of eighty feet, not counting the belfry. In order to ensure the work continued at a steady pace, the church minister had hired a scaffold company who, for a reduced fee, would erect the scaffold to the height needed to lay brick for each successive day the masons were working. I had never seen scaffold built to this height and often wondered at the soundness of this construction. On several occasions, I expressed my concerns to Father where he assured me, time and again, that the scaffold was quite safe and I should not waste any more thought upon it.

"The Hendricks & Sons Scaffolding Company has a sound reputation and there have been no accidents other than someone taking a wrong turn before they are found dead on the ground. And that, my son, is not the fault of the scaffolding. You need simply to take care where you step and you shall be fine."

This did little to assuage my concerns and I found myself at every opportunity observing how the Hendricks built each additional level, thereby becoming their greatest critic. The most frequent discrepancy in their work lay in the planking where it was not properly nailed, which would rise on one end if someone stepped onto the opposite end. This, of itself, was of no immediate danger, however, after time, the continuous rising of these planks would cause their position to shift and eventually they would make their way to the edge of the supporting members beneath them. My other concerns involved handrails that were unable to support a man's weight if he felt the need to secure his balance, which is why everyone, being well aware of this deficiency, took steps to not lean upon the rails. My complaints to their supervisor, Peter Hendricks, seemed to fall upon deaf ears.

"What's the bloody problem? Those planks move too far, you just move 'em back is all."

"You mean to say that while carrying brick and mortar up the ladders I must take constant care to do your work for you?" I said.

"Well, here I am, working for practically a farthing and I have to listen to the likes of you going on and on about how to do my job. I'll not hear another word of it. Now get along with yourself, boy, and see to your own work," he replied. As I stepped away, he scolded, "And not another word about how to do mine."

As the weeks passed and the scaffold grew to greater heights, my concern grew with it. To Peter Hendricks' chagrin, I carried a hammer and a few nails in my pocket for quick repairs whenever I spotted something loose. With the added height came the added difficulty of climbing the ladders to keep the buckets loaded with brick and mortar. Always finding planks loose on my way either up or down, I would instantly set about nailing them.

It was a Wednesday near the beginning of our shift that I was on the scaffold taking one rung at a time from the fifth level to the sixth. My head came even with the sixth level to find Father sitting impatiently upon his stool with no mortar to spread for his brick.

"That last batch of mortar was stiff within seconds of your leaving and this batch looks a bit parched already. What is taking you so long? Was that you hammering down there?"

"It was just a couple of planks that I found loose. It hardly took any time at all to fix," I said.

"Son, time is what we don't have. If you can't keep up with me then the mortar does not bond. And if the mortar does not bond, you have a weak wall."

"But Father..."

"No buts!" he barked. "Here, help me with this." Taking purchase upon a rope that ran through a block he had previously secured to the rail beside him, we waited for one of the tenders at the other end to finish loading a wooden bucket with brick. Once we had hauled the bucket to our level, Father held the rope fast while I took the other end and ran a bend around the scaffold railing. Father then swung the bucket over to the floor planking while I paid out the rope until it rested solidly on the scaffold planking. "Now, back down with you," he said. And bring some fresh mortar this time."

"Yes, sir," I said, stepping onto the ladder.

"And don't let me hear any more banging about with that hammer, do you hear? Wait a minute. Give it to me," he said, holding out his hand.

Somewhat confused, I replied, "Give you what, sir?"

He winced and shook his head. "The damn hammer is what."

Although quite accustomed to father's irritation, it was the fact that he actually swore, something I had never known him to do that took me completely by surprise. Then, it struck me. He was swearing at me like one of his men, as though I were a man.

"Yes, sir!" I said, pulling the hammer from the loop in my belt and handing it over.

The following Friday we arrived at the church ready to go to work while the Hendricks crew had just completed another level of the scaffold. We began by mixing the mortar and loading our buckets, one with mortar and the other with brick. Once we were onto the new level, we hauled up the buckets by means of a block attached to the scaffold cross beam just above our heads and began setting a work space so that Father could have good access to his materials and tools. Since our last day there, I had given the matter of the scaffold much thought and had determined that I would not let him down. I resolved to place my priorities on keeping him well supplied, even if I had to run up the ladders to do it. Perhaps I was being overly cautious with the planking, I thought. No one had been hurt thus far, so why not concentrate on my job as Peter Hendricks had advised?

It was my third trip down the scaffold to the mortar mixer and while I stepped from the ladder, one of the other tenders, Fred Ormsby, had finished loading brick into a bucket to be hauled up to Father. While I stepped over to the sand pile to shovel another measure into the mixer, Fred was taking purchase upon the rope and hoisting up the bucket of brick. I had counted off six shovels of sand when I heard an odd croaking sound escaping Fred's throat before he managed to blurt out, "OH, DEAR JESUS!"

A chill passed through me and I jerked my head around so quickly that I heard my neck crack. Fred was staring up at the scaffold while forming a speaking trumpet with his hands.

"DON'T MOVE, JOHN!"

Glancing upward, I saw Father kneeling on the scaffold planking with one hand on the rail for support while he leaned out over the edge in order to gain purchase upon the bucket of brick that Fred had just hauled up to him. What was Fred so upset about? I thought, while searching for something amiss. Then, I saw it. The planking beneath Father's knees, supported by the scaffold cross member, had slid to rest at the very end of the board.

Father glanced down at Fred with a puzzled expression and, letting go of the bucket, asked, "What d'ya say, Fred?"

At that second, the board beneath Father's knees gave way. Father's grip on the rail held him for a split second while the legs of his trousers, white from stains of mortar cement and lime, were searching for footing on the next level down. But the momentum of his weight had thrown him out and away, tearing the rail from the framing. Fred and I screamed in one long agonizing wail as Father seemed to be running with those great white legs of his through space.

I tried to run to him, thinking I could throw my body under his and soften his fall, but I tripped over a sack of lime that I had placed there only minutes before.

The wind was knocked from my lungs when I took the cold flagstone floor full on my chest and, as I lay there trying to breathe, I glanced up just in time to see Father collapsing into a pile of broken flesh. His back snapped like a dry twig and his torso folded like a sandwich. He gasped for a few seconds, the broken section of railing still clutched in his hand, while blood spewed from his mouth in a crimson spray. A violent tremor traveled through his mangled body shortly before he stopped breathing.

Crawling over to him, I looked into his eyes and, for an instant, they were penetrating and blue as the sky on a spring morning. But the blue soon faded and the eyes became clouded and distant and I knew he was gone. Though I wanted to beg him to come back, I realized he could not ever live in that mangled and broken body. His life was over and it was more than I could bear. The following moments remain blank in my memory for I only remember standing in the doorway of our home, gasping for breath while mother stood before me with a precognitive look of dread. Words came from my throat, mostly unintelligible, yet she understood what I had said and, sobbing in a low, deeply grating moan, fell to her knees while biting her hand so that blood seeped from between her fingers.

With Father's broken body carefully cradled upon a sheet of canvas between them, the masons from the church ambled through the streets in a somber procession until coming to a halt in front of our home. Lilly and I sat on the steps of our stoop while Mother stood by us, a scarf wrapped around her bleeding hand as she directed his placement on the dining room table. When we came in, he was covered with a white cotton sheet soaked through with growing wet patches of dark crimson. Mother sat beside him, her hand upon his, while staring in disbelief at what remained of her husband.

As I looked upon his shattered remains, I realized what a foolish impulse I had attempted to act upon during the accident. Had it not been for the bag of lime, Mother and Lilly would be looking upon two corpses. And, unbeknownst to me at that time, the loss of my life would have been the ruin of them both in the months to come.

The undertaker and his assistant arrived within the hour in a black wagon with padded black leather seats pulled by two age-worn grey mules. Mother met them at the door. The undertaker's dark, formal black suit with white stock gave stark contrast to his pinkish complexion. With his tattered black leather case in hand, he removed his hat and wig to respectfully bow his perspiration-soaked balding head. His hands were thin and pale and, with a quick motion, he ran his long, boney fingers through thin grey strands of hair. "Mrs. Elkins, please allow me to introduce myself. I am Travis Nivens. Dreadfully sorry to hear of your loss, ma' am, please allow me to offer my services."

Mother did not respond but only stood ghostly white in the doorway while Nivens continued.

"With your permission, I should like to see to your husband's remains." Mother nodded her head and motioned him into the parlor. Nivens stepped inside with his assistant, a young man of perhaps twenty who sported a most solemn expression which seemed incongruous for one as young as he. Once inside, Nivens glanced nervously about the room before Mother motioned him towards the dining room whereupon his nose, a thing much too large for his small head, seemed to guide him to where Father lay. While Lilly and I looked on, he took hold of the sheet and paused, giving Mother an expectant glance. Taking his meaning, she turned to us, saying, "Bobby, be a good lad and take your sister outside so that we might leave Mister Nivens to do his work."

Reluctantly, I took Lilly's hand and brought her through the front door where we sat upon the steps while the undertaker and his assistant worked on Father. For some moments, Lilly stared vacantly at her tiny drawstring shoes as a small stream of mucus traced its way from her little button-sized nose to her trembling lips. Then, cradling her face in her arm, she broke the silence with a series of long muffled sobs.

I, on the other hand, could not cry, for none of it seemed real. For me, the world had simply transformed into a very, very bad dream. Soon I would awaken and everything would be as it had been before. Before the—no, I simply must wait it out. From the doorway came a groan followed by the sound of crackling bones. For an instant, I was certain that I heard Father's voice. He was waking up, I thought. He's going to be all right, I told myself as I jumped to my feet and ran through the doorway. But when I reached the dining room, it was as though the wind had been driven from my lungs, stopping me cold in my tracks. At the table, both Nivens and his assistant were bending over Father's body. Nivens' shirt had been soaked through with blood and sweat as he held Father down by the shoulders while his assistant kneeled over Father's legs.

I shouted, "Father!" Then, turning to Nivens, demanded, "What are you doing to him?" As though I were not there, he and his assistant continued with their work.

It was as though they were a pack of hyenas about to feed on his body. I started toward them. I wanted to tear them away from him and send them running from our home. What right had they to be here—to touch Father? Before I could start towards them, Mother's hands, now cold as ice, came out from the shadow behind the doorway and held me in check.

"No, Bobby! Father is gone, son. Go outside now."

"But…"

"Go outside, she said, in a far away voice.

Walking numbly through the parlor, I found Lilly at the doorway looking like a lost puppy. The glimmer of hope in her eyes faded as I shook my head. Her cheeks went pale and, with forlorn eyes, she turned away from me before plopping down onto the steps.

I sat down next to her and placed my arm around her frail shoulder and, as we waited, realized what I had just witnessed. He was folded in half when they brought him home. They had merely straightened him out. This must surely be a nightmare. I placed the palms of my hands against my eyelids and, in a futile attempt, pressed inward to erase the gruesome scene from my mind. This is a nightmare, I thought.

Moments later, they brought him out of the house upon a stretcher with a black sheet covering him from head to foot. Next, they placed Father's body into a box on the flat bed of the carriage. In a state of dazed disbelief, we watched as the hearse wobbled and swayed down the street before disappearing around the corner.

I silently cursed God for taking my father away. And as my life went on, I would come to realize the absurdity of such a curse.

The funeral was held in the parlor. Friends, fellow masons, and some members from the lodge came and went throughout the day. Many of Father's employees took the day off to pay their respects. The majority were sitting about the street outside the house with drawn mournful faces, not quite knowing what to do now that the man who provided their means to earn a living was gone. Mother greeted them as they arrived, her fair complexion in stark contrast to her black ruffled dress.

Lilly and I found refuge by a wall in the backyard. I wore my Sunday breeches and waistcoat while Lilly wore a black cotton dress that Mother had only finished stitching together that very morning. She knew full well she wasn't supposed to sit on the ground, yet I said nothing to her for doing it. The polished steel buckles of my shoes caught the sun and reflected onto the opposite wall leaving tiny triangles of blue and green that would disperse into a starry spray each time I moved my feet. If only I could exist inside the reflected stars upon the wall, I thought. Then I would not have to be here and this wouldn't be real. Yet, though I resisted, real, it was. Even so, the triangles on the wall seemed to be somewhat magical, giving my soul a kind of safe harbor for the moment. If only I could keep them in my sight… But then, Mother put her head through the door and instantly broke the spell.

"Robert! Lilly! Aunt Beatrice and uncle Rupert are here. Do be dears and come inside to bid them hello."

With a great deal of reluctance, we dragged our feet into the house.

Aunt Bea wore a black dress with a pleated bustle over small hoops that strained beneath the lute-string fabric as she and Mother embraced, their tears streaming down their cheeks.

Uncle Rupert, solemn in his black topcoat and matching waistcoat, stiffly patted me on the back. "Bobby, your mother has mentioned to me that you haven't said goodbye to your father."

I stared down at my shoes, wishing to hide in the radiance of the buckles, yet they were now covered in the shadow of Father's great padded chair. I hoped he would say no more on it, but he continued.

"You know Bobby, it is the last time you shall see him in this life. Do you not feel the very least he deserves of you is a heartfelt goodbye?"

As I said nothing, he went on.

"Son, I realize that you are still quite young, yet it appears that the time to become a man is at hand. Show him you are capable of that responsibility. Say goodbye to your father."

Each step toward the coffin felt as though my feet were made of lead. The odor of incense mingling with tobacco and tallow made me nauseated, and if there had been a clear path to the outside, I would have run for it. Yet there was not, so I trudged on. When my reluctant feet brought me up against the cedar paneled sideboards, it took all my resolve to turn my eyes upon his face. It was as though he were a stiff piece of wood that had been surreptitiously carved by the undertaker's hand. Bending over him, I placed my lips against the cold marble surface of his forehead. I could sense that he was here, yet I knew that he was certainly no longer within this cold body.

"Good bye Father," I whispered. "I will always remember the things you taught me. I will always remember you." Turning away, my knees were no longer trembling and I sensed a new energy from within. It was as though my father's strength had left his cold broken body to take its place within me. As I neared the front door, I felt a connection to my father that I had never known while he was alive.

Glancing up, I saw Peter Hendricks, hat in hand, standing in the doorway, his thick ebony curls dangling onto his forehead. It was the first time in my life that I had the complete absence of fear.

His eyes avoided me as he brushed by on his way to the coffin.

Until now, all that had mattered was that Father was dead. I had completely forgotten why he had died. Immediately, I saw the plank sliding to the edge of the scaffold's cross support. In my mind, I could hear Hendricks' words, "Get along with yourself, boy, and see to your own work and don't be telling me how to do mine." Hendricks was a large man who towered over me, yet I tore at him, kicking and punching with all of my strength. "IT'S YOUR FAULT!" I shouted.

"Hold on there, boy! What's gotten into you?" Hendricks said with a crooked smile, his lips seemed to lose their shape at the edges like a crumpled sheet of paper. He took hold of my jacket and with one swift motion, held me kicking and punching at air, for I was unable to reach down the length of his long arms.

"YOU DIDN'T KEEP IT NAILED DOWN! Take your bloody hands off me, you bastard!"

"ROBERT!" The unmistakable admonishment of Mother's voice cut the air like a musket ball.

"But, Mother… Don't you see? It is his fault. I tried to keep them nailed down and he said…"

"Enough, Robert. Go to your room!" Mother demanded.

"He said, 'Get along with yourself, boy, and see to your own work and don't be telling me how to do mine,'" Fred Ormsby interjected.

Peter Hendricks' face lost all colour. "I ain't never said nothing like that."

"I heard you say them exact words, Hendricks," growled Jack Hanssel, Father's foreman. Hanssel leaned toward Hendricks, both arms bent at the elbows while his fists were clenched. "And I don't miss much that goes on around that job. The boy was worried about men getting hurt, his father in particular. I saw him poundin' nails, doing your work for you."

Upon hearing this, Mother gasped before bringing her fingers to her lips. "What are you saying, John?"

"He and his men didn't quite do their work as well as one might expect. Have a problem with the wages, Hendricks? Church didn't pay enough?"

Hendricks took up a defensive stance, his feet set wide, his meaty fists clenched. "My men gotta eat, don't they?"

"And we masons who were working for nothing but the

blessing—I suppose we aren't worthy of a few more nails? Why do a good day's work then? What's in it for you?" Hanssel replied, the corner of his mouth twisted up in a mocking grin.

Peter's chin trembled ever so slightly. He knew Hanssel was right. Now he did only what a self-respecting blackguard could do under the circumstances. Puffing out his chest, he blurted out in a spray of spittle, "I ain't done nothing to cause nobody to get hurt. You'll not lay this on me, Hanssel. It ain't my fault. He should've taken care to…"

The room went silent as Hanssel stepped up to Hendricks and, though Hendricks towered over him, it made no difference to the man. Pressing his face in close to Hendrick's extended chin, Hanssel's eyes narrowed. The skin stretched tight over his cheeks exposing his teeth, giving them a wolfish grin as he spoke in an even, yet deadly tone, "He should've taken care to do what?"

"I believe you should leave, Mr. Hendricks," Mother said in a strained voice. As she spoke, her bold features seemed to fade, for she had since been so worn down by her grief that this confrontation was nearly more than she could bear.

Several of Father's friends, as well as members of his working crew, had been sitting outside but, upon overhearing the conversation, had entered the house, gathering into a tightly packed crowd around the two men.

Hendricks mumbled, "I just came to pay my respects is all." Then with a glance at Mother, he inclined his head and pushed his way through the men to front door. Most of the men followed him out, giving him a shove as he made his way to the street. As Hendricks' feet hit the paving stones of Green Street, his pace turned into a full run before he reached his horse and, nearly leaping into the saddle, dug his heels into the poor beast's haunches and galloped away like a highwayman running from the constables.

As I watched him disappear around the corner, guilty as he

appeared, I couldn't relieve myself of some of that blame. I could still hear the irritation in Father's voice as he said, "Son, time is what we don't have. If you can't keep up with me then the mortar does not bond. And if the mortar does not bond, you have a weak wall."

I know I could have taken the time to drive a few nails where he stood. If I had done that he would have been even angrier but he would still be alive. I was just as responsible as Peter Hendricks, I thought. And, after many months of considering this event, I had to concede that Father carries some of that responsibility as well. Still, these thoughts would continue to plague me long after my father was in the ground.

One day after Father had been laid to rest, Mother sat us down in the parlor next to the empty space that had contained Father's coffin and, with a solemn expression, spelled out our situation. "Bobby, Lilly, I know you have endured a great deal these past days as have I. And I am so sorry to tell you that you will be required to deal with even more."

We shot a disbelieving glance at Mother. What could be worse than what we had just gone through?

"The point that I have to make is not a pleasant one. To put it simply, we will have to make do with very little money. With the loss of your father came the loss of the income which has enabled us to exist in relative comfort. He has left us with both a home that is paid for, as well as furnishings which are not owed to anyone. These things alone are a great accomplishment for a man of this age and your father was no less than a great man. There is, however, the problem of our funds. The money remaining in our savings account will not sustain us for long. I have had to use a good deal of it to pay for the undertaker and burial. In order to deal with this problem, I have discussed the situation with your father's company foreman, Mr. Hanssel. He is willing to take over the company and buy Father's equipment, as well as see to the completion of the remaining building contract. I believe it is a fair proposal, for I know nothing of running a business and, no, Bobby, you are much too young to have a hand in it.

"The house on Hereford Street is nearly completed and Mr. Hanssel will want only five percent of the profit after everyone has been paid their wages. Future contracts will be then be taken over by him, at which time our income will effectively be at an end. Our making and selling candles will not provide the things that we are accustomed to having and I will need all the help that you two can provide," she said with a strained voice. "Do you understand what I am saying to you?"

Though we nodded our heads, neither of us could, at that moment, completely understand the full measure of what Mother was attempting to convey. It had been difficult enough to accept that our father would never be returning home again; to consider that his income was at an end—the income, which provided food, clothing, to say nothing of coal for cooking our meals and heating our home in winter, was beyond us. Therefore, things such as roof shingles, curtains, and bedding linens were not even in the realm of our comprehension, for these were things we assumed would always be there. It was simply provided and that was all there was to it. We were soon to learn that things would wear out or be consumed and we would be unable to replace them. Might we, in time, begin to appear as paupers, like some of the wretches we would see on our walks through the park, or in the street near the market?

"Perhaps I should leave school and find some means of earning money," I suggested.

"Your schooling has been paid up for the next three months so you may as well take advantage of it. Perhaps by then we shall have had some turn of fortune that will allow you to continue," Mother said encouragingly.

"Cannot we ask the schoolmaster to give the money back? Would it not be best used to pay for other things?" I said. Having no desire to continue with school, for I had since completed my mathematical lessons and understood the problems to the extent that they were now becoming repetitious and mundane, I readily welcomed an end to it.

"Your father would have wished you to continue as long as possible."

"But Mother, he is gone now and we need…"

"And we must to do our utmost to honor his wishes, Bobby," she said, before I could continue.

"Perhaps there are things we might sell?" I suggested.

"What we have is little more than what we need, but I suppose we could do without some of the furniture." She paused, her hands betraying a slight tremor, "and then there is the silver Mother left me, and our fine china."

Lilly offered, "We could do wash for people."

"My dear, sweet baby, Mummy appreciates your help." Mother said, with a heartfelt smile as she gently stroked Lilly's fine, golden curls. Leaning across the table, she kissed her forehead. Then, with a far-away look in her eyes, said, "I am going to start asking around for anyone who might need a maid and perhaps you could be my little helper. And in the mean, I will continue with the candles. As for you, Bobby, your help will be required with the candles the minute you return home from school."

As the months passed, Mother was unsuccessful in finding work as a maid and we were left with our only remaining option, the manufacture of candles. We all worked hard, rising early to start the fires after which I would run off to school while Mother and Lilly went to work. Once I returned from school, I would fetch a quick bite of dinner before working well into the evening, not getting into bed until the day's batch was done as well as my daily chores completed. Upon the whole, we were only able to make enough to put food on the table while not having enough left over to purchase coal, an extreme necessity for candle production. It wasn't long before our bank account was depleted and, with winter in full progression, there were many days without heat. Mother sold her fine china, her mahogany high chest, and, most painfully, Father's great padded leather chair.

From the outside, all appeared to be fine and well. Our house was well lit from the one thing we had in plenty—candles. Yet, inside our home, things were quite another matter. When we weren't cooking tallow, we were forced to wrap ourselves inside layers of blankets to ward off the cold as we could not spare an ounce of coal for ourselves if we were to continue working. Sometimes I would spy a coal shoveler on my way home from school and, when he was about his task, sneak up behind him and slip a few chunks of coal from his wheelbarrow into my haversack. At times I was nearly caught, yet I seemed to be developing a skill for taking it. Mother knew there was extra coal now and again, though she never mentioned it to me. It seemed the luxury of keeping warm and having fuel for a fire with which to cook outweighed the need to admonish me for any wrongdoing.

It was mid-January when the hard work and cold nights had finally caught up to us and Mother and Lilly became ill. Within two days, their fevers climbed and a debilitating weakness took hold, rendering them unable to rise from bed. Mother had taught me how to check for fever by touching my lips to her forehead, or by placing the back of my hand against my neck before placing it against hers and Lilly's necks for a comparison of their warmth to mine. After doing so, and to my immense horror, I found that their skin was hot as melted tallow.

The old Clarkson clock on the mantle ticked away the seconds while I waited downstairs in the unheated parlor for the doctor to finish his examination.

"They require food and warmth." Doctor Williamson said, after leaving Mother's bedchamber. He glanced at his watch before taking hold of my chin with his freckled hand. Staring into my eyes, he tapped his finger several times on my brow. "Does that hurt?"

"No." I said.

He let go of my face, straightened up and replied, "Excellent! You will need to care for them and if you are sick as well, you won't be of any service. I would bleed them if not for the fact that it would only serve to diminish their capacity for keeping themselves warm. I suggest you build up the fires and keep their bedchamber warm, blankets and a good pint of ale when they will take it. Keep the chamber pots emptied. Have you relatives nearby?"

"My aunt and uncle have a shop in Covent Garden Market. Perhaps I could visit them and ask for their help."

"I would do so as soon as possible, lad. Only I wouldn't leave them alone too long. They must be kept as warm as possible and be given regular feedings of warm broth."

"Yes, sir! I shall take care of them. They shall have everything they need."

"I thought to ask," the doctor said, "however she drifted off before I had the opportunity. Perhaps you may know. Does Mrs. Elkins have sufficient funds to hire a maid to care for her and your sister until they recover from this condition?"

"How serious is it, sir?" I asked, while at the same time, buying myself time to think.

"Serious enough! I have seen these things develop into fatal lung disorders if not properly attended to. It is my understanding you are attending school and won't be available during the day. You must understand, son, they must be cared for around the clock."

"I shall look after them, sir. It won't do any harm to miss a few days of school."

He uttered a, "Hmm!" then, closing his black leather case, he stepped to the door. Before opening it, he turned, giving me the high brow. "Are you sure that will be acceptable to your mother?"

"Not to worry, Doctor, I shall have them back in good health in no time at all." I said, putting on my most confident face.

He shot me a disbelieving glance as he stepped onto the stoop. "I'm sure you will, however, if they should continue with this fever for more than two days, or their fever worsen, waste not a moment to call upon me—not a moment."

"To be sure, if there is any change for the worse, Doctor. Thanks so much for all of your help."

"When she awakens, tell your mother there is no call for concern about my fee until she is well over this malady."

"I will tell her. Good day, Doctor."

And with that he was out of the door. For a while, I sat on the settee in the parlor as I had some thinking to do. My aunt would not be able to leave the shop and travel across town to take care of us. They were hardly making ends meet with their new business and had already bought more candles from us than they might sell in a month. And to leave their shop closed would certainly be their ruin. No, I must think of some other way.

While Mother and Lilly slept, I donned my heavy boots and greatcoat and set out for a walk. The air had a bite, turning my breath into a foggy vapor as I set out down the street over a light dusting of freshly fallen snow. The wind pressed against me as I walked, yet my heavy woolen coat fell to just above my shoes making a good shield from the cold while keeping me quite warm. I had no idea where I was headed; only that I needed to think and walking seemed to best facilitate that process. I had been walking for about an hour, not paying much attention to direction, only vaguely aware that I was traveling east along Brook Street for a while before turning south onto New Bond. The next thing I remembered was that I was standing on the corner of Piccadilly in the Haymarket while staring vacantly at the horse traffic making its way through the intersection.

People were closing up their shops when a coach rounded the

corner at a dangerously fast pace before colliding with a stoutly made wooden crate that had recently worked free of its bindings and fallen from the bed of a freight wagon. To avoid the object, the driver had, at first, swerved his team of two horses off to one side. This, however, did not serve for it caused his carriage to rise up onto two wheels and, when he attempted to correct by reigning in his horses to the opposite direction, it was too late. The upended wheels had already struck the crate, giving the carriage just enough elevation to bring it over onto its side in a horrendous grinding crash. The driver fell heavily onto the pavers while the occupants were violently tossed about within the cab. Fortunately, no one suffered any serious injury for heads soon appeared above the framework of the uppermost door and, with dazed expressions beneath wigs all ajar, two men and one woman with a severely bent headdress frantically climbed through the upended door of the overturned cab.

Within a few seconds of the accident, chaos fell in full swing as all traffic had stopped, turning the whole intersection into something not unlike a jammed stream. In short order, a tremendous din ensued, with everyone cursing and swearing oaths while not a soul thought to lend a hand. At length, however, some of the other drivers did get off their arses and, removing their coats and rolling up their sleeves, soon had the vehicle put to rights.

Leaving the carnage behind, I continued on my way for a short distance before realizing that the sun had set and darkness would soon be upon me. How far had I gone and where I was were questions I could not answer, for nothing was familiar to me here. Berating myself for not paying attention to the streets I had traversed, I wondered how I would find my way back home. I had no money with which to hire a sedan chair and my next thought was that Mother and Father would be furious. Then the funeral came crowding back into my mind and, with a jolt, I realized just how much our lives had been so cruelly altered.

Mother and Lilly are dangerously ill, I thought, and I must take responsibility. It is up to me to care for them. Father is gone and if I can't think of an answer soon, I could lose them as well. I must find a way to obtain coal for the fires as well as food.

Crossing the next street, I came upon the Strand. Remembering that this street ran near Covent Garden Market where my aunt and uncle's shop was located, I decided to visit them. Perhaps I could explain that I had gotten turned around and lost my way and would they be so good as to give me directions for the best route home.

Yet, upon my arrival at the market, I found the shutters of their shop locked and no one on the street but women who were, as best as I could understand, frequently making some sort of business arrangement with various men who happened by. I mentally upbraided myself for not realizing that if the Haymarket's shops were closed, then it stood to reason that Covent Garden's shops would be as well. Having no idea where my aunt and uncle lived (for I had only visited them at their shop), I asked myself aloud, "Now what do I do?" I have walked all this way and still haven't come up with any ideas for helping my family, and now, to make matters worse, I am lost. A fine bit of help, I am. Well, I suppose there is nothing for it but to continue walking until I find a familiar street that will take me home. And, perhaps while I am walking, I just might still come up with some way to help our situation.

Looking about, I found that I then stood on Russell Street. As I thought most of the streets would be quiet at this hour, I was surprised to hear a boisterous commotion ahead, and, following the direction of the noise, came upon a large crowd in front of the passageway leading from the Theatre Royal by Drury Lane.

Many well dressed ladies and gentlemen were exiting the theater and carrying on about the play they had just enjoyed. One young woman stood next to a rather obese dandy and smiled innocently at him while he carried on a quarrelsome discourse about how he would have made several improvements to the play, had he been in charge. And that 'Garrick', while not the worst of actors, displayed excessive emotion for the character in his role.

"Overstating his character, completely overstating his character!" the fat man bellowed, while others about him appeared to be annoyed by his loud comments. The woman, a very attractive lady in a white dress with deep burgundy velvet trim, listened attentively to the fat man while he went on with his criticism. As she stood near him with her eyes holding him captive, she would, from time to time, incline her head, and, as she did so, the lamplight would expose the golden shimmer of her lush curls as they bunched about her shoulders.

Meanwhile, a young, well-dressed lad near my years, stood at the lady's side and, while holding her hand, dipped his other hand into the fat man's waistcoat pocket. With the speed of the flicker of a candle, he brought it out with some small shiny thing before slipping it into the pocket of his own coat. Then, back into the man's other waistcoat pocket his hand went and, before I could blink, the man's purse was retrieved and, with extreme dexterity, disappeared into one of the boy's other pockets.

As far as I could ascertain, no one around them had taken the slightest notice of the boy's unashamed thievery. The fat man then leaned over and whispered some confidential joke into the lady's ear wherein she rolled up her eyes and gave forth a loud chuckle that shivered the embroidered folds of her bustled hoop skirt. Casually, she then turned away from him while slipping a gloved hand from her muff and, taking the boy's hand in hers, bid the man good evening before stepping quickly away, leaving him with a sullen, defeated expression.

Several private coaches and taxis were lined up along the street awaiting their parties where, in the space between the horses of a coach-and-two and the rear wheels of the next chaise, I spied the pair passing beneath a street lamp where something strangely familiar had caught my eye. Momentarily forgetting my mission and, if only for the sake of curiosity, as well as the fact that the lady was extremely lovely to observe, I shadowed them from the opposite side of the street for perhaps sixty paces. As they passed under another lamp light, the boy turned his face upward to address the lady beside him and, as he did so, his features, now illuminated by the glow of the lamp, displayed the unmistakable dimpled cheeks of my old acquaintance, Pike.

CHAPTER FOUR

My thoughts were distracted by the sound of high-pitched squeals emanating from somewhere outside the door to my cell. It was a sound the rats made, which never failed to foretell of the turnkey's approach. Whether it was due to their innate sense of hearing or the vibrations detected by their tiny feet, I was not certain. Yet the rats always knew.

This time, I detected more than the usual set of footsteps. As they were fast approaching, I had hardly time to slide my manacles back on before the jingling keys came to a stop just outside my door. Instead of the usual grating sound the wooden bowl made when it slid through the slotted opening, I was surprised to hear the key straining to turn the rusty lock. With a resistant metallic grind, the door swung open revealing three turnkeys, none of whom had my gruel. One of them stepped into the cell and raised his lantern to my face. Spears of light stabbed deep into my eyes before I turned away, while some of the other men shielded their eyes and tried to go back to sleep. The man with the lantern spoke in a slow, coarse, dragging voice, as though each word required his utmost concentration to enunciate.

"Don't fret; you'll be fed soon enough. But first, we must see that you is moved to your new accommodation in the Stateside Ward. Your benefactor has reserved a much more pleasant and airy chamber what overlooks the street."

One of the other turnkeys jovially interjected, "And after we moves ya, you is gonna be fed good and proper—gentleman-like."

"Why am I being moved?" I asked.

"On account you have a friend, not to discount the fact that you have become famous," said the man with the lamp.

"Famous?" I inquired.

"Yer famous 'cause you're a young 'un and people always feels sorry for the young 'uns," said another of the trio. "They's gonna be milling about outside yer new cell under the gate so's you can wave to 'em if you like. And most likely they'll be hangin' about to see you hangin' about next week, if you get me meanin'. Ha! Hangin' about? That's a good one, if I do say so meself."

"Shut your trap!" the man with the lamp scolded. "The lad is to be our guest and needs no reminder of his circumstances."

The rats were so thick about the floor outside my cell that when I stepped out, several of them set upon the turnkeys, biting at their boots and, failing to draw blood, jumped high to get at their legs.

"What the—you little bastards!" one of the turnkeys shouted, while crushing several under foot before they grew respectful and, backing away, stood on their hind legs to squeal their protests.

As they led me down the corridor, a boy I had befriended called out, "Take care Bobby, and remember to jump high, like Dick Turpin."

As I passed one of the darker cells where they kept the pederasts, I saw a wretched skeleton of a man eyeing me through the bars before cracking a wicked smile to say, "If you could find in your heart to let him stay with us for a while, we would treat him most kindly."

"They'll get to your neck soon enough, you goddamn child fucker," one of the turnkeys said, striking the door with his leaden cane.

After we had passed through a labyrinth of dank passageways, we came to a stuffy room lit by two whale-oil sconces where another turnkey sat at an old oaken scarred desk. Glancing up, he gave me a slow appraisal before uttering, "So here's the one to be relieved of some of his iron."

"Aye, Rags is fetching the keys," said another, who, turning about, saw the stout wiry-haired man called Rags approaching with a ring of rusty keys.

Bending down, his dirt-encrusted, chubby fingers searched through the ring for the proper one and, finding it, removed two of the three sets of irons I had been dragging about for the past month and a half.

"There, that should do it," he said, setting the last set on the desk.

"Come along now. We'll be taking you to your new quarters," said the one with the lamp.

Their voices faded into the dark behind me as I followed Rags down another damp and putrid corridor. Through several checkpoints (each of which had to be unlocked and relocked behind us) we passed countless iron doors which concealed coughing and dying occupants who lay in dimly lit and dank cells, shivering as the cold from the slimy stone floor seeped up into their bones.

At length we emerged into the blinding sunlight where we proceeded across a courtyard and I was forced to shield my eyes while Rags led me along. As we crossed the open space, I passed shabbily dressed men and boys of all ages; each of whom, by their physical state, must have received far better treatment. Their donations from family and friends seemed to have made it to their rightful recipients. Several, I noticed, were pointing to me as I heard one say, "'Ere's another for the 'angman. Got the dead man's cell, has ya boy?"

"Don't pay 'em no mind, lad. Just keep on walkin'," said Rags.

Eventually we came to a large ironclad door. Rags took up a club and used it to pound the door before another turnkey on the other side opened it.

The man on the other side spoke in a high-toned voice with the manners of an innkeeper, saying, "Welcome to Stateside."

I stepped through into a large rectangular open courtyard with rows of rooms adjoining on all four sides beneath a high wall. The floor and walls were of the same dirty, cold stone as the rest of the prison and, although less filthy, this place was full of well dressed men attending various social gatherings. A most 'unlikely' scene materialized before me as servants carried plates of food to and from their rooms which were well lit with spermaceti lamps and whale oil sconces. The men were dressed not unlike the gentlemen who frequented Covent Garden Theatre or along the walkways at Ranelagh. At a glance, I could see well into their quarters which were furnished with beds—real beds—with mattresses and bedding along with wash sinks and chamber pots.

After crossing the courtyard we ascended stone steps that slumped low at the centre from being worn by time and the thousands of feet that had preceded mine. It was after we had climbed two levels and neared the top of the steps that I caught a blast of fresh air. Since my return from the trial, I had, again, become used to the sickening air of the lower levels and, as before, the fresh air now entering my lungs was intoxicating.

At the top of the stairs Rags turned and led me down a long corridor with rooms on each side. At length, we stopped in front of an iron-clad door which had recently seen a fresh coat of white paint. He gave it a shove; the oiled hinges allowed the door to swing freely revealing a surprisingly clean room. As I stepped over the threshold, I was startled to see that a chamber pot and washbasin rested against the opposite wall, but what gave me pause was the light shining through a barred window.

"This is to be my cell?" I asked in disbelief. Receiving only a chuckle from Rags, I took the liberty of stepping to the window and found that it actually overlooked the street. Fresh air, I thought. I shall breathe fresh air from now on.

Against one wall, sat a real bed with mattress and bedding included, as I had seen in the rooms below, and it amazed me how little better than a month of privation could make such a thing appear completely ethereal. No more would I be forced to sleep on damp moldy planking. My gaze stopped at the white porcelain chamber pot and washbasin resting in the far corner. Heretofore, I had had to make use of slimy old wooden slop tubs which, if we were fortunate, would have been removed only once in five days. More often than not, it had been seven to eight.

"Thank you, sir!" I said to Rags as he was met by another turnkey who came to the door. "And a hearty thanks to you, sir, as well," I said to the other turnkey, for I was feeling such gratitude that I would have thanked the rats if I thought they could answer.

The stranger spoke in a slow manner saying, "Yer breakfast will be comin' directly. An' don't be a thankin' me. It's only on account of you havin' a benefactor and bein' famous. You only gets to enjoy it fer the week. Then it's the rope an' someone else'll have this room. Jus' like someone else was here before ya. So don't you go a thankin' me."

Then, I remembered what Pike had told me about famous thieves and I had to know. "Guard!"

"What now?" asked the other turnkey from somewhere down the corridor.

"Are they going to put my head on a pike at London Bridge?"

"What gives you such a notion as that?"

"You said that I have become famous. Isn't that what they do to thieves that are famous?"

He laughed as his footsteps receded down the stairs.

"Guard! Guard! Are they going to do it? Are they?" I shouted in a panic. The vision of Mother standing before my head on the bridge was more than I could bear.

Before he closed the heavy door at the bottom of the stairs, he muttered both to himself as well as the stone walls. To my immense relief, his words echoed well up to my straining ear, now hard pressed against the door to my cell where I heard, "It'll be a cold day in hell afore they puts a child's head on the bridge." Then, he raised his voice to be certain that I could hear well and clear, "You ain't old enough and you ain't famous enough."

Letting out a deep sigh, I slipped the manacles from my wrists. Crossing over to the window, I found that my eyes were, as yet, not adjusted to direct sunlight. Covering them, I, again, filtered the sunlight through my fingers while taking in a deep breath of air so fresh that it made me lightheaded. If only I could bathe, I thought, before telling myself not to wish for more than I could expect.

After a few moments, my vision cleared enough to see that I had a bird's eye view directly down Newgate Street. Following the motion of the coaches and wagons, I was surprised to find they were passing beneath me and realized my new cell was situated above and off to one side of *The Gate* of Newgate Prison. The Gate had been constructed in ancient times as an opening through one of the old city walls and now was part of the prison that actually traversed the street above it. Below me and passing through The Gate, persons were dressed up for a day's shopping or, perhaps, even a visit to the theater.

Then I saw Pike and Laura who, disguised as beggars, were well concealed within convincing costumes. I waved for but a moment before their eyes sought me out. As he crossed the street, the wind blew Pike's rags sideways like a battle-torn flag, exposing the white cotton dressing as he crutched his way over the cobblestone surface of the street. Laura held up the hem of her beggar's ragged and torn dress as she ran out of the way of a passing freight wagon, instantly bringing to mind the many times we had run together from some irate cully. When they stopped beneath my window, I called down, "Mother and Lilly, how do they do?"

"They are holding their own," Laura replied.

I could only see the upper half of her face from the angle of the window, yet, even from that distance, those soulful eyes filled me with warmth.

Pike stared up at me, his dimpled smile displaying his teeth like ivory keys on a pianoforte. For an instant, I had the unrealistic sense that everything was going to be put back to rights and we were soon not to have a care in the world. But as I looked into their eyes, I could detect the shared pain looming behind their expressions. Pike glanced down the street and, recognizing something, nudged Laura, yet, in spite of the warning, she kept her eyes locked upon me. As Pike took hold of her arm she cried out, "We must go, Bobby. But we shall return. Do not despair. We shall find a way."

I smiled down at her and gave her the thumbs up as she turned with a wary look in the direction Pike had indicated. They both glanced up for an instant before disappearing through The Gate. My heart sank as I saw the last trace of Laura's ragged skirt trail away beneath me.

Seeing them together on the street brought to mind that lonely night when my mother and sister lay in bed, deathly ill, while I walked the streets of London. With uncommon clarity, I recalled the moments that I first spied them beneath the lamp outside the Theatre Royal. I recalled that I had been so joyous to find him that, without thinking, I called out his name, "Pike!" yet no one heard me above the din from the other side of the street.

It was then just outside the theatre where Pike and the lady proceeded up Drury Lane at a quickening pace toward the direction from whence I had just come. They were near a street from the theater before I had decided to follow. After shadowing them for four streets, I heard shouts coming from perhaps two streets behind me. Glancing back, the fat fellow with whom they had recently spoken, discovered he had been robbed and was now running, along with a group of sympathizers, in my direction. His great stomach swayed like a giant goatskin of wine, bouncing and jostling out of control, first to the left, then to the right as though it would, at any second, tear loose from his body and burst onto the street. Not quite knowing why, I found myself running toward Pike and the lady only to find that they had turned the corner of the next street. I was certain that they had been well out of earshot of their pursuers before they had turned the corner and, therefore, had no idea they were being chased.

Knowing full well they were thieves, I also knew it was wrong to steal, for my parents had long since taught me right from wrong. Yet, I felt I must warn them. I told myself that, when I caught up to them, I would endeavor to convince them to return the man's property. Yet, there was something about the situation which gave me the most exhilarating feeling I had heretofore ever had. Rather than run after them, I decided to cut over one street before continuing in the direction in which they were walking: the idea being that, when I reached the next street, I would be there well ahead of them so that I might meet them from the opposite direction.

Running down dark, unfamiliar streets was something entirely new to me and, though it gave me an uneasy sensation in the pit of my stomach, I continued on at such a pace that, while turning the next corner, I nearly lost my footing on a patch of black ice and slid halfway across the cobblestone pavement and nearly into the filthy gutter. After darting up a dark alley, I found myself at the corner of Long Acre Street and Dirty Lane. In this area the streets were completely deserted, for sensible people were, by this late hour, inside warming themselves by a fire or had already retired for the evening. Glancing to my left, I peered down the street to be sure they hadn't passed this way. As I continued down the street, I sensed they must be near and decided to wait in the shadows of a walkway between two brick homes.

While waiting, I welcomed the opportunity to catch my breath, for my lungs ached from the frosty air. Then I spied them walking at a casual pace in my direction from only two hundred paces distant. As they neared, I tried to compose exactly what I was going to say to them. I knew Pike would not know me, so I thought I might just pass by and casually mention that I had heard that a watchman was looking for a young lady and boy.

At least, that was my plan before a coach and four, pounding the street with hooves and iron-rimmed wheels, rounded the corner at full gallop. The horse's eyes were wide with fear of the coachman's whip as their great muscular haunches bunched and contracted above their powerful legs. Hanging half out of the door with one foot on the stepping board, the fat man clung to the baggage rack while the coachman took purchase on the reins, forcing the horses to slow their gallop and come to an abrupt halt in front of Pike and the lady. The sudden stop caused the fat man to be thrown, belly first, onto the stone pavers. After rolling several turns through mud and filth he was brought to a stop by colliding with a tethering post. Pike and his lady friend bolted toward me while three men with poles, whom I suspected were the famous Bow Street runners, came from around the corner ahead of them.

Realizing they were completely surrounded, they stopped directly in front of me. The lady appeared resigned while Pike gave them a cold fearless stare.

As the Bow Street runners approached, I called out from the shadows in a hoarse whisper, "Pike!"

Pike stiffened without looking in my direction. Then, he slowly turned in an attempt to see me in his peripheral yet, my being well into the shadows rendered it an impossible task. On the off chance I was a friend, for I had called out his name, he dropped to one knee as though to tie a lace on his breeches and, with his other hand out of view of the approaching pursuers, reached into his waistcoat pocket. In a flash, he withdrew a purse and gold snuff box and, while rising to his feet, used a slight but well-hidden backhand motion to toss the items to me, all the while not taking his eyes off the approaching coach and Bow Street runners. Snatching the items in mid-air, I turned and ran between the houses before I found that the passageway ended with a brick wall much too high for me to scale.

Before I could think of what to do, a window opened above my head and a man and woman in night clothes appeared. The man brandished a pistol while the woman lit a candle, lighting up the space to leave me completely exposed. To my surprise, however, they did not see me, for their attention was directed towards the goings on in the street. Ducking down beneath the window, I knew full well I was about to be undone for all that was needed was for the man and his wife to glance down, or the constable's men to look into the passageway.

The thrill of the affair suddenly transformed into a whirlwind of trepidation as the full weight of my predicament bore down upon me. What have I done? I thought. I am not a thief and here I am about to be arrested as one. Mother and Sister are deathly ill, lying at home in the cold while waiting for me to care for them. How will I be able to do that while in prison? I have done a fool thing here and now I have completely failed them. No! Far worse than that, I have killed them.

While I kneeled hunched over and pressed against the brick beneath the window sill, I felt the iron rim of a coal chute door against my knee. With the utmost care, I slid my fingers under the lip and pried it open. At first it moved easily but then, as I had it halfway ajar, I felt the rusty vibration of resistance and had to stop for fear of being heard. If I could not open it, I thought, it will be only seconds before they have me.

With a mouthful of saliva, I quietly spat upon my fingers and began working the saliva into the hinges. Then, under cover of the noise and commotion from the street, I slowly worked the iron door back and forth, gaining a little more distance with each turn, until it opened just enough for me to slip through and into the basement.

"What goes on there?" called out one of the house's occupants.

I am caught, I thought. They saw me and now they will add housebreaking to the charge. But it was not I who was being addressed.

"I am a constable," came a reply from the passageway to the street. Do you see anyone lurking around back there?"

"Why, no!" the man of the house said. "What's afoot?"

My heart rose back into my chest as I realized I was not yet doomed—at least, not for the moment.

"We have caught a couple of thieves; however, it appears they have tipped the coal to Adam Tiller."

"I don't follow, sir," replied the man from the window above me.

"What I mean to say is that they may have handed the stolen items to an accomplice. If you have no objection, I would like to take a look around back there."

"None at all! Pray, do your duty," the man of the house said.

As the passageway lit up from the addition of several lanterns, I could hear the men moving boxes and opening windows. Perched atop a pile of coal, I dared not move. When they came to the chute door, I placed my full weight against it while they attempted to push it open.

"Is this locked?" one of the searchers inquired of the man and woman in the window above.

"No, not at all, however it does hang up once in a while. Quite rusty, you know."

"Well, it is hung up quite badly now. But then, since it is, I suppose no one could get through there. All right men, there is nothing here. It appears we shall have to let them go," the constable said.

"That's preposterous!" replied someone with an indignant, high pitched exclamation who I presumed must have been the fat man. "Let them go? Let them go? Now, see here. You have them, I tell you. That little scoundrel must have picked my pocket while I was having a conversation with this young woman."

"Perhaps your wife might wish to hear my side of the story, sir," spoke the lady.

"You dare to speak of my wife! Why, you little tart. I'll not stand for it, d'ya hear?" scolded the fat man.

"I'm sorry sir. But you see, without the evidence, I am afraid we will not be able to prosecute. However, we can certainly hold them for a time while we investigate."

"Of what kind of an investigation do you speak?" inquired the fat man.

"We will inquire of the missing articles. Perhaps you or your wife can give a more accurate description."

"MY WIFE! Now, see here, you had better leave my wife out of this."

"Are you sure it was these two?" the constable asked.

"Well, perhaps I may be mistaken," the fat man recanted.

"I see," replied the constable, with a note of sarcasm.

A combination of laughter and oaths followed along with the clip-clop of the horses' hooves as they receded into the night. The window above closed with a bang and I could hear the man and his wife's muffled discourse through the floor boards. Their steps continued up the stairs and, after their voices faded, all was quiet again. After a few moments I crawled back through the coal chute hatch and rose to my feet in the dark passageway. Brushing myself off, I stepped quietly through the passageway but paused to make sure the occupants did not return before stepping out onto the street. Pike and the lady stood near a street lamp not twenty feet away with their backs to me while watching the coach turning a distant corner. No sooner had it disappeared then, in unison, they turned to face me. Standing like a pair of marble statues, their faces, now shadowed by the street lamp at their backs, appeared dark and demonic, giving me no little degree of unease as I stepped toward them.

Reaching into my greatcoat pocket, I took out the purse and snuff box and presented them saying, "I believe these are yours."

The woman slowly shook her head and, as she did so, the light revealed high arched brows above cat-like eyes that seemed to take my measure in an instant As I closed the distance between us, her full painted lips thinned into a half smile and, inclining her head, her voice carried an almost musical tone as she said, "I don't believe it. Not only does he save our lives, but he gives us back the goods."

Pike, maintaining his stoic stance, said in a low raspy tone, "Who are you?"

"I am Robert. Robert Elkins," I said, with my best effort to control the nerves that seemed to be shaking my voice.

His brows furrowed with suspicion as he said, "How do you come to know my name? I don't know you from Adam." All the while he spoke, he stepped toward me, his hands deep in his pockets while his eyes coldly threatened.

Sizing him up quickly, I could see that he stood two to three inches taller than I and at least a stone heavier, yet I decided he was not as large as my old friend, Butch. And though I thought that I could take him easily, I realized that I didn't come through this near disastrous ordeal merely to get into a scrap.

"I met you a very long time ago," I said, holding out the stolen items as though they were a peace offering. His gaze dropped to the objects in my hand whereupon his frown melted into something resembling a child given a piece of candy.

"We met, did we?" he said in a soft voice, his eyes still locked onto the objects in my hand. "Where?"

"High in the top of a tree in Hyde Park!" I replied. "Remember when we spat onto the ground?"

"Spat onto the ground? I spit on the ground all the time," he said, taking off his tricorn hat to straighten thick curly strands of coffee coloured hair. Then, as if to demonstrate this habit, he puckered his thin lips and spat onto the cobblestones. The lady immediately reproached him, the skin of her face tightening against her well-defined cheeks, an expression that gave her an air of irrefutable authority. The slight indentation in her chin seemed to give her features a delicate balance between the appearance of a genteel lady and a woman of strength.

"Pike, I have told you time and again to lose that disgusting habit." Then, as though she had turned a page, she gave me an inquisitive smile. As her eyes made contact with mine, I had a sensation of falling into a pool of deep marine water. "Are you sure that you know him?" she asked. "We have known each other for a very long while and I have no recollection of him having mentioned you."

With a degree of mortification, I thought, why should he remember me? After all, it was only a moment of his life. It probably meant nothing to him. I don't really know why I remember it so well. However, at this point I had nothing to lose and, turning to him, said, "You told me about the head you buried when you thought it was your pa. Said it was how you got your name, because it was on a pike you took from London Bridge."

"I have never told anyone of that," he said indignantly. Then, his eyes grew wide and his cheeks gave way to that dimpled smile. In a flash, his hand shot out and stopped just short of my chin, only to wipe some coal dust from my lapel. "I remember you! You are the one with the rich parents who were having a picnic in the park. Ah! Let me see," he said, placing a finger to his temple. "I remember now. Bobby," he exclaimed in triumph.

"You do remember," I said, with a good deal of relief. "I was sure you would have forgotten."

"And you remembered me. I am quite surprised at that. I must have looked like something the cat dragged in back then. How did you know it was me?"

"Your dimples," I laughed.

Pike's smile disappeared. His expression soured and he bared his teeth. "Are you making game of my dimples?" he asked, raising a threatening hammer of a fist."

"Come now, Pike, aren't you going to introduce me to your old friend before you go knocking him on the head?" said the lady.

"I wasn't making fun of your dimples. I only think they make you recognizable is all." Just as I was bracing for the blow, he lowered his fist and smiled again.

"This here is Laura," he said.

"Now, Pike, did I not teach you how to say it properly?" Laura said, a small furrow creasing the velvety complexion of her forehead.

"I am pleased to introduce you to Miss Laura Aimesley," Pike said, after clearing his throat.

"I am most happy to make your acquaintance," I said, taking her outstretched hand in mine and bringing it to my lips.

"My, but your friend is well schooled," she said to Pike. "Who is your trainer, Robert?"

"I'm not sure I get your meaning, ma'am. Do you mean school master?" I asked.

"So you have been educated in a school?" she asked. "Well, how do you come to be working with us common thieves?"

"I haven't come to—that is to say, I am not working with—I only wished to help because I saw Pike back at the theater and was curious as to how he managed to be doing so well. The last time I heard of him was over two years past when he was stealing food from costermongers and street stalls." Turning to Pike, I said, "I tried to catch up to you back then at Covent Garden Market, but you were being chased in much the same way as you were now. At least I caught up to you this time."

"And to our good fortune, I might add," Laura said, then, with a frown which seemed to nearly mar her perfectly sculpted features, "How foolish of us to have nearly been caught, and so easily. We must be growing slapdash, for we were completely unaware." Glancing over my shoulder, she studied the shadowy passageway where I had concealed myself. "You were in that coal chute after all, weren't you? How could you have known it was there?"

"I didn't plan on it. It just happened that way. I was about to call out to you when everyone seemed to appear out of thin air."

Holding out her gloved hand, she wiped some of the coal powder from my cheek and I caught the scent of roses on her wrist before she withdrew it saying, "I realize it's none of my business but, might I inquire how it is that you come to be out here alone at night? From what Pike has just said, you have parents. So I would assume that you are not in a bad way. At least you weren't when last he saw you."

Pike chuckled. "I remember. Your mother wouldn't have let you climb trees at all, if not for your father—Ha-ha! I heard them speaking of it the whole time you were climbing."

The thought of someone else having a memory of my family during one of the most cherished moments of my childhood made me feel as though the memory had been tread upon. It was as though no one should have it other than my family and me. Surprised by my own resentment, I realized I had, only a second before, wished him to remember. Suddenly brought in mind of that moment, I could clearly see my father on the grass below the tree with Mother. I could hear his laughter and then, just as suddenly, he lay mangled on the church floor. "My father has been killed, our funds are gone, and my mother and sister are very ill. I have been walking the streets to think, which is what I do best—that is to say, when I am walking."

"And what is it that you were thinking of?" Laura smiled while looking upon me with amused curiosity.

"I have been searching for some way to help them," I said. "I fear they will die if I don't do something soon."

Pike raised an eyebrow and said, "You are living on the street, then?"

"No, we live in our home in Grosvenor." I said.

"You have a home in Grosvenor?" Laura said incredulously. "My, that's a good distance from here. You did go for quite a walk this evening. So, you cannot pay your rent and are about to be thrown out then?" Laura asked, as though it were an expected sequence of events.

"No, we don't pay rent. My father has paid our mortgage in full. We own our home," I said.

"You own your own home in Grosvenor and are in need of help? There, there, you are in quite a bad way indeed," Pike said in a cutting note of sarcasm.

"Pike, hold your tongue!" Laura scolded.

I went on, "Yes, our home is fully paid for. However, since my mother and sister have been too ill to work, our funds have run out. We can't even afford to buy coal for cooking and heat. I have quit school in order to care for them but I can't do that without any money. And if I find work, it won't afford me the time needed to care for them."

Pike sighed, "Well, any work that you might find won't buy enough food to feed, nor coal to warm a mouse. Take it from me. I wound up in a parish poorhouse after my father was taken away and nearly starved on the paltry fodder provided there."

"What did you do?" I asked.

"I ran away. Which was a few months before I saw you that day in Hyde Park." A cloud passed behind his eyes as he continued. "I was nearly starved then. And things didn't get any better for me, that is, until Laura found me."

"How were you able to help him?" I asked Laura.

"The dear was quite a wretched little ragamuffin when I first noticed him hanging about in the street outside my lodging. And when I couldn't bear to look into his starving eyes, I took him in."

"Where is your lodging?" I asked.

She smiled and rolled her eyes, "At the time, and though, for all appearances, I could have been taken to be a genteel woman, I must confess I was living a miserable existence in Rat's Castle of St. Giles—as anyone's..." She winced as her teeth bit deep into her bottom lip and, as if to shake off a stinging insect, she waved her hand and said, "I'll not go into that. But, a point in fact, Pike and I are a team. We rely upon each other. I had to teach him some things at first—work on his speech—buy him some decent clothes, but it has paid off. Someday soon, we shall have sufficient funds to get away from that—that... But then, after all we have been through, we were nearly undone just now. You really did save our skins. And, if you like, you can keep that purse and snuff box."

"I could not do that. That would be stealing," I said, while offering the items to them again.

"Well, if it's stealing you're afraid of," she said while taking the items from me and dropping them into her hand bag, "you have been a most fortunate boy not to have had to live as we do. If it wasn't for stealing, Pike would have starved long ago and I would have died of the pox." She turned her eyes down and, clasping her hands, let out a long painful sigh before continuing in a soft voice.

"And if you plan on helping your mother and sister, you're going to have to make some sacrifices—sacrifices which may require you to change your way of thinking." Suddenly, she raised her head, the sad expression gone as she pulled her gloved hand from the white fox fur muff and placed a long tapered finger to her temple. Waiting for her to form her thought into words, I drew in the sweet fragrance of her perfume. She seemed to possess the rare combination of beauty and intelligence which I suspected played a great part in her and Pike's survival. She was a full eight inches taller than I, her mere presence was exhilarating. And when, at last, she spoke, I clung to her every word.

"I have a thought. We just might be able to help one another."

"How's that?" I asked.

"Well, as you have need of someone to help your sick mother and sister, understanding full well that such assistance would require a means with which to keep the house warm, as well as provide food for everyone, we also have a need."

"And what is your need?" I asked.

She smiled at me as a teacher would when given the correct answer for a test. "To extricate ourselves from the rat-hole of a lodging in which we currently reside," she said, while stroking the lapel of my greatcoat with her finger tips. Withdrawing her hand, she pulled an embroidered kerchief from her purse and wiped the coal dust from her fingers as she spoke. "And if you would be so good as to put us up in your home, we might do you a favor in turn, if you get my meaning."

Pike interrupted, his mouth twisting into a sour expression, "Takin' care of sick people?"

Laura turned and, taking hold of his brown velvet topcoat by the shoulder, said, "Yes, Pike. The very least we can do is to pay him back for saving our lives. Might I remind you that if not for him, at this moment we should be well on our way to prison?"

"My mother would rather die than take thieves into our home," I said quickly.

As though insulted, Laura exclaimed, "Thieves, we may very well be. But, from the sound of your situation, your mother and sister will die if they don't receive proper care." Placing the palm of her hand against my chest just over my heart, she spoke softly saying, "And what difference can it make to you if, through the care of thieves, they should recover?"

I couldn't deny she had a valid argument. And for all my walking, I was at a loss to think of any means to bring them succor. Perhaps there is no other way to help them, I reasoned.

"They must never know that you are thieves," I said.

"Agreed. They shall never know, isn't that right, Pike?" Laura said while jabbing him with an elbow.

"Mum's the word, I suppose," Pike said.

"And you must use another name," I insisted. "Pike will never do. She's heard of you from my aunt who owns a shop in Covent Garden Market—a shop that you and your friends used to steal from."

"She's heard of me? Well ain't that something? I am famous." Pike smiled, displaying the full splendor of his dimples.

"Agreed," Laura said. "Pike's name shall not be spoken in the house. Do you follow, Pike? Your name is to be Tom from now on."

"Tom?" he asked, his hands thrown up in a pleading gesture. "I must answer to—Tom?"

"So long as we are living in his home. Is that clear?" Laura said sternly.

"If I must! It will take some getting used to. I suppose it's not such a bad sounding name. Tom it is then," he said with a dimpled smile.

"It's settled then?" Laura's brows arched as she posed the question to me.

I recognized with faint pleasure that her aquamarine eyes seemed to wield some sort of power over me. And with scant resistance to that power, I was about to say that I must obtain Mother's approval, yet held my tongue as I realized that if I didn't take charge of the situation, they would, in all likelihood, die. It was up to me to do something and there was not a moment to be lost.

"When might you move in?" I asked.

"Splendid!" Her face brightened with the look of someone who has just won a contest. Clapping her hands, she turned to Pike and said, "Oh, this is a capital turn of events. Only moments ago, we were about to be taken off to prison and now—we have found new lodging." Then, to me, "I swear to you Robert, I will—we will, tend to your mother and sister with the utmost care." Then, with a pause, she pulled Pike's fob and withdrew his timepiece, an ornamental silver affair with intricate carvings on the casing. "There is still time," she said. "But we must move quickly. Pike, let us fetch our things."

"Now?" I asked.

"Why, yes. If we stand here any longer we will freeze. We shall hire a taxi. You'll see, it shall take no time at all—no time at all," Laura said, while turning on her heels and stepping out in a brisk pace.

"But, where are we going?" I asked, while following them.

"Why, over to Bow Street, just a couple of streets away where we might find a coachman in front of Covent Garden Theater. That is to say, if they haven't all departed. But we must hurry," she said, picking up the pace.

By the time we arrived, the last of the crowd were leaving in one chase while another hackney, a coach and two, though empty, was pulling away from the theater. Pike stooped to pick up a fist-sized stone and, even with the coach near fifty yards away, threw it with such skill that it struck a glancing blow on the luggage rack. The coachman gave a backward glance and spotted us waving beneath a street lamp. Bringing his horses to a halt, he waved us on. Once inside, we were catching our breath while Laura instructed the driver to an address whereupon he steadfastly refused to take us without payment in advance. Without hesitation, she reached into her purse, withdrew the fare, and paid the driver.

"Why did he demand payment in advance?" I asked.

She gave me a reassuring smile saying, "Oh, that is simply because we shall be entering the Seven Dials after dark."

"Is it far?"

"Far, why it is only twenty minutes by coach, however not many drivers will venture in there at this time of night.

"Is it not safe?" I asked, my trepidation growing.

"Why, my dear you shall be perfectly safe with me," she said patting my knee. "I know most everyone there and we watch out for one another. Fear not. No harm shall come to you," she reassured.

The Dials, I thought. It seems Pike has moved from St. Giles yet, from what Laura has just told me, the Dials seem to be a dangerous place as well, at least at night. So I shall finally get to see where Pike lives. Just the same, ever since my mother told me never to go there, I have harbored the desire to see the Parish of St. Giles. Perhaps I might still have the opportunity one day. Perhaps Pike might show me where he once lived.

As the coach traveled down unfamiliar streets, I began to experience a trembling sensation in my entrails. And, after we had gone several streets, I was nearly overcome by an urgent need to run home and see about Mother and Lilly. I fended this notion off by reassuring myself that in a rented coach the trip home could be accomplished in very short order. Passing Great Hart Street, we followed James Street to Cross Lane and continued down Great Earl until we reached a circular road with one, two, three—seven streets coming off of it where Laura informed the driver which street to take. Afterwards we turned down a narrow lane called Lombard Court.

At mid-street, Laura instructed the driver to stop and said, "Pike, you stay with the coach while Robert and I fetch our dunnage."

"But why must I stay here?" Pike protested.

"Because if you don't stay here, how long do you think that driver will wait upon us before he is frightened off?" she whispered.

A glance at the driver told me she was not wrong, for he sat rigidly in his seat with eyes darting nervously about while his white knuckled grip upon the blunderbuss left no doubt he was ready to fire at anything that moved.

"Just keep him company until we can return," Laura added. "Certainly you can manage that."

"I suppose so, but make it quick," Pike said with a wary-eyed look about. "If Jeb sees us leaving there's no telling what he will do to us."

"Don't you worry your little head about Jeb," Laura said with an encouraging smile. "He's most likely sitting at the Rose and Crown and by now he should be quite cup-shot. Come, Robert!"

Stepping from the coach, I found we were surrounded by refuse and rubbish. Along the side of the road were discarded gin bottles, bits of broken furniture and rotten, discarded curtains that apparently had fallen from the dirty paned windows above. The air hung heavy with the odor of gin and filth, giving me cause to cover my nose with my kerchief. The entrance to their lodging was through a heavily weathered door which hung precariously by a single hinge. Through the door were very steep stairs which creaked as though they might give way at any second.

"Take care for that missing step or you'll fall into the rat-infested cellar," Laura warned as I followed her through the door.

The air within the building was worse than outside in that perspiration, urine, and vomit were added to the mix which carried such a thickness that it seemed it would permeate my skin. Taking care not to touch the banister for it was hanging, here and again, by a loose nail, I continued upward. At the second floor, Laura ran her hands blindly over the surface of a shelf before finding a tinder box and, opening it, struck a flame. Nearby was a candle box which she lit and, taking it up, carried it down the hall. A few paces down the corridor brought us to a battered door with multiple cracks. Pieces of broken plaster lay around the floor where it had, for the most part, been ground underfoot into a dirty powder. Once the door gave way to Laura's shoulder, she entered, motioning for me to follow. Upon entering, I was surprised to find that we stood in an impressively well kept and cleanly scrubbed room with two beds near a fireplace, a closet with a sizable wardrobe and vanity complete with makeup and various perfumes.

Without hesitation, Laura pulled a large wooden trunk from a closet and began stuffing her and Pike's clothing into it. Once she had all the clothing inside, she quickly threw in her makeup and perfumes. With Laura sitting on the trunk, it took me several attempts to buckle the leather straps before it was successfully closed and ready for transport. She got to her feet, straightened the hoops of her petticoat and crossed to the fireplace. Bending down, she took hold of a loose wooden panel at the base of the fireplace and carefully slid it from the wall. Reaching into the exposed cavity, she withdrew a small drawstring pouch and, sliding it between her breasts, replaced the panel before returning to put her full weight against the trunk. Through much effort, it took our combined strength to drag the trunk through the doorway and down the hall to the top of the stairs. While we prepared to negotiate a way to manage the trunk's passage down the stairs, a door opened opposite us.

In the doorway stood a young, ivory-complexioned woman wearing not a stitch of clothing. Her ebony hair fell in rope-like strands over large gravity-defying breasts before parting to make way for the rose-hued, button rise of her nipples. My efforts on moving the trunk ceased as she placed her foot onto the trunk, giving me a most thorough view of her body.

"Got any money, boy?" she asked, in a husky tone.

Laura rose up from her efforts on the trunk like a lioness guarding her young and bodily shoved the woman back through the door. "You stupid doxie. Can't you see he's just a boy?" Then, turning to me, she said, "Well, if you can get onto the down stair side, I'll take the upper end."

For a second, I couldn't seem to move for the woman's naked body stayed firmly in my mind and I couldn't help but wonder what made it so fascinating.

The next thing I knew, Laura's fingers were snapping in front of my face while her voice broke my trance like the crack of a whip. "Well, don't just stand there with your jaw on the floor. TAKE HOLD!"

Thus reminded of the matter at hand, I gave her a sheepish grin before taking hold of one of the grips on the trunk. After we maneuvered the end over the top of the stairs, I climbed over the trunk before taking purchase on the lower end. No sooner had the bulk of the weight cleared the top step when Laura screamed, "Robert, I can't hold it. It's slipping, IT'S SLIPPING!"

I had to think fast and quickly decided my only course to prevent its crushing weight from coming down on top of me was for me to jump on top of it. The next thing I knew, I was on my stomach riding the trunk down the steps where it tore through the doorway, taking the door off of its only remaining hinge, before it came to an abrupt halt in the street. I, however, did not stop with the trunk, but instead cannon-balled, head first, into a wheel of the awaiting carriage. Fortunately, my head passed between the spokes whereupon I took the brunt of the blow with my shoulders. However, the sudden crash of the trunk had startled the horses and the driver, by way of his quick reflexes, had taken up the slack on the reins in time to prevent their running off and decapitating me in the process.

"Are you all right?" Laura asked, as she and Pike took hold of my feet and pulled me from the wheel. "I am most dreadfully sorry, I was certain I had good purchase upon it."

Getting to my feet, I took stock of myself before straightening my coat. The dull pain in my shoulders told me that I would soon have a pair of mighty bruises but, as I could move my arms without difficulty, nothing appeared to have been fractured. "Nothing appears to be broken," I said, with a smile. "That was a most capital ride."

Incredulous of my response, Laura continued looking me over.

"Not to worry," I reassured her. "I am quite all right."

Laura glanced down the alleyway before giving Pike a nervous smile and said, "Then let us lift this thing onto the coach so that we may be quickly on our way."

"I couldn't agree more," I said. "I am fearful for my mother and sister as I have been away from their bedside far too long."

"Pike, bear a hand—driver please—and Robert, take hold of that grip," she directed.

Between the four of us, we soon had the trunk secured onto the baggage rack. As the coach pulled away, a bottle shattered as it struck one of the rear wheels.

"Driver, do make haste," Laura begged, while staring through the opening in the coach door.

Pike jumped to his feet and, putting his head through the opposite window exclaimed, "He's come home early and not as cup-shot as we had hoped."

From somewhere down the dark alley a man shouted menacingly, "Where do ya think yer goin, ya little bitch?"

As the coach came to the intersection of Lombard Court and Little Andrew's Street, the driver brought it to a halt.

"Driver, make haste!" Laura cried,

"Not until you tell me where to, ma'am."

"We must go to... Where are we going, Bobby?" Laura pleaded.

Being somewhat distracted by the anger in that voice, I found it difficult to speak.

"Quickly, Bobby," she said with a growing terror in her voice, "Where?"

"Green Street, in the Grosvenor District," I finally managed to stammer out.

"Driver, to Green Street in Grosvenor. And do make haste, we have sick people to tend to," Laura snapped.

"I am sure you do, ma'am," the driver replied sarcastically before making a left turn toward the circle of the Seven Dials and bringing the horses to a fast trot.

As we circled the Dial, Laura instructed the driver again, "Take White Lion Street, please." As the coach continued past that street and, instead, turned back onto Little Earl, Laura's complexion turned white. "No, we mustn't go that way driver. Why did you not take White Lion?" she scolded

"This will be shorter, ma'am," the driver replied.

Sitting back into her seat, she let out a frustrated sigh while giving Pike a worried glance. "Perhaps he shan't see us," she whispered.

"Perhaps," Pike shrugged.

As we came to the corner of Lombard Court, thereby having come full circle of that street, a man darted out of the alley toward the coach. Fortunately, the coach was several feet ahead of him with the horses traveling at a quick trot and, though he gave it his all, he was unsuccessful in overtaking us. A glance through the glass in the carriage door revealed a man with large broad shoulders who stood with clenched fists while catching his breath beneath a street lantern. His features were heavily accentuated by the light over his head which revealed long black hair framing a wide square jaw. His eyes were fixed upon me as he shook one of his club-sized fists and muttered something indiscernible through his thick, snarling lips. Laura and Pike seemed not a little relieved when the distance increased as we sped off down Little Earl Street toward Monmouth. An icy chill passed through my veins. What had I gotten myself into? That man had pure evil in his eyes and it was quite unmistakably directed at me. I tried to reason that, with London being the largest city in the world, it is quite possible I may never see that man again. However, from deep within, my intuition told me otherwise. Yet, for the now, I told myself I must concentrate on the task at hand.

The task at hand, however, caused me to ask myself if this was such a good idea after all. Had I done the right thing? I could only hope that I had, for I was now fully committed. I shuddered to think that in utter desperation and for want of any other means, I was placing the lives of my mother and sister into the hands of these two strangers. As Laura gave me a reassuring wink, I recognized true sincerity in her expression and, feeling more at ease, mentally said, hold on Mother and Lilly; help is on the way.

CHAPTER FIVE

It wasn't until the second day that Mother regained consciousness, though only long enough to down some warm frumenty porridge that Laura had prepared for her. Lilly fared much better for she had been sitting up after only a half day of being warmed by the fires which now blazed in all three upper hearths. We kept them going non-stop for there was, then, plenty of coal in our bin. Laura had since purchased coal at first sight of the local coal shoveler on the night of her and Pike's arrival. And first thing the next morning, she and Pike had gone to the market and brought home a good stock of bread, flour, milk, portable soup, a fine joint of lamb, and salt beef.

As Mother's health improved, Laura had devised a story as to how she and Tom came to be in our home. She informed Mother that Tom was her son and, like Mother, she had recently been made a widow. Her husband had been well off but lost all their savings to gambling shortly before he took ill with consumption. Unable to work, he wasted away until he died, leaving them with a mortgage they could not afford, their house in foreclosure and they would have been left penniless if not for the trust her father had left her. The problem with the trust was that it was insufficient to pay for lodging as well as food and clothing. I had happened along when they were being thrown out of their lodging and had helped them move their belongings into a chaise. I had offered them lodging, in return for their help, which is not entirely untrue.

Miraculously, within a fortnight Mother's strength returned. With vivid clarity, I can recall one evening we five sat around the supper table finishing off yet another wonderful meal. The tall walnut paneled Clarkson clock ticked away while the fire crackled in the hearth, radiating heat throughout the dining room. We were sipping tea from serving cups which were all that remained of Mother's fine china when Laura remarked to Mother how thankful she was for her hospitality.

The milky skin bunched up around the edges of Mother's eyelids as she smiled, first to Laura and Pike, then to me as she said, "Son, I knew you would find a way to help us but I could not imagine how. I was simply too weak to think. I am so sorry. I feel as though I failed you and your sister."

"You never failed us, Mother. It is my responsibility to take care of you now that Father has gone," I said.

"No, son, you are too young to have such a responsibility." Her hand came up to wipe tears from her eyes and she stopped to restrain the tremor in her voice before speaking further, "Yet, you precious little man, you did just that. Didn't you? You found a solution to our dilemma and saved us from a dreadful situation. And this sweet child," reaching out, she took Laura's hand between hers, "has come to us like an angel from God."

Laura's eyes welled. "Now, Mrs. Elkins, Tom and I would be out on the street if not for your hospitality."

In the short space of time under our roof, it seems that Laura had grown quite fond of Mother. I knew she was adept in deception, yet this seemed genuine as I suspected those tears had not time for rehearsal.

"Please call me *Catherine*," Mother smiled. "You are welcome to stay here for as long as you like."

Laura returned the smile saying, "Are you certain we won't be putting you out?"

Mother squeezed her hand, "Not at all, dear, not at all. It is the least we can do. You and Tom can have the bedchamber next to Robert's room. It was John's study and has been out of use since he..." Unable to say the word, she bit her lip, "It is a fine room. We have a spare bed which is dismantled in the attic. It will be easy to reassemble and you shall no longer have to sleep on the parlor room floor. I hope you will be comfortable there."

"Oh, Catherine," Laura beamed, "you are such a blessing. It will be perfect for us."

Mother's eyes displayed that kind glow I hadn't seen since Father died. The deep bluish sacks beneath her eyes had receded and her cheeks were now full of their usual pinkish hue, giving her a healthy full moon glow. I loathed our deception and harbored a great deal of shame from it. Yet, like it or not, I was committed to this course, for I could not conceive of any way to turn back now.

Turning to me, Mother said, "Well, Bobby, with this arrangement, I suppose there is no reason why you cannot return to school."

Laura's eyes brightened as she said, "Yes, I have always maintained that an education is priceless."

"Does Tom go to school, dear?" Mother inquired.

"As a matter of fact, he's under an apprenticeship to a man on High Holbourn Street," Laura smiled.

"My, that is quite a distance from here. Might I inquire what sort of apprenticeship?

"Well, I have a friend who owns a business that deals with the sale of private property."

Mother sighed and, extending a finger, touched Laura's hand, "Do you mean to say, an auctioning agent?"

"Why, yes. That is exactly what I mean," Laura said, her face flushing before regaining its usual colour. "And one of his many responsibilities is to gain knowledge of how to appraise items from the estates which the proprietor has been hired to sell."

"My, what a unique opportunity for such a young man! You must be proud of him," Mother said, lightly patting Pike's cheek.

Pike smiled, yet I couldn't help wonder what he was really thinking, he being so sensitive about his cheeks.

Laura went on, "As I was saying, my friend is teaching Tom how to appraise the value of things prior to their being auctioned off. Tom is becoming more knowledgeable of property values every day."

Mother's mouth hung open for an instant as it usually did when she heard something of a surprise before replying, "Why, that seems to be a very lucrative business, and such a splendid opportunity for the boy. Your friend is doing you a great service."

Laura then proceeded to explain how, on occasion, her friend would allow Tom to take home some of the items to study them further before being questioned of their value the following day.

Mother patted Pike's hand, saying, "I have no doubt that you shall go far in the estate auctioning business young man."

Pike gave such a smile that it exposed his dimpled cheeks. Seeing the dimples for the first time, Mother could not refrain from pinching his cheeks. This is it, I thought. He hates that. Will he lose his temper? Yet, he gave not the slightest hint of it.

"Perhaps your friend could take my Bobby on, as well?" Mother blurted out. Laura shot me a curious glance and the room fell into an awkward silence before Mother closed her eyes and, placing her wash-worn hands to her forehead, said, "Oh, I beg that you'll forgive my presumptuousness. I have no right to suggest such a thing. Please forget that I ever mentioned it."

Laura smiled and said, "Think nothing of it. I will ask him first thing on the morrow." As she spoke, her eyes never left mine, all the while, arching that mischievous brow that was beyond Mother's field of vision. "But, what of his schooling?"

Taken aback by this turn in the conversation, I wondered what Mother was up to.

Mother leaned in toward Laura, her eyes widened with excitement while Laura returned her gaze with that endearing smile on her full pink lips. Strangely, Laura appeared not the least perturbed by Mother's prodding.

"You would ask him?" Mother asked, with a note of surprise. "Oh, my dear, I would not have even mentioned it if not for desiring Bobby to gain some means of employment. I know how difficult it is for a young man these days to find a means of support. He has learned all that his father had time to teach of bricklaying, yet he is still much too small to make any sort of income by it. To be sure, his schooling has been very necessary, for it has taught him to both read and write exceptionally well, yet it will not teach him a means of providing for himself. If your friend agrees to help him, I will do his wash for as long as he wishes."

"Oh, dear no, that shan't be necessary at all," Laura said. "You see, he owes me a great deal. My late husband was both his partner and mentor and made him a great deal of money before he passed. I am very certain that if I ask, he shall be most happy to repay his debt to my husband by doing me the service of apprenticing our dear Bobby here for no fee at all." Laura caught my eye again and winked as though we had entered into some secret pact.

Whatever she was getting me into, I did not like it. In an attempt at turning the direction of the conversation away from this apprenticeship idea, I said, "Perhaps, I could return to school and spend some time with Tom in the evening. Shouldn't I continue my studies, Mother?"

"We shall see, son. But first we must wait to see whether or not Laura's friend… What is his name, dear?"

"Mr. Zackery Gibbon," Laura said, drawing the name with lightning speed and, for an instant, even I believed him to be a real person.

"We shall have to wait until Mr. Gibbon gives his answer," Mother said. "Are you certain we won't be putting you out, dear?"

We? How did I come to be included in this request?

"Think nothing of it," Laura reassured.

"You have no idea what this means to me, dear. I don't quite know how to thank you."

"Nonsense," Laura smiled, "you have already given us shelter in your beautiful home which is far more than we could ever have hoped for. It is we who should be thanking you."

Laura thought it best to accompany "Tom" to Mr. Gibbon's shop due to it being such a long way to High Holbourn Street. Though I had secretly informed Laura that I desired no part in her and Pike's dealings, she gave me that wicked smile, batted her long lashes, and I was her man. It was not long after that Laura came home with the news that, after much consideration, and as Laura had vouched for my character, Mr. Gibbon had decided to take me on as an additional apprentice.

Mother's jubilation bordered on near hysteria. No sooner had the words left Laura's lips, than she took hold of me and, with a vice-like embrace, proceeded to squeeze all the air from my lungs. "My son, the estate auctioneer! Oh, just the sound of it brings me such joy. Aren't you thrilled, Bobby? You don't seem thrilled. Oh, Bobby, you have no idea what this will mean for your future."

Now I have really deceived her, I thought. If she ever learns the truth, there will be Hell to pay. I will have destroyed all trust she has in me, not to mention having broken her heart. A glance at Laura's pleading expression told me I was supposed to feign happiness and, at the very least, display some degree of enthusiasm, yet I felt quite the contrary. For I knew full well that there was no Mr. Gibbon, Estate Auctioneer, nor any place on High Holbourn Street that I would be apprenticing. I was, however, soon to find that I had been wrong on both counts.

"Lilly, what do you think of your brother apprenticing to be an estate auctioneer?" Mother said, with delight.

Lilly smiled sheepishly and shrugged her little shoulders. Of course, she had no idea of what Mother was speaking for she was still much too young to understand such things. And had she been able, I doubt that she would have any opinion upon the matter for, of late, she seemed to lack concern for most things. Even at dinner, it was difficult to coerce her to eat, for instead, she would play with her cauliflower and asparagus as though it were one of her dolls. On occasion, I have noticed her staring out of a window for long moments with a blank expression. Ever since Father was killed, she seems to have drifted further and further down some long corridor of her mind. Mother often said she would eventually snap out of it, yet I had reservations. Perhaps in the spring we three might go for walks in the park again. But then, it would most likely only serve to remind her of the one missing from the affair. I struggled to think of a means to give her something to look forward to other than the next day's chores. Recalling Laura and Pike standing in front of the Theatre Royal, I imagined that if I were to have enough money, someday I shall take her and Mother there. As for myself, I had never been but was told by Pike that it is a great deal of fun and could possibly serve to deter Lilly's thoughts of longing for Father. Perhaps, I thought, with time, her spirits will rise again.

As to the getting of that money, it did take much longer than I had surmised. To be sure, money, even for a thief, requires hard work and much skill. The hard work comes in the form of practice, as does any trade, and the skill is gained by the use of one's own wits. It was through practice and skill that I developed the ability to acquire property—property that would later be turned into money. As for the actual turning into money, someone else performed that service.

His name was indeed Zackery Gibbon, a man in his late forties who sported a powdered periwig that covered a bald space atop his head while a noticeable lump of fat protruded from under his chin that shook as he spoke. His nose was scarred from smallpox and shaped like the beak of a hawk, while his lips were thick and generally pursed as though he had been sucking on a lemon. On the street, Zack could easily appear as a wealthy gentleman and come off as quite suave in his manners if not for an unsightly scar that ran diagonally across his forehead. Of this he seemed quite sensitive and made every attempt to cover it with one of his many periwigs.

About town, Zack was always to be found in the best of attire. His wardrobe, an immense collection, was kept within a spare bedchamber and neatly hung from several pine rods spanning the entire room that were supported at short intervals by stout posts. The costume Zack generally wore comprised a tricorn hat matching the various colours of his numerous velvet waistcoats and neatly pressed culottes. Over embroidered white silk stockings, he wore shoes that always displayed a black sheen beneath buckles, of no less than silver, but usually of gold, and polished to a high luster. His fingers sparkled with diamonds, amethysts, rubies, or emeralds. Whatever precious stone he chose for the day, it was always of an intricate design and set into either heavy gold or silver mounts.

In place of a sword or dirk hanger which, of late, had gone out of fashion, he sported any number of fanciful walking sticks with hand grips of intricately carved silver or gold wolf's heads. His walking sticks, however, were no less deadly than a sword, for within their wooden staff was concealed a dirk of near the same length. Zack, being quite the swordsman, frequently demonstrated his expertise on our mannequin while allowing Pike and me to take instruction and practice under his supervision.

Zack's countenance was generally one of mirth, yet I suspected he harbored a carefully concealed ill will toward his clients that was only assuaged by his ability to profit from them.

One of his prizes, a thing which I most admired, was an intricately carved gold timepiece that he kept inside his waistcoat pocket. Zack never attached it to a fob for fear of falling victim to one of his own techniques whereupon a thief only had to give it a tug and out it came to be snipped from its chain by a small pair of scissors. Oft' times I would ask him what o'clock it was just to see him produce it.

Zack's relationship with Laura, Pike and me was, for all appearances, an avuncular one. And though he doted upon us as if we were his prize pupils, I suspected his deference was solely due to the great amount of valuables we brought him. And although we were only three of his many suppliers, most of the other thieves couldn't come anywhere near the high-priced items we acquired due to their shabby appearance, as well as lack of experience with London's upper class. We, on the other hand, had the beautiful and charming Laura who carried herself with uncommon grace while displaying the elegant discourse of a true genteel lady.

As Zack was our sole fence, I had, for a time, often wondered if the twenty percent to value he paid us for the items we brought in were on the same line as he paid other thieves. And after I had found his percentage to be the general due for stolen property, I still had my reservations as to its fairness once I had smoked his true fencing game. Oddly, most of our merchandise wound up back with the party from which it had been stolen. The reason being, Zack kept an advertisement in the London Journal offering his services to track down and recover stolen property. The payment for this service was in the form of a reward that sometimes matched or surpassed the store value of the items found, depending upon just how badly the gentleman needed to conceal the loss. For this, Zack received gratitude and respect for providing such a unique service. The fact that the thieves had not been caught was usually of no consequence to the cully, for the items were generally of sentimental value. Most items were of great expense, such as an engraved gold watch or snuff box with an inscription from the wife or mistress of which the cully had no desire to explain the loss thereof. For a cully to pay Zack his price rather than explain to his wife how he had lost the precious item was, in the least, a welcomed relief.

Pike and I spent many hours in Zack's second floor flat, a well furnished place with an office near the front of the building that overlooked High Holbourn Street. For me, it was a school of sorts, in which I was the only pupil. My course of concentrated study was the art of picking pockets, a practice that Zack would have Pike and me practice upon one another in what seemed an endless exercise.

"NO, NO, NO! I'll show you once more, but watch carefully," Zack would instruct. With Pike playing the part of the cully, Zack approached him with the skill of a stage actor, his every move displaying complete disinterest in Pike, who pretended to be standing on a street corner, very much aware that someone would wish to get their hands on his valuables. Zack walked with his head turned as though fixated on some object in a store window and bumped, ever so slightly, into Pike.

Pike appeared angry, saying, "See here, old fellow. Can't you watch where you are going?"

Zack faced Pike suspiciously and checked his pockets before declaring, "I believe my timepiece was in this pocket just a second ago."

Pike gave an indignant glare and stated, "Sir, do you make an accusation?"

Then, Zack glanced at the floor and sighed, "Dreadfully sorry." Bending over, Zack reached down to retrieve an imaginary watch. After straightening up, "Must have come out when we collided. Can't be too careful these days with all the riffraff about, now can we?" Holding the imaginary timepiece out, he checked the time, shook the timepiece, and asked. "Might I bother you with the time, what o'clock is it?"

Pike took hold of his fob and withdrew his watch while, at the same time, Zack stepped in close pretending to have trouble seeing the hands on the timepiece. In the same motion, Zack's hand slid into Pike's coat and dipped into his low waistcoat pocket, taking Pike's purse before sliding around to the other side and, with lightning speed, removing the snuffbox from his upper waistcoat pocket.

"Ah, yes. If yours is correct then mine must be slightly off. Let me see." He adjusted his timepiece to match Pike's while checking the remaining pockets of Pike's coat. "How's that?" he asked, before closing the cover.

Pike smiled saying, "I believe you have it correct now. Good day to you, sir." Pike tipped his hat and they were off in opposite directions.

"Now, I believe it is your turn. Are you ready?" Zack asked, as we went over it again and again.

We did it at least fifty times that day and fifty more the next. It became like a repetitive play with no audience. Once I had it down to perfection, Zack would create a new situation. And again we started with fifty rehearsals, and the next day, again. This went on for weeks yet, in spite of my pleading, he would not let me go out into the city to perform it for real.

"Not until I say you are ready. Don't you understand, son? If you make one mistake, you could get the tree. No! You may not touch a cully until I say you may." Though he was a strict disciplinarian, as time passed under his tutelage, I began to grow fond of him and those suspicions that I had previously harbored slowly melted away. As weeks passed into months, I practiced, sometimes with Zack, sometimes with a fully dressed mannequin that Zack had procured for just this purpose. And as I practiced, Pike and Laura went about the market places, theatres, or visited the great Rotunda at Ranelagh. As they brought back various items and were paid for them, I steadily grew envious. These items started out as merely merchandise, yet, over time, they became precious trophies to me—something I could aspire to getting my hands on if only for the sake of saying I acquired it myself.

At length, I came to a point where I could no longer contain my anxiety. I realized I must do something yet had no idea what it should be. Then, the day came when Zack greeted Laura and Pike at the top of the back stairs and I stepped alongside him to see what they had brought in. As they laid out their booty onto the oval drop-leaf table that sat in his study, I realized an opportunity.

"My, this is grand for a day's work," he congratulated. "You two have brought quite a catch for a day's work. Let us go over them again, shall we." He glanced over the table, stopping at each object to carefully assess its value until he came upon one item in particular. His eyes widened and his jaw dropped as he barked out, "What is this? Why, it is my watch, and this looks like…MY PURSE!" The colour drained from his face for an instant before he turned to me. "YOU… YOU DID THIS!" he said, slamming his fist onto the table.

Dear God, but I really botched this up, I thought. He is going to kill me. Taking up one of his deadly walking canes from the polished mahogany stand by the door, he came over to me and, laying his hands on my shoulders said, "KNEEL!"

Perhaps he will only knock me about, I reasoned. If he were going to kill me, he would have already done so. Reluctantly, I did as he commanded.

As he stood over me, he withdrew the long narrow blade rending a ringing sound as the razor sharp steel slid from its scabbard. Holding the blade over my head, he stood motionless while Laura and Pike remained silent, their expressions somber.

Dear God, he is going to cut off my head, I thought. I was about to bolt but for some reason my instincts held me there.

Then, lowering the blade, he let it rest for a split second onto each of my shoulders while saying, "Robert, I dub thee consummate pickpocket."

Then they all laughed, while Laura, clapping her hands, gave me a cheering, "Huzzah!" before wrapping her lovely arms around me and pressing me tight to her soft, rose scented bosom.

"You've done it boy! You are now ready," Zack congratulated. "If you can pick my pockets then I have no doubt you may have your way with all the pockets London has to offer." He shook his head in disbelief, "You picked my pockets, a thing even Pike here has been unable to manage."

Pike appeared slighted by this remark and could only reply with, "Unable to do it, yet, sir!"

Zack gave Pike an amused glance before turning to me. After giving me a serious look in the eye, he smiled and, throwing up his hands, said, "At any rate, you have graduated. I can teach you no more."

Zack was truly a professor of the art, for no one knew it better, nor was more practiced than he. I often wondered that had he applied himself in other more legitimate fields of study, he might have attained a professorship in Cambridge or Oxford. What a day, I thought. Now that I have the professor's seal of approval, I am sufficiently prepared to go out into the world and practice the art on real cullies.

It was not long before I was dressing up in fine attire and attending plays at one of the theatres or taking in many of the other events. Our general ploy was that Pike and I would pretend to be Laura's two nephews while she used her womanly charm to attract the attention of an unwary gentleman. Within seconds we would have his purse, snuff box, watch with fob included, and he being left completely unaware. Shortly thereafter, we would hire a hackney coach and travel to another suitable location. This we repeated until we had obtained enough booty to bring to Zack.

From that point onward, it was Laura, Pike, and I taking on the city of London. A typical day for the three of us would start with a hearty breakfast prepared by Mother and Lilly at nine o'clock, after which we would finish dressing for the day's work. Per Laura's arrangement, a hackney coachman would meet us each morning on the corner of Oxford Road and North Audley Street at half past ten. From there, he would take us to any number of market places, drop us off and meet us the next day at the same location except for Sundays and such other days that we decided to take for a holiday. This pickup location was purposefully set at three streets from the house so that the driver could have no knowledge of where we lived. Laura said that no one should ever know the location of our home, not the coachman, and especially not Zack.

"Why can't we trust Zack?" I inquired. "Is he not our most valued friend?"

Laura rolled her eyes. "So innocent are we, my little Robert. You shall someday find, and preferably without too great an expense, that in this business, as any other, you cannot trust anyone but your closest partners."

"But Zack has taught me everything," I argued. "Is he not one of our closest partners? I just don't see why…"

"HE IS NOT," Laura scolded, her eyes growing cold as I had never seen them, "and shall never be as close as are we three. Believe you me, there is nothing to gain and everything, and I do mean EVERYTHING to lose by his knowing the location of our home." In spite of my previous suspicions, I wanted to believe we could trust Zack, yet the conviction in her aquamarine eyes told me that she had good reason to believe otherwise. Thus far, she had never steered me astray, so I accepted her truth without further argument.

The places in which we had the hackney drop us were, for the most part, the Haymarket, Covent Garden, The Strand and Charing Cross. In these places we might stroll down the streets or peer into the shops for prospective cullies. On other days, we would attend performances at one of the theaters, or, from April to July, take a drive out of town to Ranelagh Gardens, a beautiful affair located just south of Hyde Park near Chelsea College. Therein lies a great piece of architecture called "The Rotunda" where people enjoy concerts while sitting in one of the box seat areas of the balconies, or simply taking a casual stroll around the circular floor that surrounds the orchestra. The balconies were splendid vantage points for gazing out over the crowd. If not enjoying a concert, we could have a picnic or take a gondola ride in the canal while observing the passersby for a potential cully. Strolling down the elm tree-lined walkways on occasion might include seeing a Duke or perhaps even a Prince, all for the admittance price of six pence.

And from May to August, eight pence gets you a river taxi from Temple Stairs across the Thames to the gardens at Vauxhall. Vauxhall is a beautiful place with many acres of shady garden walkways lit by a thousand lamps in the evening, its booths displaying art pieces by Hogarth or Hayman, as well as pictures of the upcoming plays at the theatres. Once Laura had captured a gentleman's attention, Pike and I would go to work. Usually Pike would play the acrobat by walking on his hands or standing with his tricorn hat waving high while loudly reciting a line from a Shakespearean play. This innovation was my idea, for it served to capture the attention of the people around us while Laura batted her long eyelashes at some amorous gentleman. With everyone's attention within the immediate vicinity thus diverted, I had freedom to pick the gentleman clean, as well as anyone within reach.

Once we had completed a successful performance, Laura would ask the gentleman what o'clock it was and state that she must get home before her husband, the magistrate, finds she has been gone from the house. We would then go in separate directions and meet at the river to catch the taxi across the river to London. From there we would climb into a hackney coach and make off to some other business area for more game, the idea being to get far away from the recent cully as quickly as possible.

When finished for the day or evening, we would head back home where Mother and Lilly would prepare a deliciously wholesome meal. Afterwards we would sit in the parlor by the fire and tell tales of our "work" at the liquidation shop before retiring for the evening. I didn't mind spinning the yarns of my day's apprenticing, for I had, by then, reasoned that it was an absolute necessity. For in this way, Mother did not suspect what was really going on, thereby putting her mind at ease.

And with her mind at ease, we were free to continue our lives in the manner of which we had become accustomed. To be sure, it was an equitable cooperative. Laura, Pike and I bore the responsibility of providing money for warmth, food, and clothing, while Mother and Lilly took care of the home, the wash, the mending, and prepared our meals.

On one evening in particular, we were visited by an extremely apologetic Peter Hendricks. Hat tucked under arm and wig properly adjusted, Peter stood at the door and begged forgiveness of Mother for his behavior at Father's funeral.

To my astonishment, Mother received him cordially, and asked him in for a cup of tea.

Peter accepted the kindness and, with a somber expression inquired, "Might I ask how you and your children do? I realize it must be extreme hard with the... um, the loss, and all."

Mother gave a forced smile while her eyes told me to keep my mouth shut, and said, "We manage well enough, thank you."

Peter looked about, taking in the air of abundance while failing to conceal his surprise, "I am most happy for you, ma'am. I feared you would be put out with the loss of income and all. To be sure, your funds must be heavily taxed and as gesture of kindness, I thought the least I might do is to make you an offer."

Laura was sitting with Pike and me in the parlor just within earshot as Mother gave Peter a puzzled look, "I am afraid I don't follow, of what offer do you speak?"

"Why, an offer on your house, ma'am," Peter said, a wicked smile upon his lips.

"I am afraid I have no intention of selling our home, Mr. Hendricks," Mother replied with a tight-lipped smile.

Hendricks' smile faded, "Perhaps in future, if your circumstances ever change, I may be allowed to help out in some way, such as, say, shoveling coal. I could clean up your cellar, or do odd jobs and the like about the house now and again."

One side of Mother's lips curled up in a half smile as she replied, "That is most generous of you, Mr. Hendricks."

"I would take kindly if you called me Peter, ma'am," he interjected.

"But we are in need of no such help. As you can see, things are quite well here, Mr. Hendricks," Mother continued. "And if that is all, I shall bid you good day."

Hendricks nodded and, saying no more, stepped quickly through the door, placed his hat upon his wigged head and, mounting his horse, trotted away.

We exchanged puzzled glances and Mother, her control near at end, went upstairs to her bedchamber and closed the door.

"What do you suppose that was about?" Laura asked.

"It would appear he is feeling guilty over his neglect in my father's accident," I said. "Yet, I didn't sense any sincerity in his demeanor. Did you?"

"As one thief to another, I would say that, upon the surface, he has thievery in mind. Yet, his is more along the lines of the confidence man than the pickpocket."

"I see what you mean," I said. "However, I can't smoke what he wishes to get at. And he did offer to 'buy' our home."

"Indeed, which would indicate there is something of even more value than the house that he is after," Laura said with a puzzled expression. "You don't perhaps have gold stashed within these walls, do you?"

I laughed, "If that were the case, we should never have done any business together."

With a smile worth gold, she said, "As to that, you seem to be doing quite well with this new calling."

At first, I found this new lifestyle of lying and cheating a most difficult river to cross. To be sure, I had been taught the Commandments and knew that lying and stealing were right there among the big ones. And it was only by way of numerous discussions with Laura that I was finally able to arrive at the opposite bank of that river. For no matter how I came at it, it always boiled down to the one unshakable reality, survival. And to survive as a thief with Laura was to be a thief within her prescribed bounds. It was not done by knocking someone on the head and taking his life in order to steal his meager farthings, but by lifting the purse of someone who could, for obvious reasons, afford the loss. "No physical injury, no permanent damage, not taking from someone starving, but taking from someone who will recover by his own plentiful resources," was the way she put it.

"Could you not find work as a servant?" I asked.

At this question, she dropped her head ever so slightly, her golden curls cascading onto her shoulders, and explained, "If I were to find employment in that occupation, it would only provide me with sufficient funds to purchase my meals, forcing me to take up residence in my employer's house. I would be forever in my employer's debt and I would be forced to continue this work until I was too old and feeble to perform my duties. The pay would not lend itself to any kind of savings and I would die a penniless beggar on the streets of this fine city." Raising her head, she penetrated me with her eyes, explaining, "If not for Pike, I would still be living the lowly life of a prostitute, eventually contracting the pox and, ultimately die in some indigent hospital."

So there lay our course; we three helped one another survive while Mother provided shelter. It was the only way, I finally reasoned. For, if it was wrong, then so was standing idly by and watching my mother sell the house only to have her and my sister waste away in a tenement until the funds ran out. And I would see Hell before I let it happen.

As winter turned to spring, Mother, Lilly and me would go for our Sunday walks in Hyde Park, just as we did when Father was with us. For sport, I would beg Mother to let me climb the trees and she would, at length, relent. Lilly, on the other hand, would never follow me, but instead, would sit on the blanket with Mother and sulk. Other times, Pike/Tom would accompany us and climb with me. Mother had since become very fond of 'Tom' and he had, of late, resorted to calling her Mother. As for me, it was only a short while after his stay with us that I felt towards him as the brother I had never had.

Laura always absented herself from our walks to the park for we began it with a visit to the church. For reasons she would not disclose, Laura loathed churches. And I must confess, after what happened to Father, I also felt a good deal of unease when attending services. Yet, it was for Mother's contentment that I went. Church services were, in some way, important to her and it was my wish to make things as pleasant for her as possible. As it was, life had become quite good to the five of us. We were a family, though a bit larger than before, yet a family just the same. And my home was, once again, a very happy one.

Since Laura and Pike had come to stay with us, the house had increasingly become very well furnished. For instance, there was wallpaper of a lavish floral design imported from Paris and installed in each room with its own separate theme, the new settee, drapes, linens, plate, silver, and fine china; adding many new things, as well as replacing our old and badly worn things. Mother's wardrobe had steadily increased while Lilly's and my closets were also filled with fine expensive attire. And to make our lives even better, Mother hired a day maid to do all the cleaning and assist in the kitchen while a washer woman came every Wednesday to perform the task that we all loathed. Where did the money come from? Why, the estate auctioning business, of course. I was now a full-fledged auctioneer earning half commission on High Holbourn Street.

When Mother informed me how proud she was to have her son become such a huge success, my shame grew a hundredfold—even more so when she stated that Father, God rest his soul, would be even prouder than she. Though she longed to see me at work, I informed her that it would not be possible as only the buying public may be present at such events. And I took care not to give her sufficient funds to attend as a buyer. At length, she ceased to press me further, contenting herself with shopping in the local haberdashery or visiting her sister and brother-in-law at their shop in Covent Garden Market.

On a few occasions we had taken her and Lilly to see a play. This was a most difficult affair for two reasons. First, there were the possible cullies, which we dare not touch while Mother was present. And second, there was the off chance we could be recognized by one of our past victims.

The last time we took Mother to Covent Garden Theater, Pike had stayed home to keep an eye on Lilly, as well as avoid the chance of our being recognized more easily with the three of us together.

Still, we were nearly undone when, during the intermission of a play, a gentleman who, being a recent cully, raised his voice in our direction stating, "There's the wench that stole my purse!"

Looking around, I spied the gentleman in the balcony pointing directly at Laura who stood with Mother in a throng of people. Fortunately, two prostitutes who stood nearby uttered their indignation to the gentleman's accusation as they believed themselves to be the accused.

While the crowd's attention was thus confused as to whom the gentleman referred, Laura clutched her stomach and, turning to Mother, said, "Please forgive me, Mother, but I am suddenly most uncomfortable and fear that if I don't return home directly and lie down, I shall faint. Perhaps you and Bobby should stay and finish the play. I shall catch a taxi and be home in no time at all." Then, quickly turning about, she started towards the entrance doors.

"Nonsense, my dear," Mother said, rising to her feet. "Bobby, come along now. We must see Laura home to her bed. She does seem to have grown pale, the poor dear."

In an instant, I was at their side as we hastened to the door of the lobby. Once we had cleared the door, I spied the cully shoving his way down the stairs from the balcony. Though not thirty feet behind us, his way was mercifully blocked by a line of people awaiting the next performance.

As we passed through the ornately gilded entrance doors to the street, he spotted us and cried out, "Don't let her get away, and that little bastard with her!"

Fortunately, we were through the door and into the street before anyone had an opportunity to follow the gentleman's finger. I signaled for a hackney coach and, as the driver pulled up, Laura, with the speed of a rabbit, stepped quickly inside. Before climbing into the coach after her, Mother hesitated for a second, apparently surprised that someone feeling poorly could move so quickly.

The seconds passed as though everything, the cab, Mother's feet, even the air, had been coated with glue and I fought back a feeling of panic that nearly had me bodily shoving Mother into the cab. Once she was seated, I stepped in and, reaching for the door with trembling hands, called out, "Driver, to Grosvenor District!" I managed to close the door just as the gentleman emerged from the lobby. With a crazed look in his eye, he darted to the street, first looking one way, then the other before catching sight of our coach as it pulled away.

"Make haste driver, the lady is quite ill," I prompted.

Mother gave me a disapproving glance, and, turning her attention to Laura, said, "Robert, do not speak to that gentleman in such a condescending tone. Have I not taught you to respect your elders?"

"Sorry, Mother. I was only concerned for Laura," I said, attempting to cover my anxiety.

The cully now ran after our coach and I had just managed closing the curtain at the second he came alongside. Through a slight opening at the edge of the shade, I could see that his expression was one of extreme consternation as he attempted to peer into our cab.

"That does not give you justification for such rudeness, Robert. Apologize to the man this instant and ask him to please slow this pace before he has us all tossed to the floor," Mother insisted.

The cully opened his mouth to hail our driver and, just when he was about to call out, stumbled, nearly losing his balance, and came to a halt at the intersection. Through the back window pane, I could see him at the corner, doubled over with his hands on his knees, gasping for breath as we sped away.

"Driver, I am so sorry to have spoken to you so rudely. Please accept my apology," I said, feigning sincerity.

"Apology accepted lad," the driver answered cordially.

"Now, for the Dear's sake, ask him to slow down," Mother reminded.

"Yes, Mother," I said.

To our good fortune, Mother hadn't noticed the man, for all the while Laura had occupied her full attention. And it was by some strange medical miracle that Laura's condition improved proportionally to our distance from the theatre.

"It must have been the air in the theater, dear. All those people crowded together, coughing and sneezing. It's a wonder we all didn't take ill as you did. Oh, I do appreciate your taking me, sure, for I have enjoyed the plays, yet—If you don't mind my being candid, I couldn't give a care if I ever saw another. The seating is very uncomfortable and the crowds are rakish and obnoxious at times, especially those men in the balcony with those shameless tarts."

"Well, I am relieved you have told me," Laura said, with a feigned weak voice. "We most certainly shall not have you suffer through another."

Mother sighed, "Oh! Don't concern yourself with me, dear. It is you who is in need of care." Just then, the coach hit a pothole in the road rendering a bone-rattling jar. "Oh, my poor dear, you must be feeling most uncomfortable with all this tossing about. Would you prefer we put you into a sedan chair?"

Laura put on her best pained smile, saying, "Sweet Mother, I shall be fine once we are at home."

"We shall put you to bed directly just as soon as we arrive," Mother assured. "You must have rest or you will be sure to come down with something."

No, I thought, we most definitely will not take Mother to the theater again. I had had my first close encounter with recognition and, like a fool, had not realized till then the grave potential of what might have occurred had the gentleman caught up with us. Mother would have wanted to know why he accused us. And during the time of her inquiry, a watchman or one of the Bow Street runners would have arrived on the spot. From there, we would be taken to the nearest jail while an investigation took place. Our house would be searched and some questionable items would be discovered, giving them cause to charge Mother as well. No, we would never take that chance again.

At home, Mother had seen to Laura's going to bed and informed "Tom" and me that she was not to be disturbed. After a couple of hours, Mother fell asleep in the new mahogany rocker we had recently purchased for her and, after seeing that Lilly was asleep in her bed, I took the opportunity to ask Pike to meet me in Laura's room. When I came in, Pike was already resting on Laura's settee while Laura lay in her bed propped up by a stack of deeply coloured velvet pillows. I took a seat on the stool at her vanity and took in the fragrance of her perfume while she explained to Pike what had taken place at the theater. Pike, listening intently, remained silent, a sedate expression on his rounded features. And once she had finished the account, he silently contemplated our story. Just when we were beginning to wonder if he was falling asleep, he broke the silence and said, "I had a feeling it would come to this one day."

"Of what do you speak?" Laura asked, her eyes narrowing.

"In fact, I have been thinking upon it for some time now. I didn't want to say anything for fear of begging fate," he continued.

"What do you mean?" I asked, not a little puzzled. "What is 'it'? And how has 'it' come?"

"It, my friends, is notoriety," he explained. "We have been doing this for a good while, haven't we? And though London is the largest city in the world, there are only so many places were we can work our craft. Eventually, someone else will remember us, just as they did today."

"Yes, but that was mere happenstance. The chances of it occurring again must be few to none," Laura said.

Pike lightly shook his head, paused, and said, "Today was only the beginning of it. It shall happen again. Not for a while, perhaps. A year, maybe two at best, but it will happen and we had better be ready."

"We were ready today. Even with Mother there, I thought we handled it quite well," Laura said, defensively. "And we shall never take her to the theatre again. She does not wish to go. She said that she doesn't feel comfortable there, so our problem is already solved."

"To be sure, it will be easier to run without having to concern ourselves with Mother getting caught up in it," Pike said. "But eventually, it will begin to happen. An infrequent occurrence for a time, but then it will become more and more frequent as the months and years pass."

"Since when did you become the philosopher?" Laura teased.

"It's got nothing to do with philosophy. It has to do with experience," he said, with a solemn expression.

"What are you saying? When did you experience such a thing? Surely, not since I have known you," Laura said, with an amused smile.

"I didn't experience it directly," Pike answered, his head low. "It's what happened to my old rogue of a father. Oh, he tried to ignore it at first. Said he was too quick to be caught. But, as the months passed, his expression became more and more wary. Then after a year, I couldn't remember when he didn't go to the window every now and again to see if someone was close on his trail. The last time—the last time he went out, I waited and—days passed but—I waited still. Yet, he never came home. I was of about seven years then. Later, I overheard someone saying that they had hunted him down. You know, the Bow Street runners?" his voice cracking on the name, before breaking off. He then turned away, as though turning away from an unsightly scene.

Taken aback, Laura and I glanced at one another while waiting for him to continue.

"They put him in prison, and sentenced him to hang," he said, nodding his head in an effort to accept it.

"I have grown very fond of this family and now see things differently. Before, we didn't have much to lose, you and I. But now we have so much... I have a mother, brother, and sisters. I've never had a real family and do not believe I could bear to lose this one. I shall never chance returning to the situation we both shared." It was at that moment that Laura did something I had, heretofore, not seen her do. Placing her arms around Pike, she held him in a tight embrace. Her eyes reddened, and, with tears, she kissed his forehead, rocking him slowly. With a sideways glance, she motioned me toward her and, with only a slight hesitation, I joined in the embrace.

"We must do something," Pike said, sniffing, his nose running.

In that moment, I felt almost as loved and connected to them as I did with my own family. If he was right, and we did become recognizable, we would be forced to either cease our craft, or move away, before things became too dangerous. We decided that, as a precaution, we would open a savings account at a secure bank. This would serve to support us in the event that we might have to lay low for a while. As it turned out, any incident of being recognized did not occur again for years.

In hindsight, Pike's plan turned out to be a grand idea for within a very short time we each had as much as fifty pounds tucked away in an account Laura had opened at the Bank of England.

The months turned into years, and very prosperous years at that. By the time I was fourteen, we had increased our bank account savings to well over a thousand pounds each. The saving was made even easier due to the fact that we were no longer in need of furniture or clothing, for we had previously purchased everything we needed and much more. So much so, that we wanted for nothing. If we bought anything other than food or the necessaries, it was for the most part something expensive, such as jewelry and fine clothing. I even purchased a gold watch, similar to the one owned by Zack. To be sure, I could have kept any of the ones that I had stolen, if not for the fact that I would be carrying evidence, should I ever be suspected.

Having exceeded our goal by leaps and bounds, we came to realize that we were successful beyond our wildest dreams. Actually, we had become too successful. Three times within a fortnight we had been recognized by past cullies. On one such incident, the three of us were walking out of the Theatre Royal into the cold foggy night air just after attending the popular play titled "The Beggar's Opera" when; suddenly Laura had been grabbed from behind. He was a chubby old scoundrel of very grey complexion which made his face appear a blur beneath his bushy powdered wig, pink velvet waistcoat, and gold leaf embroidered topcoat. In a high pitched, almost feminine voice, he rang out the hue and cry, "THIEF! THIEF!"

Swinging her about like a dog with a stocking in its mouth, his face came to bear and I recognized him as a recent cully from whom, one week prior, Laura had lifted his purse—a purse that contained a substantial sum of guineas. In seconds he had the entire crowd about us in alarm. So tight was his grip that, with the best of our combined efforts, neither Pike nor I could pry his hands from her. Finally, I managed to get hold of his little finger and, bending it back, applied pressure until it snapped like a twig. The man screamed even louder now that he was obviously in great pain and releasing his hold, Laura fell to the ground.

With the crowd close in about us, Laura got to her feet and stood bent over while exclaiming, "My spectacles, has anyone seen my spectacles?"

Pike and I followed suit, stooping over and searching the ground around those about us. Now and again, squatting down to give close inspection of the paving stones, we feigned concern as some of the onlookers stepped aside to allow us passage so that we may just find those elusive spectacles. As we continued making distance from the screaming man, we were soon completely out of his view, thereby giving him no place to direct his accusations. I sensed the impending approach of a watchman, yet I dared to glance back and saw that the cully had not moved from where we had left him and was now doubled over clutching his hand. Once we had made our way to the street, Laura rose up and hailed a passing hackney coach. Just as the watchman made his way to the screaming man, our coach pulled away from the multitude while the driver skillfully wove us into the traffic of the street. I could see the man pointing to the crowd about him while, with a look of desperation, searched in vain for any glimpse of us. Once again, we had made our escape due to the good fortune of a hackney coach being close at hand.

"Where did he come from?" Pike asked, while peering through the window shade of the coach.

"It was as if he simply appeared from nowhere," Laura replied, her voice trembling. Taking out her kerchief, she pulled her skirt hoops above her perfectly shaped but now scuffed knees to dab at the blood seeping through her white silk stockings.

"He must have been waiting for us," I said. "He's the one we tapped last week at the same play. I told you we shouldn't return here so soon but you had to see it. To be sure, we mustn't return here for a while."

"Oh, but I love this play so," Laura said plaintively. Then, realizing the futility of it, she sighed, "I suppose you are right," and with another sigh, said, "I shall miss it dearly." Her eyes met Pike's and she gave him a forlorn smile, saying, "Well, it appears you were right that day. Do you remember, when you said we shall someday be having more frequent close calls?"

Pike nodded, and regretfully said, "I had hopes of being wrong."

The fog was dense as we rode through the evening streets and with our coach lantern lighting up the dark doorways to reveal dim outlines of people standing in the shadows, I thought, perhaps we have been in the light too long. Perhaps the time has come for us to step back into the shadows. If we don't, we could soon find ourselves glancing about like a fox with the hounds on his trail. And if the hounds catch us, how, then, would my mother and sister survive? With that thought, I decided to make a proposal to the other two members of our trio, "Perhaps we should take a holiday from this work until our cullies have forgotten us. Either that, or we shall have to wear disguises."

"I quite agree," Laura said, a resigned smile on her full lips. "It is become far too dangerous of late. I say the time has come for us to lay low. What do you say, Tom?"

We had gotten so used to calling Pike Tom by now that we sometimes did it in private to avoid the confusion. I sensed that he had grown fond of the name.

"Well," Pike said, his fist supporting his chin while in deep concentration, "we could leave of London, perhaps for some other city where there would be easy pickings to choose from."

"I can't see us leaving London," Laura said, a note of sadness in her voice. "I have been to the south of London and believe you me, there is nothing like London—no, nothing even close to its grandeur, except perhaps Paris. And I can not speak a word of French, so that is out of the question."

"I have another thought," I said. "I believe we should give access of our bank accounts to Mother."

They both stared at me, yet neither spoke, so I went on, "Just in case misfortune finds us. Suppose we all get nabbed. Our money will be in the bank and we won't have access to any of it."

Laura's eyes narrowed and, for a second, I suspected she was angry at me for suggesting such a thing, but then she said, "You have a very valid point, Robert. Not that I believe for a second that we shall ever be nabbed, however, if we were to fall victim to such circumstances, there would be no way of hiring good counsel or being provided with decent food. Tom knows well enough about the prison fare they serve to those that have no funds."

Pike nodded with a pained expression. He had been nabbed once and spent a fortnight in St. Giles Roundhouse before the charges were dropped due to lack of evidence. Evidence he had managed to conceal by shoving between the copper panels of a roof he had climbed during his attempted escape. That was just before he lost his footing and fell into a grain wagon parked directly in front of the constable. While in jail he had gotten so sick from the food and putrid air that he had nearly died of gaol fever after his release.

"And what will become of Mother and Lilly if we are in prison?" Once I had voiced my concerns, it grew very quiet inside the cab. Soon the buildings we passed became familiar and I knew we were near the intersection of Oxford and North Audley Street.

As we stirred in our seats to collect our valuables for our walk home, Laura broke the silence, "I believe it is a splendid idea Robert. Though, as I already stated, I do not fancy us getting nabbed as we are much to intelligent for that. Right, Tom?"

"That's right. We ain't never gonna get caught," Pike said, his dimpled smile just visible in the dim lantern light.

"Mind your language," Laura admonished. "Goodness, but old habits do die hard. How many times must I tell you? You must do away with that urchin speech or you will give us away—straightaway." Then, turning to me, her irritation abated and she spoke with sage-like wisdom, "We can't ever be certain of what the future holds. We must be prepared for anything, even the worst. On the morrow, we shall all go to the bank and have the documents drawn up so that Mother may have access our funds. Do you have any objection to this, Tom?"

Pike shook his head.

That evening, Laura informed Mother the company was closing down for inventory and that we would be on holiday for a fortnight; and, that first thing on the morrow, she wished to take us to the Bank of England to deposit our hard-earned pay, as well as withdraw funds from her trust.

"I am sure the boys will enjoy the ride. I have heard that it is a beautiful bank," Mother said.

Laura inclined her head, "You haven't seen it? It is quite a grand piece of architecture."

Mother put her hands together and smiled with a degree of embarrassment, "Why, no, John used to handle all the finances and I never had any call to go there."

Laura raised a brow and said, "Perhaps you would like to come with us?"

Mother's smile vanished and she tilted her head, "Why, that is most kind of you, my dear, but perhaps some other time."

The Bank of England was a busy place with a constant stream of patrons entering and leaving through the same glass door which led into a great lobby. Once inside, one couldn't help following the contours of the walls which rose as much as twenty-five feet to a recessed and ornamented ceiling. Pike and I followed Laura across the lobby which was lit by two rows of man-sized windows that covered the entire wall facing the street, giving the great room an almost outdoor daylight effect.

We stopped in front of a long high counter where a row of clerks were serving patrons while seated at a level that allowed them to see over the heads of all the patrons in the lobby. Transactions were conducted by means of passing papers or money through the space between the narrow slats of a small wooden fence atop the counter. All about, people were elegantly dressed while patiently conducting their business in a soft cloud of tobacco smoke and perfume. While Laura did business with the banker, Pike and I strolled about the lobby.

What a capital place for picking pockets, I thought. The patrons, with hardly any concern, counted their money in plain sight of everyone else. Why weren't they fearful of being robbed, I wondered. Then, as if he had heard my thoughts, Pike caught my eyes and steered them to the men standing near the entrance door. I spotted the others, for there were at least seven more, strolling about in similar business attire, grey woolen culottes, waistcoat, shoes with brightly polished steel buttons, and the same type of composite wig. And to add intimidation, each sported a well-polished wooden club. They brought me in mind of Fielding's Bow Street runners and gave me a most uneasy feeling when they passed close by. Knowing full well our business was perfectly legitimate, I still couldn't help feeling as though they might arrest us at any second and was much relieved when Laura finished signing the papers.

After we had climbed into a hackney coach, Laura handed me the document and smiled, saying, "There, you have it."

Examining the paper, I could see it left no doubt that Mother had complete control over our account.

"Do you feel better now?" she asked, "For I certainly do."

"Much better," I confessed.

Pike punched my shoulder and, with his dimpled smile said, "Your mum will be rich if we are all knocked on the head."

I laughed, "I pray it shall not come to that, for I am having the most capital fun with you two and don't wish it to ever end."

As our coach pulled away, Laura spoke in a serious tone, "It doesn't have to end, Bobby. London will forget us shortly and we shall be back in the quick of it before you know it. However, as for the now," she whispered, "I am happy to be clear of this place. There was a bank clerk who sat three rows to my left and I prayed throughout the whole transaction that he wouldn't recognize me. He was one of our cullies from a month past."

"Did he?" I asked in a restrained voice, my heart skipping a beat as the realization hit me that all of our money was now in that bank. To think that, if he made her out, he could, at the very least, place a hold on our funds; to say nothing of calling a watchman.

"No, his eyes passed by me with only a vacant glance. I am sure that if he were not otherwise occupied and had had time to give me a good looking over, he surely would have remembered. I was near as happy to see this chaise pull away as I was during the incident with your mother and sister at the theater. I must say that the notoriety Pike foretold has truly arrived."

Our idea of relaxing at home did not fare well, for it was not two full days before we succumbed to boredom. To break up the monotony we decided upon a trip to Bath. Laura had always wished to visit the city, for it was purported to be quite a royal vacation destination, as well as a place for healing through bathing in mineral springs, a regimen prescribed by some of the local doctors. As for the aristocracy, we definitely had both the funds and the attire to fit in.

To be sure, Mother and Lilly were invited, however, Mother had no desire to ride across country, for she had traveled as a child when the roads were in very poor condition. And to state that this was prior to the turnpike system, which was now well in use, did nothing to assuage her conviction. The truth, it seemed, was that her contentment rested in the care of her home, as well as visiting with her friends in the manor. In addition, there was the local marketplace where she knew all the shopkeepers by name, as they knew her. And then there was the weekly taxi ride across town to visit her sister in Covent Garden Market that she looked forward to with undiminished delight.

As for Lilly, I believed she wanted to go but without Mother, it was out of the question. After many attempts to coerce them to come with us and, failing to make any headway whatsoever, we acquiesced to Mother's decision.

Perhaps it was for the best, for if we were to bring any lifted items back to our lodging, how were we to explain it to Mother? And now, we had an excellent opportunity to mix business with pleasure. On a day's outing, we went to the Haymarket and purchased stout luggage for the trip and, within the next day, we were packed and ready.

Mother and Lilly stood teary eyed at the door as we waved goodbye from the coach-and-two we had hired to take us to the intersection of Oxford Road and George Street. Once there, we were deposited, along with our luggage, to wait for the landau and four which Laura had arranged for a cost of 20 shillings a day. The reason for this precaution, Laura explained, was so that we could not be traced from Bath to our home, should we be pursued.

"Never, never, never leave a trail to our home! I don't care if we aren't working; it takes only one person to recognize either us or our coachman. The coachman might be easily found, and when questioned, most happy to lead them directly to our home," she warned.

All precautions taken, the landau arrived at the scheduled time and we were on our way to places that none of us had ever seen. Pike and I had never been out of the city and Laura confessed she had been only to Portsmouth. Filled with the anticipation of adventure, we took in the surrounding terrain as our chaise passed through the turnpike gate.

It was the spring of '76 and the air was crisp while flowers were everywhere in bloom. I had never seen such an array of colour and it dazzled my eager eyes as we traveled through rainbow-blanketed fields and glens. In other places enclosures had been erected, effectively fencing off large tracts of open land leaving little of common land for the yeomen farmers. Still, in the remaining commons, yeomen walked behind their plows while powerfully muscled oxen stepped surefooted through the fields, their children following in the furrows to drop in seeds. The odor of horse and cow manure added to the scent of flowers and grasses giving our noses a mixture of both pleasure and discomfort.

"Quite a different life than we have been accustomed to," Pike observed as we passed two boys laden with pails of milk on their way from a barn. The pails were of a hefty size and they managed them by means of a yoke lying across their shoulders.

"Different, indeed," I replied. Watching as they staggered beneath the load, I noticed that they had to negotiate the ruts in the path while, at the same time, taking care not to spill so much as a drop of the precious liquid.

"At least they have real milk and not the chalky slop we get in the city." Pike eyed the boys as he said, "I wonder what real whole milk tastes like? Perhaps in Bath we shall have a taste."

Fortunately we did not have long to wait, for we stayed the night at a quaint old lodge run by an elderly couple who kindly greeted us as we climbed from the chaise. While the postillion unhitched the horses, we followed the glow of their lantern as they led us to the front door of the Inn. Inside we were greeted by a warm fire before sitting down to a hearty meal of corned round of beef, pork pie, mutton chops and stewed cabbage, accompanied by a tankard of ale and a mug of fresh milk. Pike and I both took our mug into our hands and, once we had gotten the creamy contents down, smiled at one another through milk mustaches.

"Tastes so fresh and sweet," I observed. "Not at all like the milk in London."

"That's because these good people don't pour chalk into it," Pike replied.

"Why would anyone pour chalk into milk?" I asked.

"To increase their volume so as to make a greater profit," Laura explained.

"Do you mean to say that I have been drinking chalk?" I asked.

"Well, not of late. At least, since we have been in your life. You see, we are in the know of the right places to purchase milk. However, before then, well..." avoiding my eyes, she looked away.

"What do you mean, before then?" I demanded.

"Mother Elkins didn't know until I informed her. She thought she was getting a good bargain for her money and always bought milk at a certain grocer on Oxford. She didn't know, Bobby. Don't look at me like that. You are still alive, aren't you?" Laura pointed out.

"Well, I suppose I am," I said. "At least, as you say, we haven't been drinking chalk of late. I suppose I had grown quite used to it, for I hadn't noticed the change, at least until now. I dare say this is much fresher than anything Mother has purchased in London."

"Well, rest assured, you have not been drinking chalk of late," Laura said with a smile.

"Thank you, Laura. Again, you have taken good care of my family," I said.

"Just another bit of good fortune resulting from being in company of good friends. Right, Pike?" Laura smiled.

Pike nodded his head, burped, looked about to see if anyone took offense and stuffed another full fork of mutton into his mouth.

Tired and dusty, we went, with full stomachs, up to our own bedchambers to sponge off the road. After bidding Pike and Laura a good evening, I washed, toweled myself dry, and climbed into bed. Before drifting off to sleep, I took in the comforting smell of fresh linen and pondered my circumstances. Life was good, indeed. We had ample funds, fashionable clothes, and could, for the most part, do as we pleased. I had never believed that being a thief could bring one into such grand circumstances. I had always been taught that stealing was wrong and that a man must work to support his family. Well, I suppose when I am a man I shall get myself respectable employment and quit this business. However, as I sank into the soft bedding, I found it hard to imagine myself ever again doing a hard day's work. These past years had been such capital fun. Even the moments when we had nearly been undone seemed to be packed with thrills. Who knows what the future shall bring, I thought. Perhaps someday I just might become the most successful thief in all of England.

With these thoughts, I heard a din from down the prison corridor as one of the inmates cried, "Goddamn rats! They'll eat anything they gets in their goddamn teeth." Smiling at my foolish aspirations of that moment back at the inn, I thought, "Successful thief, indeed," and closing my eyes, drifted off to sleep.

CHAPTER SIX

"Your heritage, Robert," Father whispered. We were in the basement near the street side of the house, just beneath the stones of the sidewalk where the iron lid in the ceiling allowed the coalmen to drop in their loads. Father pulled aside his time-scarred toolbox from the wall near the corner of the coal bin. Bending down, he pointed to the floor and counted upward seven tiers of brick. He paused at the seventh and counted from the corner to his right seven across, except that he dropped to the next lower tier after each brick. With a firm grip, he worked the seventh brick free from the wall. With ease, he quickly had it out, placing it on the floor. His hand went into the void where the brick had previously rested and withdrew an old goatskin bag that had been secured tightly by a leather drawstring. With a tug, the knot came free and, reaching into the bag, he removed a copper scroll. After gently laying the scroll upon a nearby shelf, he withdrew a jeweled object that glittered in the candle light.

As he placed the object in my hand, I could see that it was made of heavy gold in the shape of a four-sided pyramid. Three faces of the pyramid were engraved with strange bronze-coloured figures embedded into a silver background. Upon closer inspection, I could see that the figures were set into the various courses, or tiers, of golden blocks that made up the pyramid's construction. I somehow knew that the figures represented an ancient form of writing. The remaining face of the pyramid was without pictured writing but instead contained a jeweled *eye recessed into the gold background. The stone or eye appeared to be approximately 20 carats weight emitting an intense bluish-green hue.*

Father enclosed my hands within his, pressing my fingers tightly around the object saying, "Robert, what you are holding is Hermes' Key. It alone possesses the formula for translating the writings upon the copper scroll."

As he said this, I saw the scroll unrolled before me with small, seemingly endless lines of images like the ones upon the pyramid.

*"Robert, you must understand that this Key is the one **true** Key. There can be only one in existence. Yet the Key is, of itself, much more. By containing the knowledge of the scroll, it has the power to open the portal to the mysteries of life. Guard it as I have, as our ancestors have since the day they discovered it beneath King Solomon's Temple."*

As I stared at the piece, the eye in the centre grew in size, pulsating and vibrating within a blue haze. The vibration sent waves through me until the whole of my being trembled.

It was at that point that I awoke. Drenched in sweat and trembling, I pulled myself into a sitting position and waited for the shaking to subside. In the advent of these increasingly intense dreams, I had to accept that this was by no means common. My father was attempting to communicate things to me. Things he had only hinted at when alive—some sort of ancient knowledge—an ancient 'Key' that somehow transforms itself, I thought. Yet, if he was, indeed, attempting to communicate with me, then, why of all time would he do it now? Did he not know that I was in prison and would soon be joining him?

At length, the shaking subsided when my thoughts were interrupted by the key turning in the lock of my cell door. With a reflex action, I pulled my manacles on without having a second to spare before the door swung open. Two men entered carrying a folding table, followed by two more with serving trays containing a five course meal of smoked beef, stewed asparagus, broccoli, boiled creamed onions, and beef stew, topped off with a slice of peach pie and bottle of claret.

"Compliments of a gentleman who must sympathize with your case as he has paid your meals through to the day of—eh, that is to say, to the end of your stay," said Turnkey Jim.

I could hardly believe my fortune and went about the pleasure of devouring everything before me, stopping only when I could eat no more.

Having just finished the first real meal I had had for two score days, I was startled by the thump of a club as it struck the iron plating.

"You've got a visitor," said Turnkey Jim.

Who could it be? Laura and Pike would not dare enter here, for the one who sought to bring about their undoing had eyes everywhere within these walls.

The door swung open and to my incredible surprise, stood one of the two plaintiffs in the case against me. Mr. Edmond Gibbon's complexion was of a milky shade and his eyes had diminished to sunken slits. His first reaction from the view of my quarters brought his head low upon his shoulders. Stepping through the door, he withdrew a scarlet silk kerchief from the inside pocket of his waistcoat. His dress was quite stylish and included a white brocade waistcoat and breeches that had been trimmed with expensive gold embroidery, white silk stockings and ornately carved gold buckles on his polished and now dusty shoes. Bringing the kerchief quickly to his nose, he cringed from the prison air before sneezing several times. Once the iron door clanged shut behind him, his eyes passed from wall to floor, taking in the cot, the basin in the corner stand, and finally, the window. Nodding his head, as if to accept the things he had observed, he turned to address me. However, upon seeing my emaciated form, his eyes widened and, with a shudder, the air left his lungs in a long deep sigh. His lips parted and, for a few seconds, he seemed unable to form his words.

"Robert, in all honesty I did not think it would come to this. I only wished for you to be taught a lesson." His withered eyes sought out mine and he continued, "You are so very young and needed to learn the value of earned money. It was my intention to instill into you the wrong you have done by stealing from me."

Standing before him, I felt as though I were watching a play at one of the Theatres Royal. Although his sincerity was genuine, I could not find within myself the ability to care. It was as though I were in a balcony seat observing his sorrowful features with faint amusement.

"My brother is truly the most evil person I have ever had the sad luck to have had dealings with. A month in prison was not nearly enough to satiate his thirst for revenge. I should have realized he would go to the devil for satisfaction. It has always been his way and I was foolish to think that he had changed his ways. I have always prided myself on being a fair judge of character." Throwing his arms into the air he said, "I have been such a fool to have believed him. Robert, I have pleaded with the magistrate for leniency. I have even written to the King. Since you refuse to give the location of my property and name your accomplices, let alone give them your full name, they will not consent to having your sentence commuted to Transportation.

"Apparently, my brother has connections with some of the magistrates of the Old Bailey and has seen to it that you are to be made an example for all the other thieving street urchins of the city. He even had the audacity to ask the magistrate that they place the iron weights upon you and force you to talk. Do not worry, it is no longer legal but—WEIGHTS, and you are only a child, the monster..."

Gibbon leaned back against the wall and slid down the stone surface, his greatcoat grating and bunching up as he sunk to the floor. While he sat hugging his legs to his chest, he buried his face into his knees and, in a muffled cry, said, "I can't stop it. I am so sorry, Robert. I did not wish it to be this way. I truly believed the courts were just. I nearly died inside when they gave you that sentence. I only came here to tell you that I did not, for the world, wish this upon you. Thus far you have been punished ten times more than what would have been just." He winced and, rubbing his eyes with his fists, his words came through a restricted throat, "My wife thinks me a monster... And I am not so sure she is wrong. I would take your place at the tree if it were at all possible, Robert. I can't ask you to forgive me because I will never forgive myself."

I didn't quite know how to respond. Observing him as he thumped his delicate fist into the floor boards, I said, "It is not your fault, sir. I got myself into this business long before I robbed you." Crossing the room, I sat on the floor beside him.

"I cannot give you back your property for the same reason I can't give up my friends. The one will lead your brother to the other. And he will either kill them or have the court do it for him."

Gibbon took hold of my shoulder, giving it a gentle squeeze, "But, son, they will spare you."

"And how will I live with the knowledge that I have caused the death of my friends?"

Gibbon breathed a deep sigh and nodded.

"I have been in this prison for forty days and seen a good number of people die of the fever. Unfortunately, I have not been successful in contracting it," I said.

"How can you say you are unfortunate not to have contracted the fever?"

I gave him a sideways glance. "If I had, I would not be hanged. I would not have had to live in the cold dank while lying next to my own filth for all those weeks. I have long wished it to end and this week cannot end soon enough for me. Although..."

"Yes, lad?"

"Since I have been moved to this cell, I can see the world again, smell the fresh air, and, weather permitting, even feel the sun upon my face. It almost gives one a reason to live. And yet, I am here because I am to be put to death. An odd twist, don't you think, sir?"

"I am truly sorry for this, Robert. And I daresay I shall always be. Is there nothing I can do? Surely you have parents or relatives I could contact.

"No," I said solemnly, "my parents are gone. I was living alone."

"Are you sure you want to stick to that story, even now? Would you not want to see them one last time?"

"There is no one, sir." I could still hear Laura's melodic voice in my ear, "Never give away the location of your home."

"Well, if anything, I can assure that you will have good food, as well as ample blankets to keep you warm."

"It would be most appreciated, sir, for the charities don't provide enough sustenance to feed a mouse."

"As for my brother, I will see what I can do to expose him for the villain he truly is," he said, though his voice lacked conviction.

"I am sorry you have taken this so hard, sir. And I realize your brother has done us both a bad turn. I can only advise you to keep well clear of him. He can do you great harm if he knows of your intentions."

"I have learned a thing or two of his methods and quite agree. However, I have a few tricks of my own to play. Guard!"

Pulling himself to his feet and, with the clink of the key turning the tumblers of the lock, he went to the door. I bade him good day as he disappeared into the corridor. Stepping to the window, I watched the traffic below until I saw Gibbon crossing the street, his pace slow and his shoulders slumped forward. And if I didn't know better of it, I would think he grieved for his lost wife or child. Then it stuck me, a vision of earth being shoveled upon the lid of my coffin. "Dear God," I whispered, "He is grieving for me."

A chaise pulled up and, as he opened the door to step in, I could see the rich leather upholstered interior and it brought me in mind of our landau we had hired for our trip to Bath.

A vision formed instantly in my mind of the three of us leaving the inn early in the morning on the second day of our trip. How different life was then, the sweet fragrance of Laura's perfume, Pike's dimpled smile as we took in the country air, the road ahead, and the excitement of adventures to come.

We hadn't a care in the world as we traveled along the turnpike. I had been watching the countryside go by for hours when suddenly our driver struck the horses with his whip and gave the cry, "HIGHWAYMEN!"

The chaise lurched violently forward, giving us all quite a start. Laura and Pike had been sitting opposite me, facing toward the rear before being thrown into my seat. The road had taken us into a hollow and around a sharp bend where stood a stand of large oaks. When we came to a dip in the road, I spied a coach and four off to the side near a brook on a glade of fresh green grass while its occupants stood beside it. Though I only caught a glimpse, I most certainly saw a man wearing a mask while training his pistol on the group as another man sat on his horse, his back to us.

"They are being robbed!" I said.

Laura and Pike sprang to the window but it was too late for them to see anything. Laura turned to me while Pike went to the window on the opposite side of the coach.

"Are you making game of us. Robert?"

"I swear! They were being robbed. There was a masked man with a pistol and another on a horse. He might have had a pistol as well."

Pike turned around and sat back into the seat and said, "They'll have to have more than a pistol to get my money." Then, withdrawing his small dirk from his waistcoat pocket, he ran it across his throat.

"I don't believe that would be wise," Laura warned. "Not against a pistol. Besides, we are not killers."

Pike rolled his eyes, but Laura ignored him, saying, "And it is quite unlikely they would pursue our chaise for we will be much too far away once they have completed their dealings."

I watched the road trailing away behind us and said, "Do you suppose they will kill those people? Perhaps we should go back and help them."

Pike only shook his head.

"Goodness sakes, no!" Laura said, with no little surprise that I should suggest such a thing. "They will not harm them unless they are foolish enough to resist. As for us going back, it is out of the question. We would be inviting ourselves to be relieved of our funds as well, and I don't care to visit Bath as a pauper. And I dare say, neither does our driver."

I thought on this incident for the rest of the way to Bath. Even when we were in the city, I would occasionally reflect upon whether those people were harmed and wondered if we should have done something to help them.

As for Bath, it lived up to its name by being exceptionally clean and architecturally spectacular. Although it carried the familiar odor of filth that any city has, it was not as prominent, perhaps due to the fact that the streets and houses appeared as though they had been scrubbed on a daily basis. Wondering why the city is called Bath, I asked Laura.

"It is because of the Romans, my dear," she said. "They built large bathhouses here well over a thousand years ago. The waters are fed by underground springs and most people visit them to heal any number of afflictions, or just to relax in the pools. If you like, we can visit one of the baths as soon as we have found suitable lodging."

We entered the city by crossing the newly completed Pulteney Bridge, a stone structure that spans the river Avon. Once across this narrow yet deep running green water, there stood on our left a large limestone Guildhall which had also recently been constructed. As we passed this structure, we next came upon the large gothic spires and high arched windows of the 16th century Abbey church of St. Peter and St. Paul.

Turning right at the Abbey, we passed three and four storey houses that were separated by an open limestone paved court which lay before a building called the Pump Room. This structure was fronted by five high arched, multi-paned windows separated by fluted columns whose ornate capitals supported a stone roof railing. Well dressed patrons, some in groups, some in pairs, some in sedan chairs, were entering or leaving.

My curiosity at an end, I asked Laura what they might be attending behind those high glass paneled doors. She had not a clue and, after inquiring of our driver of its use, he told us that it was where the underground springs bring up one hundred ten degree water which is used to supply the great baths within. On our way to Queen's square, we traveled down Gay Street, a long boulevard that intersects with a row of homes called the Kings Circus. The building structure was unlike anything I had ever seen, for the entire length, at least several hundred feet, was constructed in a crescent shape around a central island in the road. Queens square was a short distance farther to the west where we found it to be another of these strange crescent structures. After passing St. James' square, we decided to take a ride through the centre of the city before seeking lodging.

Traveling down Broad Street, we came upon various shops and haberdasheries. Cloth shops, apparently the city's main export, were in great abundance, as well as copper shops with various pots and kettles displayed on the street counters behind which, the coppersmiths and their wives hammered and cut away at their craft. Then there was a silversmith shop which made Pike sit upright in his seat while his eyes dazzled in the glitter reflected off the walls and onto the counter. I could imagine his mind busily turning over the possibilities. Oddly enough, the streets were devoid of the usual beggars, giving the place a fresh scrubbed appearance mingled with an air of security.

After we had come to the end of Broad Street, we found we were back at the Abbey and, as we came upon the Pump Room, we asked the driver to stop in front of the courtyard entrance. There was, as before, an assemblage of people. The women paraded about in their ruffled hoop dresses and high multi-coloured wide-brimmed feathered hats, while the men in their heavily embroidered velvet coats and satin waistcoats with glittering gold and silver fobs, sported intricately carved canes that caught the ladies eye, giving the opportunity to tip their plumed tricorn hats as they passed. Both men and women strutted proudly and unconcerned, and the men were all without boots or swords, a most puzzling thing. Without swords, how might they protect themselves? My question was answered upon noticing the ubiquitous presence of uniformly dressed fellows, their watchdog expressions eyeing everyone and everything that passed. Easily spotted, one could find them either walking in the crowd or standing on every corner sporting a long stick.

As for the lack of boots, I was later to find that they, as well as swords, had been outlawed by the late Richard Nash, a man who became the city's master of ceremonies by means of a duel and who ruled the city. Prior to his death, he had even gone so far as to have smoking banned in the presence of ladies.

How wonderful it must be to live here and not suffer the sights of poverty found in London's east end, not to mention the worry of being pilfered while taking a stroll down these lovely streets. And here we are in their beautiful city with the look of the fox in our eyes. Yet, we were there to have fun. Perhaps we shall not steal from any of these good people, I thought.

That was until I noticed Pike staring intently out of the opposite window, the corner of his lips exposed a wolfish smile and I knew he could hardly wait to sink his teeth into the action.

And there sat Laura, her face brilliant as a morning sunrise, eyes wide with surprise and wonder, staring intently from the window with her silk gloved hands clasped tightly in the ruffle of her dress. Was her smile for the atmosphere, the theater, the newness of the surroundings? Or was it for the opportunity of pilfering some foolish cully's pockets? I could not tell. Perhaps we are incurable thieves. Perhaps it is because we know nothing else. I pondered these things for several streets before deciding we were only surviving as best we knew how.

Our coach turned the corner onto George Street and after a short distance turned down Broad Street. At one point, Laura gave the driver instruction to circle round again where she bid him stop in front of a lodging house.

"Will this do for your lodging, ma'am?" the driver said as he opened the coach door. We looked at the edifice for a moment and Laura said, "Well, what do you think, gents?"

It was a three storey limestone building with a high pitched roof. On the second floor directly above us and facing the street was a room with a two foot deep iron railed balcony overhanging the entrance to the inn. The inn was located in the centre of the marketplace while the tower of the Abbey could be seen several streets distant.

Pike studied the balcony, smiled, and gave me a nod.

"We should like to see that upper room," I said.

"Let us give closer inspection, shall we?" Laura said, as we stepped out and walked stiff-legged to the entry.

I asked the innkeeper if the second floor room with the balcony was available and he replied, "It has been vacant only since this morning." Turning to Laura, he continued, "You may have it for a only a shilling per week, however, if you desire breakfast and dinner, then it is two shillings with six pence more for each of your two boys, supper being optional at twelve pence per serving."

In the parlor sat a fireplace aglow with several gentlemen sitting comfortably nearby, having their coffee while reading the local gazette. Two of the men glanced in our direction, our eyes met and we smiled.

Laura said, "We shall like to see the room first."

The innkeeper nodded and took a key off of his high desk before lumbering up the narrow staircase. We followed his bulky form to the second floor, after which he opened the door to spacious quarters, well furnished with two bedchambers and a central parlor. Crossing the parlor, I went to the small balcony and looked out onto the street. The view commanded the marketplace in both directions allowing a slight glimpse of the great Abbey spire.

"This is perfect!" I exclaimed.

Laura and Pike came to the balcony and stood beside me.

"We'll take it," Laura took the liberty of saying after seeing the smiles on our faces. Then she called down, "Driver, you may take up our things."

It was not long before we were unpacked and had the road dust washed off. In each bedchamber, we found water basins within three well polished mahogany tambour dressing tables, one in Laura's room and two in Pike's and my room. Being most happy to be clean again, I was willing to get even cleaner by experiencing the famous baths we had heard so much about from the driver.

The baths would have to wait, however, for our first evening was spent taking a leisurely stroll through the market place and over to the Orchard Street Theatre. Laura checked the schedule for the next performance, which was not to be until the following day. The play was called *"The Farmer's Return"* which had played at Drury Lane during the past fortnight while we were lying low. We all decided to attend and purchased tickets at two shillings each.

"Laura, do you plan on doing any work tonight?" I asked.

"Heavens no, Robert, we are on holiday." With a smile, she nudged my shoulder, "We must first become familiar with the city, very familiar, for we must know of all the ways of escape, all the connecting streets and alleyways, taxi access, etcetera. And that will require a good deal of time. As I said, we are here on holiday so we shall do our best to relax and enjoy ourselves while we are doing our research. Let's just have fun, boys. You can do with some fun, can't you?"

"I can always do with some fun," Pike said, a smile upon his lips. "As for now, I could do with some food."

"And you, Robert, are you ready for dinner?" No words were needed as I expressed my hunger by rubbing my stomach. Laura nodded and off we went in search of an eatery.

The following two days were spent doing a complete reconnaissance of Bath and its suburb, Bathwick, which lies on the other side of the river Avon. The surrounding countryside enclosed the city with high steep hills, giving Bath the appearance of resting on the stage of an amphitheater.

Having spent a good deal of time walking and observing the populace, we took notice that unlike London, most of the residents appeared to be acquainted with one another. Hardly a moment passed without hearing, "Good day, Mr. and Mrs. So-and-So." It seemed our only means of being inconspicuous in such a city that recognized outsiders immediately was to attend places where tourists generally frequented.

After returning to our lodging one afternoon to rest our tired feet, Laura reclined on the four-seated settee in the parlor while I sat across from her in the padded great chair. Tired though we were, rather than relax, Pike restlessly paced the floor.

"What's eating you?" I said, after he made his fifth turn from the balcony to the entry door.

"I would like to get into some of the action. There are potential cullies with pockets stuffed full of silver and gold everywhere I turn my head. What I wish to know is, when are we going to do some work here?"

Laura sighed and spoke with a tired, yet soft tone in her voice, "From what I have seen this past day, I think it wise to do no work at all. Not to argue the fact that this place is certainly a box of gems. It is an extremely well watched and, therefore, well protected box of gems."

"I ain't afraid of those bloody watchmen. They'll not see my move, and before they know something is missing, I'll be long gone," he said, while giving her a sideways glance. Awaiting her reply and, getting none, he threw up his hands and said, "If you won't go it with me, well…"

Laura sat up from her leisurely position, all the relaxation had gone from her voice when she demanded, "Well, what?"

"I'll go it alone then, is what," he said, raising a defiant chin.

"You do and it could be our undoing. You had better think long and hard, Tom." His mouth dropped open and, saying nothing, he turned toward the balcony.

Shoving his hands into his trouser pockets, he stood slump-shouldered while Laura went on, "Just think for one second that you were not easily recognized as one of the visitors from London. How long do you think that will last as our innkeeper has told everyone he knows we are from London. And everyone he has told has likely told everyone they know. The only ones who don't know where we are from are other tourists. Make no mistake; the minute something is missing, they will come for the new visitors in town. And they would surely suspect someone from London before all others."

"Well, ain't there a lot of visitors? Why do they have to come directly for us?"

"OHHH!" Laura said, throwing up her hands in resignation.

I interjected, "Because there are few tourists that match the description of a beautiful young woman with two boys." Laura rewarded me with an angelic smile and I went on, "And the constable will make very short work of finding us."

Pike made a fist and punched his hand, "Then, what are we supposed to do?"

"Perhaps we can relax and enjoy a day at the Pump Room," I suggested. "And I heard that the theater is performing a new production tomorrow. What's the name?"

"I believe it is the "Beggars Opera," Laura answered. "I know we have seen it done time and again, yet I never seem to tire of that play.

Besides, I would like to see how it is done here. I heard they have a wholly different troop of actors performing."

"Sounds like great fun," I said.

"I quite agree," Laura said, raising a delicate eyebrow. "What has surprised me most is the near absence of doxies."

"What exactly is a doxie?" I asked.

Pike gave me a sideways glance and shook his head.

I had heard the word, prostitute, doxie, whore, even seen the women in bars, as well as the theatre balconies of which Laura referred. I had an idea it was something to do with pay for immoral purposes but knew nothing of sexual acts.

"Dear me, Bobby, you have so much to learn," Laura sighed. Then, in a low voice, said, "It is a woman who is paid for sexual favors."

"I am not sure I understand," I said.

"Some day you shall. Suffice it to say, it is something extremely disreputable, as well as degrading, and I only did it so long as it was necessary to survive. And, if all continues to go as well as it has, I shall never do it again."

"I am sorry you went through that, Laura. I am so happy I found you and Pike when I did. How did you come to be involved with Jeb?" I asked.

"Oh, that's another story," she sighed.

"I would love to hear it," I said. I had always wished to know but, rather than ask, I had hoped they would volunteer their story.

"As I said, Jeb took us in. But that was after he became acquainted with me at Rat's Castle in St. Giles."

"You mentioned Rat's Castle before. What exactly is it?" I asked.

"It is a large and extremely noisome building where I lived along with other prostitutes and thieves, and that is where I came upon Pike. He had been living in the streets and I would often see his pitiful starving form passing by, or standing about on the corner, outside the building. At length, I took him in, allowing him to sleep in my room where we became good friends. Soon thereafter, I met Jeb, a frequent customer, who offered me an escape by way of providing lodging in his tenement house in the Dials. I knew that he would expect my services as payment and insisted he take in Pike as a condition of our agreement."

"Couldn't you have made your living some other way?" I asked.

She gave me a cold stare, "The only other way to survive, young man, is to live out of boxes in alleyways and hope for someone to throw out digestible garbage. No. For a woman alone in the city, there is no other way. Jeb saw an opportunity for himself and gave us a place to stay so long as I paid him by being his whore." She reclined into the settee and stared through the window to the street, "And I hope he has forgotten Pike and me, for I should hate to encounter him on the street." Then glancing at Pike, she said, "I believe we should always steer clear of the Dials, at least for several more years."

Pike returned her glance with a nod.

"Well, enough of Jeb and St. Giles. The past is the past. We are here on holiday and I have so enjoyed the sights. It has been a grand experience to have such fun without bothering to do any work," Laura said, cheerfully. "Tom, we don't have to be all the time working. What is so wrong with having fun?"

He gave her a scornful look, "My name is Pike when we aren't in company." He corrected. "What is wrong, is that we came here to get away from everyone who could recognize us in London. I fancied we might take advantage of that. Yet you act as if we are sure to be recognized in spite of the fact that we haven't lifted anything. It just seems a waste, is all. There is a lot of gold coin just walking about the streets and no one seems to take care to hide it. It's as though these people don't even have a care that someone might steal their purse. And those eagle-eyed watchmen hanging about on every goddamn corner appear to be quite smug. I'd love to twist their lips ajar. I'm not certain what I'll do but it will be something—something before we leave this city."

Laura sat back into the settee again while pointing a finger at Pike saying, "Before you do anything, you must promise you'll run it past me first."

Pike sauntered to the balcony and, leaning on the iron rail, said nothing.

"Promise me!" she demanded, her voice low and threatening.

After a long pause, Pike muttered, "I promise."

The next day, a brilliant sun played hide and seek while a light breeze pushed cotton clouds lazily toward the east, their shadows tracing across steep lushly vegetated hillsides that surround the city. We each took sedan chairs to the Pump Room, the same structure we had observed from our chaise upon entering the city. After paying the hackney men, we crossed the flagstone courtyard to the entry steps where we passed through one of two high doors which swung beneath stained glass arches.

Once inside, we discovered a spacious parlor well lit by the sunlight through those high arched window panels that rose some twenty feet from the floor. Here and there, patrons awaited their entry to the baths while lounging in reclined chairs. Laura inquired of an elderly gentleman which would be the correct course to take and learned that the baths consisted of two large pools of hot water; one being the "King's Bath" for all the male patrons, while the other titled "Queen's Bath," was for the women, it being separated from the former by a stone wall. Laura disappeared behind the partition into the Queen's Bath area while Pike and I entered the King's Bath. Once inside, we purchased our admission and were led to a dressing room which contained numbered shelves for storing our clothes.

With not a stitch of clothing, we wrapped ourselves with a towel provided by a servant and stepped through a doorway into a colonnaded room containing a large steaming pool. Within this room, one's ears are continually bombarded with either laughter or cries of, "Oh! But this is hot!" or "Hades, by God, hot as Hades, to be sure!"

and, "Jesus, God, my bollocks are boiled eggs!" For the most, their excitement was due to the fact that they were immersing themselves for the first time in their lives. And likewise, for me, a bath had always consisted of washing from a basin of water piped in from the Chelsea Reservoir, a water which had no discernable odor. However, the water in the King's Bath contained a harsh sulfuric air which, at first, assaults one's nostrils. Yet the foul odor is forgotten when confronted with the heated water.

I hesitated to venture into one area of the pool for it appeared quite deep although, to my surprise, Pike stroked like a fish and quickly went to the other side. Once there he took hold of the ledge and motioned for me to follow.

"What's the matter? Can't swim?" he taunted.

"No, I cannot. Where did you learn to do that?" I asked.

"I'll show you how but it has to be quick. This water is cooking me."

Having seen Pike swim, I knew I must learn how to do this thing. "I have never been in water deeper than a wash basin," I said.

"It isn't so difficult. First hold your breath and just float where you are. Go ahead, you won't sink. And if you did, you aren't in deep water and all that would be needed is for you to simply stand up. Go ahead!"

I followed his instruction and found to my amazement I did not sink.

"What's next?" I asked, instantly ready for my next lesson.

"Just move your arms like this and don't forget to kick your feet." He demonstrated while swimming toward me.

Attempting to follow his instruction, I was rewarded with a mouth full of hot sulfuric water. Goughing out the water from my restricted windpipe, Pike stood beside me slapping me on my back.

"Did I not tell you, you must first shut your mouth or you shall swallow all the water in the whole damn pool?" he said, with a grin.

It wasn't long before we could no longer stand the one hundred ten degree heat and climbed out to cool off on a pair of reclining chairs.

"How did I do?" I asked, quite certain I had done amazingly well.

"Oh, I suppose you did all right for the first time. Perhaps I'll teach you how to swim under water once we've cooled off."

"How did you learn to swim so well?" I asked.

"By mud-larking from the coal barges at Billingsgate. A lot of us used to do it and I was the quickest. I could dive deeper than anyone, five fathoms or perhaps even more at the peak of the flood."

"Mud-larking? What is that?" I asked, a bit puzzled for I had heard of it spoken yet never knew the meaning.

"It's what you do if you need to keep warm when you haven't any money to buy coal. The barges lose it over the side and it piles up on the bottom of the river. The bargemen don't mind so long as you don't take it off their barge, so we would dive for it."

"It must have been a hard life for you, Pike," I said, placing my hand on his shoulder.

"It was damn hard," he said, while drops of water ran from his pug nose to his short upper lip, "but it will take a lot more than starving and cold to put my bones into the ground. My mother died giving birth to me and my father was never far from a bottle of gin. That's why he got caught, I think. I think the gin made him lose the touch. When they took him away—well, that's when it really went bad. I went to live with my aunt and uncle 'til I was five and I ran away."

"Why did you run away?"

"My uncle was quite fond of gin as well and, unlike my father, he got mean when he was drunk. He beat my aunt and, when he grew weary of beating her, he turned onto me. I couldn't hold up as well as my aunt." His voice dropping to a whisper, he went on, "He kicked me hard and didn't stop till I fainted. When I woke, I thought I might shite my guts out. The next time I saw him coming from the gin shop, I took some blankets, my clothes, and got the hell out of there."

"What did you do then?" I asked.

"I lived in St. Giles, moving from one hovel to the next, eating what crumbs I could find and sleeping where I wouldn't be stepped on. They found me though, my uncle, that is. He said he was finished with me and placed me in a parish workhouse, and I told you the rest." He was about to say more but his jaw clenched. Rising to his feet, he shook it off, forced a smile and said, "Come on, let's get in, I shall teach you to be a capital swimmer."

Standing at the edge of the pool, his body, though about my height and weight, was not quite as lean, there being a noticeable layer of fat on his chest and stomach.

My reflection in the pool made me aware that I had gotten a bit soft around the edges as well, for it had been a very long time since my days of hauling brick and mortar. Examining my blond locks, now curled in wet strands upon my shoulder, I asked, "Why? I mean, I want to learn, but why do you wish me to be a good swimmer?" I inquired.

"So we can have a race. I miss racing with my mates at the river. Anyway," he said with a nudge, "once you learn well enough, you'll be in for some real competition."

"We'll see about that," I said, while jumping in.

Upon the whole, the Bath was a most uncommon experience. Everywhere there were all sorts of men, some aged and gout ridden, some young and robust, and some rather elderly sitting up in their chairs with a strange leer in their eye. If not for Pike's company, I don't believe I would have stayed long, for there were a great many who were the most gout-ridden souls I had ever beheld. And it was with great difficulty that I watched them moving about while in excruciating pain. If ever I find myself in a state such as this, I told myself, I will turn myself in and request a merciful hanging.

During our race, I attempted to beat him by swimming underwater and would have done so if I hadn't come up for air, surfacing just in time to receive a foot in the face. After we had done with our race, we had had enough of the hot water and headed for the changing room. Once dressed, we sat in great wooden lounge chairs that had been painted a blinding white which we quickly shifted into the shade of an elm.

Laura was near an hour longer before emerging from the entrance of Queen's Bath, her relaxed expression appeared as though she had dosed herself with laudanum. "You boys have a good time? I know I sure did," she said, while we stepped into sedan chairs and rode back to the inn for a warm dinner.

The hot water had given me a most robust sensation and, as I sat down for a meal of roast duck, joint of beef, stewed cabbage, broccoli and buttered toast, I wondered when next we would do it again. All in all, we returned to the Pump Room three more times where I mastered the art of swimming, as well as acquired a life-long love of bathing. To be sure, as bathing was not uncommon in the city of Bath, it was quite the reverse elsewhere, for it was thought to be unhealthy. And though I was changed by this small, yet socially unacceptable desire, it was our leaving Bath that ultimately changed us all.

That evening, we were all sitting in our usual seat of preference in the parlor, Pike in the wicker chair on the balcony where he could gaze at the goings on in the street below, Laura reclining in her evening clothes on the settee, and I quite comfortably in the great chair. The cool breeze, flowing in through the French balcony doors, intermixed with Laura's perfume and the fresh bouquet of roses standing in a rainbow coloured glass vase on the small rococo table, giving the air a sweetness that would forever lock the memory of those evenings of our stay at Bath. While the sun sank low beneath the cobalt clouds of the western sky, we were discussing the sights of the city and our experiences at the Pump Room and the Orchard Street Theatre. Pike had just given a full account of our race in the pool while placing great emphasis on my defeat.

"If not for the kick in the face, I should have had him beat," I said, while Laura made a poor effort to cover up her laughter with one of the purple settee pillows.

After taking a deep breath, she sighed before saying, "It seems we have had a grand holiday here. We must do this again next year. Oh, before I forget, the landau is due to arrive at six o'clock in the morning so we must be completely packed, dressed, and ready to go. Mrs. Jamus will have our breakfast ready at five. That should provide ample time to enjoy our meal before shifting our things down to the street."

"I look forward to seeing Mother and Lilly. They will certainly be excited to see us," I said. "I hope Lilly will like her gifts. She has become a bit difficult to please of late. Have you noticed?"

"It is only a phase, Bobby. I am sure she will snap out of it soon," she assured. "Pike, are you as ready as I to return?"

He shrugged and, leaning upon the rail, said, "I suppose I am ready enough." Suddenly, he narrowed his eyes, "Hello there, Mr. and Mrs. Shopkeeper," he said while peering down Broad Street.

I had assumed he was simply observing the goings on in the street much as I had done from my bedchamber back home. I was to find that I was quite mistaken. The truth being that, since our arrival, Pike had taken his place at the balcony every evening for the sole purpose of studying the street. Within his view were numerous shops and residences, all of which could be observed while seated comfortably upon the balcony. He had conversed with Laura and me each evening upon numerous subjects while, completely unbeknownst to us, he had been studying the comings and goings of the shopkeepers, what they did and how long they took to do it, how many servants they had and the errands they ran, all the while waiting for an opportunity when there would be no one at home. At that moment, he had been observing a store on the corner a full street and a half away.

As with most merchants in this area, the shopkeeper and his family lived in quarters above the shop. Pike remembered that this particular shopkeeper's wife, a small woman with a sharp pointed nose and a crafty set of narrow eyes, worked in the shop along with another woman of like features, whom he assumed to be her sister. And that they three shared the flat. In addition, there was a day servant who always arrived at eight o'clock in the morning and departed promptly at seven in the evening. The servant was so punctual that one could set their timepiece by him. However, this particular evening, the servant had departed at six o' clock, and shortly thereafter, Pike noticed a coach and four pulling up to the shop. Immediately thereafter, the shopkeeper, along with his wife and sister, emerged with luggage in hand and dressed for travel. The driver stowed their baggage onto the luggage rack, after which they all climbed into the carriage and away they went down Broad Street towards the Pulteney Bridge.

"It is perfect, don't you see? It will be as easy as kiss my hand," Pike said, while placing a wet smacking kiss upon the back of his hand. "No one shall know they have been robbed for it will not be reported until they return. And by then, we will have been long gone." He gave us a look of expected approbation and, we saying nothing, he went on, "I have been into their shop. They have linen and bolts of silk, expensive plate, even fine silver, well enough to make our journey worthwhile. It is perfect."

"I have been into that shop, as well," I said. "And though there is a great deal of valuable items behind his display cases—items such as plate, silver, china porcelain, I seem to recall the shopkeeper showing a customer some exquisite timepieces from a small case that he had concealed behind the counter."

Pike's eyes widened, "You see!" he said, snapping his fingers. "It's even better than I thought."

I inclined my head with a reluctant smile and went on, "I must confess, Pike; I am not sure of housebreaking. Picking pockets is one thing but..."

My reservations were mirrored by Laura's expression.

Folding her hands and twisting her lips to one side she said, "Pike, we have never been housebreakers. I don't know if we should attempt something of which we know little to nothing."

Pike shrugged, "What's to know about getting into a shop? We only have to be quiet is all."

"How do we get in without breaking anything and waking up the neighbors?" I said.

Pike smiled surreptitiously. "With a key," he said, as though we should have read his mind.

Laura sat upright and hissed, "With what key?"

Pike whistled a tune and, returning to the balcony, leaned on the rail with his back to us.

"WITH WHAT KEY?" Laura demanded.

Pike turned around slowly, his wide jaw opened, displaying a wolfish smile of pearly teeth and said, "With the key he hides under the flower pot in his window box."

"He keeps a key under a flower pot?" Laura said, quite astonished. "What a foolish thing to do! Why, he must be spotted straightaway the first time ever he used it." Giving Pike a disbelieving look, she said, "Are you certain?"

"Quite certain," Pike said, defensively. "If I hadn't been able to sleep the other night, I would never have smoked it. I was sitting right here when I saw him staggering down the street. I suppose he was on his way from some ale house. There is a street lamp just beyond his shop which gave only enough light for me to see his shadowy form in front of the shop door. He must've forgotten his key, for he went through his pockets for some time before he came to the flower pot. If not for the watchman passing by with his lantern, I wouldn't have seen him pretending to adjust the flowers. They appeared to be chatting for a few minutes before the watchman lit up the front door to assist the shopkeeper in finding the keyhole; whereby he unlocked the door, went inside while the watchman continued on his rounds."

Laura raised a brow, saying, "Are you certain he didn't already have a key and wasn't merely getting himself together to face his wife?"

Pike shook his head and replied, "His wife didn't let him in, and I know he tried the door before he went to the flower pot because he stood there for some time." Laura seemed unconvinced so Pike placed his hands upon his hips and, looking her dead into the eye, stated emphatically, "He had a key after he spoke with the watchman, I tell you."

Laura tapped the rococo armrest of the settee with her long tapered nails while she thought it over.

"I don't think his wife even knows that he keeps it there," Pike continued. "I saw him put it back after the watchman left and I didn't see him remove it before he left tonight."

Laura rose from the settee and came to the balcony and, squinting, asked, "Which shop is it?"

Pike pointed, "The one on the corner, just at the far end of the street on the right."

Laura strained her eyes to see before shaking her head and saying, "You can see that much detail from here? You must have the eyes of a hawk." Giving him a tap on the head with the tip of her finger, she smiled incredulously. "Instead of Pike, perhaps we should be calling you Hawk."

"I'm quite partial to Pike," he smiled. "But thanks for the compliment."

Laura turned to face me, "Do you see it, Robert?"

"Yes, I know the shop," I said. "It will be quite a haul if we are able to pull it off."

"What do you mean, *if*?" Pike said, with a puzzled look on his face.

"It will be quite a haul if we are able to bring the goods up here without waking up the innkeeper," I replied. "How do you suppose we do that?"

Pike thought for a moment and said, "You've got a point. It could be tricky. We'll have to think of something."

"What we need," I smiled, "is a good length of cordage."

"I spied a coil of cordage in that very shop," Pike said, confidently.

"Are you certain?" I asked. "I don't recall seeing any cordage, though I wasn't looking for any such thing."

"I am positive. It sat on the floor in the corner at the far end of the counter. After the watchman has made his round, perhaps you and I can make the drop to the street from the balcony, we could use the cordage from the shop to haul the things up to our room. Laura, we could toss an end up to you and perhaps you might tie it to a bedpost. We could then climb up the rope and use it to haul up the goods and be back in our beds with no one knowing we had ever gone out."

Laura interrupted, saying, "I could have everything packed into our trunk, ready for us to be on our way in the morning. The innkeeper would believe no one had left the inn during the night so the constable wouldn't be certain of whom to suspect."

Pike raised a brow, and with a smug expression, said, "And I have told the innkeeper that we were on our way to Bristol, so if they do send someone after us, they shall be going in the wrong direction. Ha-ha!"

Laura pointed an accusing finger at Pike, saying, "You promised you would tell me of your plans."

"I had to take precautions—" Pike argued, "just in case. I didn't know it would be possible until I saw the shopkeeper leave just now. And besides, he doesn't need to know where we are bound. He's such a nosy sort."

"Very well then," Laura said, in agreement. "Only we have not the cordage now so we shall have to find some other way of lowering you to the street. If you drop from here you could sprain an ankle.

No, that will not do," she said, placing her finger to her temple as she always did when in deep thought

I spoke up, "We can tie the sheets of our beds together. Once we are on the ground, you can take them back up and remake the beds. Upon our return, we shall toss you the rope so that you may tie that end to one of the bedposts. Do you know how to make a good knot?"

Laura smiled and said, "Once I knew a sailor, he taught me a thing or two, but I won't go into that. Yes, I know something of knots."

I looked at Pike, then back to Laura. I still didn't like the idea. Something felt wrong, deep down in my gut, yet I couldn't find any argument to present in favor of that feeling.

"Then it is agreed, we'll do it?" I said.

"Agreed!" said Laura and Pike, simultaneously.

Although I had committed to this venture, I couldn't shake the ominous feeling. It was as though you have turned down a wrong street which will, in the least, take you out of your way, costing you precious time, or, at the worst, take you into some unforeseen disaster. My aunt and uncle were also shop owners and I couldn't rid myself of the guilty feeling that we would be stealing from hardworking people. I rationalized that this was not the same thing for these people could well afford to lose the merchandise as their business seemed to be doing quite well. And besides, it wasn't as though we were entering their living quarters.

After supper, we retired to our bedchambers to get some sleep before the twelfth hour. Sleep, however, was futile, for amidst the silence, my wandering thoughts would lock onto the sound of Pike's periodic clearing of his throat, the occasional burp, and lastly, the fart that made me leave the room for the balcony's fresh air. While on the balcony, I heard a stir in Laura's room before she appeared in her night robe at the doorway. Then Pike came in, rubbing his eyes before stretching out his arms with a big yawn.

Realizing we were all too excited about what lie ahead, we decided to sit in the parlor and wait it out. As the clock on the mantle ticked away each hour, we reminisced about all the cullies we had taken and I thought about how good it would be to soon be home with Mother and Lilly. We had already packed everything but the clothes we were to wear the next day, leaving plenty of room in Laura's big trunk for what we might pilfer from the shop. The absence of man or beast on the road beneath our balcony gave the moonless night a deathly stillness. Except for our whispering, not a sound carried through the walls from the other guests. At eleven fifteen, we began tying the sheets together and had it accomplished in good time.

It was just a few minutes before midnight when the lamplighter finally made his rounds and we stood in the darkness of the parlor while he slowly passed. The glow from his lantern cast shadows onto the buildings as he walked, giving temporary life to the street about him only to disintegrate as he turned the corner. The sound of our breathing increased as his footsteps faded and, to be sure, we waited a good five minutes more before we lowered our rope of bed sheets. To our surprise, it fell some distance short of the ground. Sliding down was not difficult in the least, though I did nearly burn my hands from the friction of the sheets. Dropping the last five feet was relatively easy as well, but the second my feet struck the cobblestones, I realized we were now wholly dependent upon the cordage in the shop as a means to bring the goods, as well as ourselves, back up to our room. What if Pike was wrong?

Glancing up, I saw Laura pulling up the sheets and quickly hiding them below the balcony rail. Then she motioned us to come as close as we were able while she whispered, her words barely audible, "Be sure you find that cordage before you do anything, otherwise it is off." Making a horizontal cutting motion with an imaginary knife, she said, "Do you understand?"

We nodded, and she bent her head low to the bottom of the rail so her sound would not carry.

"For we shall have to wake the innkeeper to let you in and if anything has been stolen, we will be undone."

"Yes, we understand—shhhh!" I said, begging her to say no more for fear we might be overheard by some light sleeper.

She, at last, understood my meaning and waved us on.

Stepping as lightly as possible, we cautiously made our way down the dark street. The cool night air brushed our cheeks as we attempted, with great difficulty, to make no sound on the cobblestones with our thick soled leather shoes. If only we had Indian moccasins, I thought.

While we walked, I could envision Laura remaking the beds and nervously awaiting our return. Unlike London where there was always someone on the street at night, we appeared to be completely alone. As we neared the shop, however, we could hear the lamplighter's footsteps passing the next corner and, waiting in the shadow of an overhanging roof, we made sure he was well out of earshot before continuing on.

Laura had cautioned us to use hand signals to eliminate our being heard, but it was unnecessary for it seemed we were of one mind, anticipating each others every move. When we neared the target I was about to point to my shoes, suggesting we remove them to avoid their occasional clump on the paving stones when Pike sat down and started removing his without even looking in my direction. Now, with our shoes tied together and slung over our shoulders, we proceeded in our stocking feet. So quiet were we that I nearly stepped on a sleeping cat.

At the front of Ribbon's shop, for that was the name painted on the shingle hanging over the walkway, Pike lifted up the flower pot in the window box and I held my breath as he felt around for the key. To our dismay, it was not there. At that point, I nudged him and made a gesture with my thumb across my throat, meaning to quit the whole affair. Yet, he shook his head to the negative. Putting down the flower pot, he picked up the one next to it and felt around for only a second before producing the key. I suppose that from a distance of one and a half streets, and in the dark, even someone with hawk eyes could mistake one flower pot from the one next to it.

Pike then slid the key into the lock and slowly turned the shaft. Surprisingly well oiled, the latch turned with ease and withdrew from the catch with no more than a slight metallic click. I suppose the shopkeeper had taken pains to ensure his ability to sneak back in without awakening his wife or sister.

Entering the shop, we carefully closed the door behind us. Inside, it was black as a tomb and before our eyes could adjust, Pike took a step and stumbled over something on the floor before losing his balance and pitching forward into a stand of pots and pans. The ensuing clatter gave him such a start that he fell crashing to the floor. When the last pan had stopped banging about, the pounding of my heart continued the din through my ears.

"Are you hurt?" I whispered.

"No, damn it to hell. Has the whole goddamn city awakened? Quick, take a look but for the sake of our lives, don't move until your eyes have adjusted to the dark."

I peered through the shop window, first one way and then the other but saw no lamps being lit. The building was made of brick and I had, most fortunately, just shut the door before all Hell had broken loose. And with the occupants not being home upstairs, it seemed we were still safe. "I cannot see anything thus far," I said.

Pike remained on the floor and said, "Just watch out for a while. I'm not going to move until I can see what's what here."

Continuing my watch on the street, I noticed a figure in an upper window just across the way. I could only see a blur of white before the window opened to reveal an old woman who looked one way then the other before closing the window and, presumably, returning to bed.

"It appears to be clear now," I said, after several minutes had passed.

Pike slowly pulled himself to his feet, taking care not to disturb anything around him. By this time, our eyes had adjusted to the near nonexistent light and went to work. Within ten minutes, Pike had already found three fine bolts of linen and I had placed a case of silver by the door. On hand and knee behind the counter, I ran my fingers behind a curtain which covered the rough-hewn legs. The floor beneath was coated with a heavy layer of dust that collected on my fingers and I had to withdraw them periodically to wipe off the dirt with my kerchief. Upon nearing the end of the counter, my fingers came upon a leather box. Reaching in with both hands, I carefully slid it out from under the counter. The box now before me, I felt around the surface for a latch. Once found, I gave the metal catch a twist and raised the lid. As I ran my fingers through the contents, I felt the rounded surfaces of six watches with fobs attached along with the rectangular shapes of ten snuff boxes. The surfaces felt polished against my fingertips as they ran over intricate detail, although I could not discern the metal of which they were made.

In my excitement, I stuffed them all into my pockets and thought of how pleased Laura would be to behold this most fortunate find. Then, I was brought in mind of her instructions, "Be sure you find that cordage before you do anything, otherwise it is off."

"Pike, the cordage!"

For an instant, Pike's silhouette froze. Then he set something down onto the floor and went to a corner of the room.

After fumbling around in the dark for what seemed an eternity, I asked, "Well, where is it?"

"For all the goddamn fucking things to happen," Pike said, through clenched teeth. "Bleeding fucking shite, it was right here, I tell you. Bloody Hell! They must've done something with it—stuck it up their arse or something, because it's not here anymore."

"Well, that's it then," I said, trying to be the voice of reason. "We must put everything back in its proper place and have the innkeeper let us in."

"Not on your life. We would have to be completely mad to leave all of this. There has got to be a way."

"Well, we could always explain to the innkeeper that we had to do some last minute purchases," I scoffed.

"Oh, you're a laugh, you are. Now use that inventive head of yours to figure out a way to haul us and these goods up to the balcony."

"I don't see what is so difficult about leaving everything. So we're out of a little sleep. What's that compared to prison, or worse, a hanging."

Pike stood up. For a few seconds, he rested his hands on his hips. Unable to come up with any ideas, he threw up his arms, saying, "Think! Just think, will you?"

I looked at what we had thus far gathered at the door and it hit me. "Perhaps the bolts of linen are the answer. We'll have to tie one end to the sheets to make up the distance from the—well, I suppose Laura will have to strip the beds again and tie them back together, but when she lowers them they won't reach yet. If I sit on your shoulders, perhaps I could reach high enough to tie the linen to the hanging end." I sighed. "If not, then we shall have to retrace our steps and undo everything."

Pike held out his arms and gave me a hug saying, "I knew you would figure a way. I knew it."

We carried the goods out of the shop and, before locking the door, I spied a shiny object on the floor. Reaching down, I picked up a wonderfully carved pocket timepiece. Attached to the chain was a piece of cloth, apparently from the shopkeeper's waistcoat. It must have caught on something and fallen to the floor while he was handling the luggage, I thought. I said nothing to Pike and, while he replaced the key beneath the flower pot, I slipped it into my pocket to keep company with all the other timepieces. Taking up our booty, we slowly crept down the street towards the inn.

We returned to find Laura anxiously waiting. At length she was forced to put her head low to the base of the balcony rail while we struggled for several minutes to convey to her in whispers that she must remake the sheet rope. Once she understood, she appeared angry but, after some posturing on our part, finally cooperated. Once the sheet rope was lowered, I climbed onto Pike's shoulders. As we were near the same size, I must have tested his strength. With Pike all the while staggering like a drunken sod beneath me, catching the end of the sheet was no easy matter. When I was about to tie the knot to the new bolt of linen we heard footsteps approaching. Letting go the linen, I slid from Pike's shoulders and, while Laura pulled up the sheets, we hastily took up our goods.

With jittery nerves, we concealed ourselves within a doorway directly across the street from the inn. My mouth was so dry that my tongue stuck to the roof while we awaited the watchman's approach. Peering around the edge of the doorway, I saw to my trepidation that his progress was slow. This was due to the fact that he took the time to peer into every other doorway with his lantern before continuing onward. Pike had his hand on my shoulder while he watched the lamplighter's progress. Then his hand stiffened.

Stepping back into darkness, the thought of the lantern illuminating us while standing with our loot in hand, was a bit unnerving. It was already too late to leave it and run without drawing his attention, so we decided to chance his passing us by—a stupid gamble, for it was but a fifty-fifty chance at that. Still, with every step he made in our direction, I had a clearer image of the hangman's noose lowering over my head.

Pike handed me a silver candleholder while he pulled his dirk. I felt a fool holding it in my hands, for I was not about to cause injury to anyone, even if it meant my conviction and possible death from the noose, yet I did not release it for fear of Pike thinking me a coward.

The footsteps were near upon us and I had that ominous feeling in the pit of my stomach again, the one I had had since we decided on this course. Then the light from the lantern beamed upon the street directly across from us and I felt my heart hammering into my ears. With each beat, it seemed to be saying—IT'S OVER—IT'S OVER—IT'S OVER. Pike held the dirk ready and I shuddered at what he was about to do. I mentally vowed to stop him when, suddenly, the watchman came to a halt directly in front of us.

We stood frozen in the light of his lantern as he loomed over us. His great black coat made him appear as an immense gargoyle while his wooden staff, a one-inch diameter oaken pole perhaps five feet in length, swayed menacingly in his hand. The lantern swung forward, illuminating a short, front-brimmed hat which was pulled down over his ears making his eyes appear as dark pits tucked deeply behind a fat bulbous nose. He had us dead to rights and I feared the reach of that long staff would make short work of Pike's dirk or my candle holder. I could make out Laura, peering over the balcony across from us, the barely visible outline of her shoulders told me her hands were covering her mouth. I was about to say, "Let's make a run for it," when the watchman set his lantern and staff down onto the street. As though to straddle a horse, he placed his feet in a wide stance and commenced to scratch his arse. For nigh upon a full minute, we stared in disbelief as he dug his fingers into and raked the crack of his buttocks before letting out a deep sigh of relief. Stooping down, he picked up the lantern and, taking hold of the staff with his other hand, used it to pull himself upright before continuing onward without so much as a glance in our direction.

We waited for what seemed an eternity while he continued in a snail's pace down the street and didn't breathe easy until he had disappeared around the next corner.

Laura dropped down the sheet while I climbed back onto Pike's shoulders. This time I caught hold of the sheet and, pulling myself up hand over hand, managed to stand upon his shoulders while tying a good knot that secured the linen to it. Sliding down the linen, I motioned for Pike to go up first. Scaling the makeshift rope with ease, he was onto the balcony in seconds. I then gathered up all of our goods, wrapping up the entire assemblage, taking care to fold cloth between the things that would ring out when making contact. After securing it into one huge bundle, I tied it to the linen. Taking care not to step on the bundle, I leaned over, catching hold of the linen and pulled myself to the balcony rail where Laura and Pike hauled me in the rest of the way. Taking a moment to catch our breath, we took a good purchase upon the sheet and, hand over hand, hauled the entire bundle up and to the balcony. With one last heave, the bundle came over the rail and, before we could check it, fell to the floor with a tremendous thump. Not daring to move, we sat on the floor straining our ears for any sound. Within minutes, there came a knock at our door.

Laura answered, "Yes?"

"Is everything all right in there?" inquired the innkeeper, his voice muffled by the door.

"So sorry to disturb you. I had gone for my water glass and knocked over one of my luggage cases."

"You didn't break anything then?"

"No, everything is fine, thank you. Good night," Laura said, barely able to control her breathing from the exertion of hauling on the bundle.

"Good night," he said, while squeaking floorboards on the stairs assured us of his return to bed.

"Whew! That was quite unsettling. And that watchman," Laura said, still trying to catch her breath. "What a most fortunate itch. I never conceived we would someday be saved by such a thing as that."

"I can't believe he never saw us," Pike sighed.

"And you—there's a coil of cordage by the counter, I know there is," she taunted, rolling her eyes.

"He must have put it somewhere else," he pleaded. "Anyway, we figured a way, didn't we?"

"What he means is, I figured a way," I corrected.

"Well, let's see what you have gotten us," Laura said, her eyes gleaming like a child about to have candy. All told, we had four silver candle holders, one complete set of silver flatware, one bolt of linen a bit wrinkled from our climb, four bolts of silk, two of which were a deep cobalt blue and two a bright rose hue, all containing the most intricate patterns, one bolt of linen with a couple spools of lace.

"This is a grand haul," Laura said excitedly.

"Oh, I don't know," I said with a note of disappointment.

"What do you mean? It is truly a grand haul," Laura said, barely keeping her voice to a whisper.

In a somber tone, I mumbled, "It is only…"

"Only, what?" Laura snapped.

"Only that you have yet to see this," I said, reaching into my pockets and emptying their contents onto the bed. With the lamp lit, it was quite apparent from the familiar glitter that, though the fobs were steel, the timepieces, some double cased and intricately carved—one the shape of a banjo and one with a country scene painted on pearl shell and porcelain—were undoubtedly all of gold. The snuff boxes, ten in all, were made of silver and no less intricate in their design.

"Dear God!" Laura exclaimed, while plopping herself down onto the bed.

"And you said not a bloody thing the whole of the way back," Pike said, blowing air through his teeth. He punched me on the shoulder, saying, "Damn, what a haul! I knew this was going to be capital but I had no idea we would have such luck."

After we had completed our packing, I managed the spools and one of the candleholders in my case while Laura was able to cram near everything else into her great trunk. By the time the chaise pulled up at six o'clock, we, and our baggage, were on the street with the strongest urgency to put distance between us and the beautiful city of Bath.

Even in my prison cell, the remembrance of that moment brought with it an intriguing sense of danger that kept me awake for half the night.

CHAPTER SEVEN

The Mason Key pulsated with a dull reddish hue while the eye, turning to the shade of sapphire, penetrated my very core. Just above the eye, an old woman appeared, her time-worn features seeming to merge with the Key. Her white velvet hood, now pulled back from a thick mane of silver hair, had fallen to her shoulders. Those wizened timeless eyes, I thought. Where have I seen them before?

Startled as something brushed against my leg, I woke with such a start that I struck my head against the unforgiving stone wall. I threw my legs over the side of the cot as I sat in the darkness and waited for the fog to clear from my vision. All the while I listened for any sound other than the rain drumming against the wall outside the window of my prison cell.

Running my fingers through my louse-infested hair, I had just come upon a lump quickly taking shape within my scalp when something caught my eye. A near cat-sized creature casually moved across the floor toward the window.

"Peter, is that you, boy?" Had he found my new quarters so soon, or was it one of the other rats come to take a piece of me?

"Come on little fellow," I said cautiously. "It's only me."

The shape stopped, turned to face me and sauntered over to nudge my foot.

"Had a rough go of it, did you?" I said, while rubbing the fur just behind his ears. "Well, made it just the same, didn't you?"

Peter stood on hind legs looking first this way, then that, before wriggling his nose.

"Well, it appears now that you have found me, you will, once again, be well fed, at least for the next few days."

He dug his nose into the rotten fabric of my trouser leg and grunted.

"No, I don't have any food but, just as soon as morning arrives, you will be fed. You know the routine."

Another day was dawning, indeed—another day less to live. The wind howled through the window to my cell and, taking hold of the bars, I pulled myself up to the sill. There was just enough light to make out dull shapes taking form on the street below.

It was a day of heavy, dark clouds, low and wet, much as it had been when our chaise bounced along the rutted and potholed Bath Road. Windblown rain interrupted by short lived sunbeams frequented the first day of our return journey.

Watching the milestones pass as the wheels slipped in and out of ruts in the turnpike, I wondered how long the shopkeeper and his family would be away before they came home to discover they had been robbed. I wondered if he had sufficient funds to weather the loss and, with this thought, felt ashamed for having robbed him. I never minded stealing from the cullies on the streets of London, for they seemed to have deserved it. For them, it was always the deep captivating eyes of Laura that caused them to forget their wife or mistress who sat at home, trusting and believing in them, faithfully awaiting their return. So, the loss of a few of their valuables did not seem as though it would destroy their lives. However, no matter how I came at it, this new operation of robbing a family store did not set right with me. The thought had occurred that I might suggest taking the things back yet, knowing full well the response I would get, I kept my mouth shut. Things had always gone smoothly for us. Even when we were nearly caught, we were only *nearly* caught. I believed the reason we had, thus far, been spared was solely due to the fact that we hadn't done any real harm to anyone. Now the situation had changed. It felt as though I were being accused by the very air about me.

After a full day of travel, we were tired and hungry and most anxious to arrive at our next lodging. The sun had gone low in the sky and darkness would soon be upon us. Rounding a bend, we were hailed by a man on the side of the road who stood with his head hung low, apparently in some kind of distress. Our driver slowed to offer him a lift to the next stop which was then only a few miles distant. It was at that point that the man raised his scarf-covered face and produced a pistol. The driver went for his blunderbuss but was far too slow as another man on horseback came up from the opposite side of the coach and, reaching across, pinned the driver's hand.

Instinctively, Pike produced his dirk.

Laura shot him with a cold stare, saying, "If you do not wish to get us all killed, you will put that away."

"I would listen to her if I were you," said a commanding voice from outside the coach. Pike sighed and slowly slid the dirk back into his waistcoat.

"Out with you and keep your hands where we can see them," said another voice from the opposite side of the coach.

I stepped out first and Pike followed. Laura stopped halfway out of the coach door to take in the situation. A chorus of crickets broke the silence, while the air was cool with not a hint of a breeze and the mosquitoes and gnats were quickly upon us. We were off the side of the road in a wooded hollow near a small running brook, and I immediately recognized it to be the same place where I had caught sight of the robbery on our opposite journey.

The man who had spoken to us wore a black scarf pulled down from under his hat. He appeared to be very well dressed, wearing a blue and burgundy brocade waistcoat embroidered in silver trim under a black velvet greatcoat with silver buttons. He swung down from his mount, his black boots hitting the stony ground with a thud. His tall, heavily muscled horse had been at full gallop only minutes before and stood lathered with nostrils flaring and chest heaving. After tethering his horse to the rail of our coach, the highwayman offered Laura his hand and helped her to the ground. Standing with his pistol held loosely in hand, he appeared a full six feet in height and weighed approximately fourteen stone.

The other man, also concealing his face behind a black scarf, was not as well dressed, yet seemed respectful of Laura as he tipped his hat to her before taking up a length of cordage and binding the driver's wrists to the carriage wheels. Then, swinging up into the saddle of his grey mount, he appeared to be a yeoman as he would periodically raise his scarf before spitting a black stream of tobacco a fair distance from us. He never spoke to either of us but kept his full attention on the chaise luggage rack where, using the height of his horse to gain access, went about the business of undoing our dunnage and rummaging through our things.

Laura remained very calm while being closely inspected by the *gentleman*.

Once the two had looked each other over, Laura surprised us by asking the highwayman if she might speak with him in private.

He nodded and, before following her, pointed his pistol at us and warned, "If you value your lives, you will not move from where you are standing."

Once they reached the brook, Laura stopped and turned to face him. We were unable to hear a word of the conversation and could only wait as the spitter rifled through our things. I held onto my gold timepiece knowing it would be snatched up the instant his eyes came upon it. The moment the spitter's back was turned, I tossed it into a nearby shrub.

About this time, Laura returned with the highwayman and said, "Robert, Tom, be so good as to help these men remove our valuables from my trunk." Then, with a whisper, she leaned close, saying, "And, yes, the timepieces, Robert."

With the pistol staring us in the face, we helped him load our booty into his saddlebags and secured the rest upon two spare horses the highwaymen had hidden nearby, a wise precaution that would allow their cutting loose if a speedy escape was required.

I couldn't fathom why they didn't require our purses, nor did they search me for my timepiece. And there was that other bolt of fabric which they seemed not to take notice of. Once we had finished helping the robbers stow our goods, Laura motioned for us to come to where she stood, which was well away from our driver.

"This is a capital stroke of good fortune," she said.

Pike and I glanced at one another and simultaneously asked, "Pardon?"

"That man is Jim Bridges, the notorious highwayman. I explained that we were in a similar enterprise and were on our way to our fence in London. Being the suspicious man he must be in this business, he insisted I tell him who our fence is and, with nothing to lose at this point, I told him it was Zack. He laughed and said he would sooner see it go into the gutter than allow Zack to get his hands upon it. It seems he used to work for him years ago before he found Zack had been giving him far less than he deserved for his goods. He has since been doing business with a fence in east London who will give us twice the value that Zack will. He even offered to transport our goods to this man and, as a good faith gesture for introducing us to his fence, a Mr. Clifton, he only asks to withhold a quarter of our profit for his trouble. Mr. Clifftton runs a public house in Cheapside on Leaden Hall Street, the establishment is called the Iron Rooster. Once we have been introduced by Mr. Bridges, we shall be free to discuss future business. Speaking for the three of us, I agreed, and there you are. All is done."

A pause while she looked at Pike and me in want of some reassurance.

Having none to give, I spoke first, "You are trusting this person with everything we stole from the shop?"

"Yes."

"I don't believe it," Pike cut in. He'll simply keep everything and be on his way. We won't see a penny. Goddamn it, all that work for nothing."

Her features transforming into stone, she pressed her face into Pike's and hissed, "You don't see what has happened do you? Has he taken your purse, your clothes, your gold timepiece or that bolt of fine fabric? No, he has not, which, with that pistol pointed at us, he could do anytime he wishes. No! If he does keep the money for those things, we are still far more ahead than if he took everything, which he could have done just as easily as that man can spit. And since he has not taken everything, it only stands to reason that he is sincere in what he has told me. Think upon it."

"What I don't understand is, why didn't he take that bolt of linen or ask me for my timepiece?" I asked.

"It is because I asked him to leave those things. I wished to give the linen to Mother Elkins. And I wished you to keep the timepiece. You have always admired Zack's timepiece and it appears to be of equal or perhaps even greater value, don't you think? And since you didn't wish to go along with this venture in the first place, yet went along just the same, you deserve to have it, if only for putting your feelings aside to help us."

Appreciating her thoughtfulness I said, "She does have a point, Pike."

Pike stomped his foot, saying, "Goddamn it! This is such shite."

Laura shook a pointed finger in his face, scolding, "Now stop that cursing, young man, it will gain you nothing beyond ill manners."

Letting out a deep sigh, he ignored her finger saying, "We got no fucking choice, do we?"

We returned to the coach to find the driver facing the horses with his back to us. The gentleman raised his mask, revealing a narrow jaw with a deep cleft in his chin. He winked a rugged eye at us, bent down from his horse and, dirk in hand, cut the rope binding the driver's hands before trotting off down the road with his companion.

The driver ran for his blunderbuss, picked it up and attempted to fire only to hear a dull click, apparently his powder had been spat upon while he wasn't looking. I suppose the spitter was used to such moves and had, long ago, grown wise.

"He got away. Ma'am, are you all right? Did he harm anyone?" the driver asked, appearing more mortified than frightened. "If only I had gotten Ol' Killer here clear in time," he said, wiping the spittle from the flintlock.

"I'm sure you would have been heroic. However, we are all in fair order and would like nothing better than to be back on the road and put this all behind us as quickly as possible," Laura said, with commanding control.

She was becoming quite the lady, I thought. Intelligent indeed, how she handled that robbery, standing with the countenance of a queen, her high cheekbones, silky smooth complexion, those captivating cat eyes and those long shimmering golden locks over rounded breasts. I believe I fell in love with her then.

In fact, so engrossed was I in her charms that I nearly forgot my timepiece and had to call out to the driver to stop the coach. On my hands and knees, I received several scrapes from the thorny strands before spotting the golden glimmer reflected from the coach's lantern. Once I had taken my seat in the coach, Laura noticed the blood and, withdrawing her kerchief, held my hand and dabbed at the scrapes. Spellbound, I was lost with the sensation of her touch when I noticed Pike's knowing smile which gave me no little mortification. He could see it and he knew what I was feeling. Perhaps he felt it for her too. His eyes turned away and I could see that his smile was neither smug nor derisive. On the contrary, it seemed to be one of acceptance. Perhaps he knew what I had yet to realize—something he had already dealt with. A young boy's crush is doomed from the start.

It was not twenty minutes after our coach left the hollow that we reached our lodging, the same stop we had made on the opposite leg of our journey.

We were well received with a hot dinner of joint of mutton, roasted duck, broth and butter over fresh baked bread and cabbage. Some Bordeaux was then served followed by figgy-dowdy, a delicious raisin pudding. As the topic of our conversation revolved about the details of the robbery, our innkeeper's interest became most intense, for his questions were nearly incessant and it was with great difficulty that we were able to chew our food while he sat impatiently awaiting our replies.

"And what did you say of the robber's appearance, ma'am?" he asked.

"I didn't say, sir," Laura replied, with obvious irritation. "I have already stated that he had a scarf pulled over his face."

He sat with his hands on his hips, a childlike amazement in his eyes, half expecting her to continue, dropping his jaw to leave his mouth gaping when she did not. As Laura continued eating her meal, he couldn't wait for her to finish. "Most persons having gone through such an ordeal have had to stay and eat on good faith. And for the most part, I must confess, good faith turned empty, for it has rarely been repaid. Is that your position, ma'am? Are you, at this time, without funds?" he asked accusatorily.

She continued chewing her food but glared at him while doing so.

"Please do not misunderstand; I would not turn you out. It is just that, well, perhaps you may have something you could offer as collateral—a good faith gesture, so to speak?"

I started to speak but Laura placed her hand on my knee, giving it a firm squeeze. After a moment, she opened her mouth as if to speak but instead took a sip of her Bordeaux.

Laura's lack of response caused the innkeeper a great degree of unease and his complexion began to darken while a glistening drop of perspiration traced its way from his bushy brow to his sagging cheek. "I am terribly sorry that I must ask, madam, but do you have anything we might retain for our generous hospitality?"

With this, Laura emptied her glass and sat it heavily onto the table. "Sir, we have the funds to pay for our lodging and meals. We have had a long day on the road. We have been robbed and now are in need of rest. If you would be so kind as to ask no more questions of us, I believe that I can speak for the three of us, when I say we only wish to forget about this incident and be on our way first thing on the morrow."

The innkeeper's wife walked out of the room and motioned for him to follow. Their whispers carried over from the kitchen for a moment before he reentered the room. Apparently they had not had their fill, and like hungry dogs, they were not going away empty-handed.

"I must say, I have never seen anyone have the extreme good fortune of getting away with so much as a farthing. Wouldn't it be prudent to check your purse?"

Laura gave the man a look that I had not known her capable of. Her eyes seemed to turn black, like two pointed obsidian daggers. He stopped in the middle of his next question, mouth hanging open like a coal chute door, turned and walked out of the room.

"I have never had so many questions put to me," she said in a low voice. "It seems he and his wife must know every detail, and told to them at least five times. I believe they were committing it all to memory for the next guests," she said, while stabbing a piece of mutton with her fork.

Before we had finished our meal, the innkeeper re-entered the room, stepping as though on broken glass. He expressed his desire to send someone for the constable but Laura told him not to bother, and that we would report the robbery just as soon as we reached London.

"Are you quite sure, madam?" he said in disbelief.

"Quite sure," Laura said, flatly. "As I have said, we are quite done in and wish to rest."

"Well, if you insist. We'll leave you to your rest." However, as we rose to our feet, he put a finger to his temple and said, "In the event that the constable does happen by, you wouldn't mind answering his questions, would you, ma'am?"

Laura threw up a hand in resignation, "So long as you do not disturb our much needed rest, for we have a long day on the road ahead. I do expect we will be leaving quite early so could you have breakfast ready at six?"

Although we had had our fill of this man's inquiries, we had no wish to feed his suspicions, as the most logical response would have been to request that the constable come immediately.

Not disguising his disapproval, the innkeeper replied, "Six it shall be, ma'am."

Pike gave me a wink as we climbed the stairs to our bedchamber and, after we closed the door, said in a low whisper, "Just as sure as you'll find shite in a cesspool, that cully's going to send someone to fetch the constable."

"Let us hope not," I said. "I daresay I should not wish to explain what we were doing with those goods if that highwayman were to be captured with them."

"Exactly! And don't believe for a second that a highwayman would hesitate before giving us over to save his own neck." Pausing to collect his thoughts, Pike continued, "If they do ask that question, we must maintain we never had them—that he only took some of Laura's jewelry and, perhaps, your gold watch. It will be our word against a highwayman's. Whatever you do, do not volunteer anything more than they ask for. The more you talk, the easier it will be for them to find holes in our story. I have been interrogated before and you must know that if you are lying they will smoke it from the holes in your story."

"What holes? We shall keep our story straight," I maintained.

"How are you to know? When I'm in one room and Laura is in the other, and they tell you one of us has said something to the contrary, you won't know what to believe." Slowly shaking his head, he said, "We must talk to Laura straightaway and get it all ironclad or we'll be done for."

A light tap on her door was all that was required as she had been awaiting us. With a "shhh!" she closed it behind us and said, "I was just about to go to your door. I have been doing some thinking and I believe he plans on sending for the constable. We must get our story straight."

After a lengthy conversation with a good deal of hushed rehearsal, we retired to our beds. At precisely six o'clock breakfast was served and we were seated with a guest.

Mr. Hastings, the constable, had just happened by when our innkeeper took the liberty of informing him of our great misfortune. Hastings stood approximately five and a half feet tall, with a moon-shaped face beneath a powdered wig that I suspected covered a bald head, for it moved about while he chewed his food. After introductions were made, he lost no time in making clear that he must know everything in precise detail as he had been on the trail of these blackguards for the past two months. Our interrogation was nothing of which Pike had feared, for unlike his previous encounters with constables, he had not taken into consideration that we were the victims and not suspected to be thieves.

When asked to describe the highwaymen, I said, "They both wore scarves over their faces. I don't recall much else except for the pistols."

Hastings leaned forward so that his moon-shaped face hovered over my plate, his small hooked nose pointing at my toast, "What sort of pistols were they, son?"

Breaking off a piece of toast, I dipped it into my egg yoke and, before putting it into my mouth, said, "The large barrel sort, aimed straight at our heads."

With an insincere smile, he inquired, "What I mean to say is—did you notice the stocks?"

"Stocks?" I asked, feigning ignorance.

"Er, handles, the wooden handles. Was there any fancy work, engravings and such?"

I shook my head to the negative, saying, "All I saw was the end of the barrel—and the scarf over his face, it was black, I think."

Hastings' complexion became somewhat flushed at my response. I had given him nothing of value and he seemed desperately in need of reliable information. Thrumming his fingers on the table, he turned to Pike, "And you, young man, did you notice anything other than what this lad has just told me?"

Pike had just stuffed his mouth so full of biscuit that his dimples flattened out and chewed slowly. Hastings impatiently awaited his reply. After a minute, Pike managed to mumble some unintelligible statement through his food-packed mouth.

Hastings leaned forward and, turning his ear toward Pike's mouth, inquired, "What's that, lad? Could you repeat what you just said?"

After taking a deep breath, Pike returned Hastings' stare with a defiant one of his own and said, "Dreadfully sorry! What I said was that I seemed to have forgotten most of it except for the end of the barrel."

Hastings let slip his true frustration by pounding his fist on the table. Then, without hesitation, he swerved to face Laura, "And you, madam? Surely you must remember something."

Seemingly lost in deep reflection, Laura placed a finger to her lips before replying, "I do recall the pistol barrels, yet I also remember that one man wore a long greatcoat with black riding boots."

With this, Hastings leaned forward, the table sinking into his protruding stomach, "His greatcoat, did you notice the colour?"

"Red! Or was it green? No, it must be red, however, you must know that I have always had a degree of difficulty in distinguishing colours under lamplight."

Hastings sat back and, letting out a deep sigh, said, "Perhaps your driver might remember something. Although, I must say that with what the three of you have told me, I have absolutely nothing to go on. With exception to the pistols, it could be half of the men in England." Getting to his feet, he bid us good day and stepped off toward the carriage house.

We said nothing further to each other or to the innkeeper before finishing our breakfast. Later, as we brought our baggage out to the chaise, Hastings stood waiting by the horses, his greatcoat parting to reveal a stomach that tested the strength of his waistcoat buttons.

His face gave no indication of his intentions so we ignored him as best we could, however, with a raised hand, he caught Laura's attention, saying, "I realize this is most difficult for you, madam, but the driver informed me that one of the men had a rather nasty habit. Do you recall him expectorating frequently?"

"Oh dear, no, at least not in front of me; however, that is not to say he may have done it while I was not looking."

Hastings blank expression did not change as he continued in his monotone voice, "And what sort of things did he steal from you? The driver mentioned there were two large parcels of your belongings on the backs of their horses when they departed."

"Oh, mostly our clothes," Laura sighed, waving it off as though it were a trivial matter.

Hastings' dull expression changed as he raised an eyebrow. "I beg your pardon? Clothes, you say? What about jewelry and money?"

"I don't travel with jewelry and, as for money, it was, for the most part, spent on holiday in Bath. I had paid the driver well in advance keeping only enough for lodging and meals. Those funds I quickly placed under the rug in the coach before we were forced from the cab. I did leave a few pounds in my purse that they made off with."

"For a little money and some clothing, these must be some new culprits. The men I am looking for wouldn't settle for so little." Shaking his head, he let out a deep sigh, "That does it, then. Now I have two groups to chase. Well, I shall not detain you any longer. Sorry you had to go through this, madam."

As the coach pulled away, Laura called out, "Sorry we couldn't be of more assistance!"

While watching the inn slip from view, I felt as though a great weight had been lifted from my shoulders. I would never have imagined ourselves being questioned about a robbery wherein we were the victims. And to consider that the man who robbed us could, due to any intelligence we might accidentally divulge, be captured, made this a most uncommon situation. Though we weren't in any immediate danger, if I were to gauge what had thus far followed the robbery of that shop, I would say our future was, at best, questionable. My only consolation was to assure myself that we would return to our own professions and leave this behind us for good. However, I had no guarantees of this from Laura and Pike.

Later in the day our coach had passed through yet another turnpike gate and once our driver paid the gateman his toll I decided to bring voice to my apprehension. "Laura, I have a very bad feeling."

Her eyes had a far off look as her gaze floated over the grassy, wind-combed fields beyond the coach window while her chin wrinkled, putting pressure on those full lips, making them turn down at the corners of her mouth, as a child might when caught in a lie and knowing that punishment lies ahead. Turning her eyes towards me, her expression faded as though she were waking from an unpleasant dream and discovering it to be only just that, "And what is your bad feeling, Robert?"

Pike, who I thought to be asleep, opened one eye to let me know he was listening.

I knew he would not like what I had to say, yet it needed saying just the same, so I went on, "Well, it seems we went through a good deal of trouble to take some things—things which were most cumbersome, though, to be sure, of great value, yet the greater part of which were things we might have acquired over the course of several evenings outside a London theater."

Pike sat up and gave me a puzzled stare before opening his mouth, "Come now, Bobby, it was fun wasn't it?"

"Well," I said, pausing for a few seconds while carefully choosing my words. "It was a bit exciting although we did have several close calls."

"Close calls? What close calls?" Pike chuckled.

"Well, for one thing," I said, "there was the rope that you swore would be there. And for another, I feared you were going to stab that watchman if he had looked into the doorway."

Laura's eyes widened, "Dear God, Pike! You were actually prepared to kill him?"

"I wasn't going to kill him. At least, not directly. Just stick him so as we could make away with our goods is all," Pike said, assuming a defensive posture. "So what if I had? He would have run us in and we might've been swinging from a gallows within a fortnight."

Laura shook her head in disbelief, "You have no idea of what you are saying."

"Well, that's just it, isn't it?" I said, narrowing my eyes. "There we were, risking a hanging over some items which are hard to carry around much less sell, and we don't even have them anymore. We have nothing for our trouble save getting interrogated by a constable about being robbed. I don't know how it sits with you but, as for myself, I was a bit embarrassed about being robbed and made out the poor victim by a man whom we normally wouldn't come within a hundred paces."

Laura raised an eyebrow but said nothing, so I went on.

"And it may not be over. Those people in Bath will be looking for someone who is an outsider and we outsiders have just left town the morning after a robbery."

Laura held up her hand, "Now Robert, I believe you are giving much more thought than the situation deserves. After all, no one in Bath knows exactly where we live. Pike has led the innkeeper to believe we are going to Bristol and, although we have told them we are from London—London, mind you, the largest city in the world, how might they ever find us?"

I shook my head, "In all likelihood, the driver travels to Bath quite frequently and when he is next there, someone may recognize him and inquire as to where he dropped us off," turning to stare out of the window, I said no more.

Laura's face flushed and, searching out my eyes, said, "Robert, this will not happen. Even if they discover where we are dropped off, we will be taking another coach to the house."

"It is only that I fear for my mother and sister. I have this dreadful feeling should anyone find our home…"

"Come now, Robert," Laura said, tilting her head, "no one shall ever discover our home. I would sooner die under torture than give it up. And the same goes for Pike."

Pike mumbled, "Here, here! So why not forget all this nonsense and start thinking about how grand it shall be when we are soon home?"

Still, I couldn't shake the feeling and went on, "If they find our home, it will never be the same for Mother and Lilly. No matter how ironclad our story is, Mother will wonder at first, but as time passes, she will start to put things together and become suspicious. I will lose her trust, which I already do not deserve."

Pike threw up his hands and shook his head.

Laura sighed, "Robert, if it should come to that then we will leave. You now have enough funds to keep your mother and sister free of debt. Perhaps it would be wise not to have the liability of us around. I would so hate to see you lose your mother's respect."

Suddenly, the flow of dread pulsed through my veins. The thought of them leaving was not an option. "I would never ask you to leave. If not for you, my family might have perished and for that I shall be forever in your debt."

"Don't forget, Robert, that it was solely due to you that we were able to break free of the Dials," Laura pointed out. "Thanks to you, we are well off and wish for nothing. You have more than met your end of our agreement."

I sighed, for this was not the point I was attempting to make so I tried another tack, saying, "Forget our agreement, for upon that point we are both on good footing. You must know that I consider you both to be part of my family. I have grown to love you dearly. Pike, you have been the brother I never had and Laura I..." I had to stop myself for I was on the brink of exposing my newfound passion to her. I knew it would change everything between us and this as well as other reasons made me realize it was pointless to pursue the point. "All I am saying is that, although I can't put my finger on it, I believe we made a mistake by doing this last job. I do not like how it has gone thus far and it seems we should steer clear of this sort of thing in future."

Laura gave me a penetrating stare. Had I given myself away? Could she see my passion for her through my façade?

Pike placed his hand on my shoulder and said, "Well, I don't have any problem with that. It was capital fun but I prefer our regular profession. I was only making do with the situation is all."

"And I would like to see if that gentleman Bridges makes good on his promise of giving us our cut," Laura replied with conviction. "And of all things, I should like to meet his fence. For if he does make good on his promise, I daresay we may do far better by his fence than with Zack."

It was late afternoon of the following day when we stood in front of our home. The sky, blanketed with streaks of high sheeted clouds, filtered the rays of the sun on our smiling faces. Our arrival was received with embraces and kisses.

My gift to Mother was a leather handbag with an intricately beaded design of an albatross which produced yet another hug.

"You didn't have to bring a gift, son. Your coming home safe was all the gift I could ever ask for."

I handed Lilly her gift. She sighed happily as she pulled the pair of embroidered silk slippers from the bag.

Pike presented Mother with a bright green scarf embroidered with red and pink roses, a sight that made her eyes light up as she took him into her crushing embrace.

His head buried between her breasts, he cried out in a muffled voice, "Mother Elkins, please, you're crushing me."

Releasing her embrace, she took him by the shoulders and teased, "My dear Tom, I didn't think you were breakable. I suppose I shall have to go easier on you next time."

We five walked, hand in hand, into the house while the coachman brought up our bags. While seated in the parlor, we sipped tea and recounted the events of our journey along with the wonders of the beautiful city of Bath.

The following day we rested while a washer woman came and did our wash; a task we had always dreaded, but with our new prosperity, it was now a delight to see someone else perform it for us.

On Saturday we decided to go in pursuit of the establishment mentioned by Mr. Bridges. Once there, our plan was to seek him out and make acquaintance with his fence. After dinner, we told Mother and Lilly we were going to Covent Garden Theater to see, *"Much Ado*

About Nothing," a Shakespearean play we had seen time and again and were better able to answer any questions she might have of its content.

Mother wished us well as we left the door and proceeded down the street passing some of the children I used to play with. Butch had since moved away and most of the faces were no longer familiar. I gave a nod to the few boys I did recognize as we rounded the corner to Brook Street, receiving only one wave in return. At one time this would have bothered me a great deal; however the fact that I was no longer the leader of the gang did not concern me in the least. As we hailed a hackney coach for Cheapside, I realized my days of playing games had died with the passing of my father.

Leaden Hall Street was a fairly clean causeway with many gentlemen dressed in smart business attire returning from or in route to various offices, one of which was the honorable East India Company.

Our first impression of the Iron Rooster was that it was a boisterous establishment, for we had arrived in the midst of much commotion and goings on. The air wafting from the entry assaulted us with smoke, ale, vomit, unwashed bodies, and thick, suffocating perfume. The inside of the bar was solid from end to end with both surly looking Jack Tars and doxies, the tables and chairs having all been fully occupied. Those that couldn't find a place to sit were standing about singing while a man sitting on top of the bar played a lively tune on his fife.

We had to take care where we stepped for there were two fellows lying unconscious on the floor soaking up their vomit with their clothes. It was quite obvious that Laura's attire was too upscale for most doxies, as many of the tarts gave Laura a stare that could burn the hair off a hog. It was generally understood that no respectable lady would dare enter such a place without her husband or a man to escort her. After seeing Pike and me alongside, I believe the lack of protest could be attributed to the idea that she was a wife bringing her boys to assist in fetching home her husband. As it were, Pike and I tried to look our toughest while not coming anywhere close to fitting the bill.

Our "wife with her boys" act lasted all of ten steps before a mighty bastard who, too drunk to catch on to the idea, took hold of Laura's arm and attempted to cover her face with his massive, slobbery lips. Laura had had much experience in these matters and was quite capable of protecting herself. This cully was quite numb however, and could neither feel her knee slamming into his groin nor the bash in the nose from her elbow. He kept at her with hands as huge as baskets, one nearly passing completely around her waist. His grip was so secure upon her that there was nothing for it but to pick up the nearest full bottle of claret and bash him over the head. The immediate effect was the release of his hold upon Laura, whereby his attention turned to me. His mammoth features fell upon me for a few horror ridden seconds before his eyes rolled up, displaying the whites. A few seconds passed before he wavered and, toppling like a fallen oak, crashed headlong into the floorboards, giving the building a thunderous shake.

This might have been the end of it, had it not been for the presence of one of his mates, another large powerfully built man with a bald tattooed head. In a second, my face was immersed into tattoo covered, tree-trunk sized biceps, his armpit odor filling my nostrils while forearm hair enmeshed my face into blue inked skin. Taking hold of my neck with one hand, he lifted me high into the air above the drunken mob. While suspended thus, I could see that nearly all of the men below me were sailors who, for the greater part, displayed tattoos upon their arms, faces, and even exposed bald patches of scalp. This brute would have snapped my neck if not for a word from the tall, well-dressed man whose smile displayed an oddly familiar cleft chin. I supposed him to be either the owner of the establishment or the sailors' captain, for he seemed to command respect. The brute turned to him and replied, "With you, is he?" before lowering me to the floor and quickly brushing me off with a poor attempt at straightening my shirt and waistcoat.

Very much shaken, but oh, so grateful for the assistance of the tall gentleman, I quickly went over to where he stood with Laura. Pike was handed his dirk, for he would have stuck him with it had not one of his friends taken it away from him. As I turned to look back, the brute had disappeared into the drunken crowd and the man I had struck over the head had been pulled up into a chair, yet he remained quite unconscious. During the incident, the fife had never ceased playing while not more than four or five sailors had even taken notice that I was nearly killed. It was as though it had never happened.

The gentleman introduced himself and, upon hearing his name, I was disappointed I had not smoked his identity.

"Why, it's Jim Bridges, the man whom you last saw with a mask," Laura said, her voice trembling. "Robert, are you all right? Did he injure you?"

Clearing my throat, I turned my head, first one way, then the other before hoarsely replying, "It seems I have not gotten my neck broke."

Pike came up to me and apologetically said, "I'm sorry, Bobby. Had it not been for his mates, I would have gutted that cully."

Bridges bent down and, looking me in the eye, said, "I am most sorry for this, it usually isn't so rough in here but for tonight. You see, these fellows just came off a long voyage having just gotten paid. As for the fellow you took out with that bottle," he chuckled, "have no fear, for as sure as the sun will rise on the morrow, he will remember nothing. Come! Let us go where we may discuss our business."

Taking Laura's hand, he led us to the rear of the bar where he pulled back a pleated velvet curtain to expose a heavy oaken door. He inserted a key into the lock and, giving it a twist and a shove, swung the door wide to allow us entry.

We stepped through the doorway and were greeted by a crackling fire that burned within a large stone hearth. Framing the hearth was a mahogany mantelpiece supported by cherry-veined polished marble columns. The walls were lined with a dark oak wainscot above which hung several scene paintings set into intricately carved gilt frames. In the centre of the room stood a long baroque table surrounded by four shield-back chairs while near the hearth rested three high-back heavily padded chairs of leather upholstery. Next to these sat a small walnut table upon which rested a Bavarian style pipe of carved ivory, tobacco pouch, ash tin, and tinder box.

"Please have a seat," Bridges said, then, turning to me, "I must say, that was quite a gallant thing you did, young man. One would not expect such quick thinking and force from one as young as you."

Then, to Laura, "I would like for you to meet a dear friend of mine. He is the owner of this establishment and the most reasonable fence of which I have ever had the pleasure of doing business. But before you meet him, per our agreement on the road that night, I shall give you your share."

He stepped over to a bookshelf, took up a large leather-bound book and, setting it on the table, withdrew a heavy pouch from its hollowed out pages.

Pike's mouth fell agape as he emptied the sparkling contents onto the table.

Bridges drew up one of the shield-back chairs, offering it to Laura before seating himself beside her. With long dexterous fingers, he separated the coins, stacking them into piles of ten until he had lined up a total of twenty, saying, "I hope this is to your liking. I was quite surprised at the value. The silver was from a rare and prized collection. And those timepieces are exquisite works, not a pinchbeck among them for they have been tested and found to be gold of high quality. Their detailed embellishments make them worth well more than their total weight. Then there was the fine silk, a most exquisite weave."

Laura turned to me and stuttered, "T-Two h-hundred yellowboys?"

"Well, yes, as a matter of fact three of those bolts of silk were of a quality rarely seen in London," he said, speaking in a low voice. "French imports, you know, black market and illegal to sell." He gave a knowing smile. "Bath always manages to get the best that Bristol has to offer. And with the opulence of that city, there are many there who can afford such luxuries. That is why I travel such a great distance to do my work. Those particular bolts will bring as much as £5 a yard."

Laura nodded, her eyes still transfixed on the stacks of gold. It was with apparent reluctance that she turned her attention from the gold to address Bridges saying, "Then, why not live closer to your work? What I mean to say is, why not take a residence in Bath and save the bother of the long road back to London? Oh, to be sure, your fence is here but might you simply store your loot before transporting it here? Perhaps you could even transport it by ship from Bristol?"

Bridges' eyes widened and, slowly shaking his head, said, "Bless me, but you have, in short order, sized up my situation entire. There is one thing you have not taken into consideration. To live in Bath would place me much too close to my work. With the roaming eyes of the city's watchmen, I would soon be recognized. No, it would not do. You see, people such as we have not been welcome in that city since the days of Richard Nash. And, though he himself was a former highwayman, he pledged to rid the city of all thieves. As Nash was successful in that endeavor, the city has remained nearly crime free to this day. Besides, I do well enough by staying clear of the city. Thus far, I have managed to reap its rewards without risking its noose."

"As for you and your boys, I am amazed at what you pulled off. And to work within the city of Bath is brazen indeed. I must take my hat off to you, madam. I pray you have left no trail. The constable is quite relentless when it comes to tracking down people of the craft who do business within his city. As for your loot, it was quite wise of you to conceal those bolts of silk within the linen. French silk of that rare quality would most certainly have brought a great deal of attention. And to conceal it within bolts of linen was good insurance, indeed." He gestured toward the coins, saying, "Feel free to count them again, if you like."

Laura accepted Bridges' compliment without letting on that it was a complete surprise to us how wise we were. Perhaps it was the shopkeeper's wife who took the precaution of concealing the silk before they departed that evening.

Glancing at the door, he said, "My friend should be here momentarily. I must say that he is most eager to meet you and has indicated that he might be interested in conducting further business. Oh, here you are," Bridges said, facing the door.

Through the door walked a thin man of forty-plus years who, having poor posture, stood approximately five feet tall with a shiny freckled head that was bald except for a thick line of gray hair above thick cup-sized ears. With a serious expression, he adjusted thick spectacles upon his saliently hooked nose.

Bridges said, "I have the honor of introducing you to my dear friend and business partner, Mr. Sam Clifton. Sam, this is the woman of whom I spoke. Her name is Laura and these are her associates, Pike and Robert." Then, turning to us, he asked, "Is that correct—Pike and Robert?"

"Indeed, it is," Laura affirmed.

"Pleased to meet you, sir," we all said.

"And I, you," Clifton said, before seating himself at the centre of the table.

Until that moment, Laura had resisted touching the gold coins that sat glistening in the lamplight before her, but now she cupped her delicate fingers around the stacks and, pulling them to the edge of the table, let them fall heavily into her purse, causing it to sag.

"I take it, then, that the price is to your satisfaction?" Clifton said, breaking the silence with a smile.

"Oh, quite satisfactory indeed, Mr. Clifton," Laura offered.

"I must say, Mr. Bridges was quite surprised at your silk, yet he did not wish more than five percent for himself, which is most unusual," Clifton said, giving Bridges a sideways glance.

Bridges thrummed his fingers on the table, appearing somewhat perturbed.

Laura smiled, fluffed her long golden curls and batted her eyelashes at him.

Bridges cleared his throat and explained, "I was merely interested in helping her out. You see, she has been doing business with Mr. Zack."

Clifton's smile vanished, "Zackery, is it? I hope you realize that he will be most displeased at our conducting business."

"I believe we may keep this between you and me," Laura replied. "He doesn't need to know."

Clifton stiffened, "I daresay you don't know Zack well enough." Then, with a sigh, he said, "Please forgive me if I have spoken out of turn. I have known others who have had dealings with him and can only assert to what I have heard. And solely based upon those allegations, I would gather that if he discovers your deception, well, let me just say that he can be most unpleasant."

"Zack and I have had a business relationship for a good many years," Laura defended. "And I don't believe he should hold such a thing against us for long. Sure he might be a bit disappointed but he would soon let bygones be bygones. I am certain of it."

I wondered who Laura was attempting to convince more, Mr. Clifton, or herself. And I wondered how Zack would take the news, especially if we had taken pains to deceive him.

"Well, I shall leave that for you to deal with," Clifton frowned. "I can only advise that you take great care to conceal that fact. As for our doing business, few things could please me more. I might add, if you plan on more travel, it would be wise to forewarn Mr. Bridges so that he might avoid approaching you as he did. Do you generally deal in heavy items or was this an exception?"

Laura shook her head, "We have no immediate plans for obtaining more heavy goods, for we prefer the lighter merchandise such as timepieces, snuff boxes, rings, and the like."

"Splendid," Clifton said. "I can move items such as those quite readily. Then is it agreed, we shall do business?"

Laura looked at us with a smile and we happily nodded our consent.

"Agreed!" she replied.

"Splendid, when next you have need of my services, just come by the back door of the saloon around two o'clock. I am generally here, however, if not, there will be a string tied to a nail on the door. The number of knots in the string will signify the number of hours I will be gone." You may reach the back door by use of an alley. Jim will show you the way out. Now, if there is nothing further, I must bid you good day."

Jim took us through the door and walked down the alley to the street where our hackney coach waited.

As we stepped in, he took Laura's gloved hand and, kissing it, said, "I hope to see you soon, and if I may be so bold, in other than business. I realize you have a ride, but I would consider it an honor to give you a lift home in my carriage."

Laura looked full into his hopeful eyes and, her cheeks flushing, smiled as she replied, "Most kind of you to offer, sir, perhaps another time."

His brows arching, he persisted, "If there is to be another time, where shall I find you?"

"Perhaps it is I who shall find you." Laura teased while the hackney pulled away.

I remember the look of longing in her eyes and it was then that I realized the futility of my jealousy. I had to face the facts. She was eight years my senior and I was only a boy. Still, every time I see her, even from these prison bars, I feel a short stab of heartache.

As the sunlight faded into dusk, I lay on my cot and dreamt of what could not be.

CHAPTER EIGHT

"*You must find the Key, Robert. You are the last of our line. If you do not, it will be lost forever,*" my father warned. The Mason Key glowed and vibrated in my hand, rendering a low hum that climbed ever higher until it reached an ear-piercing pitch. Just when I thought my eardrums would burst, the Key fell silent and vanished. *My feet dangled in the air beneath the gallows, twitching and jerking as I struggled to draw air through my crushed windpipe. As my vision faded toward black, I saw the brick wall in our cellar, cold and silent for centuries and no one came to retrieve the wisdom of the ages.*

I awoke to find myself drenched in sweat and, as my blurred vision cleared, the brick wall in my dream faded and was replaced by the stone wall of my prison cell. How can I find it, Father, if I am to be hanged? I thought. Hanged! "What day is it?" I said, aloud.

In prison, where one is forced to remain continuously idle, boredom must surely be the greatest punishment of all. After spending many weeks here, however, I find that my mind is continually at work. Whether I am planning my escape or my death, I am continually contemplating how best to accomplish both the former and the latter.

To be sure, time in prison can move quickly or slowly, depending on one's circumstances. Suppose you have a date of expected release; it passes second by tortuous second. You can do nothing but anticipate that coming moment and wish nothing more than to walk through the gate to freedom. If, on the other hand, you are a dead man—a man awaiting his execution, then time is a racehorse, galloping ever faster to the finish line with no second slowed to the slightest degree. Not that we don't all have our remaining days before us, yet to know when the last day will come can truly be a curse.

I have spent many days either staring through the bars or at a blank wall in the dark, or at a piece of straw on the floor while my mind traveled at lightning speed to places and events of my life. At these places, I attempt, through the workings of my mind, to change the events—to mentally mend the fractures and stitch together the tears of soul. Yet, when I come out of my trance, though the shadows in my cell have traveled a very noticeable distance, those places in my life remain unchanged. It seems there is a sort of madness hovering over me with an invisible scourge, whereupon, if I refuse, the lash will cut and tear my bleeding flesh until, in vain, I do it all over again. Try as I might, I cannot will myself to do anything else. So, I shall go back to where I left off and perhaps I will see where I should have changed something—anything that might help me repair this broken life.

As our coach carried us back home from the Iron Rooster, I reflected on Bridges' offer and, for a second, wished Laura had taken the gentleman up on it. He seemed such an interesting sort and she had no *real* gentleman callers. The only men interested in her had been our cullies, and they could not count as real.

However, she remained hard as steel in her conviction to not give up the location to our home. And deep down, I knew she was right in doing so. Even Zack with whom we had been doing business for years did not know where we lived. We had all agreed long ago that our home was sacrosanct and nothing would soil it.

"Two hundred pounds!" Laura breathed. "Can you believe it, boys? Two hundred pounds! And Pike, you were so concerned about not seeing a halfpenny of it."

Pike smiled, displaying his dimples in the light of the coach lantern. "I wish I could be wrong like this all the time. Then we'd all be rich," he said, slapping me on the knee.

"I suppose your scheme was worth it after all, Pike. My misgivings must have been amiss," I said, half believing my words, yet knowing full well I still harbored misgivings just the same. I could only describe it as a sense of having dug my way into an underground tomb filled with treasure while knowing all the while that I will have to run a gauntlet of scythe-wielding tomb guards in order to take any of it out. Yet, in light of this evening's events, barring the moment when that brute had me by the throat, we were on our way home with five times what we had dared hope for.

Pike leaned over toward me and said in a low voice. "Maybe we should go back to Bath for another go."

"Oh, no! Don't even think about going back there for a good long time," Laura snapped. "They will be looking for us around that city for months to come."

"How could they possibly know we did it?" Pike said, a smirk on his lips.

"Just think about it. Who left the very next morning?" I said.

Pike shook his head, "The shopkeeper and his family left with luggage, perhaps for a holiday, and for all we know they could still be away, even now. And when he comes back and puts out the alarm for the constable, there will be no way of knowing which night it took place. And if they don't know that, well, they won't know who might have done it, will they?"

"Our quick return to Bath could put someone in mind of when we were last there," Laura said. "Before long, we might find ourselves being watched at every turn. No, Pike, I don't like the idea of going back, at least not until a good deal of time is passed."

Pike scowled. Turning away, he stared through the window at

the passing street lamps and muttered, "I might as well be talking to the horses pulling this coach."

Laura placed a reassuring hand on his knee and, speaking softly, said, "Perhaps your idea does have some merit. Suppose we were to use it in a different city, such as, say, Bristol, or even a bit farther away, Glasgow or Edinburgh? Do you get my meaning?"

Pike turned, his eyes brightened and his dimples framed that smile. It always brought me in mind of a child about to get his hands on something sweet. "We could travel to a different city, perhaps every month or so. What d'ya think of that, Bobby? Come on now, don't piss on that too."

What could I say? It was a plan. We had just made a great deal of money using it. It worked once, it could work again. I shrugged my shoulders and said, "Sounds all right, I suppose."

She went on, saying, "And if we kept to this long enough, we could soon be forgotten around here." Taking hold of my hand, she gave it a squeeze. "We could do just as we did in Bath. Pick a place to stay with a good view of the marketplace. Wait for the right opportunity while seeing the sights; get the lay of the land and, when the moment is right…"

Pike took up the slack by adding, "Off we go back home, bright and early the next morning. And no city is going to be as tight as Bath. It's got to be a good deal easier. Mind you, the goods are likely to not be as pricey but it will be well worth our while if we continue to use Mr. Clifton's service."

Laura's eyes smiled at me and, sensing my reluctance, attempted to transfer her enthusiasm by squeezing my hand again.

I found it difficult to resist, they were so excited, yet I still couldn't shake my feelings of foreboding.

She said, "We could have a good deal of fun taking in the country. Oh, we shall have to think up some excuse for Mother Elkins. She will not like us being on the road so much with the highwaymen about, which brings up another problem. In future, we might not be so lucky as we were with Mr. Bridges."

"We could get some handy pistols to bring with us," Pike suggested.

"Oh, heavens, no, we must think of something else. Perhaps we can send our loot by ship. It would take a good deal of time to arrive, but, that is of no import. We have plenty of time. What do you suppose, Robert?"

"I am not too keen on housebreaking. We had a good deal of close calls with that," I said, hesitantly.

"That was because we were inexperienced." Pike said, cheerfully. "We'll have to think the next one through a bit more—bring rope instead of tying bed sheets together, get a set of lock picks, carry cloth sacks to put the goods in, bring a scarf to hide our faces. Like Bridges and his friend."

"Well, perhaps it might work," I said, reluctantly, while still having that feeling of hell to pay. "But for the now, I would like to try our luck at the local markets for a while before we get rusty. What do you say?"

Pike and Laura nodded.

"It's settled then," I said. "We shall spend some time at home, work the streets a little and at the same time we can give Zack just enough of our business that he won't think something is amiss. The really good stuff should go to Mister Clifton though. What do you think, Laura?"

"Oh, there could be a problem there, all right," she sighed. "If Zack gets wind of our dealings with Clifton, I do not believe he will take it well at all. We must use the utmost care to not let on what we are about. Perhaps we shall give old Zack what we produce in London and save the proceeds from our travels for Mr. Clifton. That way, Zack won't notice any change. And when it happens that we must go to Cheapside, we will be far from where Zack lives and, therefore, he will have no way to hear of our dealings there."

"He'll be wondering why we haven't brought anything from Bath," Pike pointed out.

"We'll have to come up with a good one there," Laura said, placing a finger to her cheek. "Have you any ideas, Robert?"

"We could tell him the truth," I replied. They both looked at me with incredulity and, smiling, I went on, "What I mean is to tell him the truth about everything up until we pulled the job. Do you recall that we were about to go home with nothing?"

"Because of their watchmen, you mean?" Pike said. "Always poking their noses into everyone's business, at least everyone who happened to come from out of town, that is."

A slight furrow formed between Laura's brows as she said, "I suppose he might swallow it. And I believe he has been there—I mean, to Bath. I recall him mentioning something about a relation he visits from time to time. And, if he has, then he would know that much is true. Pike, you will have to be yourself when I tell him. That is to say, you must appear cross because we came back with nothing. You wished to make a haul but I cautioned you against it, that sort of thing."

"I get it," Pike said. "He just might go for it." A serious glance at me, he said, "What do you think, Bobby?"

"I suppose it could work," I said.

The next day, after bidding Mother and Lilly good day, we took a chaise to High Holbourn Street where Zack kept a well furnished second storey flat next to the Old Pine Boar Inn. Inside the street entrance were stairs that led to a parlor, a room we had only heard of and had not been allowed to enter. This, he used strictly as an office for meeting with clients. These clients were not "thieves such as ourselves," he had informed us, but cullies who were seeking his assistance in acquiring their lost property.

On the surface, this gave Zack the advantage of appearing to be the hero to the unsuspecting public. Whereas, in reality, he was a master, using thieves like us to take the items, then, using the London

Gazette to advertise his ability to find the items that were stolen. The grandest stroke of all was to use the cully twice. First by having him lose the items, then by having him pay to get them back. What a circle we created, I thought. Every time we took something we were creating revenue for not only ourselves, but also for Zack, not to mention the London Gazette. How he had managed to keep up this game over the years must surely have been, from day to day, a near run thing. It would only take one observant mind to smoke the whole operation.

Passing the street entrance to Zack's place, we went around to the rear of the building by means of an alleyway that led to the Old Pine Boar Inn. It was at the rear of Zack's building that a separate stairway was used whereby his contacts could enter relatively unseen.

To let him know of our presence, he had run a black leather cord over the door through a small hole in the brick wall at the door jamb. When the cord was pulled, the force would travel up the stairs to a bell, which was fastened at the top of the stairs, causing it to jingle. If Zack was not busy entertaining, he would come down and let us in. Otherwise we would have to return at a later time. If he was not at home we were informed of this by the absence of the strap over the door. This time, the strap was in place and we were about to pull on it when the door suddenly opened.

Standing in the doorway, Zack, still in his bed clothes, had a woolen robe pulled tightly about his neck, a kerchief to his cherry red nose. He hacked a deeply congested cough, sniffed and said, "Come in."

On our way up the stairs he said between coughs, "I was wondering when you would make it back to our fair city. I trust the trip was not too long and you didn't suffer any misfortune?"

"Not a mishap the entire time," Laura said, reaching the top of the narrow stairs.

"Well, at last you have come home," Zack smiled behind his kerchief. "Did you have a good holiday?"

"Oh, a delightful holiday," Laura replied. "Bath is a most beautiful city."

"Well, lads, did you enjoy yourselves as well?"

I spoke first and cheerfully said, "We had a grand time. The place is quite different from London."

"My boy, every place is different from London. However, Bath is a most unusual city," he said, motioning us through the door at the top of the stairs. Laura went first with Pike and me in tow. We entered his small parlor where it was common practice for us to unload our goods onto his oval drop-leaf dining table. The leaves of the table were up and, the three of us walked slowly around it, stopping to face it for an awkward moment. Zack blew into his kerchief while we looked at one another for some encouragement. The table stood before us, silent and empty, as though waiting for us to display the goods which, of course, we did not have.

There followed a dead silence until Laura broke it, saying, "Zack, I am afraid we have had a most unsuccessful time in Bath. The people there, though mostly cordial, are very conscious of outsiders. I am afraid I cautioned the boys to do nothing for fear of suspicions being cast upon us."

Pike stuffed his hands into his pockets and kicked a chair.

I sat in one of his roundabout chairs, rested my chin on my fist and put upon it the most disgusted face I could manage.

More silence followed as he studied each of us. Then, he broke the mood by putting on a jovial grin, saying, "But you did have fun?"

"We most certainly did," Laura smiled.

"Well, that is what you went there for, is it not? After all, you were on holiday and one cannot expect to enjoy a holiday while working. And if my memory serves, you didn't go there to work. For if that was your intention, I should have cautioned you against it. You see, Bath is a capital place for taking a good restful holiday. The people there are, upon the whole, generous fun-loving souls who, at the same time, are most suspicious of outsiders." Turning to face Pike and me, he put the kerchief to his mouth and coughed up phlegm before saying in a wheezing voice, "You did right by not working. You should be thankful, boys, Laura has a very well-developed instinct. Trust it!"

Breathing a sigh of relief, I nodded my head to the affirmative while Pike shrugged his shoulders reluctantly.

"Still, Bath is the target for many a fool, in spite of the fact that they are frequently apprehended and quickly rewarded with prison, or the gallows. Only this morning the London Gazette had an article about someone who's shop had been robbed of a good deal of valuable property. Surprising as it may seem, they have yet to catch the man responsible for this deed. I suspect he was either extremely intelligent or just plain fortunate. For, you see, their constable doesn't know where to begin his investigation because the family had been gone three days before returning to find they had been robbed. In that time so many have arrived and left the city that it will be near impossible to track everyone down."

He sneezed while crossing over to Laura who had been sitting in an overstuffed chair by the window overlooking the alleyway. All the while Zack spoke, Laura stared absentmindedly out of the window. At length, he stepped between her and the window. Placing his hand upon her shoulder, he stared into her eyes and asked, "When did you say you left Bath?"

Without so much as a flinch, she replied, "Why, I hadn't, but it was four days past. It was such a pleasant journey, you would have enjoyed it, I'm sure. This time of year everything is in bloom and the countryside is spectacular, for the colours are glorious in the sunshine."

"Four days. That would have been the day after the shopkeeper and his family left on holiday. There was a woman who lived across the way who said she heard a loud clanging the very evening of their departure. You may have even come across the fellow who masterminded the robbery. I should certainly like to meet the gentleman for he has accomplished something most uncommon—a thing that is rarely done these days—a successful robbery in Bath." Throwing up his hand, he punctuated his comment with, "Ha!"

Though something seemed out of sorts, I breathed a well-hidden sigh of relief, as did Pike.

Upon leaving Zack's residence, we decided to walk part of the way before hailing a hackney. We couldn't quite smoke whether he suspected us of doing the job or had simply been innocently happy for our vacation enjoyment.

"If he suspects we did it, he would be expecting the goods. And since we were empty-handed, he should suspect nothing," Laura reasoned.

Still, I felt uncertain and said, "Then why did he fire that question at you—'When did you say you left Bath?' I must say, Laura, you handled it pretty fine back there."

Pike nodded, saying, "A bit finer than I could've managed."

"Oh, I was ready for that. That is just his way of confirming his suspicions. He is pretty good at smoking things out and I think he was in a quandary between what he suspected and what he knew to be the truth." She had a satisfied smile upon her lips as we walked down High Holbourn Street and, after a moment, said, "You see, he knows the profession he taught us is far removed from the job pulled in Bath. Still, he wonders, either through instinct, or simply due to his own suspicious nature, how we could have somehow pulled it off. Mind you, he will ask around but will never be quite sure of himself unless he some way finds proof that we have done it. And the only way that will happen is if we tell him, because only we know. For the moment we are quite safe. My only apprehension is what the future may bring once we begin traveling the country and eventually cease our dealings with him. We shall have to find a way to break free of him. As to the how, I have yet to find the answer, but it shall come. It always does."

"How do you know that?" I asked.

"Pardon?"

"How do you know the answer always comes?"

"Well, because it always has come."

"Every time?" I asked.

"Why yes," she smiled. "Just as it has always come for you."

"For me?" I puzzled.

"Don't you recall when you were in a spot with what to do about Mother and Lilly? Well, it is just like that. You see, Pike and I were also in a spot when we met you. The answer came then just as it will come for our situation with Zack," she explained. "For me, it has always been that way, ever since I was a child. The answer may not be pleasant, but it is an answer just the same."

"I always meant to ask. Where are you from? I mean, before you were in that spot in Rat's Castle—when you were a child."

Pike turned his head away and said nothing while Laura seemed to be searching for words.

"It seems so long ago and so far away. York is where I am from. I grew up there. And it may surprise you to learn that I come from a respectable family."

"It doesn't surprise me in the least," I said. "I have always known you to carry yourself with dignity and grace, a quality that only comes from a respectable family."

She smiled, and said, "Thank you, Robert."

"Why have you not gone home to visit your family?" I asked.

"It is because I can never go home. For I left without my father's blessing to marry a man whom I had foolishly believed loved me. Later, I found that he only wanted me for his mistress. You see, as it turned out, he was already married." Her voice broke for a moment as she fought back the feelings that were attached to those bad memories. After a long pause, she continued, but in a low, disconnected tone, "And once he tired of me, he cancelled payment on my lodging and left me with nothing."

"Could you not go back to your parents, still?" I puzzled. "Surely they would take you back."

"You don't know my father," she said, under her breath. "He would have had me disowned which he most assuredly has since done. And then, there is the loss of respectability for my family. It is better that I never come home. Then they have no shame to deal with. They can say their daughter is missing or dead and be done with me." A tear traced its way down her fair cheek.

"I am so sorry, Laura," I said.

"Oh, don't be, Robert. If not for our circumstances, we might never have met and I would never have come to know the love your mother has given me. You see, my own mother was never concerned about me or my sisters unless one of us were about to be marrying someone of reasonable wealth." She paused, and, with a frown, continued, "She had not a loving thought within her soul. It was your mother who gave me that which I never had. No. I have no regrets. And I have always said, 'For every problem there is always a solution.' Generally a good deal of time and planning is required, but sometimes it is as quick and simple as our meeting that evening near the theatre."

"I am so happy to have found you and Pike that night," I said.

As we three walked arm in arm down the busy street, I felt a deep sense of belonging. Though, to be sure, not in any way comparable to what I felt towards Mother and Lilly. Yet, Laura, Pike and I, had become dependent upon one another. So much so that I might best describe us as a very close second family.

Crossing Drury Lane, we entered a marketplace and were soon passing haberdasheries with their wary shopkeepers. The air was filled with the scents of fresh vegetables, fabrics, and pipe tobacco. It was shortly after we entered this area that our feet began to ache from the constant uneven step on the cobblestone. I spied a coach and four for hire sitting at the curb just a street ahead so we sped up our pace for fear of it leaving before we might arrive. Pike and I decided to run ahead, for Laura was much too slow with her cumbersome hooped petticoat bouncing along, catching wind and, not unlike a sail, forcing her back at every gust. Reaching the coach first, I had gotten the driver's attention when Pike came up beside me.

Taking hold of the lead horse's bridle, I called up to the coachman, "Sir, if you could wait for only a moment, our friend will be coming up as soon as she catches her breath."

Pike turned to see what progress Laura had made when his eyes went wide.

"Hell and death!" he screamed, and tore back down the street from whence we had come.

Letting go of the horse, I instinctively ran after him and, to my horror, found that Laura was nowhere to be seen.

At the far end of the street, a green paneled wagon pulled by two whip-scarred and poorly fed horses approached the corner at a quickening pace. At first, I couldn't make out the driver, for his back was to us and all that was visible was a dirty black leather greatcoat fitted tightly over large powerful shoulders. Then, as the wagon turned the corner, the driver turned his head and I was struck by something vaguely familiar. The hair fell in oily black strands while he bared his teeth to form a spiteful grin. It was not until I caught sight of those shadowy black eyes that I broke into a full run. While I ran forward, my mind raced backwards to that cold evening I had helped Laura and Pike escape their lodging in the Seven Dials. There was no mistaking the hate-filled eyes of the man who had darted out of the alley behind our carriage.

Always the fast runner, no doubt from years of practice while evading angry shopkeepers, Pike tore after the wagon. Still, I managed to keep up the pace, only lagging behind a few paces. As we reached the corner, we could see that the wagon had moved at a fast trot and was already two streets distant.

Although we ran at our best speed, the ever-increasing distance from the wagon made it apparent that we were losing our chase. Our only chance would be to find a coach for hire, yet none were to be seen on this street. At the next corner we looked in both directions but could see nothing resembling a taxi. There was, however, an aged man with white unmanaged hair, threadbare coat and breeches only a few paces down the street.

He was holding a feed sack to his mare's muzzle and, as we came upon him in a heated dash, he slipped the strap over her head, securing it behind her long white, spotted ears. Ointment seeped through the horse's bandaged knees while her hooves were worn and cracked from many years of traveling on cobble and paving stone. Harnessed to her, was the old man's cabriolet, a light, two-wheeled vehicle, and if in fair condition along with a fast horse, capable of very good speed. And although the cabriolet appeared just as scarred and aged as the horse, we were desperate for anything that might travel faster than we could run.

"Sir, might we hire you to follow that wagon? We can pay you well."

The old man continued feeding the mare while speaking in a barely audible tone, "Gertrude does not run anymore, and she won't be doing any more pulling today. Will you, dear?" he said, stroking the rough sinews that protruded from the old beast's neck. Giving a sideways glance, he said, "You lads had better run along now."

"But sir," I said incredulously, "it is a matter of life or death. Our friend is in extreme danger. She has been kidnapped. We must catch up to her captor immediately or it will be too late!"

The old man turned away from the mare to glare at me. The corners of his mouth twisted up in a mocking grin. "I heard a lot of stories from the likes of you young guttersnipes who got nothing better to do than throw bottles and garbage at me and my Gertrude." His eyes widened as his rage seemed to build with each word. "You had better run along now before I take this strap to ya," he said, pulling down the leather rein from the horse's back to swing it menacingly in my face. His eyes tightened to slits when he realized I hadn't moved. His mouth drew open wide spraying spittle as his voice cracked, "Now move!"

"But I'm not making it up!" I cried.

At that moment, Pike placed his arm around my shoulder and pulled me away.

The old man maintained his stance, swinging the strap threateningly above his head so that there was no mistaking his intentions.

"Never mind that old sod, Bobby," Pike whispered. "We'll not be needing him."

"What do you mean?" I said, not a little confused. "Jeb is getting away. He could hurt her, even murder her."

"Not if we have anything to say about it," Pike said confidently. "I know where he lives and it's not far from here."

"How do you know he will be taking her there?" I asked.

"Because it is the only place he has. He might be a landlord but he is the landlord of a broken down old rat-infested, shite of a building. He never had anything else."

"That night we moved you out of there," I said, "I could see then that he is a very large man and we are only half his size," I said, my voice quavering. "How do you propose we go about the business of getting her away from him, Pike? We'll need help, and soon, very soon."

Pike frowned. "For someone who put down a man twice his size with one swing of the gin bottle, you surprise me."

"That was blind luck and you know it," I said with no little irritation. "We'll need a good deal more than luck to get her away from him."

"You leave that to me. It'll be dark in a quarter hour. We must move quickly," Pike replied.

"Yes, but we are on foot and I have no idea how far the Dials are from here," I said.

"It's only a few more streets," Pike said. "That's probably how he found her, just mere happenstance. Likely on his way from the market, just rotten luck is all. It was foolish of us to be on foot through here. So much time has passed since we left him that I had hoped he'd long since forgotten us."

Through ever darker streets, the air took on a chill which soon bit through our clothing. We were unprepared for the evening as we hadn't brought any warm clothing, thinking we would be at home having supper with Mother and Lilly by this hour. Supper, by God, surely they will be worried.

Brushing the thought aside, I told myself nothing could be done about that now. In a second, our life had been turned upside down. We had known danger before and had always made our escapes, yet this was a totally different matter. This was something that cut to our very core.

Our tired feet were now pumped with renewed energy. My pulse pounded with every step as I agonized over what he might do the second he had her indoors. Laura was in danger for her life. It may already be too late. I shuddered at the thought. No! I refuse to accept that, it is not too late.

Running, sometimes walking, we said nothing to each other while our thoughts raced through nightmarish scenarios, driving us on ever harder. After what seemed an eternity, the surroundings had changed to a rundown and unkempt manor, none of which looked familiar. I broke the silence to ask Pike where we were.

"St. Giles," he replied in a short breath. "This is my old manor."

Speaking in short sentences while pausing to take air into his burning lungs, he continued, "I may still have friends here—we must find them—we will need help if we are to take Jeb on—he is good with a knife—even better than I."

Rounding a corner from Broad Street onto Dyot, the manor went from poor to decrepit. Filth from chamber pots of days gone by lay everywhere, while the rancid air made the back of our throats burn. Shabbily clad children with gaunt faces, some black, some white ran in groups, like miniature football teams after an elusive ball, from one gin soaked drunkard to the next with hands outstretched hoping for a morsel of anything to fill the bottomless pit of hunger.

To those around us, it became immediately apparent our attire was an advertisement, saying here are a couple of easy cullies. Fortunately, the darkness descended upon us quickly. The fog then rolled in, mixing with the heavy odor of the surrounding filth and, though noxious, gave us good cover. Though I had no idea where we were, one glance at Pike's set and determined jaw was all the assurance I needed.

Turning the corner at Ivey Lane, we stepped cautiously down a narrow street. After we had gone one street to a point where the street ended at a narrow gated passageway, we came upon a large brick building upon our right that appeared incongruous with the other slum houses around it. It appeared the building had once been some ancient hospital that had gone to ruin over the centuries. All the windows were aglow while shouts of laughter mixed with anger filtered down to the street.

Pike stopped at the entrance, looked up at the building as though he were visiting an ancestral grave and exclaimed, "Rats' Castle." Turning to me with mournful eyes, he said sorrowfully, "Where Laura and I once lived."

So, this is the place she told me about, I thought, remembering our conversation back in Bath. Laura was a prostitute here.

"Is this where she took you in?" I asked.

Pike stared up at the building and slowly nodded, "I believed I would never have to come here again," he said, with a half-hearted smile. "I was wrong."

Entering through a large doorway, we stopped in front of a wide staircase of hand-worn heavy oak banisters that led to the second floor. The entry led into a large, well-furnished parlor with various gilt-framed paintings upon the walls, plush and intricately designed Indian rugs covered in bright hues of red, indigo, and green upon the floor. The air was heavy with tobacco blended with stale perfume, gin, and body odor, as well as a rather gamey odor I had yet to recognize. At the top of the stairs stood three women, most likely prostitutes, who were pushing a balding middle-aged man down the stairs towards the front door. The man wore nothing, save his knickers, while he stomped his bare feet and screamed in an indignant high-pitched whine that he had been robbed.

"Go on with yourself, now!" one red haired, scantily clad doxie warned.

Another large breasted woman with an olive complexion beneath a thick crop of hair dark as tar that draped in ropes down onto her white breasts taunted in a husky voice, "And don't you be comin' back or we'll not let you keep your knickers next time."

The man was pushed through the door and onto the street by two large men who, reeking of gin, turned to Pike and me with intent to give us similar treatment.

I was prepared to dash out the door, thereby saving the men the trouble, yet Pike stood his ground as though he had nothing to fear from these blackguards.

"I wish to see Sally!" he proclaimed.

The larger of the two stopped short of backhanding Pike and, with a look of bewilderment, said, "You know Sally, do you?"

Pike's expression turned to irritation while several young boys of perhaps six to ten years wandered into the room. Some of these boys were holding clothing that presumably belonged to the man recently thrown into the street. Apparently they had been in the process of divvying up the goods when they had overheard Pike. One came up behind me and tried at my purse with extremely poor execution. Catching his cold oily hand at my pocket, I took a firm hold, bending back his wrist until he cried out in a shrill pitch that brought the other boys to his side. Soon they had us surrounded while pressing in with daring fingers and looks of ill will.

"My name's Pike," he said, in a commanding voice that effectively stopped them in their tracks, leaving no doubt his reputation remained intact.

"My God, it is you!" cried a woman's voice from the top of the stairs.

Not unlike mice discovered by the lamp light, the boys scurried away into one of the other rooms. Being thus put at relative ease by the absence of these rascals, we glanced in the direction of the woman's voice.

"Hello Sal," Pike said with a smile, his dimples prominently displayed.

Down the stairs flowed a well-formed and fashionably dressed woman with long golden hair that fell forward over her shoulders in tightly rolled curls that gently bounced at each step. Upon her large, yet well-formed facial features, sat a distinctive mole just above the right cheek. She reached the bottom of the stairs and was upon Pike in a single bound. Taking him in an embrace, as though he were her long lost child, she rocked him from side to side while her alabaster complexioned breasts pressed against his face. After a moment, she seemed to recover and, holding him at arms length, looked him up and down with a smile saying, "Why, look at you. It appears you have done quite well for yourself." Then, upon seeing his sullen expression, her features took on the coldness of a marble sculpture as she asked in an icy tone, "Where is Laura?"

"Laura is why I have come. Jeb has gotten his filthy hands on her."

A dark cloud passed behind her eyes as she asked, "When?"

"Not half an hour ago. He snatched her up on High Holbourn. I believe he took her to his place in the Dials. We would have gone there straightaway but Bobby and I could use some help," Pike explained. "Could you spare anyone?"

While giving me a quick once over, she frowned and, biting

her lip, said, "I am shorthanded at the moment but am expecting Big Bones within the quarter hour. He could take on ten Jebs, if you get my meaning."

Pike shook his head and, starting for the door, said, "We must go now. We cannot afford to lose any more time."

Sally raised her ivory palm, saying, "He has another house now. It is here in St. Giles. He may have taken her there."

Pike stopped at the door and, turning round, asked, "Where?"

"I believe it is a house over in Jones Court, between Bainbridge and Buckridge Street," she said. Then, with a look of concern, "Do not allow him to get his hands upon you. Just as soon as Bones arrives, I shall send him in search of you."

"Thanks," Pike said, as we darted through the door.

"I can only hope that you are not too late," Sally said, mournfully.

I followed Pike through a narrow gate which opened onto Carrier Street, a dark lane with many tenements where cries of wailing and curses filtered through poorly shuttered windows. On one dimly lit corner, a man uttered curses while he struck a woman with a walking stick, yet she relentlessly held fast to his purse. Turning onto Buckridge Street, we passed an alley where a prostitute knelt in front of three men who I thought were about to do her harm but, instead, handed her several shillings. I started to ask Pike what was afoot but he only motioned me on. Following Pike closely, I glanced warily to my right and left and wondered if we would ever find Laura in this part of the city. What if we were wrong? What if he took her to the Dials?

Suddenly, Pike's pace slowed as we approached a shabbily dressed black man that eyed us as though we were lambs come to the slaughter. He was a filthy man with large wide eyes, stubbly chin and, by the smell, coat sleeves that had been soaked with fish oil. He stepped into our path and produced a surprisingly shiny dirk that was in stark contrast to his heavily soiled clothing.

We came to an abrupt halt.

The man spoke in a low gravelly Irish brogue, saying, "Now where might a couple of dandy dressed lads such as yourselves be headed in such a hurry?"

Stepping back we found our retreat had been blocked by two of his dirty friends.

I tried to control the trembling of my chin while, in his usual confident tone, Pike said, "That is none of your affair. If you don't step aside, I believe you will soon part with something dear to you." The sod's eyes darted down to his privates where Pike held his razor-sharp dirk already inserted into the ragged pants.

The man's mouth fell agape while a voice from behind me, said, "You got yourself in a good fix, ain't ya, Joe. Now suppose we takes this 'un here and guts him while his mate does you?"

Not unlike a very bad dream, when you find yourself in the clutches of a monster, I felt a tremor pulsating from my core that traveled outward to my extremities like ripples in a stone-struck pond and, within seconds, my feet and hands trembled out of control. This is it, I thought. We were going to be carved up like a Christmas goose while God only knows what is happening to Laura. A fine pair of knights we turned out to be.

I am not going to go to my death without so much as a whimper, I decided, and was about to grab and twist the bollocks of the man who threatened me when Pike spoke with an unbelievably calm voice, saying, "And a pleasant evenin' to you, Willy."

Willy, apparently the one with his dirk to my back, laughed out saying, "Pike, you little scrap, is that really you?"

"Last time I checked, I was still me," Pike said, with a chuckle.

"I thought you was dead," said Willy. "It's been a long time since I laid eyes on you and those dimples of yours. Joe, you got to see this little nipper's dimples. Let him have a look, will ya, Pike?"

"Enough with my dimples, you old sod. How've you been?"

One moment, I had stood with my blood pumping through my

ears ready to die, and in the next, I had become part of some long lost dirty family. The dirk disappeared from my stomach as quick as it had come and these deadly creatures suddenly became our mates. To be sure, I had no desire to keep company with these filthy cutthroats, yet I was extremely grateful for their transformation.

Willy seemed to be the one in authority. As for the other two, I couldn't make out much of their faces except that they were covered with much hair while few teeth remained to grace their pitiful smiles.

One of the three, who Pike addressed as Giles, towered above us all and, with a willowy bending motion, brought his head down to look Pike in the eye while addressing him with a heavy lisp, "Pike, whooths yer mate, here?" He smiled at me and I didn't quite know how to take it. It was a queer sort of smile with a fat tongue protruding through his thick drooling lips.

"This here's Bobby. We been workin' together these last three and a half years. He's got a quick 'and and can cut every bit as fast as I. Lucky for you, I gave him the signal or he'd a 'ad you gutted and skinned as quick as I can spit."

Within a second, Pike seemed to have lost the respectable speech Laura had gone through such great pains to teach him.

"If he tho quick, then whyth he thaken like a tree in a thtorm?" replied Giles.

"Shakin' is how he moves so fast. If I hadn't stopped him, each of those shakes woulda' been one more slice from your hide."

Giles smiled stupidly and, while displaying open hands, stepped a few paces backward saying, "I ain't gonna try nothing, Bobby. Justh you thettle youthelf down now."

Forcing a dead-eyed smile, I pretended to sheath a dirk under my shirt. They were noticeably uneasy at the smile and I felt it best to keep quiet, maintaining the face whenever they glanced my way.

The one called Willy said, "What are you fellows up to tonight?"

"We're going to collect a debt from an old friend," Pike said.

"Say, how is Laura?" Willy asked. "I sure been missin' her pretty little face around here. You know she saved my arse once and since she left, I can't deny there's been many a time I coulda' used her help. Remember that time I got run down by the Bow Street boys, Joe? She stepped between me and the boys using them eyes of hers to capture their attention and I was gone three streets before they could pry themselves away. God, but she is pretty."

Giles and Joe gave out a deep sigh until Pike cut in and softly said, "It's Laura who we are looking for."

Willy quickly sobered and said, "What d'ya mean?"

"Jeb's got her and I believe he means to do her serious harm."

"You know that for sure?" Willy asked.

"Snatched her up right off the street just over an hour ago. Must'a hit her over the 'ead and stuffed her into a wagon we saw him drivin'," Pike replied, his old street accent taking over again.

"Was it a green wagon?"

"Green it was and we're headed for his place this minute."

"Ya know, he ain't in the Dials no more," Willy said.

"Sally told me as much," Pike said.

As though he hadn't heard Pike, Willy went on, saying, "He's got 'imself another house over on Jones Court. Don't know why he bought it 'cause it ain't much better 'en his old 'un. Come on, I'll take you there. If he harms one hair on her sweet head, so help me, he's a dead man."

"An' dyin' thlow, he will," Giles put in.

Joe said nothing and obediently followed along.

We walked down Buckridge for another street where Willy motioned for us to turn into Scott's Court. Pike hesitated, though Willy kept on.

"Why are you going that way? Jones Court is another street farther," Pike asked, irritably.

"Cause there's a secret entrance to his building that even he don't know about. And we can get to it from one of the houses here," Willy replied. "Come on, you're wastin' time."

Pike hesitated for another second before making up his mind and, giving me a frustrated glance, stepped out into their wake.

Scott's Court was a dark narrow row made even darker still by the fact that the roofs of the houses completely overlapped the court. In making our way through, we were forced to step over a group of gin-soaked men and women who had apparently gotten themselves too cup-shot to make it to their quarters. I thought of how I had always wished to see St. Giles and now realized what my mother had meant when she warned that it was a very dangerous place.

Passing several occupied buildings, we could hear laughter from within, while the thick smoke of freshly cooked meat combined with tobacco to waft in bilious clouds from the windows as their chimneys were in dire need of repair. The caustic odor of vomited gin permeated the air the whole of the way and, as I forced back a surge of nausea, Willy motioned for us to stop. Directly ahead sat a neglected and abused old house with no visible signs of occupancy, for the windows were dark. Willy approached a boarded up window and, taking good purchase upon a loose board, pulled it aside and bid us enter through the glassless frame. Stepping across a floor of shattered glass, I nearly tripped over a poor soul who slept curled up near the wall. Willy took up a candleholder and, producing a tinder box, lit the candle before motioning for us to follow him down precariously rickety stairs into the blackness of a basement.

"Is this his new place?" Pike whispered.

Willy motioned him to be silent and crept across the stone floor to the other side of the basement where a legless table lay on its side propped against the wall. Taking hold of the table, Willy slid it to one side exposing a jagged hole in the basement wall. He then knelt down and, on his hands and knees, crawled through. Unfortunately for the rest of us, the candle light went with him. Pike and I got down onto our hands and knees and followed, while Giles and his silent partner trailed behind us. After we had crawled through, we found ourselves in another basement.

Willy motioned for us to be quiet and pointed down where there lay a few loose boards set over the dirt floor, "That's for the magistrate what tries to chase us through here. Don't step on them boards. It's set to help you into shite up to yer neck."

A cesspool for the Thief Taker or Bow Street Runner that happens upon a chase through here, I thought. It is little wonder there is no evidence of any law in this place. It's set up for escape at every juncture. And I can't imagine the fool who would wish to crawl through a hole in a dark basement after one of these cadgers.

Stepping carefully around the stinking pit, we made our way over broken gin bottles, newspapers, boxes of discarded and long forgotten rubbish, to the opposite side of the basement.

Willy stopped there and motioned for Pike to come close. Pulling aside an old wooden crate, he exposed yet another square opening and said, "We is now under Jones Court. Jeb's place is on the other side of this wall. We got to be real quiet from here on.

As we pulled ourselves through the opening into yet another basement, we paused to strain our ears for any sound. Within a moment, muffled steps from above caught our attention. Then there came a sound like the slap of a whip followed by a thud as something hit the floor. A woman's voice whimpered above us while we could hear the legs of a chair raking the floor, most likely being righted after it had fallen.

"Thought you would never see the likes of me again, didn't ya? Run out on me without so much as a word, will you? Well, you'll not get away from me this time, you damn bitch. Just give me one reason why I shouldn't slit your throat, just one." Another slap cut the air and the chair thudded on the floorboards.

"Well, you got yourself some fancy clothes and some money in your purse so I suppose you been doing all right. And there you were, walkin' down High Holbourn just as easy as you please."

The chair scraped across the floor before stopping with a thud as it was righted again. "Think you're better than me, now? Got yourself another man, do ya? Ha!"

Another slap cut the air above us and I whispered, "We must get to her before he kills her."

In the meantime, Willy had found the stairs and, after making our way over to them, we stood at the ready.

From above we could hear Jeb, saying, "I figure you owe me plenty, plus interest. I only want what's mine so I'm only going to ask you one more time, woman. WHERE DO YOU KEEP YER GODDAMN MONEY?" Then, another slap as the chair heavily struck the floor.

While Jeb was in the act of pulling her chair upright, we took advantage of the noise and ran up the stairs.

"You think you can walk out on me, do ya? Think you're better 'n me, do ya? Think you're too pretty to be seen with the likes of me, do ya? Well, I'm gonna fix that," he snarled.

Willy carefully slid open the basement door and, one by one, we followed him through.

The room was barren while a few discarded paint pails sat in one corner. We could make out his shadow on the opposite wall from where we stood as the light came in through an arched opening to an adjacent room. Stepping lightly, we crossed the floor and went through the opening into the next room. Unlike the previous room, this had scant furniture. An old table sat in one corner while in the other stood a hearth with a stack of coal burning within.

The light from the hearth illuminated Jeb's form as he stood with his back to us. His hair was unbound and hung to his shoulders in thick strands, while his broad shoulders were tilted downward as though he were carrying a heavy sack of grain. Standing over Laura, he had her pinned to the chair by resting one knee on her bound thighs. Though out of view, it was apparent that her hands were tied behind the back of the old splintered crook-back chair in which she was seated. As we neared, we could see that he was holding a long shiny dirk to her eyes and, muttering softly under his breath said, "I'll fix yer face good. That way no one will ever want to be seen with the likes of you, ya little whore."

As we came up behind Jeb, I could see that Laura's milky complexion had turned red as an apple. Her lips, swollen and puffed out, distorted her once perfect features while a stream of crimson oozed from the corners of her mouth. Though she had gone through hell during the time it took for us to find her, she held her head poised, bloody chin high, in utter defiance. Her nose, though not broken, added to the flow of blood as she exhaled, spraying a fine scarlet mist into Jeb's face. In one hand, he held a fist full of her lovely blond curls, twisting them so that each turn forced her swollen and bruised eyes closer to the tip of the knife. The bodice of her sapphire dress appeared as though she had spilled a tankard of ink upon it. And it was with horror that I realized the ink was, in fact, her precious blood. Though he taunted her thus, her expression remained blank, like an indifferent bystander, as though he was not worthy of her attention—as if he didn't even exist. Seeing her here, under this animal's hand caused my blood to boil, and when I went for Willy's pry bar, he caught my meaning and quickly withdrew it from my reach.

Then, as Laura caught sight of us beyond Jeb's shoulder, life poured into those hopeless eyes and, smiling through cracked and battered lips, she spoke in a slurred, almost drunken voice, "Thank God! I feared you would never find me."

"Well, find you I did," Jeb replied, still unaware that we were upon him. "And don't be thanking God for that, you silly wench. Don't you see? It's too late for you. My patience has run its course and even if you tell me where the money is, God cannot help you n—," his words were cut short as Willy tapped him lightly on the shoulder with the iron bar.

Startled, Jeb swung his head around just in time to meet the curved end of the bar as it hooked him in the mouth like a fish, rendering a cracking sound not unlike broken china underfoot. Willy attempted to extract the bar from Jeb's teeth but it had caught into his cheek, making the skin rise out to mold around the claw-shaped steel within. Jeb grunted from the pain and, tripping over his unbalanced feet, fell to the floor while his knife, falling from his grip, stuck into the floorboards beside him.

Laura, though bound to the chair by multiple strands of rope, managed a glance down at Jeb and warned, "Willy, the knife!"

Within the split second it took for Willy to react, Jeb already had the knife back in his hand and, undeterred by the pry bar still in his mouth, swung the blade at Willy's legs, leaving a dark line of blood where it had cut through the stocking to graze the skin above the ankle. Willy, in turn, had a good purchase on the pry bar and, with one great tug, pulled the end through Jeb's cheek, spraying blood and chips of teeth as it exited his face. His head free of the pry bar, Jeb's mouth gaped open exposing his broken teeth in a bloody macabre grin as his torn cheek hung in a flap of skin below his jaw. Undeterred by his terrible wound, he lunged like a cat at Willy, the knife flashing through the air. Sidestepping his deadly thrust, Willy brought the pry bar down hard across Jeb's knife wielding wrist before skillfully slamming it into his nose. Jeb's head shot back from the blow and, dropping the knife, clutched his flattened nose as Willy, wasting no time, swung the bar around in a long arch to come up hard, rendering a hollow crack as it sank deep into Jeb's unprotected groin. Jeb doubled over and, with a deep groan, fell headlong onto the floor.

Pike had his dirk out and quickly cut away Laura's bonds while I searched through the kitchen and found a water basin with some linen towels. As Pike removed the rope, I gently dabbed at the blood seeping from her mouth and nose.

"How ever did you find me? How could you have known he moved to this awful place?" she asked, through bruised and swollen lips.

"Never you mind about that now," Pike said. "It is over. We'll have you out of here and back home in no time at all."

Her pain-filled eyes fell first upon Pike, then me as she said, "I don't know what I would do without you boys." Then, with a sigh, "I suppose I would be dead."

"If we had kept a closer eye on you this would never have happened," Pike said, with trembling chin. "One of us should have stayed with you. We are both to blame for this."

"Don't go blaming yourself," Laura said. "It was no one's fault. He would have killed you. And if you hadn't found me, he would have killed me eventually. He told me as much. He was going to torture me until I told him where we lived and then he was going to kill you, Pike, but not until he had your money, as well. That is why I am still alive. I told him nothing," she said, while staring transfixed at Jeb's bloody form on the floor.

While helping her to her feet, her dress opened at the thigh and my eyes fell upon a small stream of crimson, stark against the ivory skin of her leg. "Dear God, what has he done to you?" I said, my anger now burning tears of empathy.

"I will be good as new, Bobby. Just get me home," Laura said, her breath heavy and voice shaking. Then, turning to look down upon Jeb's shattered face, she gasped as she met his loathing eyes. Clutching Pike's hand, she whispered, "Pike, he will come after me again. You know he will."

Pike and I stared with detestation as Jeb writhed and moaned on the floor, his hands clutching his groin.

"You leave him to me, missy," Willy said, his jaw seemingly

locked. "Don't you even think on him no more. A bad memory is all he is about to be."

Upon hearing this, Jeb moaned through clenched and shattered teeth, saying, "I washan't gonna kill her. She wouldn't ansher my queshtions ish all." Then, with mangled face upturned, he begged Willy, "Ain't you done enough to me?"

Taking hold of Laura's arms at the shoulder, Pike and I shored her up as she walked between us, her knees wobbly and trembling.

Giles, upon seeing Laura's swollen and battered face, exclaimed in his muffled voice, "That bathtard!"

At the front of the building, I heard Willy speaking quietly from within, "Come on boys, we got work to do."

Through the dimly lit door opening, I could make out Joe's unforgiving smile, as well as the dirk shimmering in his hand. Giles, in his willowy pace, stepped through the doorway while Joe followed, silently closing the door behind him. As we made our way through the darkness down Bainbridge Street toward a distant streetlamp, a hulking giant of a man came panting up to us.

His heavy features and unusual height of near seven feet were enough to frighten several armed men. Yet, upon recognizing Laura, he stopped and beamed a wide-toothed smile. In a surprisingly gentle tone, he asked, "You all right, then, Laura?" And seeing she was not, Big Bones' smile faded as he said, "If you want, I'll fix him good for what he done to you."

"No, Bones, it's already being taken care of," Pike said, as a bloodcurdling scream cut the air. Then, without a word, we continued on our way.

CHAPTER NINE

Sliding back the old tool box, Father counted the bricks from the floor upward to seven, then, across one and down one until he had reached the seventh in that order. Turning to face me, he smiled and held out the small leather bound book. "This book contains the knowledge referred to by the symbols on the Key," he said, opening the book to a page with seven lines. "See here, the seven principles of life." As I looked into his eyes they changed, growing aged and narrow. His hair went from black to silver and his skin became pale and transparent with blue traces of small veins near the surface. The face was no longer Father's but had transformed into that of an old woman. The paper-thin lips creased and smiled and the voice was light and musical. "Meet me there, Robert. I will explain it to you." She reached out and touched my forehead and, in doing so, sent me falling backward into a river. Gasping for air, I fought to keep afloat as the current took me, dragging me to the bottom and holding me there till I thought my lungs would burst. Then, from above, I saw a blue light and the current ceased. As I swam toward it, the light grew brighter until I could see that it emanated from the eye in the triangle of the Mason Key. As I neared, almost within reach, a bolt of lightning shot out from the eye, striking me hard in the chest and, waking, I sat up cold and shivering in my prison cell.

Again, I thought. I am to die, yet my father exudes such confidence in these dreams. With a sigh, I surmised that these dreams were most likely due to my own wish to be free; to have the power to break free of this hell. I must face it, they are only dreams and nothing more.

A narrow iron plate, situated in the upper centre portion of the door to my new room, was periodically slid to one side allowing the turnkey to observe me at his leisure, presumably to assure I had no designs on cheating the hangman. This feature, coupled with a turnkey who stepped lightly, was cause for me to keep my manacles on throughout the day.

It was before I received my breakfast that this rusty plate grated to one side exposing a rotting set of teeth that, in a voice like a squeaking wheel, said, "Do ya know what day it is? I say there. Do ya know what day it is?"

"I don't know what month it is, much less what day," I said to the teeth.

"Never you mind what month it is. Never you mind, 'cause it ain't important to you. It might mean something to me and the other bastards what works in here but it don't mean nothin' to you. You know why it don't mean nothin' to you?"

Realizing there would be no reply, the teeth continued their goading, "Cause regardless of what month it is, it's the day that's important to you. You know why it's important to you?" I say. DO YOU KNOW WHY IT'S IMPORTANT TO YOU?"

Growing weary of these rotten teeth invading my space, I replied, "No! Why is it so goddamn important to me?"

"'Cause it's the day before you dance on the rope's end is what day it is. Ha-ha-Ha! It's your last full day on this earth—time to make peace with God. Better do it soon 'cause you'll meet him soon enough and it'll be too late then."

It became apparent that this turnkey's cordiality thus far had been solely dependent on the value of my benefactor who, with his funds about to cease at my execution, made me less worthy of respect. "If you've nothing further to say then I would much appreciate your absence."

"Oh, it slipped my mind. You have another visitor. He's a Grub Street gentleman who wishes to draw your likeness for the Gazette," the teeth said in snarling mockery.

"I don't wish any such portrait," I said, with growing irritation.

"Got no choice. All the condemned gets his bloody portrait for the Hangin' Fair," he said with a grin.

The door opened and a short man with medium build, threadbare waistcoat, breeches, and patchy periwig entered. With a sketching pad in hand, he smiled nervously, saying, "Clarence Tolliver at your service, sir."

"Will this take long?" I curtly inquired.

"But just half the hour, if you please," he replied.

I sat near the window and while he silently sketched away, I realized I hadn't known the correct day of the month simply because there was not sufficient time to count the marks on the wall of my old cell before they had moved me to this one. As I had previously mentioned, time moved at lightning speed in here, for I had somehow imagined there to be two full days remaining before my execution. Two more full days, but now, one of those days is gone. I shall be dead on the morrow. On the morrow they will come for me and I will be taken to Tiburn Tree. The thought of being choked to death by the weight of my own body sent icy chills up my spine. Wiping the perspiration from my hands onto my ragged breeches, I sat for a moment further, then, wiped them again before rising to my feet.

"I must take a minute to stretch my legs," I told him.

"By all means, do so at your ease, sir," he said while controlling his irritation. It was obvious he wished to be here no longer than was absolutely necessary.

Inhaling the fresh air from the window, I took it in as far as it would go, holding it as long as I could, mentally counting the seconds until, after a minute had passed, I started to ache from every part of my body. After two minutes, the pain increased to an unbearable degree while my heart pounded, increasing in force with each beat. When I could stand it no more, I exhaled and sucked in precious air.

The realization struck me. A hanging death may take only a few minutes but those few minutes will be an eternity at the rope's end. No, it is most certainly a slow and painful death. When the time came, I would not have the luxury of resumed breathing. The pain would go on until... I recalled that a couple shillings to the executioner could be rewarded by having him take hold of your legs and pull you down in order to snap your neck. I didn't think to ask Edmond for those shillings. But then, I was planning on doing the Turpin, jumping high into the air above the cart to gain sufficient momentum on the fall to break my neck. What if I can't do it? What if—I went to my chamber pot, vomited, and sat down.

Clarence took up his instruments and continued without a word. After he had done with my sketch, I sat for some time attempting to get my thoughts under control.

When my breakfast arrived, a piping hot meal of eggs, toast covered with a thick layer of butter along with a slice of ham, I found that I could not bring myself to eat it. Why feed a body that's going to be dead soon? It'll only serve to give me the grace of shiting myself in front of the crowd.

As I got to my feet and stared through the window, my heart rose into my throat. Down the street, Mother, Lilly and—I couldn't make the other person out, stood in the visitor's line while looking my way. As I waved through the bars, I could see that the third person was indeed a woman. Her head covered with a large brimmed hat that sloped down at the edges to conceal her face, she wore a faded blue dress. The dress appeared strangely familiar until I suddenly recalled that it belonged to Mother, leaving no doubt as to the identity of the third person.

Dear God, I thought, Laura is taking an awful risk coming here. If she is recognized, she will be executed along with me.

In a short upward turn of the brim, Laura glanced from beneath her hat and, seeing but not acknowledging the frantic wave of my hand, motioned for Mother and Lilly to look up. They each returned my wave and, with the sun full in their faces, I could see their tears. After a moment, the line ahead of them shortened and they proceeded through the visitor's gate.

Dear God, I thought. Above all things, I wished to see them, but not like this, not here. Slumping down to the floor, I clutched my knees and silently wept. After some time, I heard steps approaching from the corridor.

Behind me, the observation slot opened and the rotten teeth spoke, "You'll have more visitors today. The usual lot of ladies come to see a boy what's about to be hung."

Of course, I thought. There is always a throng of women to see a man or boy off to the Tree. Mother, Lilly, and Laura would blend right in. Not having spoken to them since my arrest, I couldn't fathom what I would say. To think they should have to come to this awful place to see me; not only come here, but, then go through the pain of seeing me executed and put into the ground on the morrow. Dear God, would Mother and Lilly come to see me hang? I prayed they would not. I couldn't bear to see their faces in that mob. God, but I have put them through hell. If only I could have stopped my dealings before this had happened. If only I had listened to my intuition…

My intuition had come in the form of a sickening pain in my entrails that night we brought Laura home from Jeb's building in Jones Court. I knew she had nearly lost her life. I knew we saved her from a horrible death. I knew Joe, Willy and Giles had killed Jeb for his fiendish deed. And I knew that Jeb had died slowly for what he did to her. Yet knowing these things did not give me solace, for it only served to make me more ill. If we had quit the business, none of this would have happened. My intuition was right on the mark, housebreaking was a bad thing. Stealing was a bad thing. I shouldn't have given it a second thought. I should have insisted we quit the business. It has brought nothing but pain to all of us. The pain began the night Jeb found Laura and I can still see my mother's and sister's faces when we brought Laura through the door of our home that awful night.

"Oh, my poor darling, what has happened to you?" she said, her voice tired and her eyes red from being up half the night with worry. "Come! Let's get that face cleaned up. Lilly dear, fetch a bowl of water and a washcloth."

After cleansing the blood from Laura's battered face, we could see, to our relief that her nose was not broken as Pike and I had feared. The seductive lips I had come to admire were now distorted from the swelling and lost in a purplish black mass that spread across her entire face, rendering it unrecognizable. Mother gave us some relief when she said that Laura's wounds, though unsightly at present, would most likely heal with no permanent effects. As for the bleeding from her legs, she told Mother that she had began her menstrual something or other and Mother dismissed my question as to what that meant. She seemed to understand immediately and sent Lilly for another kind of cloth before ushering Pike and me from the bedchamber.

After making several trips to the kitchen to put together a poultice from her copy of Culpepper's English Herbals, Mother came to us and asked, "Just what in the Dear's name has happened to her?"

During our taxi ride from St. Giles, we made use of the time to develop a very convincing story to explain both Laura's condition, as well as our extended absence. We informed Mother that we had decided to take a scenic ride through the surrounding countryside before returning home. While out on the road, our coach lost a front wheel and we were flung into a ditch. Unfortunately, Laura had been facing the direction of travel and the sudden impact had sent her flying to the opposite side of the coach. After we gathered ourselves, we found that the coach axle had broken, the horses gotten loose of their harnesses and off into the countryside. And to make matters worse, we were on a seldom traveled road. As our luck would have it, a good deal of time passed before someone happened along who was willing to take us back to the city. Once on familiar streets, we gave our thanks to the good Samaritans before hiring a hackney that would bring us home.

"Well, I have never been so worried," Mother exclaimed, wringing her hands. Thank the Dear for bringing you home." Then, turning to me, ordered, "Robert, you must fetch the doctor."

"Mother, do you think it necessary," I said. "He will wish to bleed her and she has lost a good deal of blood already."

She sighed and said, "Yes, and it seems the least we can do is to feed her some breakfast." After giving Pike and me an assessing glance, she said, "You must be famished. I shall make a fire and prepare breakfast, eggs on toast?" We both patted our stomachs and moaned. "I thought as much," she said. Then, pointing her finger at me, said, "However, as soon as you have eaten you must go and fetch the doctor."

As she said this, I realized that a doctor could soon smoke that what had happened to her was no accident. He would have questions that we could not afford to answer. I was brought in mind of Constable Hastings at the inn. His questions had seemed to never end. If the doctor called for a constable, things would only become worse, for we haven't the time to reinforce our story. I must attempt to change her mind. As I followed her up the stairs to Laura's bedchamber, I said, "Mother, don't you think that good rest and warm soup has cured more ailments than any doctor. Remember when you and Lilly were taken ill. The doctor did little to nothing for you. It was Laura and Pike who nursed you back to health. It seems the least we can do is to return the favor."

"Oh, Bobby!" Mother said, hovering over Laura, with her finger to her chin. "Perhaps you are right. For the now, we shall forget about the doctor, only for the now. Though, mind you, you shall run for the doctor as fast as ever you can the moment her condition changes for the worse."

My heart skipped a beat at those words. Had I done the right thing? Perhaps she really needed to see a doctor.

During the following fortnight, Laura received around the clock care from everyone in the household. It soon became apparent that her injuries were not extreme and no doctor was consulted. For a good many days her features were sorely distorted with she in much pain. Eventually, however, and ever so gradually, the swelling receded and the black skin gave way to purple. The purple bruises remained for an entire month before giving way to yellow and completely fading away.

On the second day of Laura's injuries, Pike and I had gone out, presumably to work, yet only strolled the streets and shops long enough to return with the story that we had both been excused from work at the property liquidation house; and that as soon as Laura had regained her health, we would be free to return to work without any fear of losing our employment. As far-fetched as our story was, Mother, most surprisingly, accepted our explanation without any reassurance. As the time passed slowly, I took it upon myself to daily purchase the London Evening Post so that we had some good reading during our time of idleness.

It was then that we discovered that the rebellion in the colonies had progressed into a full scale war. Fortunately, England appeared to be making short work of it, winning battle after battle, for the rebels had suffered numerous defeats. Yet, in spite of this, they doggedly continued their refusal to acknowledge the Crown as their sovereign. Why did they detest their own country's laws, I wondered, and remembered how Father had shared with us his own confusion when reading about their situation.

It was not three days after our encounter with Jeb that Mother had taken Lilly to the market leaving Pike and I to watch over Laura.

I had been perusing the London Evening Post when I came across an article that read, "Murder in St. Giles." From there it went on to explain that, "A Mr. Jeb Whittcomb was found dead in a building he had recently purchased on Jones Court. The victim had been murdered in a manner too gruesome to describe on these pages. Suffice it to say that Mr. Whittcomb suffered long before surrendering to the Almighty. His killers, for it is believed there were no less than two, remain at large. If anyone has intelligence of this murder, it is your duty as a citizen to bring this information to the authorities."

As I read the article aloud for the benefit of Laura and Pike, our feelings could best be described as a mixture of both sadness and relief. The relief to know Jeb would never again hurt Laura brought a sense of liberation, for we three had, heretofore, never been free of the fear of his finding us. As for his slow death, Pike sat with a contented smile upon his lips while Laura sobbed. And as I viewed the dark shadows upon her bruised features, I felt nothing of Jeb, as he was no more to me than a rabid dog just put down.

As the time passed, we busied ourselves with household chores and, while not occupied thus, Laura and I read the Gentleman's Magazine, as well as books I borrowed from a nearby coffee house.

This did much to pass the time for Laura and me but did little for Pike, who had never had the opportunity to learn how to read. And seeing Pike's consternation, Laura and Mother took it upon themselves to teach him the basics. Surprisingly, Pike was an amazingly quick study as, within just six weeks, he had made his way through the London Gazette sufficiently to pose questions such as, "Laura, what does this mean?" or, "Mother, how is this pronounced?"

We were in the parlor one afternoon when Pike who, taking up a recent copy of the London Evening Post, pointed out to us that the French had, on the thirteenth of March, announced a treaty with the American Colonists. While our surprise was congratulatory for his great reading progress, we were, at the same time, quite taken aback by the news.

"What does this mean?" I asked Mother.

Mother's complexion turned pale and she answered, "It means, son, that the rebellion in the American Colonies is no longer just a rebellion."

Laura's tender brow, the bruises now faded to a light blue, turned up as she asked, "What will the French do?"

Mother shook her head with an expression of deep sorrow and said, "They will go to war against us now, just as they did in the Seven Years War."

Laura and Pike shared my puzzlement and I asked, "But their treaty is with the Colonists," I puzzled. "What has it to do with?"

"What it means, son, is that we will be fighting the French while, at the same time, attempting to put down a rebellion." She gave out a deep sigh and said, "We can only pray it is over quickly. For, if not, they will be dragging every hardworking man from his family to fight them." With a smile, she glanced from Pike to me and said, "At least the two of you are still too young to be taken. And that is why I pray it is over soon."

I recalled having read of the last war we had with the French. It had received its name from its duration of seven years. Perhaps this would be shorter, I thought.

As the weeks passed, Pike continued his reading while keeping up on the progress of the yet undeclared war. And when the time came that Laura had recovered sufficiently for us three to return to work, Pike could not get enough material to read and would, each day, insist on stopping into any nearby coffee house for a minimum half an hour's reading time.

With the healing of Laura's wounds came the forgetting of my remorse over our life of stealing, as well as the potential danger in which it had placed my family. For a few weeks, we worked the theater at Drury Lane, Covent Garden, and the shops in the Haymarket before taking some of our accumulated goods back to Sam Clifton at the Iron Rooster. Prior to this we had carefully set aside a lesser part of our booty for Zack.

This time, we went to the Iron Rooster during the early part of the day and found the place somewhat sedate compared to our first visit.

Sam Clifton stood behind the bar, an apron covering his thin frame and, as we entered, greeted us with a smile. Adjusting his spectacles, he reached over the bar to take Laura's hand while the sunlight, coming through the window, reflected off his bald head. "Welcome back," he said, his hooked nose pointing to the bar. With Laura's hand in his, he shook it vigorously saying, "I was beginning to wonder if I would ever see the likes of you again."

A quick glance from him was all that was required for the patrons sitting nearby to rise from their chairs and move to the far end of the bar.

"Well, it is good to see you, as well, Mr. Clifton," Laura said, a warm smile upon her lips. "We would have come sooner if not for my taking ill."

"I am most sorry to hear that you were ill. Is everything good now?" Clifton frowned with concern.

"Dear, yes, and it is most kind of you to ask," Laura said, then, in a quiet voice, "However, we went back to work just as soon as I recovered and we should like to conduct some business with you. I am fairly certain it will require but a moment," Laura smiled.

"Think nothing of the time. It would be my pleasure, ma'am," he beamed. Then, raising his voice for the benefit of the men at the other side of the bar, "Why don't you and your boys come back to my parlor and tell me all about your trip to Paris. Franklin, be a good fellow and watch the bar for a few."

Franklin, a short Irish fellow with thick red hair, appeared from a storage closet behind the bar and, jumping up onto a stool, made himself appear quite tall to anyone who sat on the opposite side of the bar.

"Your wish is me command, sir. And what will the lady and her boys be havin'?"

Laura smiled, "Bordeaux, if you please."

Sam motioned with his thumb toward the back room, "Just bring it into the parlor, Franklin." Then, leading us past the bar, he said, to Laura, "I am most anxious to hear of Paris."

The room appeared much the same as we had last seen it. The baroque table still sat at the centre and we each pulled a chair to it. The large fireplace was not lit yet we were quite comfortable.

Franklin brought in four glasses of Bordeaux. Setting them onto the table, he gave a nod and returned to the bar.

Clifton sat across from Laura and said, "So, what have you for me?"

"Well, not quite a haul as Mr. Bridges has brought you. We have been toning down our travels of late. Bye the bye, how is Mr. Bridges?" Laura asked.

I smiled and glanced at Pike who raised a brow.

"Oh, Mr. Bridges has been out on the road and I haven't seen him for some time now."

"Is it uncommon? That is, for him to be away for so long?" Laura said, with obvious concern.

"On the contrary, it is quite common indeed. Sometimes I don't see him for weeks on end. And then, as though no time has passed at all, I walk into the bar and there he sits with a big smile on his face. When he has been gone a long time, he always has a wagon waiting behind the building for he generally stores up a good deal of merchandise before bringing it to town. Do you desire me to give him your regards when next I see him?"

"Why, yes. I would like that very much. Please do," Laura said, with a smile.

After we had concluded our business with Sam, we left by the front door and I couldn't help noticing a cully who seemed vaguely familiar. Seated at a table near the far end of the room, his face hovered over a tankard of ale. Beneath the pug-nose, his long upper lip dripped beer onto the table after he drank. There was something familiar about the old threadbare wig he wore but I could not quite put my finger upon it and thought to ask Pike if he might recall the man.

After we had crossed the street and gone some distance down the street, I mentioned him to Pike who turned and looked back in the direction of the Iron Rooster.

The door opened and the man in question appeared. His large buttocks swiveled as he turned and walked away while his short legs forced his long stiff neck into a reckless gait, possibly from some sort of spinal malady. Walking with his hands in his pockets, it appeared as though he must pull his bulky buttocks along so that it might catch up with the upper part of his body. I knew I had seen that gait before yet could not recall when or where.

As Pike had no recollection of him, I decided to let it go.

After another street, we hailed a hackney and, during the ride to High Holbourn Street, we took stock of the remaining items that we had kept aside for Zack.

"I don't think he will like it," I said. "For all the time that has elapsed, he will be expecting much more than this."

"Not to worry," Laura said. "We shall simply tell him that we have had a slow go of it. And that we had to take more care due to our increased notoriety."

"I sincerely hope he does not smoke it," I said, as the chaise pulled up to the alleyway leading to the backdoor of Zack's flat.

After dismissing our driver, we stepped down the alleyway, pulled on the cord, heard the familiar jingle at the top of the stairs and shortly thereafter, the door opened.

Zack appeared at the door dressed in fresh powdered wig with a blue velvet waistcoat over black breeches. His gold shoe buckles shone brightly as we followed him up the stairs to his parlor where we placed our goods onto the table. After he examined the items, he stood up and looked each of us in the eye before asking, "Is there anything you wish to tell me?"

"I don't quite understand what you mean," Laura said, displaying an innocent smile upon her full lips.

I stepped to the window for an excuse to get away from his stare while he asked the same question of Pike. The reason behind Zack's question came with a jolt as I looked upon the street below. There was a man walking away from the front street entrance of Zack's flat. And although that, in itself, was of no importance, what caught my eye was the way that he walked, the slow twisted gait, the oddly shaped buttocks and long torso, while his hands were all the time secured into the pockets of his breeches. Now I remembered seeing him on this street corner some weeks past. In fact, I had seen him several times but never thought for a moment that he worked for Zack. How had he come so quickly from the Iron Rooster, I wondered? He is such a slow walking fellow. Could there be another similar to him, I reasoned? But then, a sleek cabriolet pulled up in front of him and he stepped in. The horse was a well groomed thoroughbred that stood at the ready with shimmering black mane and well-formed, powerfully muscled legs. The lather around the harness told me he had recently been driven hard. So he was one of Zack's men, most likely sent to spy on the competition and had just delivered the news of our transaction. I had to think quickly.

"I don't know what you mean," Pike answered.

I turned to face Zack's penetrating stare as he asked, "Well, Robert, have you nothing to say, as well?"

Glancing first at Laura, then to Pike, I said. "It's only fair we tell him the truth."

For a millisecond, Laura's eyes opened wide as the shock of my words registered. Pike, on the other hand, did not flinch, standing his ground like a stone statue.

"Sir, we have recently been to visit one of your competitors, a Mr. Clifton."

Laura and Pike's mouths dropped open simultaneously.

I went on, "We were given his name by a man who robbed us on our return from Bath. You see, he told us. That is, the man who robbed us, that for the right price, we might recover our belongings from the man we met today." Laura and Pike remained silent.

"I see, and did he?"

"Sir?"

"Did he return your things to you?"

"Why, yes, as a matter of fact he did, although we had to pay as much for them as though we had purchased them anew."

Zack paced the floor, hands behind his back folded into a knot while taking in my story. Then, turning, he stepped across the room to face me before turning to glare at Laura. "Is this true?" he hissed.

Her complexion had taken on the rose flush of blood while a V-shaped vein rose from her forehead as she hesitated, but then answered, "Why, yes," while her pleading eyes glanced at me.

"I must tell you, I suspect you are not being wholly truthful with me and if I find otherwise, I will be sorely disappointed. And you do not wish to find me in that state. It would be most distasteful for you all. Do you get my meaning?"

"Yes!" Laura and Pike spoke in unison. Then Laura carried the ball. "We are dreadfully sorry, sir. We were a bit mortified about the situation; allowing ourselves to be robbed by another of our profession, albeit a highwayman. You see, we were too ashamed to tell you."

Zack turned and faced me with a look that sent needles down my spine. There was rage behind those eyes that shouted so loud I could practically hear it.

Turning away, he stepped toward the window, paused to look upon the street below and said, "Recently, I received intelligence that the three of you were at the Iron Rooster and, therefore, had to assume from this information that you had betrayed my generosity. Naturally, I did not wish to believe this, yet, when you three said nothing, I feared the worst." Laura started to speak but Zack held up his hand, saying. "What Robert just told me has gone some distance in regaining my trust in you, yet I find that this pittance of items on the table is most unbecoming of your trio."

With a discernable tremor in her voice, Laura explained, "Well, sir, it has been quite difficult of late, due to our becoming recognized. It was mainly on that fact that we decided to go on holiday to Bath—primarily in hopes that the passage of time would allow our recent fish to forget our faces."

"So this is it. Well, if this is all you can do, perhaps you had better consider some other line of work," he said. Turning from the window, his features were distorted into a Shakespearean mask of tragedy as he shouted, "Is it Clifton that has the good merchandise? AM I TO RECEIVE ONLY THE RUBBISH THAT HE DISCARDS?"

Pike spoke up, "We had thought of going on the road and hitting other cities where we could bring our goods back here to you—just until things cooled off, that is."

"On the road," he mocked. "Well, that might be worthy of some future consideration, yet I find it will not do for the now. Haven't you something to give me as a gesture of good faith?" he said, punctuating the question with a long draw of his sword, then, sliding it back with a snap as the blade hit the hilt.

Laura and Pike stood mute.

The air within the room became tense and I wanted nothing more than to be back on the street. What would Zack do if we could not give him anything? Why couldn't we just leave and do business elsewhere? What did we owe him anyway? What did he mean when he said that we would find it sorely distasteful if we disappointed him? I had long suspected him capable of doing great harm if provoked. He always carried that wolf's head walking stick and now he was pulling the sword from within. First showing a few inches of blade, then sliding it back in only to withdraw it an inch or so farther each time—as if to display his growing ire.

Laura was visibly disconcerted and Pike had his hand on the dirk in his pocket.

Perhaps if I could give Zack something to show good faith, we may yet leave here with all of our parts. The timepiece from the Bath jobb was in my pocket and, giving it one last touch, I held it out as an offering, saying "I held onto this because I wished to keep it for myself. Perhaps you might take it, sir. I'm sure it will fetch a good price. Whatever you feel is fair, we will be most happy to accept."

Zack's eyes lit up as the gold glimmered in the sunbeam from a nearby window. Picking it up ever so gently, he cradled it within his heavily ringed fingers. A smile formed upon his lips as he took in the intricate carving upon the cover.

I knew he must find this piece delightful for its quality and craftsmanship were so close to his very own timepiece, which is exactly why I had wished to keep it. Giving it up was most difficult for me.

Opening the cover plate, his expression suddenly changed. Taking a deep breath, he sat down into one of his two heavily stuffed chairs. Closing his hand around the timepiece, he turned to face me and motioned for me to sit in the chair opposite him. In a tone of resignation, he called, "Laura, Pike! How did you come by this timepiece?" Then, holding up his hand, he cautioned, "Before you say anything, I must tell you that I know for certain that it was taken in the Bath robbery. So, you see, it is most coincidental that you happen to be in possession of it."

Dear God! I thought, I only wished to assuage his anger and, instead, have only made the situation worse.

Laura spoke up, "How can you be certain that it came from Bath? We only happened to lift it from a gentleman the other day."

"I do not care to hear any more lies. I have a gentleman who would like to purchase not only his timepiece but also anything else taken in the robbery—particularly several bolts of LINEN. He is willing to pay a good deal for them and if you give them to me, I will take care of it, returning your share in kind. Do you have them?"

Laura stammered, "I don't see how…"

"STOP!" he barked, and, withdrawing the hidden sword from his walking stick, pressed the tip of the blade against Laura's throat.

Laura stood like a marble statue, her arms stiff at her sides.

While I searched for something to take hold of, Pike reached for his dirk.

"Don't even think of it. Either of you!" he warned, pressing the blade so that the tip made an impression against her delicate throat. Pressing his face close to Laura's, he hissed, "If you deny any more of this I will end you now."

Then, without warning, he withdrew the blade and turned his full attention on me. With a twisted grin, he asked, "Is there anything left of the merchandise from Bath that you haven't sold to Mr. Clifton?"

Swallowing hard, my throat being extremely dry, I confessed, "We only have a bolt of linen. The rest is gone and I don't mind telling you we got a good price for the lot. Much more than you would have given us, which is why we have given him part of our business. And we had decided to continue giving you a share due to our appreciation of your having taught us the craft. We only refrained from telling you of our situation because we didn't wish you to feel slighted. And, seeing as you have pointed a sword at Laura, it is apparent that we have overestimated our appraisal of your feelings, for, not only do you not feel slighted, you obviously feel nothing for us. If it pleases you, we will give you that bolt of linen, and, after that, do business with you no more."

His lips smiled but his eyes betrayed them, "You will do that, will you? That would please me extremely. I am sorry to hear you no longer wish to conduct any further business with me. As a parting gesture of good will, if you bring me this thing, I shall trouble you no more. If Clifton is to be your new partner, then, so be it. How soon may I have it?"

"I will see to it that you have it on the morrow," I promised.

He searched out my eyes and, in a lowered tone, asked, "What time might I expect you?"

After a pause, I said, "Noon."

"Fair enough," Zack smiled through gritted teeth, "noon it shall be. Pray, do not keep me waiting."

We all left in grim silence fearing we had narrowly escaped with our lives. Once on the street we hailed a taxi and were on our way back home.

As the coach wheels rattled against the paving stones, we silently sat in our chairs and mentally assessed our situation.

At length, Pike punched me in the shoulder and admonished, "You did us up good, didn't you? Why did you have to tell him everything?"

Laura interrupted, "He saved our lives is what he did. Zackery knew from the start what we were about. What I don't understand is, how did you know we were undone, Robert?"

"It was the cully from the Iron Rooster. I spied him from the window. He was stepping into a cabriolet."

"The one with the queer gait?" Pike asked, in disbelief.

"The same," I said. "And it was touch and go from then on."

"I am just relieved we got out of there with our skins," Laura sighed. "He says he will leave us alone but don't you believe it for one second. He will have us working for him and find some way to do in Mr. Clifton. He is ruthless when you are his enemy. We must get that linen to him and ask his forgiveness—tell him we will no longer do business with Mr. Clifton. You were mistaken to tell him we were not doing business with him any more. We can never stop. With him, it is a lifetime commitment. We can never leave."

"Why not?" I asked. "What can he possibly do to stop us?"

"Didn't you see that dirk? If not him, he will get someone else to do his dirty work. No, you don't tell him you are quitting. I didn't say anything at the time, Robert, because I needed time to think. I don't know what it was that made him change his tune but he acted quite strangely after he laid eyes upon your timepiece. And for him to settle on a bolt of linen is more puzzling indeed. Oh, to be sure, we'll have to get back into his good graces or we are undone in this city. Certainly, it was all right to do business with Clifton as long as he didn't know what we were about but now... And then, there is that odd behavior of his," she said shaking her head. "I don't rightly know what to make of it."

Upon our arrival at home, Mother and Lilly had another deliciously hot meal prepared for us. Throughout supper, the three of us said little to nothing while Mother brought us up to date on the events of the new construction in Grosvenor.

"They are to add onto Green Street and continue it all the way to Tiburn Lane, then build new houses on either side. Why, if you walk down just one street you will see the load of bricks and cement set up for the work. If your father were alive, bless his soul, he would have enough work to last him for years. Oh! Bye the bye, I received a post from your aunt and uncle and am happy to find they are doing quite well with their shop. Isn't that capital?"

"Pardon, Mother?" I asked, attempting to recall what she had just said.

"I said, don't you think that is capital, Robert?"

"Yes, the new construction will provide jobs for a good many people," I replied.

"I was speaking of your Aunt Beatrice and Uncle Rupert. Where is your mind, Son?"

"Sorry, Mother. I have had a long day and am very tired. What were you saying about Aunt Beatrice?"

"I said, they are doing well in their new business," she replied.

"That is splendid news. And it is most comforting to know they are managing. I am very happy to hear it. May they have infinite success."

As Mother talked on, my mind drifted backwards to the events of the day. It seemed I could think of nothing more than to get that bolt of linen to Zack so that our life would return to normal.

When the morrow came, we found it to be a wet and drizzling day with a sky of low lying grey clouds. Though we dressed warm, I couldn't seem to shake off a persistent chill that traveled inward from my extremities. With the bolt of linen folded into a canvas bag, Pike made his way past Mother's distracted eyes and awaited us on the stoop. With our package tucked under Laura's arm, we held our umbrellas together and dodged mud puddles on our way to the road. As we walked, the rain steadily tapped on our umbrellas while the air felt heavy in our nostrils. After a short wait on the road, Pike and I spied a hackney and stepped into the street to get the driver's attention. Within a moment, the driver turned his horses around, bringing them to a panting halt in front of us. We climbed in and, as we pulled away, I could smell the lingering odor of whiskey throughout the coach. At first, we suspected the odor had come from the coach's previous occupants, but within the first few streets we heard curses from other coach drivers. It seemed our driver was heavily cup-shot, striking posts, scraping and bumping the wheels of other coaches. We were violently jostled about and bid the driver stop at the next main intersection so that we may send him home with his pay and thence, hire another coach. Pike put his head out of the door and gave him the instructions, yet to no avail. Pike, then, repeated the instructions, however, the driver insisted he would get us to our destination. As we demanded he stop the coach, the driver, as if to further show his determination, drove the horses even harder.

Now Pike's blood was up. His jaw extended, he hailed, "Goddamn your drunk arse. I said, let us out!" and proceeded to climb out of the coach door after the driver.

Turning onto High Holbourn Street at a very fast pace, one of the wheels caught into a rut and, with our sideways momentum arrested, the coach was forced upward and onto two wheels before toppling over onto its side. After collecting ourselves, Laura and I found that, other than being shaken a bit, we were relatively unharmed. Unfortunately for Pike, this was not the case, for the upset had occurred just as he was stepping through the cab door. Once we had climbed onto the upward side of the coach, we found that Pike had not been thrown clear, but had gone down with the carriage, the upper part landing on his leg. Fully conscious, he was not aware of any pain though his complexion had grown very pale. Within seconds, enough men had gathered around to effectively right the coach, thereby freeing his leg.

There was much damage below the knee as his foot was turned in an impossible direction. As he tried to move, his foot flopped around as though disconnected.

Laura asked for a doctor and, as no one knew where to find one, we wasted no further time and soon had him into another hackney coach.

"I believe the bones are broken," Laura said, with tears streaming down her cheeks. "I must take him to a hospital. We can only pray they are able to save the leg. Robert, you must go on without us. Can you do that?"

"I will come as soon as I have finished our business with Zack," I said, as Laura stepped into the carriage.

"Do take care, Robert. Give him his gift and don't upset him with any more ill talk. We must make things right with him now. And please do explain why Pike and I cannot be there. Forgive me for not being there with you."

"There is nothing to forgive. Rest assured, I shall make things right," I said.

"I have every confidence you will, Robert," she said, the strain of worry upon her features. Then, to the coachman, she ordered,

"Driver, take us to Middlesex Hospital in Marleybone Fields and do make haste."

As the coach pulled away, I glanced about to get my bearings. Tucking the package under my arm, I set off down High Holbourn. With the rain having stopped for the present, I decided to continue on foot as Zack's lodging was only five streets distant.

As I walked, I couldn't shake the sight of Pike's mangled leg from my mind. Will they take off his leg, I wondered. And if they did, what would that do to him? He is a strong-willed soul, I decided. And he would, in all likelihood, overcome it with ease; as he has overcome everything that life has thrown him.

On my way I passed several thieves who eyed my package and I had to give them the "look," which they readily understood and left me to my business. The "look" is, in and of itself, a form of recognition. There is a code amongst thieves, which does not allow them to steal from one another. Once something is stolen, it becomes the property of the thief and no one else may steal it from him without far reaching consequences. All thieves are taught this in their training and I had yet to hear of anyone breaking this code.

After I passed the last intersection, I noticed amongst the hurdy-gurdies, fiddle players, beggars, and those vendors who sell hot and cold viands at the street corners, a strange group of men standing in an alleyway. One of them carried a long stick and I instantly recognized them as Bow Street runners. The next thing I took notice of made me most uncomfortable. Five doors down the street, a watchman sat on his horse while looking at his timepiece. I passed him without any noticeable distress and kept up a steady pace until I turned into the alleyway that led to the rear of Zack's office.

It was noon by my estimate, judging from the faded glow of the sun through the clouds directly overhead, and I pulled on the black leather cord. Within seconds, the door swung open and Zack appeared with walking stick in hand and wearing his best attire. He sported one of his many powdered wigs, apparently on his way to conduct some important business. Peering past me, he said, "Where are they?"

"Excuse me, sir?" I said, politely.

"Where are your friends?" he asked, while resting his hands on his hips. "Do you have it? Well? DO YOU HAVE IT?"

"Oh, you must mean the package. Why, yes. As I said, I shall not let you down, sir."

Appearing even more perturbed by this information, he repeated his first question, "Where are they?"

"I am sorry to say that they will not be able to make it, sir. However, as promised, I shall make good our agreement."

Turning, he motioned for me to follow him upstairs. Reaching the top of the stairs, we continued on past a room that had heretofore always contained large amounts of merchandise stacked in various piles throughout. Yet the room was now empty, save a small stool in the corner.

"Are you moving, sir?" I asked.

"Why do you ask such a silly question as that?" he said, a smile creasing his lips while looking out of the window toward the street. "I have no intention of moving at all. I only decided to tidy up a bit."

"But, sir, all of your merchandise—surely you could not have sold it all? You must have moved it to some other place. But, why?" I asked innocently.

"Nonsense, I am not moving I say, and that is that," he insisted, a note of irritation in his voice. "Well, let us see what you have brought me."

I opened the package and handed him the bolt, saying, "I hope this meets with your approval, sir."

"Oh yes, it does, indeed. See here," he said, uncovering the end of the bolt to show me an inscription written by the shop owner. "It says, received by Mr. Edmond Gibbon from Kingston supply house on 7 May, 76. Oh, this is capital, complete confirmation that this is Eddie's property."

"Well then, you see that we have made good on our part, sir," I said, respectfully. "And sir, I do apologize for my poor behavior. I am sure that I speak for the others when I say, from this point onward, we shall never do business with anyone other than yourself. Sir, who, may I ask, is Eddie?"

"Eddie is the shop owner you robbed. Edmond Gibbon, you know?"

"No, I don't know Mr. Edmond Gibbon, sir. But I am happy it pleases you to have it. We should like you to keep it as a token of our sincerity. And in our future business transactions…"

"Oh, I don't believe there can be any more transactions between us," he said, with an evil grin. Then, returning to the window, he waved at some unseen person on the street below.

"I don't understand, sir. I thought we could let bygones be bygones."

Raising his voice, he said, "There will NOT be any further business between us, Robert, for Edmond Gibbon, the man whose shop you robbed, is my brother."

It was as though I had just been decapitated by an invisible scythe. Completely stunned, I could only stand mute.

"Quite a coincidence, don't you think?" Pausing, he bent and stared deep into my eyes for some sign of guilt. At length, he straightened up and, letting out a deep sigh, said, "You did not know, did you? I had suspected your trio planned this all along knowing, through some intelligence, that he was my brother. I couldn't guess at your intentions. Perhaps, out of some deep seated hatred, you wished to do me injury and, perhaps thought it good measure to throw my family into the bargain." To be sure, he shot another glance at me and, satisfied, went on, "Yes, you didn't know. But I'll wager your partners did, and kept it from you because you might not have wanted any part in it. I spent the better part of my savings to start up his business. A good deal of what you stole was a gift from me. You see, after working non-stop for the past five years in order to make a go of their business, he and Mother—yes, my mother—and my sister-in-law, left on holiday.

And it was a well deserved holiday for they had done it. The business was successful; solely due to the fact that they put every farthing right back into it. Five years hard work and sacrifice, along with my savings, is what it took to make a life in Bath, a city I chose for its low crime rate, only to be taken away by your damned robbery."

He paused, seemingly considering something, and turned to me with a raised brow, saying, "Well, I have decided that, due to your ignorance in the affair, I am willing to not charge you for this crime provided you lead me, this instant, to Pike and Laura, as well as the stolen property, of course."

I knew it was out of the question and, pleading for their lives, I said, "Sir, they are my friends, you have been my friend. This is all a mistake. They knew nothing of your family. It is simply an odd coincidence. Cannot we pay you back? I realize it will take a good deal of time, but the merchandise is all gone, save this bolt and the watch—"

Cutting me off in mid-sentence, he drew his sword from the walking stick scabbard, leveled it at my face and demanded, "You will tell me now or you will die. Do you understand? You will die."

Standing my ground, albeit on trembling legs, I defiantly stated, "I will tell you nothing."

His complexion transformed to a purplish hue and, tapping the hilt of the sword three times upon the drop-leaf table, said, "Then I must tell you this. Regardless of your ignorance in the affair, I shall make you and your friends pay dearly. You will not die by my sword, for that would be too easy. No, I shall see to it that you die at Tiburn Tree." The door at the front stairs opened with a thud followed by many footsteps. The footsteps came to an abrupt halt and a long silence filled the room.

The door swung open and, as though in a play carefully rehearsed on stage, I was quickly encircled by five men, one being an aged constable wielding a long stick. I stared in disbelief as Zack handed the bolt of linen to the constable.

"Here, you have proof," Zack said, trembling with anger. "You saw him come in. You saw the package under his arm. Here it is." Tearing at the bolt with scratching nails, he pulled the fabric aside to expose the label. "See here, received by Edmund Gibbon. He—they have stolen this from my brother's shop in Bath."

"They?" replied the constable.

"He has two accomplices who did not come. But he knows where to find them," Zack glared at me, baring his teeth.

"We shall take it from here, Mr. Gibbon," the constable said, while a big burly fellow secured a set of manacles onto my wrists. "And I shall need you to come to the Old Bailey to make a statement. Perhaps your brother should accompany you. We shall require his presence to verify his property. I shall hold onto the timepiece as well; further evidence, you understand."

"Must you?" Zack's voice broke and, throwing his hands out like a praying mantis, pleaded, "My brother will desire it be returned immediately. It is very dear to him."

"Well, perhaps as only a formality, we shall keep it until he arrives. Mind you, we shall need it again at the trial."

Zack stroked the watch for a few seconds, and before reluctantly handing it over, said, "You shall take care not to misplace it, I trust?"

"Not to worry, sir, it is in good hands. A most damning piece of evidence, to be sure. This alone will get them to the Tree."

"Damn little thief! I shall enjoy seeing him swing. I shall enjoy seeing them all swing," Zack said, pounding his fist into his palm. His enraged eyes struck me like daggers as the constable and Fielding's Bow Street men pulled me down the stairs to the front of the building.

"Damnlittlethief," I thought, the pot calling the kettle black, indeed.

CHAPTER TEN

The gate swung open wide, ringing as it hit the stop, the vibration disbursing a sprinkle of rusty white paint flakes into a pile onto the ground below. Shuffling easier with the reduced weight of my single iron bondage, I entered the large common courtyard where all the other prisoners of the Stateside ward were waiting to meet with their friends, families, or admirers.

Waiting beyond another, though smaller, gate on the opposite side of the yard, were Mother, Lilly and Laura, mixed in with a barrage of women dressed in a wave of velvets and feathered hats with their hair piled so high that the breeze threatened to topple them with each gust. Most of the women, along with their gentlemen, were standing impatiently in the line ahead shielding Mother from view when, at last, the gate swung open and all the visitors filed through.

I smiled as they caught sight of me while my eyes searched everywhere for signs of Mr. Zackery Gibbon. Thus far, I hadn't seen him anywhere, though this did little to assuage my apprehension.

Mother was holding a kerchief to her nose to filter the sickening odiferous air when she spied me and broke into a run with open arms. The sun played on the blue and white brim of her wide velvet hat while it swayed until she came to a halt before me. For precious moments, I was enveloped within those loving arms. If not for my manacles, I would have reciprocated by putting my arms around her but could only stand in her embrace with the cold iron pressing into her tender stomach. Fitting somewhat tighter upon my wrists since my change of diet from putrid tasting prison gruel to the daily bounty of the past week, I had just managed to get them on in the split second before the turnkey opened the door to my cell.

"Dear Heavenly Father, what have they done to my son? If only, your father—" her words cut short realizing the mention of Father would only serve to add to my misery.

In an instant, her warmth and the familiar sweet scent of her perfume hurled me back to the days before my arrest. Clinging to the touch of her breath upon my cheek, I wanted that moment to never end. But then she released me while Lilly and Laura gathered round and we stood in a circle holding hands. For a few moments, it was, alas, as though we had never parted.

"Mother, I am so sorry," I said, dropping my head in soul-wrenching shame.

"Son, you broke my heart. You broke my..." she said, her voice cut short.

"I am so sorry," I sobbed. "And—I cannot ever expect you to forgive me."

She took me by the shoulders and, with a hand to my chin, raised my face to meet hers. Returning her gaze, shameful as I felt, I could not turn away; for not only did those eyes see me, but saw into my very soul. Yet, now they were teary red from the pain I had given her. I did this to her, I thought, heaving another shovelful upon my wagon of guilt. She came to this hole of filth to see me. And it is solely my fault that she is here. I knew the foul stench of the prison was on my clothes, permeating my very skin, yet she looked upon me as though I had recently bathed, taking no notice whatsoever of my foul odor.

"You are skin and bone," she said while assessing my appearance. "It's a miracle you haven't died from the gaol fever." Turning her head slowly from side to side, tears traced runnels down her cheeks while her lips formed a distant smile. As though she were seeing me in another time and assuring me with her eyes that I will, and shall always, have her unconditional love. Her smile transcended words that seemed to say, "Remember, it is I who gave birth to you."

After a moment, she said, "It is I who should be asking your forgiveness, son. If not for my own failure, you would not have had to deceive me that night when we had taken ill."

"But Mother, I lied to you every day."

"Yes, and you did it to keep us off the street. Laura told me everything."

I glanced at Laura and asked, "Everything?" I couldn't believe she told her everything.

Laura nodded.

"And yet, you still love me?"

"A mother's love is forever, son. It is stronger than the iron in this prison and shall remain long after these bars have turned to rust."

She knows, yet she forgives me, I thought. Tears welled in my eyes turning everything into a blur and she held me again, this time only tighter.

"Mother, I don't want to die."

"Son," she said, "you shall never die. Hurt a great deal, yes, but you shall never die, for your soul lives forever."

I had fully accepted my inevitable death yet, now before Mother, try though I might, I couldn't stop my tears. I wanted her to take me home, to protect me the way she did when I was an infant. Yet, I knew she could not. And I knew she felt my pain, doubling it with her own. My nose ran and, I became a child for those few seconds before the wind hit me full in the face and brought me back to my senses.

"Sorry Mother," I said, wiping my face with the filthy sleeve of my ragged shirt. Straightening up, I spoke with as much confidence as I could muster, saying, "I shall be fine. Do not worry about me."

Her eyes clenched shut and she squeezed me once more, saying, "I shall be with you son, always."

"Mother, I do not wish you to see me hang. I couldn't bear it. Please don't come to Tiburn, please."

She held my face in her warm hands and said, "It will be the last time that I shall see you in this life, son. How can I not be there?"

"Would you go to the park and sit in the grove near the trees I used to climb. You know, where we all used to picnic with Father. I would much prefer you were there. Could you do that Mother? Could you do that for me?" After a long pause, she looked deep into my eyes and, with great inner pain, held my dirty hand to her lips and nodded.

Turning to Laura, I said, "I want you to turn over my portion of our bank account to Mother as we discussed on our return from Bath."

Her eyes smiled as she took hold of my arm with those long silken fingers to pull me aside. Several of the other women visitors made their way toward me but stopped in their tracks with one threatening glance from Laura.

Turning away, they quickly made their way to one of the other condemned prisoners.

Once they had left, she faced me again and, in a whisper, said, "I have already done that, Robert. Forget about that for the moment. I must speak to you of the morrow. I have a plan that might—" she stared at a passing turnkey and waited until he had stepped out of earshot, "I say, might work. You need look for a butcher wearing a bloody white apron. If in some way, you are able to get free, you must run to the butcher and dive under his apron. That is all I can do, Robert. You must find a way to get free before they put the noose around your neck. I can't promise it will work but I shall do my bloody best to make a distraction. When you see the distraction, you must jump off the platform and run like the devil to the butcher and do as I say, Robert. Dive beneath his apron." The whites of her eyes had grown scarlet and, quickly welling as she spoke, tears spilled over onto her cheeks. "I want you to run like the devil, Robert. Do you understa—" her voice broke and she held me close for a long moment.

At length, I said into the sweet scent of her hair brushing across my lips, "Laura, if there is any chance at all, I will do it. After all, I have no other options. However, I will not show the white feather. If I cannot get away, I will go to the Tree with courage. I will not shame my mother and father."

She winced before whispering into my ear, "Do wait for the distraction. Do not attempt anything before then. Promise me you will wait for it, Robert."

"How shall I know," I asked. "Suppose there are other distractions. How am I to be certain it is the right one?"

"Oh, there will be no mistake," she smiled. You shall know beyond all doubt. Now, promise me."

"I promise." Quickly glancing about the courtyard, I said, "I pray Zack doesn't find you here. The disguise is a most effective one but it wouldn't fool him. He comes and goes here all the time. I have heard his voice echoing through the corridors. I believe he has done in others like us when he has had something to gain by it. It makes him look the stern enforcer in front of the magistrates. Did you know about his brother? He set the trap for us all."

"Yes," she said. "I read of it in the Evening Post the day following my return home from the hospital. We, that is, Pike and I have taken precautions for us to come here. Fortunately, we do have friends."

"How is Pike, and his leg?"

"Oh, it was broken just below the knee but the doctor set it and he has been healing quite well—no fever or infection, bless his soul."

Lilly stepped up behind Laura and I reached out for her. She held out her thin pale arms and I took her cold hands into mine, saying, "Lilly, I want you to take care of Mother. It is up to you now."

"I shall, Robert. I promise. I have missed you so." Staring at the stone floor, she asked, "Will you come to see me after you are in Heaven?"

"Of course I will," I said, "each and every day. And when you are in bed at night, you have only to look up. You may not see me but you must know that I shall be smiling down upon you."

She squeezed my hand before wrapping her arms around me. I gently kissed her tear streaked-cheeks before she went sobbing over to Mother's embrace.

The turnkey announced that visiting time was nearly at end.

Laura kissed my forehead and said, "Wait for the distraction. I am—Pike and I are counting on you to make it. I realize you were against the robbery from the very beginning and accept full responsibility for your situation. You could have given us up at any time yet, here you stand. Trust that I will do all that is humanly possible to help in your escape. I can only pray it will work. I don't believe I can handle the thought of you hanging, Robert. I don't think I shall ever be able to handle much of anything if you do. You will make it, Robert. You must—" her words cut short and she bit her lip.

"Does Mother know of this plan," I asked.

"No! Should it fail, I did not wish to give her any false hope," she said before turning away.

I followed her over to where Mother and Lilly stood and it seemed we spoke for such a short time before visiting time was at end. My heart sank as I watched them disappear through the gate and I walked back to my cell. When I got to the window, I could see them standing at the end of the street. Soon, ever so soon, a chaise pulled up and they were gone. I couldn't take my eyes off the space of street where they had stood only seconds before and I longed for them with all my heart.

Just as I started to turn away from the window, I noticed another chaise arriving through the gate below, coming to a stop where Laura, Mother, and Lilly had stood. The wolf's head cane appeared as Zack stepped out. He seemed to be in a hurry, for he glanced in each direction before scolding his driver at length. Something had happened to keep him away. He missed his opportunity to catch me with my family, as well as getting his hands on Laura and Pike. Was it divine intervention? No, Laura and Pike had cooked something up and he was furious.

"Don't worry, you conniving old bastard. You may have yet another opportunity on the morrow," I said, knowing he was much too far away to hear. I am certain he would not miss my hanging for the world. Suddenly, I was struck by what I deemed to be his next course. He will be waiting at Tiburn, not only to observe my execution, but, at the same time, look for a grieving mother. And, if she were there, it would not be too difficult for him to smoke her out. Once he found her, he would follow her home and make plans to destroy them all. I pray she does not come. I can only hope Laura will see to that.

Yes, he is a most venomous sort of reptile, I thought, as he stood on the sidewalk gazing this way, then that. As I watched, his countenance transformed from his usual self-confident smirk to one of ire. His brows furrowed while the eyes narrowed into slits and the fat lips protruded like an angry baby who had just soiled his britches. Glancing at his timepiece, he stuffed it back into his waistcoat pocket, took hold of his cane and struck the coach with such force that it severed the wolf's head, sending it bounding into the street. Without considering the danger, he darted into the street to recover it. Reaching into the cracks of the cobblestone, he was caught in the shoulders and slammed backwards by a passing horse and rider. After the horseman tipped his hat and continued on his way, Zack got to his feet, picked up his tricorn, adjusted his wig and glared straight at me. I do believe he knew I was watching, though with the sun in his eyes, he could neither see me, nor the smile on my face. A hackney coach passed, momentarily blocking my view, yet after it had gone, his eyes were still fixed on the window to my cell. After another moment had passed, he turned his attention back to the street in search of the head to his walking stick. There it lay, flattened by the coach's wheels. He stood there in the middle of the street holding the object in the palm of his hand like a man whose child had been killed. Then, before the next coach was upon him, he jumped up into his taxi while giving the coachman some instruction that brought the lash to the horse's haunches and the coach lurched forward down Newgate Street in the direction of Snow Hill.

"Zack, you relish the thought of watching me hang, don't you?" I said to myself.

Even after a fitful, sleepless night, the morning came much too quickly. Like clockwork, I was, in good order, given my last meal. Laura had somehow managed to give the turnkeys a hefty sum, enabling them to provide a small banquet from a nearby eatery. Leg of mutton, carrots, cabbage and peas, along with a bottle of claret is a meal that the average prisoner only dreamt of. That is to say, anyone that is not about to leave this world. Still, with the possibility of my escape, I realized that, if by some slim chance I made it, I would need to eat now for it could be a long time before I might have another opportunity.

It was with much difficulty that I finished my meal. All through it, my mind continually conjured up visions of my strangled body suspended from the tree while shite ran down my ragged breeches. The thought that my manacles could grow even tighter also entered my mind, yet I quickly dismissed the possibility, for I knew it would take more than the few hours I had remaining for my wrists to grow in size. And, should the opportunity present itself, I had every confidence that I could get them off within seconds.

My meal finished, I watched Peter eat until he had his fill. Sauntering away, his belly bulging, he settled down beneath the bed while I called for the turnkey to carry away the plates, cup, empty bottle of claret, pewter flatware, and the little bits of food Peter and I were unable to get down.

Eying my stomach, he shook his head. Then, looking about the room, asked, "Near put it all down, did ya?"

"Yes, it was quite good, thank you," I said with a smile.

"Yer stomach ain't just a little bit squeamish?"

"Why, not at all," I said.

"You ain't been thinking about the Tree?"

"Well, yes. It shall be good to be out in the open again, fresh air and that sort of thing," I said."

Once he had stuffed the last of my utensils into a burlap sack, he shook his bald head and left the room. After the door had clanked shut, he eyed me through the observation slot for a moment.

Paying him no mind, I stretched out on my cot and let out a most voluminous burp.

The observation slot slid shut with a clang and, before the sound of his shoes scraping upon the wooden floorboards faded, I heard his muffled voice say, "Mighty big bollocks for such a young un' as that."

A very short time passed before the sound of the turnkey's footsteps returned as they came to collect me up for my journey. In a large courtyard sat a two-wheeled cart enclosed by sun bleached sideboard rails that stood as high above the bed as a man's shoulders.

Five men and two women stood in the cart and, as I approached, I could not help but notice the wet stain streaking down the ragged dress of one of the women. She held her manacled hands to her face, covering her eyes, mumbling something like a prayer, though I couldn't discern any complete words.

As I climbed up to join them, she dropped her hands, exposing pale clouded eyes that hadn't seen the sunlight for many months. After only a glimpse, just enough perhaps to take in my shape, she covered them again. "So young, you are, and I, crying for myself. You shame me, lad," she said, while her knobby fingers kneaded the skin around her eyes, leaving bits of dried crust that flaked onto her cheeks.

The executioner stood tall and gaunt with eyes sunk deep into their sockets. With a sideways glance over his shoulder, he took in the shabby stench of his cargo. With a slap of the reins onto the horse's haunch, the cart lurched forward. The sun bore down from a cloudless sky onto my shoulders and neck and I turned my face upward to feel the warmth penetrate my pale skin. It had been a long time since I had contact with the great star and I took it in like a sun worshipper while, in contrast, the executioner cursed as he sweltered beneath an oilskin coat and leather hat, and I wondered what purpose such a garment had for him.

Nearing the main gate, we were preceded by two prison gaolers on horseback while another wagon came up behind us bearing eight coffins. The other woman in the cart caught sight of the crudely constructed boxes and, burying her face into my chest, began a low wailing. I could think of nothing to say that might console her as I, too, was destined to fill one of those boxes.

Behind the wagon that bore the coffins, six more gaolers took up the rear, each carrying a wooden staff of approximately five feet in length, while their swords, hanging at their sides, slapped against the saddles as the horses skittered from side to side in anticipation of the gate's opening. As the massive iron gate swung wide, a large crowd stood in wait, forming a kind of gauntlet on both sides of the street. Through the sideboards I could see that the crowd on either side of the street contained several persons who bore baskets of rotting food. Within the cart, two men were tied to the front so securely that they were unable to move while the rest of us packed into the small space to the rear.

Once through the gate, the rotten vegetables and animal excrement started flying, the bulk directed at the two men tied to the front of the cart, making perfect sense that our driver wore an oilskin overcoat and hat. Within moments, the two men were covered from head to foot with odiferous slime. I knew not who these men were and did not wish to know. The fact that we were all to be hanged at the end of our little journey was enough to consider, let alone pay any notice to their present condition.

The few streets to Holbourn Street bore a tightly packed throng who cursed and spit at us while the cart squeezed by them. Holbourn Hill was taken slowly, allowing many food throwers time to take good aim yet I was able to dodge the bulk of it. As we made our way past Zack's office, I could make out the dim interior through half-closed curtains and realized he must have gone well ahead of the cart to Tiburn Tree in order to assure a good seat in the Marble Arch. As the cart rumbled down Holbourn toward Oxford Road, the size of the crowd varied from large groups of people to scarcely two or three. As we rolled along, I fixated upon the distraction and turned over a seemingly endless line of schemes that Laura may have conjured up. As the cart turned onto Oxford Road I realized I must be ready the second it occurs. This street was heavily crowded and progress was slow. I knew this was my last mile testified to by the bile coming up from my stomach to sear my throat. My heart seemed to be beating louder than the crowd's roar while my blood flowed like ice through my veins. My vision grew a little clouded and I feared that I might faint. Something must happen soon if Laura were to make good on her promise, I thought, as the seeds of desperation began taking root.

What happened to my acceptance of death? What happened to the consolation of, at last, being out in the open air and free of the stench of Newgate, I thought, as I realized that nothing mattered more to me at that moment than to find some means of escape. My pulse raced through my veins like a caged animal searching for some opening to dart through while the only thought within my mind screamed over and over—I don't want to die, I don't want to die, I DON'T WANT TO DIE!

At mid-street, the cart struck a rut in the cobblestone that set us all ajar and momentarily shook my thoughts from the blind alley of terror I had been trapped in. In the next second, I caught a glimpse of a butcher who stood leaning against an old house just a few doors farther up the road. The butcher turned and I recognized the tall man with the gaunt face. Giles wore a long bloodstained butcher's apron while his dirk hung loosely at his side.

This is it, I thought, while scanning the street for the distraction. I must get these manacles off now. I tried to do it quickly but, in my haste, found I was pulling unevenly as the skin on my wrists bunched against the iron. After a momentary wave of panic, I realized my error and corrected with an even back and forth twist.

I had no sooner accomplished this when I heard a loud commotion as the executioner cried, "Hooo!" while pulling on the reins and bringing the cart to a halt.

The distraction, I thought, I must get them off now. As I lowered my hands to my sides, the manacles dropped heavily onto the floor of the cart. A quick glance told me that all eyes were to the side of the street opposite from where Giles stood. In one second I was upon the rail. Before jumping over the side, I froze.

Laura stood directly across the street atop a wooden crate. All heads had turned towards her. All eyes glared, mouths agape. No one said a word, only staring in disbelief. The gaolers were dumbstruck as they sat transfixed upon their mounts.

Her milky white complexion, illuminated by the sun, accentuated the dark protruding nipples of her full firm breasts. For a second, it was as though they pointed straight up to the gaolers, first paralyzing them and then, gluing them to their horses. Her hips, swaying from side to side, slowly turned in a tight circle, first displaying the rounded firm cheeks of her buttocks atop long tapered thighs, then the dark curly "v" shaped mound of blond hair. The brick building behind her became her stage backdrop as she swung her arms and hips in a steady even movement to an unheard melody. Upon the whole, it was a performance not to be matched on any stage, at least, not in this land. The whole crowd had gone dead quiet. All six prison gaolers sat motionless upon their horses, completely forgetting their duty.

This was my chance; however, like everyone else, I couldn't take my eyes off of her. Paralyzed on top of the rail, my hands locked onto the boards of the cart, I heard, "Hmph!" as Giles cleared his throat, not eight feet behind me. Coming to my senses, I dropped to the street completely unnoticed. Running low, I crawled beneath the apron where I found an open iron hatch leading beneath the street to a coal bin in the basement of the building Giles had been leaning on. I dove through, landing on a pile of clinking coal as the iron lid fell into place above me. It was dark as pitch and I searched with my hands to find my way through the room when someone uncovered a well lit lantern. As my eyes adjusted to the light, I could make out the handsome features of Jim Bridges.

His eyes told of the danger in which he had placed himself, yet he smiled and pointed to the stairs. Placing a clean shirt over my shoulders, he said, "You must run like lightning up those stairs and through the back door. There is a board covering a hole in the back fence. Put these breeches on and, here are your shoes and stockings. Wear this hat down low on your face. You must not let anyone get a good look at you. Turn away if someone appears to take notice. Walk steadily and if pursued, run. Here! Take this purse. Wait, you shall need this as well," he said, handing me a small dirk. "Forget about hiding in the city or the rest of England. They shall track you down if they have to search every town, farm, or rabbit warren. You must make your way to the Thames and get yourself aboard a ship—any ship that is leaving port. You shall have to stow away. It is the only way to assure your escape. You must never stop running until you are well away. Now go, quickly—go!"

"Tell Laura I shall always be in her debt, and you as well, Jim," I said, as I ran up the stairs while buttoning my shirt.

"Pike sends his regards. He is sorry he couldn't be here. It's just as well, his injured leg would have slowed us all down," Bridges said, as I topped the stairs.

The house appeared to be vacant and I could hear the frenzied commotion coming from the street. The back door led into a small walled yard with a wooden plank leaning against the wall, just as Bridges had described. Within a second, I was through the opening and into another yard. Before continuing, I reached back through and moved the plank to its previous position. On this side, I found another small yard which opened onto a house with a narrow walkway to one side leading out to the street beyond. Once on the street, I stepped across, forcing my legs not to run, though I could hear angry voices and horse's hooves coming from the next street. On the next corner, I spied a sedan chair and hesitated before dismissing the means of transport as being far too slow. Walking at a fast pace, I turned the next corner and cut across to the next street. Suddenly, I realized I was in my own manor. Standing on Green Street, my heart ached as, not half a paces distant, I could see the protruding steps leading up to my home. The traffic in the street was fairly light with a few coaches slowly rumbling by, a lone sedan chair on the lookout for a potential fare and a few people on their way by foot that took no notice of me.

As I stood pondering my next course of action, I was startled by a hand on my shoulder. Bunching my fists, I spun 'round ready to strike out. However, beneath the dark hood of her silken gown, I spied the familiar face of Mrs. St. Clair.

Though her frame appeared frail, she stood firm and I was not able to break free from her grip upon my shoulder. "Robert," she said, "there is little time. You must come with me this instant."

Unable to speak, for my thoughts were in a whirlwind of panic, I wanted to run, yet I only stood there with my feet strangely anchored to the paving stones.

"Come with me Robert," she beckoned. Then, seeing that I hadn't moved, she brought her face close to mine and, piercing me with those aged eyes, whispered, "Come!"

Reluctantly, I drug my feet behind her. No one on the street seemed to take notice as I followed the old woman. Soon we came to my home and, walking to the door, she turned the lock with a key, saying, "Do not be concerned, your father gave me this key for just such an emergency."

As the familiar creak of the door slid open on its hinges, I had the strongest urge to run upstairs to my bedchamber, crawl between the sheets of my bed, curl up into a fetal position and fall asleep. Perhaps then I might wake up to find it had all been just a very, very bad dream. Without the act of falling asleep, stepping into my home did feel like entering a dream. The familiar smell of Mother's cooking emanated from the walls and it appeared as though nothing had changed since my absence. Father's great chair sat in the parlor, the clock ticked away the seconds above the fireplace, the brass chandelier that lit up so many conversations hung above the dining table. Still, the absence of my family gave the house a strange, ghostly presence. I knew Mother and Lilly would most likely be somewhere in Hyde Park, hopefully a safe distance from the gallows. Still, I yearned for their precious company. Did they know I had escaped? No, there wasn't time for them to have received the news.

Outside, I could hear the screech of iron-rimmed wagon wheels on the paving stones while horses at a quick gallop shot past the window. The hunt was on and I was right in the middle of it. Soon they would be searching all the houses. Why had I listened to this old woman? Have I lost my mind? What are my chances of escaping now? I knew I should run from here yet was reluctant as uncertainty held me.

Opening the door to the cellar, she motioned for me to follow.

Why was she so familiar with the inside of our home, I wondered as I hastened down the stairs.

At the bottom of the stairs, the kitchen was alight with candles and, in the hearth, a large pot of water hung above the fire. Taking up the pot hook, she withdrew the pot of water and placed it upon the board and dresser next to a stack of folded towels and said, "Take off that hat, we must wash the filth from your hair."

I stood quite dumbfounded and didn't move.

"Off with that shirt!" she commanded, then, taking up a towel, began scrubbing my face while I unbuttoned the shirt. "Here, lower your head!" she ordered while pulling my face down into the pot of warm water. After toweling my face and hair, she attempted to brush the tangled mats and knots free but, being unsuccessful, gave a sigh and handed me a clean shirt.

Taking me by the hand, she said, "Now, we must move quickly. Your father and I were going to wait until you were of age but, under the circumstances, there simply is no time."

"You know?" I asked, quite confused.

"Yes, I was at your trial and, yes, I know."

"And what is your relationship with Father?" I asked.

"Your father's ancestors trace back to the Knights Templar, as do mine. We are connected by the knowledge brought by the Knights from their excavation of Solomon's temple which lies beneath the ruined temple of Herod in Jerusalem."

"Father told me of the copper scrolls," I said.

Saying nothing in reply, she stepped quickly to the end of the basement and stood beneath the iron coal chute door that led from the street above. She drew back the white hood exposing her long silver hair. The luminescent strands glittered in the candlelight and I realized she was the woman who had appeared in my dreams. She stooped down low and, with a grunt, pulled Father's old toolbox aside. Tracing with her long knobby fingers, she passed them over the surface of the floor where the outline of a mason's square intersected by a compass had been etched into the stone.

"I have never seen that before," I said, incredulously.

The square lined up with the corner of the wall where she then counted upward seven courses of brick. Pausing, she gave me a sideways glance, and I said in a faint whisper, "Seven across each lower than the previous."

"Very good, Robert," she said, a relieved smile on her aged lips, "Your Father has already told you of the Key?"

Shaking my head to the negative, I said, "I have had dreams."

"Ah—dreams, of course," she knowingly nodded. "Bless his soul. He has kept his promise, even in death."

"What promise is that?" I asked.

"At another time, I shall explain it to you." With a sigh, she said, "Help me," and began picking at the brick with her pale bony fingers.

Stepping to her side, I took hold with my fingertips, working it from side to side. Inch by inch it gave way until we had it free. I placed it on the floor while Mrs. St. Clair reached in and withdrew an old goatskin pouch.

Taking it carefully into her hands, she worked the leather strings loose from the slipknot, just as my father had done in the dream. Setting it on the table, she tenderly opened the pouch and withdrew two familiar objects; a copper scroll, along with a pyramid-shaped gold piece.

Gently taking up the scroll, she said, "This once belonged to my ancestor, Hughes De Payen, and has since been passed down through our family to the first born son of each generation. My father, however, having no son, entrusted it to me. Unfortunately, I am barren and, in order to protect our family's heritage, decided to make your father the 'Keeper of the Key'. As I have said, he too, is a descendant of our family of Templars, a man named Andre De Montbard who was a close friend of Hughes De Payen and his wife Catherine St. Clair. It has been in safekeeping down through the centuries in the Templars Preceptory, the Rosslyn Shrine on our family's estate near Edinburgh but in the last century, the secret was betrayed and the Key had to be removed for fear of it being stolen."

Setting the scroll on the table, she carefully plied the copper while slowly unraveling the sheet as she said, "The symbols are of ancient Egypt but I have long ago deciphered them. It begins with the First Principle of the ancient mysteries. Only with the Key, will you be able to read it. Touch it now and read the first line to me."

Doing as she instructed, I rested a finger upon the golden pyramid when, suddenly, the symbols upon the scroll transformed into liquid. I stood transfixed as the inky liquid ran about the scroll until it settled into words of plain English. Upon the page was now written a heading and I read it aloud, saying, "The Seven Hermetic Principles. The first Principle, the Principle of MENTALISM. The universe is mind. The ALL is mind. The universe exists within the mind of the ALL. "What does this mean?" I asked.

She rolled up the scroll and placed it back into the goatskin pouch, saying, "Someday you must read this, however, for the now, we must move quickly. Where you are bound, you will not be able to protect it so we must return it to its hiding place. But first," she said, "hold out your hands."

I did as she ordered and, just as my father had done in my dreams, she placed in my hands the gold pyramid, its jeweled eye staring placidly into my face.

"Since you do not have time to study the copper scroll," she said, pointing to the book, "you must receive the knowledge through Hermes' Key. It is the Ancient One, the True One, passed down from his very hand through thousands of years, long before even the Christians walked the earth. Feel its truth, Robert."

Examining the object, I said, "The Key?"

She replied, "The Key of Hermes Trismegistus, the great Ancient Master of Masters, the True Speaker."

"Father has mentioned Hermes to me," I said.

"There exists false replicas of this Key only meant to confuse those who would steal it for their own illicit gain. This, however, is the only true Key. It was discovered while the original Knights Templar dug into Solomon's Temple in the year 1126."

As she spoke, I felt a vibration as well as heat emanating from the metal. The eye, staring out from the centre, seemed to have a consciousness of its own. As I beheld the object, I had the uneasy sensation of one being observed, not unlike the magistrate's glare while I stood before him at the Old Bailey Courthouse. As I held it in my hands, Mrs. St. Clair stood with her fingertips touching one another as though in prayer.

Her lips pursed, I saw that the lines of her chin took on a marble like rigidity while her expression became tense and her eyes appeared as pinpointed diamonds.

My first thought was to put the object down but my body went rigid and I could not move.

As I stood transfixed, the vibration grew until it became an audible hum. Increasing in intensity, the hum grew to a loud roar before climbing to an ear-piercing shrill. Just when I thought my ears would burst from this horrendous sound, it left the range of my hearing and the vibration, now so high that I could scarce feel any movement, caused the object to turn from its glimmering gold luster to a dark dull red. At first I thought it must be from heat but realized it was not burning my flesh. Within seconds, the colour transformed to a bright red before melting into orange, then yellow, green, blue, indigo, and finally, violet. No sooner had it reached this last colour then it faded into what appeared to be a black void. Surrounding the void were pulsating shafts of light which revolved around the triangle while the object grew so cold that my hands went numb. And just as I thought my hands would freeze if I held it one second more, the object vanished.

"What has happened?" I asked, realizing that I could once again move.

She placed her fingers to her temples, her eyes were now pale and sunken as the experience appeared to have drained her. With a deep sigh, she said, "The Key is within you now. And there it shall remain until you have fully understood the knowledge."

"What knowledge?" I asked.

"The knowledge of the ages—the answers to the mysteries of life have been given to you so that it may be carried down through time." Smiling, she said, "You see, Robert, you are to be the next Speaker."

Seeing that she wavered, I took hold of her arm to steady her and she continued, saying, "You are the next in the line of Speakers which left off with your father. When you have a son, the Key will leave you and return to its physical form. At that time you must protect it until your son becomes one and twenty years of age, for he will be the next in the line of Speakers. Tell no one of this, but use the knowledge to teach only those who are ready to receive it."

Turning away, she raised her withered arm and pointed to the steps that led up to the parlor, saying, "Now you must go. They are near. You will do well to take the sedan chair that is about to pass by."

"But won't that be dangerous? What if they recognize me?"

"Walk out of the front door and hail them just as you would on any day you wished to go to town. Appear as though you have business somewhere and they will not suspect a thing."

Hesitating at the door, I felt distant and confused and through it all, realized that I must know what had happened, "What happened—down in the cellar?" I asked. "I feel strangely different—inside."

She smiled, "You are different. As time passes, you shall come to realize it."

"But, why me? Why am I to be the one to receive the Key?"

"You will come to understand."

"But—"

She shook her head, saying, "Enough! Now, GO!"

Stepping from the front door, the sedan chair was nearing the house and I did as she suggested. I hailed them and boldly stepped into their chair.

"To Grosvenor Square," I ordered.

At Grosvenor Square, I directed the men to transport me to within a street of Saint Giles parish. If they were to be questioned later, I am certain they would volunteer the information, thereby leading my pursuers here to spend days scouring every inch of the cellars and cesspools before giving up on the search. As the sedan chair men stepped away, I ran toward St. Giles leaving them with puzzled expression on their faces. Once they had turned the corner, I doubled back to Broad Street and caught a hackney coach. I decided on making my way to Smithfield. My newly concocted plan was that, once there, I may have a good chance at making my way through the cattle yards toward the edge of the city. For, contrary to Jim's advice, I had no desire to leave England. Although London is my home and I knew I must leave, I also knew that I would someday return. And if I managed to get free of the city, there was a good chance that I could make my way to Bristol or some other large city. The purse Jim handed me proved to be ample funds for a long stay in a simple lodging house and I needed only to find a suitable place until it became safe to return.

After traveling several streets, I discovered the driver was taking me onto High Holbourn, a street that would not only take me toward Smithfield, but by Zack's office. Although I had no fear of running into Zack, for he was sure to be awaiting my arrival at Tiburn Tree, yet I did experience a degree of trepidation when passing his building. The taxi had gone another street when, from a freight wagon ahead, fell a large wooden crate that broke into several pieces as it spilled its contents onto the street. One of the sections, a large pianoforte secured to a broken corner of the crate, tripped the taxi's horses and drove its wooden legs up into the springs of the carriage beneath my feet.

The coachman shouted, "You fuckin' bastard, look what ya did to my coach!

The freight driver returned in kind and the coachman stepped down with fists clenched. Taking off his coat, for it was a very fine piece with laced velvet done up with an intricate design on the lapels, the coachman paused while looking for some place to set it down. But this was his misfortune, for the freight driver took this opportunity to deliver a crushing blow to the temple. A jagged cut that spewed blood down the coachman's face brought him to drop the coat into the filth of the street and, without hesitation, leap upon the freight driver. The coachman straddled the big man around the waist; his legs locked into a scissors hold, and proceeded to beat him heavily about the head and face. The freight driver attempted to extricate himself from the coachman's scissors grip but to no avail for, each time he had nearly untangled the coachman's legs, the coachman delivered another smacking blow into the man's nose, which was gushing blood as it had since been flattened out across his face. Within seconds, a crowd poured out from the surrounding buildings and public houses to observe the fight.

Stepping out of the coach, I placed a shilling upon the coachman's seat before continuing east at a steady pace down High Holbourn. Once I had crossed the intersection of the next street, I noticed a man stepping out of a bar. He seemed strangely familiar and, as I walked by, he shot a glance at me, revealing the pug nose and long drooping upper lip. I continued on my way, pretending not to take notice but, in the reflection of a shop window, could see him staring rather intently as he tugged gently at his long lip. It was the worn and barren wig that struck a cord and, stretching out in a fast pace, I jutted down the next street before turning to see if he followed. His ungainly gait brought me back to the day we had left the Iron Rooster. At that time, I thought he was a slow walker. But that was before he arrived at Zack's place well ahead of us. Not to be deceived again, I broke into a run. When I reached the top of Holbourn Hill, I caught another taxi and headed east. Glancing back as the taxi pulled away, I saw Zack's man trying to get the attention of another taxi before I crested the hill. After we crossed Fleet Ditch, I stepped out onto Snow Hill. The coachman took his taxi north up Cow Lane so I went south, ducking into a doorway as the hackney carrying Zack's man turned the corner to pursue him. This should give me the time I need to get well away, I thought.

After a few streets of mud splashing from beneath the uneven paving stones onto my stockings and breeches, I realized I was nearing the vicinity of Newgate Prison. I can't be certain whether it was excitement or fear, but I felt the irresistible urge to face it. Boldly walking down Newgate Street, I stopped just short of The Gate that stood directly beneath my old cell. After a moment, I turned and walked back to the corner of Old Bailey to stare at the bars where I had sat awaiting my execution only a few hours ago. Awash with jubilation, I thought to myself, this must be how Jack Shepherd felt after his escape. It was a most powerful sensation for the whole of twenty seconds before the drum of horse's hooves beating heavily down Snow Hill brought the gaoler guards around the bend. Turning away from their approach, I walked at a steady pace northward up Gilt Spur Street. In seconds I could hear the guards slowing at the entrance to the street I had just turned down. God what a fool I was to come back here. I thought. I am undone. RUN, RUN! They will take you to the Tree and finish the job! How could they have known I would be here? Surely, this must be the last place they would expect to find me. Ready to bolt, I glanced over my shoulder in time to see them turn in the opposite direction onto Old Bailey Street. No, they were here to see the head magistrate to obtain a warrant for a citywide search. Deciding that my best chances were to distance myself from here as quickly as possible, I continued northward. Though the streets were unfamiliar to me, I knew I was nearing Smithfield, for there was the familiar odor of manure and there stood the tall spires of St. Sepulcher's Church. I recalled how, years ago, my father had brought me here in a sedan chair because I wished to see where the herds of cattle that periodically disrupted traffic on Oxford

Road were bound. We stopped at the church along the way and I distinctly remember the cattle yards were not far from here.

The streets were busy with coaches and two, coaches and four, and sedan chairs all hurrying to and fro. Fairly certain the news of my escape had yet to arrive in this part of London, I knew that it followed close in my wake. If I stayed too long in one place, it could be my undoing. For now, speed was my only advantage and that advantage grew lesser by the minute. Soon, gaolers, watchmen, and the Bow Street runners throughout the whole city will be fast upon my heels. No, I must keep walking—no stopping, no running, just a steady pace so as not to draw attention. And If I wish to remain alive, I must keep moving away from everything of which I am familiar.

As I walked, the odor of manure grew ever stronger and I realized that I was nearing the cattle yards of Smithfield! Well, I hope my plan work, I thought, as I turned the corner and came up behind a small herd of cattle in the middle of a dirt road. These huge beasts were all around me in seconds, all walking with wary eyes and tense step. Although I feared being trampled, they seemed to be aware of my presence and kept only inches from stepping on my feet. I was attempting to make my way out of the herd when, just ahead, at the next corner, appeared Zack's man. He was stepping from a hackney and talking to a coachman who had stopped to purchase feed for his horses. A strange twist of fate, I thought. I had just left that coachman in hopes of losing my chase. Little did I suspect he was on his way to Smithfield.

On the corner to the right of the coachman, not ten paces away, stood two watchmen, and now Zack's man approached them. One of the watchmen had with him a sketch and, as I made my way past them within the cover of the cattle, I watched Zack's man pointing to the taxi I had previously left. The watchmen handed Zack's man one of the sketches and commenced to showing another to the coachman. As I rounded a corner in the road, I could still see them motioning with their hands to indicate the height of... Could it be they were speaking of *my* height? Dear God, could they be looking for me here, and so soon? If so, they now had Zack's footpads to assist them. Ducking my head as low as possible, I continued down the street within the herd.

"There 'e is!" came a voice from directly above as a boy with ferret features, perhaps two years my junior, leaned out of an open window while, clutched in his hand, was one of those sheets of paper.

As it flapped in the breeze, not six feet from me, I could make out the sketch. It was a well-drawn likeness of a boy with an indifferent look in his cold blue eyes while, beneath his neatly tied-back shoulder-length blond locks, his seriousness was accentuated by an aquiline nose that gave purpose to a well defined and slightly protruding chin. Above the picture was a caption that read, "Robert the Thief." I recalled the concentration on Clarence Tolliver's expression as the Grub Street hack had had me sit whilst sketching my picture in Newgate.

Fortunately, no one heard the boy's hail above the din of the cattle. As the herd rounded the next corner, I could see the boy still attempting to gain someone's attention. The news has traveled ahead of me now, I thought. It is no longer safe to continue on the streets. I must find a place to hide, and soon.

The cattle were being driven by someone to the rear, as well as ahead, for I heard the distinct crack of a whip now and again. After entering a large corral, the gate was closed behind by unseen hands. Sensing the cattle's distress immediately following the closing of the gate, I stroked the two standing on either side of me. Whether the stroking was for the cows or for me, I knew not. Yet it gave me a small degree of comfort and seemed to be well received by the animals. If only I could get out of this corral before that boy successfully shouts out my location to those men, I thought.

Making my way between the gentle beasts, I found the edge of the corral to be blocked by a high wooden wall. Perhaps the other side, I thought, as I turned to coax the cattle to open a path in that direction. The brown spotted white face of one of the cows, a recent recipient of my strokes, appeared from the herd. Lowering her head, I extended my hand and stroked her long nose while her egg-sized nostrils flared to take in my scent. While I made my way across the yard, I felt her occasional nudge against my back and would, now and again, stop to stroke her while I searched for my next course of action. As I reached the opposite side of the yard, I found that it was fenced in by an equally high wall. What to do next? Retreating was not an option. The gate to my rear, if not yet, would soon be covered by the watchmen to see if the boy's story had any merit. The only way to go was in the direction that the cattle were headed and, the fact that they were being prodded by the men to my rear gave me little comfort. Bessy, for I had since given her this name, and I made our way through the mass toward what appeared to be a narrow opening that seemed it would only admit one cow at a time. What was beyond that opening remained to be seen and I hesitated, wondering if someone wasn't waiting on the other side. Looking about, it became apparent there was no other way out so I nudged Bessy toward the opening. None of the other cattle seemed to be in any hurry to enter and Bessy, with a little coaxing, reluctantly went through ahead of me. Giving her a reassuring pat on her rear, I followed through.

Once inside, the odor of manure became so thick that it burned my nostrils, making my eyes water. Glancing down, I realized that I was ankle deep in it. We were surrounded on both sides by high wooden fences that had seen much wear as testified by long gouges into the boarding made by the hardened tips of horns. Upon closer inspection I could see the wood had splintered to catch tufts of hair within the sharp edges while the lower planking was heavily scored from being struck by an endless stream of hooves. As Bessy boldly trotted ahead, I was now the reluctant one. Stopping momentarily to step up onto the fence boards and peer about, I could see numerous cattle pens, some containing small herds while others were empty. The pens were covered by a high roof while a series of catwalks ran over the pens throughout the structure allowing the cattlemen to traverse the area without having to get their feet filthy as I had been doing. While I paused, I realized that the rest of the herd were coming through the opening and, were I to remain, I would soon be trampled beneath their hooves. As my friend Bessy was, now, nowhere in sight, I sprang down the narrow chute just a few steps ahead of the bovine column.

The manure, straw, and urine combined into a muck that clung heavily to my shoes and mercilessly slowed my steps. Realizing the beasts were fast gaining upon me, I took one desperate leap and caught hold of the fence rail, attempting to pull myself up as quickly as I could. It wasn't quick enough, however, for the cow to my rear caught me with its massive chest and, slamming into my back, pinned me to the fence before scraping by on her way down the chute. The wind knocked from me, I clung to the fence for a brief second before the next cow butted me, one of her horns raking my arse and sending me up and over the fence. Landing on my back, I saw my fall had been cushioned by more manure and I lay in it for some time before catching my breath. At length, I managed to get to my feet and staggered to the nearest fence. As I struggled to pull myself up the fence boarding, pain shot down my backside and I feared something had been broken. As I gained my footing, the discomfort soon subsided and my breathing came more easily. Much relieved to have gained the catwalk, I sat above the cattle pens and took in my surroundings.

With the approach of voices, I made my way in the opposite direction. I soon reached a gate which led to a large ramp that appeared to be used to move cattle from one corral to another. Crossing the ramp, I found another gate farther down the way and entered it. For a good distance ahead, I could see this walkway continuing into an area containing pigs which were penned below. Retracing my steps back to the ramp, I then followed it to an area where cattle were being loaded onto a large wagon hitched to a team of six horses.

With the wagon fully loaded, the driver was coaxing his team away from the ramp. With only a second to spare, I leaped across the gap and managed a handhold on the rear rail. Ahead was an opening in the barn where sunlight penetrated and I could see through to the street beyond. Easing my way between the legs of the cattle, I concealed myself between low sagging udders as the wagon stopped at the gate before entering the street.

"I still don't see why we have to haul 'em," said the driver to another man at the gate who, upon writing a count upon a board, replied, "Got too many complaints from the people of Wapping about the piss and manure on the streets. People say they're fed up with cleanin' up after us. So we got to put 'em on the wagons until we is told otherwise."

This was my way out of the city, I thought. Out in that glorious countryside where I might find a stream and wash the filth from my body. Then, if I managed to dry my clothing in the sun, perhaps I might catch a ride on some passing coach and secure passage to another city. Yes, all I must do now is keep myself concealed for perhaps an hour or two and, when the time is right, off this goddamn wagon I shall go. The wagon slowly rounded a turn and all the cows moved their feet slightly to brace themselves when one hoof would have stepped on my hand had I not moved in the nick of time.

If only I can hold on, I thought as one cow, three feet from me, relieved herself onto the floorboards. I crawled well under the belly of the cow nearest me in an attempt to get out of the way. I shall never get this smell off my clothes, I thought.

After perhaps half an hour had passed, I was certain we would be nearing the edge of the city yet, above the manure, I smelled the distinct odor of the Thames. Perhaps we are going to cross the bridge. Of course, the wagon driver must be taking the cattle across the London

Bridge to Southwark. Peering out from between the cattle's legs, I could see nothing familiar to me. We were definitely nearing the waterfront as testified by the smell of the fishmongers stands. Something is wrong, I thought. If we are not crossing a bridge, then, where are we going? The wagon came to a halt upon a long wharf where a ship was tied alongside. The sign above read, "Shadwell Dock." The cattle are going aboard this ship. What was I thinking? I asked myself. Cattle are brought to London to be butchered and not taken out of London unless they are being sent aboard ship as provisions. I must get out now and be damned if anyone sees me. Within a second, I had leaped from the wagon with my feet hitting the planks of the wharf in an all out sprint. After perhaps twenty yards, I slowed to a normal pace and, glancing back, found that no one had taken notice. A short distance farther, and I was strolling through a boat repair yard where sawyers worked in pits, sawing great beams, or up on a scaffold, driving nails through hull planking into ship frames. Fortunately, the smell of lumber and fish was much stronger than the cattle shite and urine on my clothes, so no one paid me any notice as I made my way out of the yard onto Fox Lane. Breathing a sigh of relief, I walked past piles of fish in huge stalls where the fishmongers were preparing to take them to markets throughout the city. My heart dropped when I saw the man with the long rod coming around the corner in the opposite direction. I could do nothing but turn and run.

  A cry of "STOP! THIEF!" ensued and I ran faster. Unfortunately, ahead of me and running in the opposite direction came another watchman, as well as several more men who had taken up the cry. There being nowhere to go but back to the Thames, I turned down a passageway which displayed a sign with a pelican figure, and ran toward the river. As I passed the building on my left, I had an odd sense of my father's presence. Glancing up at the edifice, I was momentarily taken aback, for there stood the Old Dundee Masonic Lodge of which my father had been a member with the title of "Master Mason." He had told me many a story about his meetings in this place and had, at length, expressed his desire for me to become a member one day. How disreputable my first visit to the lodge has turned out to be, I thought.

With watchmen hot on my heels, I ran down the pelican stairs and did not hesitate for a second before plunging headlong into the filthy Thames. The chill of the icy water stuck me like a wall of broken glass but I quickly recovered and, reaching out for a few strokes, caught my breath before diving beneath the surface. With the cries of the men muffled by the water, I took ten more strokes before bouncing my head off the hull of a grain barge. Disoriented and confused from the blow, I came to the surface and instinctively took hold of the gunnels. After gaining my senses, I pulled myself up onto the barge and crawled into a pile of grain.

"There he is! Stop that barge! The little bugger's getting away!" cried an ape-faced man with a gravelly voice. I could see a group of scrubby looking coves not a stone's throw distant who, with nothing better to do and with no ground to follow, sat on the stairs calling out for a water taxi. From what I could tell, the barge was headed up river.

One man sat slumped forward at the bow, apparently asleep, while a lethargic helmsman steered the barge with absolutely no deference to my pursuers. He must surely hear them, I thought. At any second, he must heave to. Yet, the helmsman only stared at the sail, a blank expression on his face. More shouts ensued as a river taxi pulled up to the stairs, allowing the men to board. In quick work they had the boat turned with oars pulling hard toward the barge. Fortunately, the barge was moving steady under sail at a faster speed than the small boat. After rounding a bend in the river, the helmsman turned his wheel which brought the big yard swinging across over my head, and in doing so, made the boat lose a good deal of headway. Looking back, the men in the boat had brought up a sail which soon increased their speed. Soon they will come around the bend in the river and lose their wind as well. Perhaps this barge can still outrun them, I thought. But then, once again, they hauled upon their oars. Seeing that they were fast gaining, I realized that if I didn't get off the barge, they would have me in minutes. Crawling to the side shielded from the pursuer's view, I slipped over the gunnels and into the cold water without making a splash. So penetrating was the chill of the water that it nearly took my breath. Knowing I could not survive in it for long, I swam as Pike had taught me, diving under the surface when the oarsmen came alongside the barge. Under water for as long as my lungs could hold out, I must have managed to cover perhaps fifteen yards before surfacing. Taking in precious air, I watched the men who had just come aboard the barge. Instead of searching the water, they were searching the barge while a watchman had his hands around the helmsman's throat.

"Why did you not heave to when we hailed you? Are you deaf?" Then, the man who had been sitting at the bow came up behind the constable and, swinging a strangely shaped club, knocked him to the deck. Standing over the constable, he bellowed in a deep trumpeting voice, "Goddamn lubber, that's my brother yer chokin'. And, yes, he is deaf!"

Reaching out in slow even strokes, I swam toward the middle of the river. Upstream, London Bridge loomed with coach and foot traffic beneath recently lit overhanging street lamps as dusk was quickly falling upon the city. Father had told me that before I was born, people lived upon the bridge in rickety old houses. And that their occupants would dump their chamber pots directly into the river causing much admonition from the people below in the river taxis. Even with the houses gone from the bridge, I knew that the greater part of the city's filth was floating all around me. How much longer before they search the water for me, I thought, as the cold seeped into me, causing a tingling and numbing sensation in my fingers. While treading water, I thought of making my way to the other side of the Thames, but like a heavy woolen blanket, a dense wall of fog rolled down the river towards me until, covering everything, disguising everything, it took every discernable thing from view.

With no reliable sense of direction, I treaded water, listening for anything that might give a hint of where the shore lay. If I just struck out, I thought, I might only be swimming down the river and not across it. For eternal moments, I strained my ears while fighting back the urge to cry out for help, knowing full well the only help I could expect was to be returned to Tiburn Tree. The cold penetrated me deeper and the numbness took hold, making me shudder. Then, I heard something. At first, it was only a whisper, but then grew steadily more distinct. It is water slapping against the wharf. Yes, it must be, I thought, as I stroked out hard for it. Suddenly I could see a great wall coming at me through the curtain of fog. The sides hung out above me while the rushing water took hold, forcing me away as the ship sailed by. It nearly left me in its wake when I felt a rope grazing my side. Taking hold, it pulled me slowly through the water. By now, my hands had grown so numb that it became extremely difficult to maintain my grip and, as a precaution, had to pass it around my waist. The force of the water against my body only served to make the cold penetrate even further and I knew that if I remained this way much longer, I would be doing the hangman's job for him.

In silent desperation, I used what little strength I had left to pull myself, hand over hand, toward the craft. As it gradually loomed into view, I could make out the great hulking mass through the haze, but then my fingers gave way, releasing my hold. Determined not to let it go, I lost several yards as the rope slid through my hand before I managed to wrap it around a leg and squeeze it between my shoes. Clamping on with my legs, I held fast as the line pulled me along in the vessel's wake. From somewhere aboard, a bell rang out every minute as a warning to other craft in the river and, though I felt my life in extreme danger, I dared not cry out. The sensation in my fingers gone, I willed them to work and, once again, pulled my way along the rope. At length, I feared I had lost more than a few yards, for I was certain to have covered at least thirty or so feet. Just as I had decided to give it up, the fog thinned and there it was, not twenty feet distant. In desperation, I kept pulling against its slow even wake until I passed the rudder, making my way alongside to where appeared a kind of makeshift ladder built into the ship's hull. In order to take hold of this ladder, I knew I must let go of the rope. I also knew that my hands were so numb that they would soon let go for me. But could I hold onto the sides of the ship's ladder? Pulling myself a few yards farther up the rope's length, I hoped it would allow me sufficient time to catch hold as I drifted down upon the ladder.

Realizing that my life depended on this one act, for I had grown too weak and numb to keep myself afloat, I held fast, attempting to gauge the speed of the water as it cut past the hull. I knew I would have very little time to release and take hold before being swept away. As though leaping into an abyss, I let go. The current swept me toward the ladder with lightning speed and I had only managed to catch hold of the lacquered rope with one hand before being hurled against the hull with a violent, thrashing force. Parting my lips to breathe, the full current of the filthy Thames flooded into my mouth and, had I not restricted my throat, the river would have forced itself down my throat. My hand slipping and chafing on the stiff lacquered hemp cordage, I managed to find a foothold beneath the water's surface, thereby bringing my thrashing in check. With utmost care, I flattened myself against the ship's side and through a battle with the current, steadily brought my other hand to bear. Though the feeling had left my hands, I could see my fingers close around the ladder rail. With my feet planted firmly onto the step below the waterline, I pushed myself upward to the next step. Upon close inspection, I could see that the entry ladder was made of wooden strips set into the hull, much like a set of shelves, while red, baize-covered rope was strung through the outer ends of the steps to make a most shallow sort of hand rail.

Clinging to the ladder with the water tearing past me like a rock in a raging stream, I glanced upward and traced the broad curving line of the hull to where it gave way to an opening in the ship's rail. Step by step, I made my way up the ship's side. Once free of the raging water, my progress improved until I found myself at eye-level to the main deck. My left hand, numb with cold and no longer able to function, gave way and brought me completely off balance. Wavering for several heart-wrenching seconds, I nearly fell back into the river before regaining my balance by the slow steady pull of my right hand. One desperate push from my legs brought me prostrate onto the deck where I lay catching my breath. Without hesitation, I crawled between groups of casks and managed to conceal myself just as my body went into a violent series of tremors. Pulling my knees to my chest, I hugged my legs tightly to suppress the shaking while taking in the situation on deck.

Nearby, there were several men at the bulwarks. Farther forward, and barely visible, were at least three more who stood at the bow, all attempting to see through the thick wall of fog while, no more than ten paces behind me, another manned the wheel. At intervals, a man with a deep froggy voice called down locations of various objects such as, "Sail, two points off the starboard bow!" or, "Barge, dead ahead!" The voice of the man aloft seemed to echo the tension of all the other men on deck as they anxiously leaned over the ship's rail.

"Fog clearing a half cable ahead!" came the call from aloft.

"Huzzay!" sang out the men on deck.

Realizing I must get out of sight before the fog cleared, I made my way from cask to cask until I found a hatchway and slowly stepped through. Inside the hatch, I found a ladder that led directly down at a near vertical angle to the deck below where a lamp was lit, illuminating a large cargo hold. Reaching the bottom of the ladder, I found there were stacks of various sized casks in long rows that ran down the length of the deck to the far ends of the ship. Below the floor grating,

I could see that the hull tapered inward to a point of being near horizontal, allowing no more space than for a couple feet of water to wash back and forth with the motion of the boat. So this is some sort of flat bottomed supply barge, I thought.

In my search for another place to hide, I came upon a large container and, finding its lid securely fastened, took up a pry bar that hung from a nail driven into an overhead deck beam. With my arms very weak, I struggled with the weight of the bar before getting purchase sufficiently to force the top off the container. My throat restricted as the odor of its contents assaulted my nostrils. Most likely spoiled meat, I surmised and, tapping the lid back into place, felt pity for the poor bastards who will have to eat this. Noticing another container of similar size, I took the bar and pried the lid free, half expecting more rancid smelling contents, yet was surprised to find it contained only water.

With the assistance of the pry bar, I managed to lever the cask over onto its side where all the contents spilled into the bilge. Once empty and much easier to manage, I soon had it secured to the rope which had previously held it fast. With the lid in hand, I lowered myself into the cask and leaned up against the sides while pulling my knees up to my chest. This will have to do, I thought. Pulling myself up to a standing position, I quickly looked about and, through a narrow passage between the casks, spied a coil of hemp cordage. Sliding my dirk from its sheath, I sliced through the hemp, taking a good sized length back to my hiding place. After coiling the cordage, I carefully dropped it into the cask and climbed in on top of it. Carefully sliding the lid into place, I took care to leave a small section open so that I might hear if someone came down the ladder. Within the darkness, I shuddered in my cold, wet clothes and leaned against the slimy staves. At first, I squirmed around while attempting to situate the cordage into a comfortable cushion beneath me. This proved an extremely difficult task and I soon gave it up, for I had little to no strength left. After twenty plus minutes, I could no longer withstand the discomfort and climbed out. My hands trembling and my knees wobbly, I held onto the banister rails and made my way back up the ladder.

Poking my head through the hatch of the main deck, I had to wait for my eyes to adjust to the darkness before I found the fog had cleared. The city lights were slipping silently away and, under my breath, I gave thanks to Laura for helping me escape the clutches of Newgate and, ultimately, the hangman.

The men were everywhere on deck while others were climbing into the rigging. The moon, now at its zenith, was nearly full, bringing into view an occasional building on the passing shoreline.

Ahead, and on my right, sat a group of three-masted ships which were moored off the river in some sort of narrow man-made channel. After we had made our way past the channel, a man who stood at the bow hailed a ship that lay at anchor directly ahead and opposite a line of warehouses. On shore, I could make out a large sign, which read, "King's Victualing Office & Ware Houses."

"Ahoy, *Deception*!" the man at the bow called out. Then, came a reply from the other ship, "What ship is that?"

As the high sides of the large ship loomed above the deck, I crept below to my hiding place. On my way down the ladder, I heard the helmsman answer, "Hogue. Victualing barge, Hogue!"

PART TWO
—∞— THE JOURNEY —∞—

1. Jib 2. Fore topmast staysail 3. Main topgallant staysail
4. Main topmast staysail 5. Main staysail
6. Mizzen topmast staysail 7. Mizzen vang block
8. Mizzen brail

A. Fore topgallant sail B. Fore topsail C. Fore course
D. Main topgallant sail E. Main topsail F. Main course
G. Mizzen topsail H. Mizzen course (spanker)
I. Spritsail topsail J. Spritsail

CHAPTER ELEVEN

"HAUL AWAY!" came a cry from somewhere above, while the men of the supply barge were scrambling everywhere below deck. From what I could make out, they were now at work loosening the bindings of the casks and rolling them across the floor to a space beneath an open hatchway. Peering through the slightly raised lid of my cask, I spied a large sling of netting that dropped down through the open hatch wherein they placed several hogsheads before calling out for the men above to, "Haul away!"

It was beginning to look as though the larger portion of casks in the hold were slated to be taken aboard the ship now tied alongside. Perhaps when they finish with these, I thought, I might have an opportunity for escape.

Suddenly, it struck me that the cask I was in might be slated to go aboard that ship as well. If I didn't get out soon and find another hiding place, I may have a lesser chance of escape on that ship than I do here. At least this barge will be returning to its loading dock, whereas that ship, taking in so many stores, is most certainly bound for distant shores. Unfortunately, each time I raised the lid just enough to look about, I found I was in close proximity to several men.

After perhaps an hour, I noticed a pause in the activity and carefully slid back the lid, just far enough to stick my head through. To my amazement, I found that the deck had nearly been cleared. I was halfway out of the cask when I heard the drum of feet coming down the ladder.

With the lid back in place, there was nothing to do but await the opportunity to run. The only difficulty there being, if I am fortunate enough to make my way to the main deck, then it would be over the side again. That filthy water had nearly killed me once, dare I try it again?

The answer came when my cask was tipped and spun round and round across the deck. With my knees drawn up, I used my feet to thrust my weight against the sides, thereby wedging myself in place so as not to be thrown about. At length, the spinning stopped, though the sensation remained for some time afterward. Once I felt I could make my move without falling on my face, I heard someone call out, "HAUL AWAY!"

Suddenly, my cask was on the move, although not merely spinning as before, it now swung to and fro while I could hear blocks squeaking from the strain of the load.

The sound of men calling out, "Two, six, HEAVE!" drew nearer.

The call repeated with each movement of the load until I had been set down onto the other ship.

Is it too late? I wondered. I had been carried into some dark void where the cask came to a rest on its side. Once stationary, I waited while voices and the sounds of footsteps began to fade. It was not until all was quiet that I slid open the lid and, letting it fall, attempted to see into the darkness. The most I could discern was that they had placed me on top of a tier of casks while directly opposite the opening of my cask sat another, separated by only inches. There was only one problem to solve now. How was I to get out?

As I lay on my stomach contemplating this dilemma, a thick odor of decomposing meat mixed with that of sewage wafted into my barrel. Brought in mind of my old cell in Newgate, I wondered if I had escaped from one prison only to find myself in another?

With my shoulders bunched up against the bottom of my barrel, I placed my feet against the cask opposite the gap and tensed my thighs. With all my strength, I pushed against the other cask until I thought my back would break. Not knowing if anything had moved, I rested for a moment and tried it again. Curling into a ball, I spun around and stuck my head through the opening. In the dark, I could feel with the tip of my nose that it had moved, but it wasn't enough.

After getting back into position I found that my shoulders no longer reached the bottom of the barrel and could only push with my arms. After several tries at this, I found that I had made absolutely no progress. Realizing my arms were not as strong as my legs and back, I pushed the coil of cordage against the bottom of the barrel, and, using it as a spacer, was able to gain purchase by using my legs and back.

However, with all my strength, it would not move. Drenched in sweat from the fetid heat of the hold, my lungs heaved as I struggled to take in air. Sinking back into the cask, I lay catching my breath and wondered if I would ever be able to move it farther. No, I thought, there was nothing left in the barrel to push against.

With an icy chill, I realized that if I didn't get out, I would die here. A wave of nausea swept through me and I fought the panic building within me.

I closed my eyes in exhaustion, and felt utter despair at my predicament. I had come through so much only to find myself continually challenged just to survive. I felt as if all the terrible events of my life were contained in this moment—stuck in the physical confines of a cask and unable to break free. Grief of my father's death, sorrow for the disappointment I had caused my mother and sister, placing my friend's lives in danger by allowing them to orchestrate my escape. Everyone and everything I loved was gone. I laid down my head and became lost in a flood of the tears.

The image of Mrs. St. Clair startled me. She was holding out the Key and talking to me but I couldn't make out the words. I focused on her mouth and realized she was repeating the First Principle over and over. "The universe is mental, Robert. The universe is mental."

Once I understood her, I began to hear her voice. I was sure I had begun to hallucinate from lack of food, strength, and my complete loss of hope.

"Robert, the entire world is made and remade as we perceive it to be. You must believe that there is no physical entity that can contain your spirit—that can prevent you from freeing yourself in the darkest of moments. You need only to believe that freedom is a state of MIND. Freedom exists without physical restraints."

I had much difficulty reconciling her words to my current state of imprisonment. She made it sound as if I had only to believe that I could get free in order to make it so. The weight and pressure of the casks surrounding mine was so oppressive that it made her words seem ludicrous.

Her image returned, her hand outstretched, palm up as if for me to take it. I reached out to hold it and felt the neighboring cask give slightly.

Reaching out, I rested my hand upon the neighboring cask and felt it move. Sticking my head through the opening, I surveyed the space. I could feel that it would be extremely tight and wasn't sure I could manage it.

Gathering my resolve, I crawled through on my back until I was forced to bend my neck while sliding my head upward against the end of the cask opposite me. Once I had my shoulders through, I reached up with one hand and took hold of the lip of the barrel. With one hand below and my other on the lip, I slowly pulled myself into a sitting position. With both hands above me, I hauled my weight up until my head was above the casks. Now it was time for my feet. Bending at the knees, I inched up with my toes until my legs were clear of the opening. Now I had to push up with my thighs and force myself through. Once I had one shoulder through, I knew there was no turning back. The strakes were now pinning me between the ends of both barrels and I could move no farther.

Unable to go back down, while unable to pull myself above the casks, I prayed the load would not shift and struggled to achieve some purchase. With my feet resting on the cask's edge, I realized I could use the situation by pushing with my knees. With that, they moved ever so slightly, allowing barely enough room for me to push myself through to my chest. Now, my knees were shaking and my muscles cramped from the contorted position they were in and I knew I had to do something fast. The cordage was straining and popping like a timepiece, clicking away the seconds, growing louder and sharper with each pop as if to warn me that very little time remained. The opening was so tight that I had to let out all the air from my lungs while pushing hard with my legs. Even still, I left some skin on the strake ends as I raked my back and ribs slowly through the tiny gap. As I pulled myself free of the opening, the load shifted hard. Cordage snapped and popped and the tier of casks beneath me moved. Searching with my fingertips, I traced the area below where I had just extracted myself and found that no opening, not the least of which had any dimension large enough for even a rat, remained.

As I lay on my stomach in the darkness, I could feel a deck beam against my back and realized I was on top of the stack. At least I would not be crushed if any more shifting were to occur. As it was, my back and chest were sorely cut and chafed and I could feel the warm wet of my blood soaking into my shirt.

I decided to try and make my way down the length of the hold in hopes of escaping through a hatchway. Reaching out into the darkness, I felt around for any open space ahead.

Maneuvering was painstakingly slow, for the deck was just inches above, barely allowing room to squeeze past each beam. At length, I had crawled over numerous casks before spying a faint glow filtering in through the rows ahead. Scraping my shins and elbows, I slowly made my way toward the light of a glim. It was not until I had come to the last two tiers of casks that I heard someone speaking.

"I expect this completes our stores, Mr. Bengs."

Then another voice replied from above, saying, "Prepare to weigh anchor. We must lose not a minute if we are to make the morning ebb."

"Aye, aye, sir," was the response. Then someone else called out, "Fleet the messenger!"

Of what do they speak? I wondered, as the lamp was extinguished and a grating slid over the hatchway. I was, again, in total darkness. The darkness, of itself, did not frighten me for I had been well accustomed to being locked up in such spaces. What was of concern, however, was the strange conversation I had just overheard. Try as I might, I couldn't understand a thing they had said. Which way is the anchor? And how does one make the morning ebb? I must get off this ship, I thought. And though I didn't know what they were speaking of, I felt an odd sense of urgency.

Suddenly there came a clanking of some device that reverberated throughout the ship while, at the same time, someone was playing a strange tune on a fife.

"At long stays!" someone announced, "Heave cheerily!" said another.

What kind of English is this? I wondered.

"Short stays. Dry nippers for the heavy heave. Heave and pawl."

Does someone named Paul need dry knickers? Have these people gone mad? By the bloody Christ, I am locked below the deck of a ship of madmen. And to make matters worse, it is soon to be sailing down the Thames and into the channel.

"Up and down," that same voice said, as the clanking sound increased its momentum.

"Anchor's awash."

Now they are washing the anchor. If that is true, they will soon be drifting down the Thames.

"Cat's two blocked. Well the cat."

Just when I thought I had something understood and now they have a constipated cat. What insanity goes on up there?

The pipe music stopped. I've heard that song before. Hearts of oak, or some such melody, I recalled, as I made my way on all fours across another endless row of containers. If only there were some light.

"Get the ship underway. Rig the fish! Man the fish! Walk away with the fish!"

The ship is getting underway. I understood that much, but why at this juncture do those fools suddenly wish to go fishing in the Thames? The river is awash with the city's filth, evidenced by my own reeking stench.

"Bosun, make sail! Topmen, aloft!"

They are making sail. We are underway. And to where? It was at that point that I was brought in mind of Jim Bridges' instructions, "Forget about hiding in the city or the rest of England for that matter. They will track you down if they have to search every town, farm, or rabbit warren. You must make your way to the Thames and get aboard a ship—any ship that is leaving port."

Here is my opportunity. Though I had no intention of following those instructions, it seemed that in spite of myself, I had done exactly that. And now I must undo it. I must get off this ship or I may never see my family again. Jim's advice may be sound indeed yet, I simply could not will myself to adhere to it. The mere thought of Mother, Lilly, Laura, and Pike growing more distant each day was almost unbearable.

Feeling my way down to a small open space on the deck, I sat with my back against a barrel and waited for the dawn. The steady swaying motion of the ship soon made me aware of my exhaustion from the day's events. Though soaked through from the swim, my climbing about in the hold had made my blood warm and the tremors had finally ceased. It was not long before sleep overtook me.

As I drifted off, a flood of memories ran rampant through the fissures of my mind. A gaunt man in an oilskin coat held before my face the hard twisted fibers of a noose while a woman in a urine-soaked dress kneaded her sunken eyes and said, "You shame me, lad." Then, I was with my father during a mason's gathering. The *crusher* contest was held and Father was the victor. The other men were offering their congratulations when he suddenly fell from the scaffold in the church. Rushing toward him as he fell, I tripped over a sack of lime and watched helplessly as he crumpled into the stone floor of the church.

It was the familiar touch of tiny padded feet on my arm that finally brought me round. "The turnkey will feed us soon, Peter," I said, while trying to remember why I was not lying on my cot. Perhaps I rolled over and fell out of it during the night.

Then, like a venomous snake, a seething wave of nausea crawled through my entrails and I had a vision of being afloat within some putrid barrel of sewage. Up and down, the motion went, then left and right, almost at the same time. No wonder I am on the floor, I thought, the gaol fever has finally taken hold of me. I have seen its effects, as well as heard the slow death cries from the afflicted. But this is much worse than I had imagined. Pike had once told me that precious few, he being among them, have ever survived it. Reaching out into the darkness, I felt the cold iron hoops of a cask. Now the walls are moving in on me. Dear God, please let me die soon, I mentally pleaded.

What's that, I thought while feeling a rope's end swaying against my hair. Reaching up, I took hold and, puzzled how a rope could be in my cell, suddenly remembered the events of the previous day.

"I am on a ship and I have the fever," I said. "If I am discovered, I will surely be recognized and sent back to hang. That is, if the fever doesn't take me first."

"Who's there?" called a man's voice.

I bit my lip. Now I've done it, I thought.

"Who's there?" he repeated. "If you think you can hide, you got another thing coming. The captain gives out a dozen as easy as kiss my hand to those who shirk their duty. If you come out now without me having to go in after you, I won't breathe a word to anyone. But if

I have to crawl into that goddamn hold to get you, I'll take great joy in seeing your hide laid open, I will."

This proposal did not sound the least bit reasonable and I was not about to deliver myself into this man's hands, whoever he may be. At that moment, all I wanted to do was to be off this ship so that I may crawl into some other hole, preferably on land, and die. My fever was taking hold with every movement. And if I have anything in my stomach, it shall soon be forthcoming.

"I'm not going to ask you again," he continued. "If I don't hear from you this minute, I will have to report you to the first mate. I say, IF I DON'T HEAR FROM YOU—THIS MINUTE."

As if in response, my stomach gave a retching heave and sent what little remained of its contents onto my legs, there being no room to vomit onto the deck.

"I heard that," he said. "Sounds like water. If you've opened any of those casks—well, then you're into some real trouble mate. You might as well come out, the rum's not anywhere near you."

If there was another way out, I thought, I hadn't found it. And it appeared there was no use in hiding any longer. After coming so far, only to give myself away in such a foolish way was both humiliating and shaming. In order to save me from the noose, Laura had done for me what no other woman would ever conceive of doing. And Jim Bridges, who barely knew me, put himself in extreme danger. Giles was a complete surprise until I remembered how he adored Laura. The fact that he did it for her did not, in the least, reduce my debt to him. I was undone, for there was absolutely no way out but through the hatch where that man was standing. I was actually calling out. It must have been the fever. Well, I did give it my best. Perhaps I may get another chance at some later time.

"I am coming out," I said.

"Well, be quick about it then. I don't have all goddamn day."

When I had made my way to the top of the tier of casks, I could see the light of day shining down onto the bald head of a man who, squinting through leathery eyes, did his best to make me out in the darkness.

"And while you're crawlin' around back here, you best keep in mind what cask you opened. I told you there's no rum in there." After a pause, he said, "What in bloody hell is keeping you? My grandmother was old but not quite as slow."

It was extremely painful, crawling like a spider over those last three tiers. The previous day had taken a heavy toll on my body and now the cuts and abrasions to my shins, arms, ribs, and back had grown quite tender. Adding to this was the wretched state of my stomach. With no options, I raked my chafed and bleeding body over the tiers toward the bald man who stood in the light of the hatch.

As I made my way over the last tier into the open space beneath the hatch, he said, "One of the nippers—I might have known—and a might young to be going after the grog. What's your name, boy?"

The instant my feet touched the floor, my legs buckled under and I slid down onto my back where I found yet another tender area of my anatomy. Reaching out, I managed a hold upon the cordage used in securing the tiers and pulled myself upright. No sooner had I gained my footing than the blood seemed to have drained from my head and I dropped, this time only to my knees.

"Well would ya look at you?" he said. "You got your clothes all torn and bloody for your efforts. That'll teach ya."

My stomach convulsed and I spewed another stream of bile into the bilge.

"Ah! So that's it, is it," he smiled. "You got the sickness. Well, we'll put you to work and in a couple days you'll be good as new. What's your name boy?"

He doesn't know who I am, I thought. I've got to come up with a name. Suddenly, I had a vision of my father laying stone onto a fresh bed of mortar.

"Mason," I replied.

"Mason, who?"

My father's name was John, I thought. And I always liked that name. "John Mason, sir."

"Well, I don't recollect a Mason signed on, but there being so many new faces aboard, it is damn hard to remember them all." He scratched the back of his neck and asked, "And your watch, Mason?"

"I have no watch, sir. I believe it fell into the river."

"Your watch! What watch are you on?" he repeated, now very irritated. After receiving only a blank stare for a reply, he said, "Your assigned duty station, for the bleeding Christ—your watch! Don't look at me that way, boy. Can't you see I'm trying to prevent your kissing the gunner's daughter? There still might be a chance we can get you to your crew before the mate finds out where you've been…"

"I must tell you, sir, I haven't a clue as to what you speak. I was seeking warmth and crawled into a cask and fell asleep. Only when I awoke, I found I had been loaded aboard this ship. Could I trouble you for help in getting me ashore? I have taken ill and if you could assist me ashore, I have money enough to hire a chaise back to London where I might fetch a doctor."

"We got our own doctor, boy," the man said, while curiously looking over my face. "Was you knocked on the head? Cause you must be knocked on the head to try and sell a story like that." After a slight hesitation, he spat onto the floor and turned about to face a ladder that led up through an opening to the deck above.

"You wait right here, Mason. I don't recall your face but it don't mean you ain't on the register. I'm going to check the roster and be right back, so don't you go scurrying back into the hold, ya hear?"

After waiting several more stomach-wrenching minutes, I heard a number of footsteps approaching the ladder before the bald man descended.

"It seems you are not on the ship's register, Mason. You shall have to come with me."

"Where are you taking me?" I asked.

"I am bringing you to see the lieutenant," he said.

"Must we disturb the other passengers? Could you not just put me on the next river taxi to shore and all will be forgotten?"

"Up the ladder with you. You can forget about your river taxi, for there are none to be found here."

Swallowing hard, I pulled my aching body up the ladder behind the bald man.

The ascension of the ladder was a sickening experience, for every movement I made felt as though gravity threatened to pull me back down. After nearing the top, my feet slipped and, if not for my grip on the smoothly polished rungs, I would have fallen backwards into the hold. As it was, I struck my swollen shins against the hard wood, sending lightning bolts of pain up my spine.

Once I had gained the top of the ladder, I found that I was in a dimly lit part of the ship where partitioned spaces hid various compartments. Taking a quick look around, I noticed what appeared to be some sort of quarters for the sick, while another space that was curtained off carried the heavy odor of gunpowder.

A tug on my shirt returned my attention to the bald man who bid me follow him up yet another ladder. With trembling legs, I managed the climb to the next level where I came upon a group of uniformed persons standing on a deck that was lined with huge iron cannons. I say persons, for they were not all men. Three were boys near my years. None of the group spoke, but only looked on with haughty unforgiving smiles. Did they recognize me from the picture? I wondered.

A tall, lean man eyed me indignantly before crossing over to where I stood. His uniform differed slightly from the others in that the tail of the blue coat was much longer and stopped at the knee. His nose was long and thin with large nostrils that flared slightly as though he were perpetually sniffing the air. Once his round protruding eyes gave me a thorough looking over, he turned his back and, in a tone that was slightly nasal, said, "You will come with me," and strutted away.

I followed him, staggering and stumbling down the double rows of cannon to another ladder situated near the centre of the ship.

After gaining the top of this ladder, I again lost my footing. Gravity seemed to have gone awry for, instead of down the ladder, I fell sideways, slamming my hip into the unforgiving iron knob on the back of another cannon.

The uniformed man, completely indifferent to my plight, only eyed me with disgust and, at length, snapped, "Pull yourself together, boy. You are about to meet the captain."

Getting to my feet, I had had enough of this bruising and was determined to not fall down. With a firm grip upon the ladder rail, I set my legs in a wide stance.

The uniformed man gave a slightly discernable smirk and continued up the ladder.

I climbed the steps taking care to hold fast at each step and, before reaching the top rung, a knotted rope was thrust into my hand by the uniformed man who said angrily, "Take hold of this until you have gotten your footing. Do you understand? Do not let go until you have your footing!"

I nodded my understanding before continuing up to the next deck.

As I stood at the top of the ladder, it became apparent why he had been so insistent upon my taking a firm hold upon the rope. With my head through the hatchway, I clung to the knotted rope while the wind slapped me in the face like a great wet hand. We were in the open sea, the bow ramming through huge waves as they burst over the gunnels carrying spray and great deluges of water down the length of the ship. Each succeeding wave sent the ship's bow high into the air before falling violently back into the sea.

Straining my eyes to see through the spray, I glanced in every direction as the ship crested a lofty wave. To my horror, I could not see land.

Dear God, I thought, as the forlorn ache of grief rang throughout my soul, will I ever see my family again? My stomach churned and I started heaving just as a stout fellow who, taking a firm grip of my arm and shoulder, plucked me from the hatchway and walked me to the side of the ship, saying, "To leeward, mate. Always vomit and spit to leeward."

Once I had relieved my stomach, I turned round and faced the cold unforgiving stare of the uniformed man. He said nothing and stepped out toward the back of the ship. I wanted to stay where I stood, holding onto the rail. To let go seemed madness as I would surely be blown into the sea by this great wind, yet the fellow who had helped me to the side gave me a nudge. Reluctantly, I let go the rail and, with my legs wide as though straddling a horse, I made my way past many an amused stare from the ship's company.

We passed uncounted ropes that ran from the ship's side up masts to the billowing and taut sails and I couldn't help wondering how anyone could possibly know what each was for. At the end of a narrow gangway, one of two that ran along both sides of the ship over a section of the deck below, I came to the officer who had given me the cold stare. Avoiding his eyes, I looked down at the deck below and noticed another row of cannon. So this is what the London Evening Post referred to as our walls of oak, I thought, just as a wave broke over the bow sending spray and a raging river of seawater down the length of the ship.

"Watch where you are stepping, you fool," the officer said, his hand taking hold of my shoulder as I nearly fell over the side of the gangway. "Sorry, sir," I mumbled, half doubled over and ready to heave again.

"And I have to present this lump of shite to the captain," he said with disgust. "Bosun, lend a hand here. Rig a sea pump and see if you can't wash off some of this filth. The captain is in his cabin and I will not be responsible for fouling the air with this miscreant's stench."

"Aye, aye, sir!" the barrel-chested man said, as he plucked me up with one arm and carried me like so much baggage, my stomach retching all the while.

Two other men produced a metal contraption and secured a section of hose to it while one began thrusting upon a lever connected to the top of the contraption. Within seconds a gush of ice cold seawater hit me full in the face, driving me to the deck onto my knees. Choking and gasping for air, I struggled to keep my wits as the unforgiving blast continued.

After being thoroughly soaked, I was carried back to the officer and set upon my feet. With much difficulty, I followed him back down the ladder to a doorway at the back of the ship where stood a sentry in a uniform of another kind, red jacket with white waistcoat and breeches over black high-top boots.

The first lieutenant, as I was soon to learn was the officer's title, told the sentry that the miscreant was here to see the captain. The man then tapped the cabin door with the hilt of his sword and announced our presence.

After a short pause, an angry, deep voice from within said, "Enter!"

The sentry opened the door and Bengs motioned for me to step into the cabin.

As I followed the lieutenant through the captain's quarters, I noticed that this part of the ship was not unlike a proper lodging, complete with bedchamber, dining room, windows across the back above a settee, much cabinet space, and a large desk in the centre of the room where the captain was seated while peering over some papers.

Post Captain Thadeus Cole was a stout man with thick untamed brows and midnight black hair neatly tied back into a club-shaped configuration. As I stood before him, he appeared quite unaware of my presence and I took a miniscule degree of comfort in this; I had no more desire to be the object of this man's attention than I would that of a hangman. He picked up a quill, dipping it into a small ink cup recessed into the desktop and, with his short, thick leathery fingers, made a few notations onto a ledger. The sleeve of his coat displayed wide gold embroidered ribbon patterns embellished by gold anchor buttons that raked the desktop as he wrote.

Perhaps he needn't notice me at all, I thought. If only I could scurry away like my old furry friend Peter and conceal myself within the ship again.

But then his deep-set weathered eyes left their focus in the ledger and fell upon me. I am not sure whether it was the lurch of the ship or the stare from those eyes that made me nearly lose my footing again. The last time I had felt such command of power was in the presence of my dear father.

"So, this is our stowaway?" he said in a deep resonating voice.

A brief silence fell until he broke it by thrumming his fingers on the desk, saying, "Miscreant, criminal, guttersnipe?"

"Yes sir," I replied, realizing he must have recognized me from the posters scattered about London.

"And I could have you hanged from the yardarm of this ship on the morrow, perhaps even today, if I saw fit to do so. That is what we do to spies."

"But, sir!" I exclaimed, wondering how, in spite of my escape, I had still managed to be facing the noose.

"Silence!"

I felt a grip upon my shoulder from the first mate and, as I looked up, his expression was most threatening.

"However," the captain went on, "you seem a bit too young and stupid to be a spy."

His mouth soured for a second, as though disappointed, before he went on to say, "So I will rate you ships' boy and put you to work. Once you have been signed on as such, you will be subject to the discipline of this ship." After a pause, he said, "You will sign aboard?" which was more a statement than a question.

What choice did I have? They obviously don't know who I am and that, in itself, is a precious bit of good fortune.

"Yes, sir. I would be most honored to sign aboard and serve the King," I said. Being completely out of my element, I thought it prudent to lay it on thick. As in Newgate, these people had me with no possible means of escape.

"Very well, then. Mister Bengs, have... What is your name, boy?"

My true name nearly left my lips before I remembered the name I had decided upon while in the hold. "John Mason, sir!"

"Have Mason sign aboard and ask the doctor to look him over. I am sure he will want to disinfect our new recruit." Rate him boy, third class and, if the doctor finds him fit, place him on the larboard watch in the waist."

"Aye, sir!" Bengs said, while taking hold of my ragged sleeve.

"Oh, thank you, sir!" I said, doing my utmost to sound appreciative.

"Oh, you will not be so thankful by the week's end. Now get out of my cabin."

"Yes, sir! But there is one thing, sir."

"What is it?" A fat bottom lip protruded, his expression turning to steel.

"I believe I am dying, sir."

"Dying?"

"Yes sir. I feel deathly ill, sir. I believe I am dying."

His fingers resumed their thrumming as he said, "While on this voyage, I am certain there will be many occasions where you will wish to die. And, at some point, your wish might even be granted, but not today."

"Yes, sir," I said, realizing there would be no sympathy for me.

Turning to Bengs, he said, "Mr. Bengs, be so good as to see that Mason is seen by the doctor."

"Aye, sir," said Lieutenant Bengs and I followed him through the door.

Once out of the captain's cabin, Bengs turned and, bringing his long thin nose close, said with spraying breath, "From this moment forward you will say, 'Aye, Aye, sir!' when addressing an officer."

"Aye, aye, sir!" I said, while wiping his spittle from my eyes.

Apparently satisfied with my response, he straightened himself and said flatly, "Come with me."

"Aye, aye, sir," I blurted out while following him out onto the quarterdeck.

There we came upon a tall, powerfully built man wearing short canvas breeches with black and white striped shirt, a costume which appeared to be worn by most of the crew. Sporting a lump of tobacco in his cheek, he spat with great skill directing the black wad downwind and over the rail without coming into contact with any part of the ship.

After studying the sea and sky for an instant, Bengs adressed him, saying, "Mr. Douty, take in the t'gallants and courses and single reef the tops'ls."

Near Bengs stood a thin boy of perhaps twelve years who, beneath a low leather hat was dressed in white breeches and buckled shoes with a weathered blue topcoat. When Bengs had finished with Mr. Douty, he turned to the boy and said, "Mister Tomkins!"

"Aye, Sir!" the boy snapped back while stiffening his small body into a wishbone posture.

"Wait here and keep an eye on Mason until I return," Bengs ordered, before stepping behind a door whereupon he returned with a board and paper. Taking up a quill, he dipped it into an ink bottle that was set into a notch in the board and, handing the quill to me, said, "Sign here!"

The sheet contained a list of signatures from the entire crew, some signing with an X, some with their names, however most were done with either an odd scribble or an X.

"An X will do!" Bengs said with irritation.

"May I sign with my name sir?"

"So, you are not illiterate," he said, somewhat surprised. "Very well then, be quick about it."

It was the first time I had signed my name as John Mason, a name I would carry for the rest of my life.

Addressing Tomkins, he said, "Take him to see the doctor. Give the doctor my compliments and would he be so good as to examine our new ship's boy." After a pause, he raised a hand and said, "Before he sees the doctor, find Mister Sawyer and see that he is provided with slops. If the doctor finds him fit, take him to the waist and give my compliments to Mister Hershel, and would he place Mason on the watch bill assigning him to the larboard watch in the waist."

"Aye, aye, sir!" Tomkins' stiffness relaxed slightly after we left the lieutenant and, taking hold of my arm, he pointed to a hatchway not ten paces from us.

I staggered toward it and, though my stomach wrenched, I willed myself to get there.

Once at the hatchway, Tomkins handed me the end of the knotted rope above the ladder. Upon seeing my hesitation, he said, "We haven't all day. Now get down the ladder."

"Give me a moment, I'm going to vomit."

"Damn lubber!" Tomkins uttered in disgust. "Over here then," he said, pointing to the ship's side, "and be quick about it. Here—into this pail." He handed me a wooden pail which had been hanging from a rope tied to the rail. "That's it. And when you're finished shitin' through your teeth, empty it over the side. And do take notice that this is the leeward side."

My blank stare gave him pause.

"Lubber, the leeward side is the downwind side. Remember that or your shite will end up in your face, which I am not concerned about, mind you. It is the ship that I care about and don't want your vomit all over her clean decks.

After heaving my stomach's contents into the bucket, I tossed it overboard,

"Here, drink this," he said, handing me a ladle of water he had drawn from a cask that was secured to one of the vertical black ropes along the ship's side. The black ropes, upon closer inspection, appeared to be taking up the strain of the masts as the ship rolled from side to side.

"Thank you," I said while taking the ladle.

"Thank you, SIR!" He reminded me. "And don't put your mouth on it, you goddamn blackguard. Tilt your head back and pour it into your mouth. Everyone shares this and no one wishes to drink your spit."

It wasn't for not being accustomed to being called a blackguard that I took offense, but that it came from someone I could have easily thrown over the side had I not been in such a wretched state.

I took a splash in the mouth, as well as across my face before the wind took the rest of it back to the sea. Handing the ladle to the little bastard, I said condescendingly, "Most obliged for your generosity, sir," and climbed down the ladder.

Two decks below the fresh air of the ship's waist, my nostrils took in the dense putrid odor that had wafted up from the ship's hold, a mixture of sweat, farts, and tar which combined with the residual of the vomit at the back of my throat. If not for the dominating aroma of tar, I could have closed my eyes and fancied myself to be back in my old filthy cell in Newgate.

Mr. Sawyer, the purser who, a man of perhaps eighteen stone, sat with his ponderous stomach resting upon a scarred mahogany desk while poring over his ledger. With the wave of a heavy hand, he stated he was not to be disturbed.

The purser's mate took us to one of several large trunks and, opening one, withdrew some of the odd clothing along with a straw hat that I had seen the non-officer sort wearing on the ship. My only consolation was that I would not be seen in this attire on the streets of London.

With the new, though extremely stiff, clothes stacked and folded, I carried them as Tomkins led me to another cabin whereupon I was told to remain outside the door.

Tomkins knocked and, after a few seconds entered the sick berth.

While I waited, a resonant voice penetrated the door saying, "You would bring a louse-ridden street urchin to my sick berth?"

"I am under orders from Lieutenant Bengs, sir," Tomkins explained.

"Orders? Well, I suppose I shall have a word with Mister Bengs when next we speak. Still, orders or no, it does not excuse you from thinking, young man. To be an officer is to have the capacity to THINK, is it not?"

I could hear the doctor tapping Tomkin's head with some wooden object and I dared not peer into the room to see what the object might be.

"Take him back up to the waist and rig the wash deck pump," he ordered. "I'll be up directly with the delousing powder."

Wash deck pump again, delousing powder, this doesn't sound good. Do they mean to freeze me to death?

Following Tomkins up the ladder to the gun deck, I struggled to avoid collision with cannons or snaring my feet in coils of rope while stumbling along the ever-pitching and slanting deck. The banistered ladders were no less difficult to traverse due to their steep incline as it combined with the tossing motion of the ship to throw one's feet clear from its steps.

"See here, Tomkins, sir," I said, "I have already been washed. Must I do it again?"

Tomkins smiled and said, "I know you have."

Being carted through the streets of London to a gallows could not be more humiliating than standing naked before a ship of strangers and being hit with blasts of icy seawater. Each pulse of the pump drove uncontrollable tremors through my body. In short order I lost my footing and fell face down onto the deck, while my stomach wrenched forth bloody bile that the pump quickly washed into the scuppers and over the ship's side.

Just when I felt I could take it no more, an authoritative voice said, "Enough!" and the pumping ceased. The blank stares from the seamen involved in the operation, as well as the few idlers who were looking on were a bit puzzling, for I half expected sadistic laughter to be added to my degradation.

"He's a livin' skeleton!" I heard one wide-eyed man say while another muttered half aloud, "White as a sheet, he is too! Been kept in a cellar or a gaol for a long time to get like that."

It was the bosun who stepped up and gave the coves the choice of either returning to their duty stations or suffer the rope's end.

"Cover your eyes!" the doctor said before throwing an awful concoction of powdery substance over my head and brushing it onto my body with a stiff bristled brush. It was not until after this final baptism that Tomkins handed me my new attire. Sitting on the deck, I quickly donned the stiff, nearly wooden breeches and shirt before staggering to my feet.

"Get him to sick berth!" the doctor ordered. "He'll be no good for a day or two. Once you've installed him into a hammock, have the cook send down some portable soup. Lean, mind you, yet hot."

Tomkins responded with, "Yes, doctor!" which puzzled me that he hadn't used the, "Aye, aye, sir!" that I had been instructed to use.

Two decks below the open air of the quarterdeck, I found myself back in sick berth.

"There's your berth. Or should I say, your beddy-bye?" Tomkins sneered, throwing out his thin calloused hand to indicate a five foot length of canvas. Hanging at shoulder height, it was secured at each end by a section of rope tethered to an iron bar that had been nailed to the overhead deck beams, apparently for that purpose.

"What am I to do with it," I asked, while another surge of nausea forced me to double over.

"What do you think, Johnny Newcome," he sneered. "You can puke into it but you will have to clean it up afterward. That is, unless you like wallowing in vomit."

What in God's name does he speak of, I puzzled. Everything was now spinning, as well as up, down, and sideways. If he doesn't start making sense, I am more than willing to direct my next fountain into the little jackass's face.

"Just take hold of the bar and pull yourself up so as you are straddling it like a horse."

"Like a horse?" I asked.

"Look," he said angrily, "I will show you. Mind you, you had better watch closely for I shall only do it once." Taking hold of the iron bar above his head, he swung his body upward and hooked one leg over the midsection of the canvas before letting it take his weight. Then, using his feet, he pried the folds apart near the centre and sank into it like a moth in a cocoon. It actually appeared comfortable, I thought. I was later to find it to be the only thing of comfort on the entire ship.

After several attempts, I found I was too weak to raise my legs into the air and, exhausted, I dropped to the deck. After a minute passed, I attempted it again but to no avail. After two more failed attempts, Tomkins was at the end of his patience and he reluctantly offered assistance. Taking hold of my legs while I maintained a firm grip on the iron bar, he pushed my butt upward until I could get my legs over the mid-section of the hammock. As I rested there, he spread the canvas and shoved my legs into the end so that I could further spread the hammock with my feet stretching the cloth wide enough to contain me. Once I had myself securely in, I thanked him and almost instantly fell into the depths of sleep.

I slept for what seemed an eternity, waking at intervals to be fed soup and swallow water. At other times, a ghostly figure would help me down so that I may sit upon a seat of ease which was comprised of a wooden bucket covered by a flat plank with a hole in the centre.

Each time I woke and sipped the hot gruel, a concoction given me by the ghostly figure who I had found to be Mister Tims, the doctor's assistant, I could feel my strength return in degrees. It was during the naps that I passed through a myriad of dreams of walks through the park with my family, or evenings at the theatre with Laura and Pike. Yet, each time I woke with the fresh sense of being so close to home I was confronted with the unsettling fact that, as I had slept, all the people that I loved, all those places of which I was so familiar, were farther away still.

CHAPTER TWELVE

Sick berth was an eerie compartment situated deep within the ship and, although its function was to care for the sick, it reeked of urine, tar, vomit, and things in various stages of decomposition. The stench was not unlike that within the walls of Newgate and, if not for sleeping within the confines of a hammock, I would not have fared well there. This strange manner of rest, however, was made ever stranger by the frequent babble from Rudy, the cook's mate who had gone insane from the effects of an elixir he had purchased while in London, a potion which was supposed to relieve him of seasickness. Although I had heard the ravings of many tortured minds while in Newgate, this was the first time I had observed its effects.

The doctor had done all he could to flush the evil liquid from his stomach and could only sit by while Rudy fought to free himself of his bonds. After two days of his screams, his gaping mouth at last fell silent. Hours later, his jaw locked with the muscles of his mouth twisting into a convulsive rictus. Another hour passed before he vomited blood through his nostrils with such force that it squirted between his clenched teeth. Unable to breathe, although the doctor made every effort to pry open his mouth, Rudy drowned in his own blood. The next day, he was sewn into his hammock with an eight-pound round shot at his feet, the final stitch oddly being placed through his blood-encrusted nose. Soon thereafter, I was told, he had a decent service before being put overboard.

The whole ordeal was so disconcerting that it left everyone within the sick berth drained and exhausted. The odor of Rudy's expelled blood remained to decompose with the other aromas beneath the floorboards long after his tortured corpse was sent to the bottom of the ocean.

It was three full days before I had recovered to the extent that I could keep down solid foods. Having daily eaten nothing but the gruel referred to as loblolly, I feared my skin would soon be taking on the greenish chalky colour that it left in the bottom of my bowl. But then they brought down a dish called lobscourse, a combination of salt beef, stewed vegetables and spices mixed with crumbled biscuit and my mouth filled with saliva from the first waft of its aroma. And it was with this meal that I became acquainted with the seagoing bread commonly referred to as "ship's biscuit" or "hardtack." It was not anything near the warm wheat flavored loaf found in most London chop houses. Indeed, this item was rock hard all the way down to the Royal navy's broad arrow which is scrupulously branded into each piece. In fact, it is so hard that, if not carefully nibbled at, one can expect to break one's teeth upon it. It is recommended to first let it soak in hot coffee or soup before making any contact with your teeth.

Another discovery I made was that I could stand on the deck in sick berth without falling down. To the inexperienced observer, it may seem to be a simple feat, yet getting to the deck of a ship from a hammock does take a degree of study. First, you must take hold of the hammock rail and let yourself down. Before you set your feet onto the deck, you must hang there for a few seconds to get the feel of where the deck is, for the ship is in continual motion. The motion of the ship is generally from side to side while your hammock is following the pull of gravity, keeping it more or less even with the horizon, rendering one within it the sense of not swinging at all. It is not until one's feet are planted on deck and he has let go of the hammock rail that he feels the greater part of the ship's motion and must endeavor to find balance within it.

Shortly after Rudy's death I was brought up to the quarterdeck to take in fresh air. I must say that the doctor had managed to improve the air in sick berth by having some of the men rig air scoops from the gun deck above. The air that made its way down to us, however, was in no comparison to the brisk clean air of the open sea. As I stood on the pitching, rolling deck feeling the sun penetrating my pale skin, I had to shield my eyes from the burning glare. As my eyes fully adjusted, I found myself surrounded by a spider's web of rope running to and from all points of the ship. Men were everywhere, bare legged and bare foot climbing the masts and on deck, while some were hauling on ropes as thick as my thighs. Beyond the ship, I saw the endless expanse of water with no hint of land in any direction.

The doctor, standing to my right, glanced up at the sails while the sun caught the red hues of his disheveled hair making the strands appear as though on fire. He said, "Mason, I have notified the captain of your progress and, for the now, you may return to sick berth until the end of the first dog watch. When the bell strikes the second dog, you will begin your usefulness by reporting to Lieutenant Bengs for duty. I believe he will be placing you on the larboard watch in the waist."

"Aye, aye, sir. I shall be most happy for the opportunity to earn my way," I said. "Where might I find them, sir?"

His winged brows arched upward as he asked, "Find who?"

"The dogs, sir," I replied.

"What in blazes are you speaking of, boy?" he asked. Then, clasping the back of my neck with one hand, he pried my eyelid open with his fingers, staring deep into my eye, and asked, "Have you been bumped on the head?"

"Why, no, sir. Did you not mention there were two, the first and second dog, which the bell shall be striking. Perhaps while I am watching them," he turned my head slowly from side to side while I went on, "I might endeavor to keep them away from the bell so as not to disturb the crew with that annoying ringing I have heard since I first came aboard."

"Hmmph!" the doctor murmured while his lips fought desperately to restrain the half-smile forming beneath his hand, "I am sorry to say there are no dogs on this ship, though we could do with a few to keep up morale."

Releasing his hold on my neck, he withdrew a tobacco stained ivory pipe from his waistcoat, inserted it between his teeth and produced a pouch from his other pocket. Taking care not to lose the tobacco to the wind, he shielded it between his coat and, bringing the pipe down to it, poured a measure into the bowl. "The dog watch is a station of two hours duration," he said, replacing the pipe between his teeth, "where you will be kept quite busy." Then, he spoke in a low tone as though it were a carefully kept secret, yet I suspected he did so as not to alert the surrounding ears of the crew to my innate ignorance of sea life. "The bell you hear is the signal for the end, as well as the beginning, of each watch."

"How long are these watches, sir?" I whispered, in keeping with our secret.

"Generally four hours," he said, "however, the dog watches, as they are called, are two hours in duration so that the men won't be working the same hours of every day."

Placing a firm hand upon my shoulder, he went on, "You see, each day their dog watch is rotated from the first to the second and back respectively. This alternates their duty time as well as their hours of sleep, making it fair for everyone aboard."

"Approximately how many are aboard, sir?"

While scratching through the black stubble of his chin, he replied, "Well, if you were to include the marines, of which there are forty four, there are exactly three hundred and six men and boys aboard. Which, I am told by the captain, is a good complement for a frigate of this size, that is, being a fifth rate man-of-war."

"Is your work governed by these watches as well, sir?" I asked.

"No, no, I am the doctor and, as such, not bound by any rules of the crew. I shall ask the captain to appoint you a sea daddy to teach you how a ship is run for I am not the one to be explaining such things as I do not fully understand it all myself, being primarily a medico before a seaman. And I shall advise your watch captain to go easy on you for the first day but after that, you shall be expected to pull your weight as well or better than any of the other men, that is, the other ship's boys. Oh, to be sure, you will have a great deal to learn but there will be plenty of time for that."

"How long will we be at sea, sir?" I asked. As long as he was giving me his confidence, I may as well glean as much information as I can.

"Well, I suppose we will be on this leg of the voyage for close on two months."

"If you don't mind my asking, sir, when will we be returning to England?"

"I cannot say," he said, his forehead furrowing. "No one knows for sure, perhaps not even the captain. We could be sent back straightaway, or we could be required to stay for a year. With this war with the Frogs, it's no telling how long we may be away."

"We are at war with frogs, sir?"

"The bloody French! Christ! Where have you been these last two months, boy?"

"I'd rather not say, sir."

He gave me the raised brow and smiled, saying, "I suppose on this ship, it is of no concern what you have been up to. You are in the Royal Navy now and are bound to the captain who will be your god, so to speak, for as long as you are on this ship. I am about to turn you over to him this evening. Better go below and get what rest you can before they put you to work. And be sure to eat your full portion at dinner for you shall need it."

"Aye, aye, sir!" I said, while descending the ladder. Once on the lower deck, I was surprised to see that I no longer had difficulty keeping my footing. The whole motion thing had come to feel quite natural to me.

Until recently, I feared I would die from the gaol fever and I could not risk telling the doctor of my suspicions without revealing to him my criminal past. All the while me thinking he was wrong in his diagnosis of seasickness, I found he had been right all along. I shall live after all.

How capital, I thought. No hangman's noose, no wasting away to a horrible death from gaol fever. True, I was in strange surroundings but, upon the whole, it mattered little when considering that I had a new chance at life. The idea struck me that it was not entirely without possibility that I may someday see my family again.

Heeding the doctor's advice, I ate all of my dinner using my wooden spoon to scrape clean the bottom of my one foot square wooden plate. They all displayed the broad arrow brand to remind one that the Royal Navy owned everything aboard. I would not have been surprised to find it on the fatty slab of salt pork that I had just consumed and I must confess that I did look for it.

After dinner, I went up the ladder to the quarterdeck to report for duty. Attired in my stiff and chafing slops, I was amiss to find my duty station. Men were gathering forward, aft, (terms I surmised meant the front and the back of the ship) and in the middle. Remembering the doctor's statement of my being part of the larboard watch in the waist, I determined that I must belong to the group in the middle, given that the ship could be likened to a person's body. As I neared the middle of the ship, Lieutenant Bengs stood near a mast with a slate in his hand. Catching my eye, he motioned for me to continue forward toward a group of men.

"Mason!" he said irritably, "See that man there."

As I approached the group gathered about the middle of the

ship, I heard my new name called out. Raising my hand high so that I could be acknowledged, I waited silently for a reply.

A red faced man with thick fiery golden brows barked, "Mason!" even louder while glaring straight at me, though I kept my hand raised, shaking it well in his view so as to leave no doubt that I was his man.

As the man's countenance changed to that of a footpad bent on clubbing me to the ground, a fellow ship's boy, much my junior, elbowed me and whispered, "Say 'Aye.'"

"Aye, aye, sir!"

The man retorted, "Don't you ever call me sir! It's Maxwell to you. You is number twelve. Next time I won't say yer name, I'll just say 'count' and you will say twelve once somebody says eleven. Ya got that?"

"Aye, s—! Uh, Aye, aye, Maxwell!" I said, hoping I had it correct.

"Just an 'aye' will do. We meet here at the beginning of each watch and if yer late, you'll be kissing the gunner's daughter. Is that understood?" Maxwell growled.

"Aye!" I blurted. I could not imagine there were any women aboard and harbored no desire to discover the consequences of his statement. From that point onward I resolved that I would be religiously on time.

After he had given assignments to the rest of the waist and mainmast crew, he turned his attention to me, saying, "The lieutenant has ordered that Harvey, here, is to be your sea daddy."

I addressed a copper-skinned man harboring a wide stiff-set jaw. His large ivory teeth displayed a pleasing smile as he held out a heavily calloused hand. Placing my hand in his where it nearly disappeared within his horny skinned grip, I shook it as well as I could and said, "Pleased to make your acquaintance, sir."

Shooting a glance to the other men of the crew, he said with a chuckle, "At least he's got manners."

One of the boys stepped out from the group and, with an impish grin, mimicked me like a parrot, saying, "Pleased to make your acquaintance, your majesty!"

Harvey's opened hand shot out in a flash, cuffing the boy on the cheek saying, "Enough of your lip," and I noticed several strands of his ebony locks had gotten free from his tied club catching the wind as he turned his head back to face me.

While we waited for our instructions, I observed Harvey from my peripheral as he stood with his legs slightly spread while his hands, large and powerful, hung out away from his torso as though ready to take hold of a line or rope at a second's notice. His attire was similar to the other sailors but what set him apart was that he displayed neither judgment nor condemnation in his weather beaten eyes.

"By being your sea daddy," the mainmast captain said, while aiming a long callused finger at Harvey, "I mean he will be teaching you how to be a worthy *Deception*."

I was extremely confident in my ability to deceive, for I had excelled to the highest approbation of my former teacher and betrayer, Zack, yet I could see no place for it on a ship of His Majesty's Royal Navy. To have a new teacher, or "sea daddy," attempting to teach the art to me placed me in most awkward position. Therefore, with no little trepidation, asked, "Please forgive me, Maxwell but—why must I be worthy of deception?"

He stared in disbelief, saying, "By the nailed Christ! You been on this ship for three days and nights and don't know the name of her?"

"Well, er—no, I suppose I do not," I shamefully confessed.

"That's it!" Maxwell said, throwing up a hand. "He's all yours, Harvey. I don't care what it takes, just get 'im in shape by the week's end or it's the daughter for 'im. We need every hand and I'll abide no shirkers."

"Aye," Harvey said, his wide jaw jutting out with conviction, "I'll get him into shape." Then, turning to me, he said in a low voice. "We don't wish to see your backside bloody now do we, lad?"

"Not if I have any say in the matter," I said.

"Very well then, come with me and, if you do everything I tell ya, you just might be able to keep your hide."

After taking several steps he stopped, and turning to face me, said, "Well, to start with, this ship is named *Deception*. And every man jack of the crew are called *Deceptions*."

After a long pause, whereupon he looked me over from head to foot, he scratched his scalp, which was somewhat visible beneath his thinning brown hair, and said with degree of disappointment, "You've never been near a ship, much less aboard one, have ya?"

"Well, I've been to the Thames and have many times been aboard a river taxi but, as for ships—no, I have not been nearer than that," I admitted.

Letting out a heavy sigh, he shook his head, saying, "Why am I always the one?" Then, taking in another deep breath, he slapped his meaty hands together, grimaced, and with newfound acceptance, said, "All right, we've a lot of work to do. Take hold of that line."

Within the vicinity of the mainmast, I made my way from pin rail to cleat while repeating the names of each line as Harvey called them out.

The enormity of what I must learn between now and the week's end became painfully apparent. If I didn't learn the prescribed information within the required time frame, I would suffer the beating of the gunner's daughter, presumably much more forceful than what I was used to from my school teacher back in London. Thus I was driven day and night to be continuously identifying, verifying, and putting to memory the various ropes and lines.

As I worked my way down the *Deception's* length, I found that the most impressive thing about the ship was her masts and rigging. The standing rigging which supported the masts alone encompassed miles of rope. A combination of shrouds and backstays, the tarred rope ran from various points on the mast to the ship's sides as well as down the length of the ship to connect to other masts so as to give support to each other.

The thing I needed to learn more than any other was the location on deck of the running rigging for setting and stowing the sails. Ropes or lines called "sheets" were used to hold the lower corners of the sails to the yards; halyards to heave the yards aloft in order to pull the upper portion of the topsails up tight when setting that sail; clewlines to lift up the clews at the lower corners of the sails when they were to be taken in; buntlines to haul up the bunt, or middle of the sails to the yards and leech lines to pull in the leech or side of the sail. For the fore and aft running triangular sails there were downhauls to haul down the sails and brails which were used to bring them into the mast or stay. Additionally, there were the many braces that led to the ends of the yards and which were used to pull the yards round to the most desirable angle so as to trim their sails in order to the take the wind on the best point.

Although there was much to recall, I found that with continual familiarity, the whole configuration contained a feasible logic. The ropes or line for the lowest sails, or courses, ran down the forward stay in a set order. The lines of the next sails, or topsails, which were set above the courses, ran down topmast stay in the same order and so on. Topgallant and royal sheets along with their clewlines and bowlines were run down and belayed on deck at the fiferails along with the sheets and halyards.

Though I needed to learn a great deal, I felt confident that I could, for there was within me a strong desire to know everything about the ship. In addition, I harboured an increasing compulsion to scale each and every one of those masts.

Oddly, Harvey repeatedly cautioned me about going aloft, saying, "Are you certain you're not going to come all froze up on me when you are fifty or a hundred feet above deck? I don't relish the job of prying you loose from the shrouds, nor do I care to be the one who has to haul you down while you cling to me like a cat what's gone mad."

"Oh, I have climbed hundreds of trees, even taller than these masts. It must be glorious up there," I said.

"It ain't like no tree in the park, boy," Harvey warned. "Them masts are swinging in a circle whilst the ship rises and falls in the swell; the farther up, the more the swing. You got to have one hand for yourself and one for the ship at all times," he said, while searching my eyes for any hint of fear.

He went on, still maintaining his stare, "You're gonna either fall into the sea where you will drown before we get a boat hauled out, or you're gonna hit a few spars, snapping off an arm that gets caught in the riggin' before you hit the deck in a pile of bloody bones."

Suddenly the image of my father lying broken on the church's stone floor came to mind and I gained immediate respect for what he was telling me.

"I understand, Harvey. I will never let go of the ship. Please believe me, I have no fear of heights and I do love to climb," I explained.

We went up. Taking hold of the great main shrouds that support the mast from either side of the ship's hull, I placed my feet into the ratlines, a series of horizontal ropes sewn to the shrouds so that they may be used as a ladder.

Making my way upward with Harvey trailing behind, we came to the area called the futtock shrouds which is just below the fighting top, a platform which functions in spreading the topmast shrouds, as well as supporting men who fire muskets at enemy ships during battle. This was the most difficult part of the climb for, in this section, the shrouds travel away from the mast upward and around the fighting top before angling back toward the topmast cross trees, the junction where the topmast connects to the topgallant mast. When climbing this section of the shrouds, one must time his ascent to the roll of the ship and, when the time is right, take hold and climb quickly while the ship is heeling away so that the futtock shrouds are more toward the vertical. Otherwise you might find yourself hanging by your hands beneath the futtock shrouds with no foothold. The girth of the futtock shrouds at the topmast are so thick that I could not get my fingers around them, forcing me to hold onto the ratlines, a dangerous hold should another sailor climb down from above and step onto my hand. As a consequence, one must call out that he is coming aloft before climbing this section of shrouds.

The view from the fighting top platform was the most beautiful I had heretofore ever seen. Standing on the platform, I was surrounded by miles of running and standing rigging; the sun-bleached canvas billowed out like fluffy white pillows on all three masts while, far below, the bow battered through wave after wave, each throwing up a streak of water that disintegrated as the wind caught it, taking it leeward and transforming it into a mist which caught the rays of the sun to form a magnificent rainbow.

The brilliant red coats of the marines' uniforms on deck below were a deep contrast to the sailors' white duck trousers and striped shirts. Officers in their marine blue coats and white waistcoats were stepping about the ship relaying orders from the poop deck, where the lieutenant conned the ship making sure that every man did his duty. The tall masts heeled over from the pressure of the wind upon them, forcing the fighting top platform to lean nearly forty-five degrees from the horizontal.

Taking a firm grip on the shrouds, I could feel the tension increasing within the twisted fibers of the tar coated hemp as the ship leaned over, or heeled, for these lines were taking up the strain from the leaning weight of the entire main topmast. When we had gained the topmast crosstrees, we stopped to lay out onto the topsail yard, a long tree shaped horizontal member that supported the great square sail.

The footropes running beneath the yard were nothing like stepping out onto a tree limb. Not only did the narrow rope cut into the arches of my bare feet but, when Harvey stepped down onto a nearby section, his weight, taking up the slack, thrust me upward. Had it not been for my heeding his instruction of one hand for the ship, I would have been thrown over the yard to the deck some sixty feet below.

The thrill of this traverse became more breathtaking each second for, when we reached the end of the yard, or yardarm, we were at one moment in the chilly shadow of the sails above the leaning deck, and the next, suspended some eighty feet over the foam crested waves with the warm rays of the sun on our skin.

I wanted to stay there but Harvey put a leathery hand on my arm and, with a tobacco stained grin, said, "We ain't there yet mate. Come on!"

Our next stop was at the topgallant yard, the uppermost spar. That is, the topgallant was the uppermost yard for the moment. For at any time, wind permitting, and if the captain is so inclined, a royal mast and yard might be rigged. A royal mast is a temporary mast that is placed above the topgallant in order to gain more speed. It is a light spar that is hauled up and set in place above the topgallant whereupon another, though smaller sail is installed or, bent on. At the top of the topgallant mast was a cap which is called the truck. A glance from Harvey told me that I might get upon it and I was there in an instant.

This being the uppermost part of the ship, I was forced to take a firm hold upon the rigging as I was struck by the full power of the wind. Cutting through my hair and blurring my vision, a stiff gust battered me about like a flag yet I couldn't take my eyes off my view of endless sea.

I was so taken by the majesty of the moment, that the absence of land in any direction concerned me not in the least. Perhaps it was due to my recovery from the dreaded seasickness, a condition that places everything in a most disagreeable light.

I could feel England slipping ever farther away, and I took comfort in the thought that my mother and sister were in relatively good financial ground, as I had left them a sizeable sum from my bank account. As for Laura and Pike, they should be fairly secure, providing they can outwit Zack, which I was certain they were most capable of doing. If they can manage to have a condemned man escape the noose, I had no misgivings for their ability to outwit the old bastard.

As for my own ground, some would find being forced into service aboard any ship a stroke of ill luck, yet I found it to be quite the contrary. This very stroke of luck had given me protection from those who would have me killed.

To be a member of the Royal Navy may not be the aspiration of most men of sense, but it had, thus far, given me an opportunity to stay alive and, at the same time, learn something of the world beyond England. Believing that anyone can remain safe aboard a fighting ship is a fool's notion; we were now at war with the so called "Frogs," an encounter with one of their ships could mean the end of everyone aboard.

Then there is this immense ocean. It is so vast that the odds of happening upon one of their ships would be dubious at best. I realized the captain must be an intelligent man to have such a position in the Royal Navy, but it would seem, even for him, an impossible task to find an enemy ship in this vast watery expanse.

I suppose some would look upon this ship as another form of imprisonment, yet I find that the experience of being aboard this rocking, swaying, forever uncomfortable, unforgiving, yet magnificently ethereal machine was more stirring than any trip across England or any escape from a constable. Here is the experience of the Atlantic with its endless line of seas, their foamy crests catching the wind and spraying skyward like plumed helmets worn upon the heads of an endless column of soldiers as they swept toward some unseen distant battle. I felt I had found a second home, a place where I belonged.

As the days passed, I continued to learn the name and use of every rope, sheet, and halyard on the *Deception*. I knew it was only in learning quickly that I could keep my arse from meeting the gunner's daughter. Even with the threat of that punishment aside, life aboard ship was anything but easy. I never had a free moment unless I was in my hammock; and when I was not on watch, I was repairing or washing my clothes, making oakum from excess rope fibers found to be irreparable, or trying to keep out of the way of the men who were on watch. During a stiff gale, I may be called from my hammock in the middle of the night when the bosun announced, "ALL HANDS!" to haul on a brace or halyard.

Life aboard was as strange to a landsman as living on land is to a mariner. Not even *time* is the same. A typical day in the Royal Navy starts at noon and runs till noon the following day. The Navy pay, which is issued for each month of service, is based on lunar months of which a year contains thirteen. A ship's boy, however, was not paid by the month, but instead by the year, and my rating, ship's boy third class, was the lowest, paying a mere £7 a year. I was putting on weight quickly, however, and with my strength returning, I had only to become a quick learner to be raised in rank to my goal of rated Able Seaman. This rank would earn £1, 13s, 6p per month. I had a good deal of study and experience ahead of me.

Harvey said that I had as much an opportunity as any man aboard. As to how long it could take was strictly up to me.

An income of this measure was nothing compared to that which I had become accustomed to as a thief, yet for the first time in my life I had the opportunity to earn my way at the expense of no one else. Strangely, the idea of making an honest living carried a degree of intrigue. Remembering my father did well with an honest profession, even supporting our family, it occurred that I should be able to do the same, possibly as a mariner.

"Larboard watch ahoy. Rouse out there, you sleepers. Hey, out or down there!" came the call of the bosun's mate.

After moving from sick berth, my hammock location was now

on the gun deck under the number eighty-seven painted on the hammock rail. Being part of the larboard watch, I knew it was now 4 a.m., or 0400 hours, and if I did not get my feet onto the deck, the bosun's mate would soon cut my hammock down with me in it. I had only a few moments to get my hammock down, pull my clothes from my trunk and get dressed, all in complete darkness. After I had managed this feat, I had to tie up my hammock with seven good turns in order for it to fit through the ring measure, a wooden ring used by the bosun to assure each hammock did not take up any unnecessary space.

Once I had it properly tied, I then had to carry it up the ladder to the quarterdeck so that it could be stowed into the hammock netting, a rack at the ship's sides or bulwarks. The netting with the hammocks stowed within served as a protection from enemy ship's small arms fire.

My first duty of this day was to assist in heaving the log chip from the taffrail, a rail that is on the poop deck at the aft end of the ship.

Harvey held the twenty-eight second glass, and I threw the triangular shaped board or "chip" that contained a weighted side along with three attached lines, one to each corner, connecting it to the main line from the reel, much like a kite. The chip being held in this way was stopped dead in the water causing the line to run out from the reel.

When a mark on the line representing 100 feet went over the rail, Felix, the other seaman involved in this operation said, "Mark!" and Harvey turned the sand glass.

When the sand ran out, Harvey said, "Stop!" and I gave the line a jerk which pulled a plug from one of the three lines attached to the chip, rendering it flat on the ocean surface, thereby allowing me to pull it in.

As I took in the line, Harvey counted the knots, each representing a nautical mile.

We performed this no less than three times before Harvey was satisfied enough to report seven and a half knots to Midshipman

Lewis, a brutish, fat faced boy of sixteen who had, throughout our exercise, repeatedly berated us with, "Come on now, you sluggards, what is it? Oh, not again. We'll all be in pluperfect hell before you've done with it."

And so it went, while Harvey continued without as much as the slightest inkling of annoyance. The boy was not half Harvey's size, yet Harvey returned his derisive comments in the most congenial manner in spite of the fact that he could, with little to no effort, have thrown Lewis overboard.

Later, we were on our hands and knees holystoning the deck. A holystone is a bible-shaped block of sandstone used to scour the deck clean. The stone is cursed to some extent in that it must be dipped in saltwater, which softens the skin making your knuckles prone to tearing when raked against any cornered object. As each day passed, this morning ritual caused the skin around my fingers and palms to crack open and each dip into the bucket of saltwater made those cracks burns like fire, a pain that lingered throughout the day and was made even worse by the numerous other hand-chafing tasks required of me. While Harvey had the holystone, I followed behind him with a hog-bristled deck bumper and asked, "Why do you take such abuse from Lewis?"

"Watch your mouth," he whispered. "That little shite-sack can have our backside bloody any time he has a mind to."

"Under what authority?"

"On the first Sunday of the month they will read a paper called the Articles of War. In them articles there's one that states, I think it's number nineteen or twenty, but I'm not sure, anyway, what it says is, anyone who uses contemptuous words to a superior officer can be charged with mutiny and get flogged or even hung, depending on what mood the captain is in when he gets word of it."

In some ways, I thought, those Articles were not so different from the law of England where I had nearly been hung for stealing. Even more ludicrous was the fact that it only took the word of an impish shite like Lewis to get your skin ripped from your back. I couldn't help but wonder at the absurdity of giving one of such temperament this much power.

It was at that moment the wash pump hose turned on me, soaking me from head to foot, while Lewis' unmistakable hoarse laughter cut the air.

I paused momentarily and made eye contact with him before continuing my work. Having no desire to hang for this turd, I bore the wet and cold and reserved my revenge for some future opportunity.

Lewis, however, was having none of my inaction and, desirous of causing me more irritation, stepped over to me and with his hands resting on his backside, leaned backward and gave me a stinging kick in the hand that sent the bumper flying across the deck.

"Mister Lewis, do come here for a moment," said Lieutenant Bengs, who had just stepped to the rail of the poop deck.

Lewis abruptly turned and darted up the ladder to see to the lieutenant.

I retrieved my bumper and continued working. Even though my clothes were soaked through, and the ever freshening morning breeze blew up my backside, I was relieved to see that Lewis also had his superiors to answer to.

"You done good not to go off at him. I could see you were willin' but you held your own. You done good," Harvey said under his breath, while we made our way to the end of our assigned deck area.

"I have dealt with much worse than the likes of him in..." Dear God, I thought, I nearly said Newgate.

"What's that?" Harvey asked, "In what?"

"In London," I said, "I have seen his kind."

"I suppose we all have," he said, shaking his head. "Anyways, watch out for him. He seems to have taken an interest in you and if the lieutenant saw what he did, well, he will have a few words with him and Lewis won't like that at all. Next thing he'll be wantin' to take it out on you so…"

"Take it out on me? He has no right to take it out on me!" I argued.

"Just you mind what I said," Harvey cautioned. "Watch out for the little piss."

Once we finished holy-stoning the deck, we were piped to breakfast. By breakfast, I must clarify that it was less wholesome than the worst chop houses in London, yet better than prison fare. Burgoo was the general issuance, a sort of oatmeal mixed with water and served along with Scotch coffee, a concoction that tasted like no coffee I had ever known and smelled of something burnt mixed with hot water.

It was not until after breakfast that I had the opportunity to put on a dry set of togs. Fortunately, before I had left sick berth and had regained my senses, I mentioned my missing purse to the doctor and he had since seen that it was returned to me. This made Mister Sawyer, the purser, extremely pleased. To see that I was not without funds with which to pay him, as so many pressed men and previously jailed men aboard had not, came as quite a pleasant surprise to him. He had gladly opened his store, giving me opportunity to purchase everything I would require in addition to the set of slops with which I had gone to sick berth. It was then that I purchased a tarred hat, three trousers, four shirts, two pair of sturdy shoes, a belt, five pair of wool stockings, a mess kit, and a sea chest in which to store everything. And, it was then that Mr. Sawyer, after seeing that I still had a good deal in my purse, suggested I have the initial "M" embroidered onto my shirts and trousers thereby rendering them easily identifiable should anyone attempt to steal them. I had no doubt in Sawyer's desire to squeeze another shilling out of me, yet I felt it to be a wise suggestion and bid him use crimson thread.

This left me with twenty guineas remaining, which Mr. Sawyer suggested I give to the captain for safekeeping. I would not be in need of it until allowed to go ashore, which might not happen for months.

Although it made sense, I couldn't bring myself to part with it. After all, the captain was not the Bank of England, and, once turned over to him, what kind of song and dance would I be expected to perform in order to get it back? I decided I would take my chances by keeping it buried in my sea chest.

It was not until after breakfast that I was relieved from my watch. I then had four hours to stay out from under foot and occupy myself with learning the different functions of the running rigging. To assist me in my education, Harvey lent me his copy of *"Falconer's Dictionary of the Marine,"* as well as a diagram he had made naming the different belaying racks and pins about the masts. Armed with this literature, I sat near a twenty-four pound gun and read by the sunlight coming through the gun port. My method of study was quickly improved by periodically running up on deck to verify what I had memorized and quickly returning without drawing notice from any of the watch captains. I was informed by Harvey, that if the watch captains suspected I was without anything to do, they would put me to work at some task regardless of whether I was on watch or no.

Once I had the belaying points put to memory, that is, the places where the running rigging lines are tied until they are to be hauled upon, I began climbing the rat lines to study the function of the standing rigging. Those lines consist of shrouds, which run from the ship's side to the masts, as well as the stays, which support the masts by running from the front of the ship to the back of it, or fore and aft. Then there were the studding sails; sails set upon the ends of the spars to catch additional wind. I noted how they were made fast to the yards, as well as how they were struck back to the cross trees. I also made note of how the masts were stepped and wondered how they could be struck, that is, taken off and tied to a lower mast, so as to prevent them from "carrying away," which Harvey said must be done before a heavy blow. It seemed that hardly any time had elapsed before my watch was to begin again, now being called the "afternoon watch."

It was during this watch I was surprised to find that after we had eaten our dinner we did not go immediately back to work but, instead, we remained seated on our chests while being served our daily ration of grog while the bosun's mate played a tune on his brass fife.

In stark contrast to the ordinary routine of a Royal Navy ship in the service of His Majesty, in this short time of rest we were ordinary people, each with our own ideas, opinions, dreams, and woes. It was also during these short intervals that I came to know the superstitions, jealousies, and resentments of my shipmates, as well as what it is to be a tarpaulin, or foremast jack.

On one of these occasions I was knocked to the deck when a burly man named Bill Ryan decided I was sitting on his trunk, apparently too drunk or stupid to notice that it was, in fact, mine. I had gotten quite used to being battered about while in prison, but this was not supposed to be prison, and though Ryan was not an officer, had I had another eight stone, I fancied I would have beaten him bloody. Although I fancied doing a lot of things that were beyond my measure, I had the good sense to know when to let it go, as it was not in my best interest to add fuel to this man's drunken rage. There were, however, few things aboard a ship that went unnoticed. If there was an infraction of any sort, someone knew of it and, ultimately, someone would pay.

On the forenoon watch of the following day, all hands were called upon deck as Lieutenant Bengs gave the order that we must witness ship's punishment.

While standing in the waist with the entire crew, I looked on while the bosun and two of his men hauled up one of the deck gratings and lashed it vertically to the mainmast. The marines in their clean uniforms were in formation, the sun illuminating the red coats with white lacings, their polished buttons glistening while they maintained a mechanical gaze with muskets at the ready.

Ryan, preceded by two marines, was taken out from below decks and made to stand before the grating. The captain stood at the rail of the poop and, after reading the nineteenth Article, ordered a punishment of two dozen lashes for the offense of being drunk and using contemptuous language to a superior officer.

The bosun, after receiving a nod from the lieutenant, tore Ryan's shirt from his back and tied a leather apron around his backside to cover his kidneys and buttocks. Then, two of the bosun's mates pinned Ryan to the grating, he being held in a spread-eagle position, while they tied him to it with spun yarn.

The men who stood about me wore sullen expressions and it was clear that none took pleasure in what was about to occur. My eyes were absently drawn to the pin rail where, from pure habit, I began my process of identifying, one by one, the various lines tied to it when I came upon a red, baize-coloured bag hanging from the rail.

Once Ryan was sufficiently tied, and a piece of rope placed between his teeth, the bosun opened the drawstring of the red bag and withdrew from it the most hideous of instruments. The handle was an oval loop of served rope which concealed nine strands of knotted rope seized together. The stock of the cat o' nine had a section of about eight inches in length which tightly bound the strands to it before allowing them to separate into eighteen-inch lengths. The bosun gripped the loop while running his fingers through the strands with his other hand.

I remember with most vivid clarity the humiliation in Ryan's face as he stood, pressed to the grating, in front of the entire ship's company. Others had informed me that this was not his first and would, in all likelihood, not be his last performance in front of the cat. In light of this information, I fancied he would be somewhat inured to this form of punishment, but I was sadly disappointed. Even with the first stroke upon his whip scarred back, he was powerless to withstand its force.

The bosun, taking care to position his feet for good balance and maximum effect, came down with all of his weight. The first twelve cracked like musket shot and slowly turned his back from red to purple with cross hatched whelps. With heavily muscled arms shining from sweat that even the cool Atlantic breeze could not dry, the bosun worked at his task with such conviction that, had he held anything stouter than a whip, Ryan would have been dead by the end of the first dozen. The lieutenant then ordered the bosun to trade places with one of his mates, and from that point Ryan's condition deteriorated rapidly. Each stroke that struck now made a slapping, wet sucking sound as it merged with the long furrows already cut into his skin before drawing, from those same wounds, bits of bloody flesh. Within these lines, more blood would well up and fill the void as it tried to feed the flesh that the cat had stolen. By the fifteenth blow, the smell of Ryan's blood was in the air for the wind caught the spray from the cat when it swung over the bosun mate's head. Ryan's chest heaved with quick short successive breaths as though he had been running hard. He clenched his eyes shut only to have them reappear like glazed ivory balls as the cat tore off more of his flesh. He bit down hard, his jaw muscles twisting in a rictus that threatened to sever the strands of the rope between his teeth. Rope muffled his gasping groans while the muscles in his shoulders contracted, pulling the swollen skin tight over his partially exposed ribs. When I saw the taut sinews of his back being exposed by the absence of his skin, I feared he might die from the force of the next blow. The leather apron around his waist was no protection against those merciless tearing strands of the cat. It was at that point that I turned away for, even though he had given me offence on the previous day, I would not wish more than one of these lashes upon him, let alone twenty-four.

"Avast!" Bengs ordered.

Thank God, I thought. He has finally taken pity on the man.

The lashing ceased and, to my confusion, all eyes were on me. Lieutenant Bengs stepped to my side and, taking hold of my arm with a less than manly grip, said flatly, "Mason, you will witness punishment or join him at the grating. Is that understood?"

"Aye, aye, sir," I said, quickly turning my eyes back to Ryan. I've done it now, I thought. They are going to flog me as well. Dear God, I don't know if I will be able to hold up to that kind of torture. I'll probably shite myself.

As I waited for Bengs to give the order to have me seized, I saw through my peripheral that he turned to the bosun and, as though observing a friendly game of whist, said in an even tone, "Continue."

And the flogging resumed with the count of eighteen. By the time the last blows were struck, Ryan no longer flinched. His near lifeless body slumped against the grating as his back oozed streams of crimson down his trousers and onto his feet. Two of his friends untied him and brought him directly to the sick berth where he would be cared for until the doctor deemed him able to return to his watch.

If the reason that we witnessed this torture was a warning, the point was run home, for Ryan's bloody back remained in my mind's eye long after his wounds had healed.

We were having our daily ration of grog, and I was sitting on my sea chest next to one of the long eighteen-pound guns while examining my hands. The previous nights hauling on halyards and braces had rendered them chafed and bleeding.

Bently, a wiry framed, bug-eyed man with hardly a hair on his body, whispered in a deep resonating voice, "It was that goddamn Lewis what got him flogged this time. I swear some 'uns gonna send him to meet Davy Jones if he don't learn to look the other way once in a while."

"Keep yer voice down. Yer so goddamn loud that even yer whisperin' can be heard on the quarterdeck," cautioned one of the men who sat in the shadows.

"Anyways, Ryan got himself cup shot and he knew the consequences. 'Sides, ain't the first time he's had his bloody arse on the grate."

"Lewis seen him drunk before and ain't said nothin'. What got his blood up this time?" asked Bently.

"I know vat done it," said Schultz, the gunner's mate who stood with his huge arms folded while leaning against a deck knee. Pointing at Bently with the stem of his unlit pipe, he said, "I vas dare on da quarterdeck ven Bengs give him da verd."

"What *verd* you talking about?" Bently mocked.

"Da verd! He says, 'I ketch you playing dis shite on da men again ven day yust trying to do dare verk, I gonna ask captain to put you before da mast,' vas da verd he give him."

"Who was he fucking with this time?" Bently asked, no longer mocking Schultz.

"You know," Schultz said, pointing his pipe at me.

"Me?" I said. "What have I to do with it?"

Harvey breathed a heavy sigh, "Oh, the shite's gonna be on you now. Mind what I said, you watch your back."

"Oh, I can handle him," I said, feigning confidence.

"No you can't. Just you remember Ryan's backside. All it took was a word from Lewis."

"Well, Ryan was cup-shot," I said. "He gave him an excuse. I'll give him nothing. What can he do with that?"

"Just watch out for him, that's all," Harvey warned.

"I vould listen to him, if I vas you," Schultz said.

The rest of the day was filled with fire drills, sail drill, and gunnery practice. The pain in my palms intensified as the watch progressed. There was no time for my hands to recover and I could foresee no such time in future. As if to make matters worse, I now had Lewis taking every opportunity to watch over my shoulder so that no matter what the drill, I should always be hauling on a rope.

There was no avoiding him and if I averted my eyes he would place his face within an inch of mine while periodically grunting into my ear, "Do your hands hurt? Do you want your mummy?"

Later, at gunnery practice I stood with chafed and bleeding hands while Lewis ordered me to handle the training tackles of one of the long eighteens, a gun that weighed over four thousand pounds. The training tackle is used to shift the muzzle so as to line it up with a target. I could see the well-concealed concern in Schultz' eyes when he noticed the bloody rope in my hand.

Lewis must have taken note of this for he instantly appeared and, eyeing Schultz with contempt, started in on me again. "Come now you sluggard, you're making your gun crew's time as slow as a bleeding snail. Get your back into it, damn you! What's the matter, have you gone deaf? I said, get your back into it!" he screamed, saliva spraying from his ragged gaping mouth.

"Excuse me, sir, but don't he supposed to be der powder monkey fer dis crew?" inquired Schultz.

With blood rushing in, Lewis' face seemed to grow even fatter, taking on a turnip hue as he stepped up to the big man and, with a voice like a squealing pig, shouted, "He'll be a gun crewman if I say he will be! Now keep your mouth shut and mind your gun crews." Then turning to me, he placed his wet mouth to my ear and said, "Now, haul on that training tackle you little shite, or I shall have you flogged."

Along with the burning, throbbing sensation in my hands, I felt loathing that I had not experienced since that terrible night we came upon Jeb torturing Laura. It took every bit of restraint I possessed not to turn on him like a rabid dog. At first, I entertained the image of my bloody hands crushing his fat neck, but this gave me no surcease and I soon found that I could use the pain to concentrate on other things. Soon the image faded, giving way to glimpses of my past.

First, there was my father falling down the wall of the church, then, Mother and Lilly near death from sickness; Laura, Pike, and I in a hackney riding away from the constables at Drury Lane, myself in that moldy rat-infested hole beneath the courtyard of the prison, Mother's eyes on that last day in Newgate, and finally, Mrs. St. Clair standing before me with the Mason Key in her age old hands. Although Lewis continued hounding me, the images I saw brought me to realize what really mattered in my life, and his insults eventually carried no more irritation then that of a pesky insect buzzing around my ears. At length, the call came down to "House your guns!" and his fun was at an end.

While I worked with my crew at securing our gun, Lewis leaned over me and whispered, "You must know this is not over. Before I am finished, you will wish you had never been born."

CHAPTER THIRTEEN

The life of a newly aboard a British man-of-war is a brutally painful existence; the price for want of familiarity with the things about him is painfully exacted by the bosun in the use of a knotted rope's end. The term for its use, "starting," though a seemingly innocent-sounding word, is meant to describe an evil act that is so ancient that its origin dates back to biblical times. Most puzzling is the way it is dispensed, for it is in direct contradiction to all other manner of disciplinary action on the ship.

Without seeking permission from a superior officer, the bosun may, under his own discretion, strike a seaman with this device on the head, back, or arms. Though it does not always draw blood, it can raise a purple welt upon the skin that will ache down to the bone for two to three days, depending on how near you were to the bosun when you received it.

Within the first few days as a boy third class, I received no fewer than a dozen of these aching vipers that nearly drove me mad from the continual pain they caused. As though this were not enough to endure, I was required to be continually ready to run, climb, or haul upon lines, leaving my hands in a constant state of being chafed and bleeding. In addition, my knees and elbows were covered with blisters from kneeling while doing the morning's holystoning of the deck where I would periodically rake my elbows across the saltwater-washed deck. My feet, if not for the shoes I had purchased, would have made me a cripple, for the footropes upon the yards cut into the arches, embedding bits of tar into the skin which, in short duration, will raise a nasty blister. By the end of my first three days out of sick berth, I staggered about like a feeble leper in hopes of finding some place to rest my battered and aching flesh.

The sad truth, however, is that there is no place on a man-of-war for a seaman to rest. The deck is continually pitching and rolling. Saltwater sprays over you and burns into the cracks of your chafed skin. And if you manage to find someplace on deck that is out of the way, you may not lie upon it for long before the motion of the ship pulls the skin of your back, first one way, then the other, until it feels as if it will tear from your body. During the day, you dare not even dream of getting into your hammock, for it is stowed into the hammock netting where it will remain until everyone has been released from the evening's battle stations, but not before the ship is declared by the captain to be in order.

Was this worse than Newgate prison? I asked myself, and after pondering this question for a moment, I could state unequivocally, "NO!" Unlike Newgate, I had been fed sufficiently to steadily gain weight and, except for the time spent below decks, I breathed fresh sea air, the purest of the world. No matter how foul your lungs may become while below, they are cleaned anew at your first breath on the quarterdeck.

Fortunately, after only two weeks afloat, I found I was becoming accustomed to shipboard life. My hands no longer chafed and bled, for the skin had since thickened to form heavy calluses; while I found more resilient strength in my limbs. What eased my way through the day most was my increased familiarity with the routine. Harvey had, until then, taught me a seemingly endless amount of rope handling, knot tying, rigging functions, and terms of the various parts of the ship; hinting at teaching me his knowledge of signal flags if I kept up the good work, which meant doing my utmost to follow his instruction and commands both quickly and efficiently.

Though my abilities had improved, I had yet to attain perfection, a condition of which, if attained, Harvey would let me know the moment it occurred. After promising Harvey I would be worthy of learning the use of signal flags, as well as anything else he might care to teach me, he smiled and vowed to teach me everything that he knew regarding ship handling.

To be sure, learning and hard work go hand in hand aboard ship and once I had gained both familiarity and speed with these things, I no longer received the rope's end, not to mention the accompanying aching bruises. Soon thereafter, the absence of those bruises afforded me much needed sleep, which in turn enabled me to deal with the hard work of the following day.

The sleep I came to experience, however, was in no way the peaceful rest that I had envisioned. Once I had at last grown accustomed to sleeping soundly amongst the mixed odor of tar, soup farts, and timber-sawing snores, I fell victim to a recurring dream. This was a dream that distressed me sorely in that it involved both my father and me. It began with Father as the main attraction in the *crusher* contest, the same contest I had witnessed while working as an apprentice tender.

The contest started off rather harmless with my father crushing a brick within his hand just as in the previous dream; yet as I ran forward to congratulate him on his victory I found the scene had changed to the horrible moment my father fell from the scaffold to his death.

Each time I reached this point in the dream, I would try to break his fall by throwing my body beneath his, only to be tripped up by the bag of lime which had been on the floor directly in my path. Lying on the floor of the church, I was forced to re-experience this horrible event while watching helplessly as my father slowly fell to his death. As the nights passed and the dreams repeated, a new detail emerged in the split second before Father collapsed onto the stone floor.

As I looked up at Father, just beyond him and to the side of where he fell from the scaffold, stood the tall lean figure of Peter Hendricks. His form became clearer each night and, at length, I noticed a tightly bunched group of nails clutched in his hand. The nails he clutched were not straight, but instead, bent and uneven. I pondered the bent nails until one night I woke to the realization that they were nails that had once been driven in prior to being pulled out! As it struck me, I cried out and received a poke in the ribs from one of my hammock swinging neighbors. There was no doubt that Hendricks had removed those nails—the very nails that I had so painstakingly hammered into the scaffold planking beneath my father's work station. My heart turned in my chest and I felt as though I might suffocate. I dropped from my hammock and ran up the ladder to the quarterdeck. I nearly cried out again but caught myself as I made out the silhouette of one of the officers standing nearby. Instead I stood at the rail and stared with complete confusion into the darkness of the evening sea. It could only mean that Peter Hendricks had murdered my father.

Returning to my hammock, I lay in frustrated turmoil. I was now more than a thousand miles from London and could do nothing about Hendricks, nothing but lie wide awake until the bosun called us out of our hammocks with the usual, "Rouse out there, you sleepers. Here I come with a knife. It's out or down there!"

While I worked through each subsequent day, I could see those nails in my mind's eye and envisioned dealing out innumerable forms of justice for the man whom I knew had killed my father. Yet after I had killed Hendricks for the hundredth time, I still couldn't answer the question of why he had done it. I could only take solace in the hope that someday I would nail him to a wall and ask him that question.

Fortunately, my dreams weren't solely of Father's death, for many were of Mother and Lilly, yet the ones I treasured most were of Pike and Laura. Sometimes we were walking down a London street or enjoying a play at Drury Lane or Covent Garden while they generally ended with a run from either an angry constable or an angry cully. Then there was the one dream that, above all, tore my heart out. In this dream I stared into Mother's grief-stricken eyes the day before they were to take me to Tiburn Tree.

It seemed the farther from London I sailed, the more I dreamt of my life there. With the exception of Newgate, I missed the city dearly and wondered if I would ever stroll down those streets again. Would I ever see my family again? I was a wanted criminal with a death sentence hanging over my head. No, seeing them again would jeopardize both my life and theirs. Yet, knowledge of this fact alone did not persuade me to give up hope. Perhaps when I am older and have grown into a man where, along with my new name, no one could recognize me, perhaps...

For now, I must continue regaining my strength. Already I had gained a good deal of weight. My clothes no longer hung on me like a shirt on a wash-line. My wrists were thicker and, had I worn them today, I am certain those manacles would not slide past my hands.

As my familiarity with the ship and its duties grew, so did my ability to get along with most everyone with whom I worked. If not for the encounters with Midshipman Lewis who kicked, punched, and tripped me whenever we were beyond the watchful eyes of his senior officers, life in general was fine.

Controlling my temper under these assaults was a thing that became increasingly more difficult as the days passed. I harbored thoughts of hurting him, such as a good knock down blow to the head. As time passed, however, that fancy quickly changed to doing him severe harm. I found myself entertaining a vision of Lewis tied to the grate with his teeth biting into the rope as the cat tore his miserable pimpled flesh away. It bothered me that I could harbor the same ill will that had caused me to feel disgust for those on this ship who condoned it, yet I felt it just the same.

It was on Sunday that we had scrubbed the decks to the white of old ivory, coiled all lines into neat spirals upon the deck, and polished all the brass to a glistening shine before donning our best and cleanest duck shirts and trousers. Using every bit of our spare time for cleaning and braiding each other's hair, we were nearly prepared for the captain's inspection of divisions which would take place after the chaplain's prayer.

I was on my way to the officer's mess with a pot of portable soup when Lewis stuck his foot between my legs and sent me flying to the deck. Before I could get to my feet, he proceeded to call me a shite-licking guttersnipe, dog fucker, horse shite eater, and so on while stomping my arched back and sending me face first into the hot soup. As the dark beef broth soaked into my best white duck, I heaved myself up before he could get another kick into me.

Just as I gained my footing, he spat in my face, smiled and said, "Well, my little turd, what are you going to do? Are you going to strike an officer?" Lewis' contemptuous smile displayed teeth that were large, dirty and carried the odor of rancid meat.

I was about to go for his throat, certain that if I could get a good grip, he would not be able to get free before I choked him into unconsciousness. Then, I remembered Harvey's words, "He's not worth getting yourself flogged over."

I had a vision of myself being tied to the grating while Lewis looked on with that same pig-faced smile. I knew then that merely choking him would not be enough. I wanted to kill him. I couldn't condone lying in wait and attacking him from some unseen quarter. No, I must meet him eye to eye. It is imperative he knows who is killing him, and I wanted to kill him slowly. I had never fancied myself a murderer, but then, I had never been under the thumb of a demonic imp. From that point on, the thought of seeing him dead entered my mind on numerous occasions.

As I gained control of my anger, I picked up the pot and returned to the galley. With a reproving stare from Griswald, the peg-legged ship's cook, I shrugged and said, "Ran into our dear friend, Mister Lewis."

Rolling his eyes, he said nothing and, giving a heavy sigh, sent me to my chest to get a fresh change of togs while he refilled the pot.

Shortly after the second dog watch of the following Tuesday we were called to reduce sail. Due to my improved performance, I had been given the opportunity of joining the men aloft to reef the main topgallant which, if deemed acceptable by the second lieutenant, could gain me a recommendation for promotion from Boy Third Class to Boy First Class, thereby gaining me another two pounds per annum in salary.

Although the day's sun had warmed the deck, I found the wind carried a brisk bite. Being in a most earnest mind to show my ability, I was at the topgallant crosstrees well ahead of the other hands and, as the order came from the deck, "Trice up! Lay out!" I quickly ran with relative ease along with the other men out onto the windward end of the yard.

As I reached my position at midway on the yard, I found that Lewis had ascended the mast well ahead of everyone and now perched himself above us at the royal crosstrees in order to give me the benefit of his special attention and criticism.

The helmsman steered into the wind just enough to luff the sail, that is, to spill wind from it, allowing us to gain purchase of the loose canvas.

With the bite of the wind on my hands, I soon felt my fingers tingle and knew I must work fast before they went numb. Reaching down over the yard, I, along with the other men, took hold of one of the reef points.

"Haul out to windward!" the call came from the deck. Turning to leeward, we pulled the sail up toward the weather side which allowed the weather earring to be passed; the earring being a length of rope used to tie the outward end of the sail to the yard. Once sufficient turns were made around the weather earring, the man at this station raised his arm, signaling for us to haul the sail out to the leeward side, or downwind.

By this time I could feel numbness seeping into the ends of my fingers and prayed I could maintain my hold on the sail.

Once the earrings were secured we could let go the reef points and haul up the sail, keeping it under our chests in folds as we pulled up each successive fold until we had the last pleat up tight. Next was the most difficult part, keeping in mind the saying, "One hand for you and one hand for the ship!"

With the last fold under our chests, while holding the forward point of the reef line, a line that is attached to the sail in rows along its width at several points, we must reach under the yard and pull the after end of the line to it so that we could join them together in a square knot. The danger in this maneuver was that it allowed no hand for you, for both were fully occupied with the securing of the reef line. One false move could send you plummeting to your death.

"Move your skinny arse, Mason! For the bleeding Christ, my grandmother is old but not half as slow. What are you waiting for? Mason, you're as useless as tits on a boar!" Lewis went on and on while I managed to complete my task ahead of four of the eight rated seamen on the yard.

Once the reefing of the leeward side of sail had been completed, the bosun hailed, "In and down," and we sidestepped our way to the mast where Lewis ordered me to wait while he made his way down the ratlines to me.

"You failed, Mason," he hissed. "You bloody well fucked it up and I shall see to it that you never have another opportunity. Rest assured, I will inform the lieutenant that you were a bloody stumble fingers who lost his hold, nearly falling off the yard."

"I thought I did quite well, sir," I said.

"What you think is of no concern to me, you sour little shite-sack.

You will never do well for I will be on your back to bloody well see that you don't."

"Why is that, sir?"

"Cause you made me look the fool in front of the lieutenant, is why. Like my father, I shall be made Post one day and YOU cost me."

"Just what did I cost you, sir?"

"Time, you little guttersnipe," he snarled, "time that I will now have to make up. If I am to make lieutenant, I must obtain a favorable report from the captain. You have fucked that up for me; and for that, my little shite, you are fucked. Yes, fucked. In fact, so fucked that before I am through with you, I shall see your backside bloody. Do you understand me? By the month's end, I shall spit into your blood as it runs to the scuppers."

His face, though not a foot from mine, turned a fiery red as tiny blood vessels rose to the surface around the pus-filled pimples. Just as it seemed the pimples would explode from the pressure, he relaxed his brow.

In that instant, I realized his frustration had grown to the point that merely berating me with words was not doing it for him. When he shot a quick glance to my chin, I knew this must be his target and when his fist jumped out, I was ready for it. With a firm grip on the paunch matting ropes, I pulled myself sideways to the mast. His thrust was surprisingly quick as I felt the edge of his fist graze my cheek.

With no impact to check him, the momentum of his weight carried him past me, tearing the royal halyard from his grip and sending him headlong, arms swinging like a bird attempting to take flight, into the empty space between the masts. But for only a millisecond, he teetered on the yard before being upended as his feet slipped from beneath him. He let out an ear-piercing scream that was cut short when his knee caught on the topgallant yard's foot rope. For a second, he was suspended by one leg where the footrope had caught him behind the knee. Had he been in better physical condition, he might have maintained that hold simply by keeping his knee bent; yet, with his excessive weight coming to bear, it was too much for the muscles in his leg to hold. His knee was losing the battle. The footrope slid toward the chubby calf and would soon slip past his heel.

It was more reaction than thought that caused me to untie one of the reef points nearest him and secure a hastily made slip knot around his ankle. Just as his knee gave way, Lewis let out a blood curdling scream as the reef line brought his fall up short, leaving him dangling from the yard by his foot.

While the ship rolled in the swell, Lewis screamed incessantly as he was swung, first one way, then the next.

I checked the knot and found it to be holding, though, due to the nature of a slip knot, Lewis' own weight was tightening the rope so that the flow of blood to his foot had been cut off.

Suddenly Lewis cried out even louder, but this time I sensed it was more from pain than fear. Here was this snot-nosed shite, a near fully grown brat, in authority over me, yet crying and screaming like a banshee. While strangely feeling more like an observer of the incident then one taking part, I asked myself, just what exactly am I doing? Here is my opportunity to be rid of the bastard.

While part of me wished to cut him free, something within, seemingly greater than myself, said, "No!" He had given me ample reason to kill him, but to do so, to cut this useless bastard's life short was just not in me. Although I have been a thief, I have never been guilty of murder, I told myself. I have been chosen to be the "Keeper" of the Mason Key and as such, must be worthy of the honour.

Watching him swinging his arms in a useless attempt to take hold of anything within reach, I still had to wonder if letting him live would be doing the world a disservice.

When the bosun called the men to the mainmast, it struck me that an uncommon length of time had passed since Lewis had first started his screams. Though I had, on numerous occasions, seen them all scale the shrouds with lightning speed, the men seemed to be moving like snails. It made perfect sense. They were enjoying the show, for they loathed the little bastard every bit as much as me.

At long last, the first officer cut in with his speaking trumpet, "Damn yer eyes, I'll have every man jack of you on the grate if you don't get a move on!"

"Maxwell, what took you?" I asked, as his familiar golden locks appeared in my peripheral.

Soon, more men arrived on the yard, quickly taking hold of Lewis' legs and hauling him back onto the footropes. It was then that the stench of Lewis' urine-soaked trousers and shirt hit us.

In a patronizing tone, Maxwell asked Lewis, "Do you want us to rig a bosun's chair to get you down, sir?"

Lewis puffed out his bottom lip, "No, I do not!" before turning to me and stating, "And untie this goddamn rope, you piece of shite."

I attempted to work the knot free but it had cut into the skin so deeply that I could scarce see it.

Maxwell took out his marlin spike and Lewis broke the air with more curses as the spike probed around until it found the buried knot.

Once the knot released, Lewis massaged his ankle for a few seconds before taking hold of a backstay and sliding to the deck, but not before muttering, "I'll have your backside for this, Mason."

"That's gratitude for ya," Maxwell muttered before calling after Lewis, "Would you like us to fetch you some clean britches, sir?"

Surprisingly, Lewis did not reply but only glared up at me while on his way to the deck.

"Is you all right, lad?" Maxwell asked, placing a leathery hand on my shoulder. Oddly, his voice carried a note of concern and I wondered at his sincerity for I was not used to anything like it since being on this ship.

"I believe so," I said.

Out of the corner of his mouth, Maxwell whispered, "Why in

bloody hell didn't you just let the little devil go? He'd a' been all right, going back where he come from—which is in hell."

The deep voice of the bosun boomed from his speaking trumpet, "Mason, on deck, NOW!"

I'll get a starting for sure, I thought as I slid down the backstay. I may even receive that lashing Lewis promised me. Damn, I thought. It is just as he said, I am "totally and completely fucked."

On my way down, I caught a glimpse of Lewis who, standing in the waist, was having words with First Officer, Lieutenant Bengs. He appeared quite red-faced and barely able to control his voice, while aiming a chubby finger at me. Once my feet reached the deck, a quick glance about revealed men who, unable to control their grinning expressions, were forced to cover their mouths and feign sneezing.

Then I saw Lewis, standing before one and all in his piss stained uniform. "The goddamn bastard!" he said in a squeaking pitch.

"I'll have no blasphemy from my officers, Mister Lewis," Lieutenant Bengs reproved.

"But he..." intimidated by Bengs, Lewis struggled for words. Then, finding his voice again, blurted out, "Mason pushed me off the yard, sir."

Bengs raised a brow and said, "So that's it, then? You are charging him with the attempted murder of an officer?"

"Aye, sir!" Lewis coldly affirmed.

"That is a very serious charge," Bengs said, an entertained smirk forming on his pale thin lips. "Are you certain of it?"

God! Forget the cat. They are going to hang me, I thought. No, they will most likely flog me to near death and then hang me.

"Are you injured?" Bengs asked indifferently.

"No, sir!" Lewis replied, after raising his foot to massage his ankle.

With mild curiosity, Bengs eyed the bruised ankle and said, "In that case, the captain wishes to have a word with you. He is in his quarters, do not keep him waiting."

"But, sir..." Lewis said in a pleading voice.

"Yes, what is it?" Bengs answered impatiently.

"May I first see to my, uh..." Lewis motioned to his shirt and trousers.

Bengs followed Lewis' motion to the urine-stained trousers just as the wind momentarily shifted, slacking the sails and wafting the acrid odor into Bengs' flaring nostrils. Taking in a brief sniff, Bengs gave Lewis a contemptuous glare and ordered, "The captain will see you NOW!"

Lewis obediently knuckled his forehead and, moving stiff-legged, hobbled aft toward the captain's cabin.

"Mason!" Bengs snapped.

Instantly coming to attention, I said, "Aye, aye, sir!" This is it, I thought. Perhaps they will throw me in irons first, while pondering how best to kill me.

"You did well up there," Bengs stated, as though the act of giving an approving comment were painful to him, "and if you are not charged with attempted murder," a slight pause ensued before he stoically continued, "I shall recommend to the captain that you be promoted to boy first class."

"Aye, aye, sir," I said. Bloody wonderful! I will either be promoted or hanged. "Thank you, sir!"

"Don't thank me yet, Mason," he warned, as Second Lieutenant Newcomb came over and whispered something in his ear. With a disinterested expression, he turned to me and said, "The captain wishes to see you, Mason. Don't keep him waiting. Run along now."

As I made my way aft beneath the side gangways in the ship's waist, I could feel eyes upon me. The captain's cabin was but a few steps away and I realized with each of those steps that I was nearing either promotion or damnation. The marine sentry at the cabin's entrance stood in his scarlet coat with boots and buttons polished to a luster. Holding his musket by the muzzle with the butt resting on the deck, he stepped forward with a knowing smirk on his pox-scarred face and, sniffing the air about me, chided, "What, no pissy pants on this one?" Shrugging the comment aside, I stepped toward the cabin door but the sentry threw out his musket, the muzzle landing flat against my chest, and said in a more serious tone, "Captain said to wait here."

Taking in a deep breath, I waited while reflecting that I had not been in the captain's cabin since I first came aboard. Since that day, I observed that no one entered, other than his coxswain, who was not an officer, unless it was for something of great importance. In that room, I had been instantly transformed from a stowaway to a volunteer. In that same moment, however, had the captain been in London that afternoon, he might have sent me back ashore to hang. He still might unwittingly carry out the sentence of the court by ordering my hanging.

I mentally chastised myself for not letting the bastard Lewis fall to his deserving death. At least then he wouldn't be here to bring charges against me. Why couldn't I have let him fall? My thoughts were suddenly interrupted by the captain's booming voice from the other side of the partition.

"PUSHED, BY GOD! Mister Lewis, you shall see to the feeding of our animals in the focs'l and, whilst you are there, I suggest you tell your story into the sow's ear."

"Feed the animals, sir? Isn't that Parker's duty, sir?"

"The odor you exude will fit right in with that of the manger. You are dismissed now. See to your new duty, Mister Lewis."

"But, sir, my charges against Mason…"

"DAMN YOUR BLOOD! I saw the whole thing. You dare lie to me? You request charges against a boy who saved your pitiful excuse of a life—even though you took a swing at him! If it weren't for my friendship with your father… Relieve Parker and stay out of my sight until I can decide what to do with you."

"But, sir!"

"Dismissed!" The command was punctuated by a thump, most likely the captain's fist onto his desk.

"Aye, aye, sir!" Lewis submissively replied.

The door opened and Lewis stepped out, his face white as new bed linen. With his wide mouth hanging open like a gaping pouch, he glared at me but said nothing and slowly stepped around the sentry.

Returning his glare with a smile, I said, "Sorry about the ankle, sir." What the hell, I thought; I am sure he now desires to kill me. And since the captain isn't going to hang me, much less flog me, I suppose the least I can do is give him a little nip. Sniffing the air, I glanced down at his stained breeches.

Lewis screwed his gaping mouth into a teeth-baring sneer that much resembled a mad dog. Raising a threatening fist, it was kept in check by the sentry who quickly swung his musket between us.

"You may enter now," the sentry said with tongue in cheek.

Stepping over the watertight threshold, I made my way to the dining room, or officer's mess, such as it is called, which, though small, could accommodate as many as ten with servants included. Pausing at the door to the main cabin, I knocked lightly before announcing myself, "Mason, sir!"

"Enter!" Captain Cole said in a soft voice, which was quite a disparity from the tone that had boomed through the bulkhead only a minute earlier. Though his tobacco-stained ivory pipe was not lit, the sweet odor hung in the air. He was seated at his desk with several stacks of paper upon the freshly polished surface. With quill between thick fingers, he glanced up after finishing an entry into, what I surmised, was some sort of ledger. "Mason, give me a moment," he said, and continued writing while a strand of his ebony locks dangled and bounced alongside his chin as he wrote. After making his last punctuation, he set the quill into its engraved brass holder and leaned back in his chair. Taking in a deep breath, he glanced at the ship's wake through the gallery windows and, turning back to face me, let the air flow from his barrel chest like the rush of wind through the trees of a forest. "You may not be aware but, though I am in my cabin or on the poop, I see all goings on. There is little that escapes me. You have made a good deal of progress for someone who has come aboard with absolutely no knowledge of ships. It is my understanding that you desire a promotion." He paused and it was not until he said, "Is this true?" that I realized this had been a question.

After two seconds of finding my voice, I managed to blurt out, "Aye, aye, sir!"

"Merely desiring a promotion will not get you one," he said. "There is a good deal more to attaining a promotion on a ship of the Royal Navy than memorizing ship terms and hauling upon a line. It takes a will in which those who have been impressed from the bars or taken from the gaol generally do not contain."

I froze on the word, "gaol," and, as a bead of sweat slowly traced its way down my spine, wondered, did he know?

"And that alone will not do." He continued, his thick brows furrowing. "One must apply himself in a manner that exceeds his desire for self preservation. He must apply himself in a way that the preservation of the ship comes before all else."

He paused to look me dead in the eye with the most penetrating inspection I had known since my father was alive. I supposed a promotion was premature. Harvey must have been mad to even mention it to me. How presumptuous of me; I haven't a snowball's chance in hell. With his hands palm down on the desk, he examined them while he spoke. "Over the past three weeks, I have observed your progress both aloft and alow and have seen you become more of a seaman each day. What you did up there today was what a real seaman would have done." Inclining his head, he paused, seeming to reflect before continuing, "No, most would simply have let him meet his maker." Another long pause as he seemed to be searching for the right words. "To have the ability to put aside your differences in order to save a man's life while risking your own is a rare quality, even among officers. What I mean to say is that you showed you have real bottom, son. I must say, however, the rating of Boy, First Class is out of the question." Taking in a deep breath, he let it out slowly.

Perhaps, I might at least rate Second, surely after this speech...

"I am unclear concerning the circumstances that brought about your coming to be on my ship," he stated.

Now I am going to be questioned about things I can't answer. So he's going to hold my promotion for information, I thought.

He continued, "And, at this juncture, do not particularly care to know. It seems that whatever you were running from hasn't prevented you from making the best of your situation." His eyes left me and went to the ledger before him where he began writing.

After several silent minutes, I wondered, was I done here? Did he forget to dismiss me?

I was about to knuckle my forehead and quietly disappear from his sight when, as if to the papers before him, he said, "I am entering you into the ship's register as ordinary seaman."

Did he say, "ordinary seaman?"

"Sir?"

After penning another note, he replaced the quill and, glancing over the page, said, "From this point forward your duties will be much more demanding." A brief pause, then, "So do not think for even a second that I have done you a good turn, for I do no such thing. Everyone on this ship must pull his own weight. I have no doubt that you shall soon find yourself wondering if you are up to the task. If I find I have erred in my expectations then so be it, we shall always have need of another boy." Leaning over his desk, he peered deep into my eyes and asked, "You will not disappoint me, will you, Mason?"

"No, sir!" I said, thinking for a moment that I must be dreaming.

Was I, only a few moments past, expecting to be hung from the yardarm?

"That will be all. You may return to your duty station," he said, his eyes returning to the papers.

I knuckled my forehead saying, "Aye, aye, sir!" and retraced my steps to the quarterdeck.

As I passed the sentry, his smirk had been replaced with a genuine smile as he said, "I expect we shall not see you hang from the yardarm this day, Seaman Mason."

Though the captain had, at no time, raised his voice, this man already had full knowledge of everything that transpired. By the time I made my way back to the mainmast, I was not surprised to find that nearly the whole ship knew of my promotion.

CHAPTER FOURTEEN

To pull my own weight as a ship's boy was a thing that I had learned to do well during my first three weeks aboard the *Deception*. The tasks I had to perform under that rating were both difficult and often grueling. Although the work was designed for boys, allowances had been made to exclude heavy work such as lifting of extreme weight or hauling upon topsail halyards.

To pull my weight as an ordinary seaman, however, an occupation generally held by men, was quite another matter. The position required I pull as much weight as the next "man" and therein lay the inequity. I could not bear the thought of disappointing the captain after he had seen fit to reward me with such an advance in position. I would handle the weight of sail to be furled or reefed, halyards to be raised, braces to be hauled upon, bowlines to be set, masts to be struck and then stepped again, as well as the other duties of holystoning the deck or manning the wash deck pumps.

There was also the higher pay rate to consider. Unlike the wage of £7 per annum I had earned as Ship's Boy Third Class, my new position paid £1 5s 6p each month which, at sea, there were thirteen. I realized it was a paltry sum compared to what I had taken in as a thief, but it was honest pay, earned by my own hand and the first wage I had truly worked for.

As Ship's Boy, I had honed my abilities in sail handling, while gaining the strength and endurance of which I formerly wouldn't have believed myself capable. I initially believed that experience had fully prepared me for the position of ordinary seaman. To my surprise, however, my first week as ordinary seaman was so backbreaking and muscle straining that the instant I crawled into my hammock each night, I was fast asleep as soon I closed my eyes. Once asleep, it seemed as though my allotted four hours had vanished as I felt the nudge from my crew captain. To make matters worse, the exhaustion I endured was exacerbated even further by my never-ending hunger. To be sure, the meals were dealt out in equal portions, yet, of late, the biscuit had become rife with maggots and the salt beef both stringy and tough as shoe leather.

Fortunately, after four long days, my name appeared on the roster for mess duty. The work in the kitchen was extremely hot and without respite but there was generally food to be had. This, I thought, must be the answer. If only I could be placed on permanent mess duty, my hunger would be at end.

It was by mere coincidence that I befriended the peg-legged cook, a Mister Julius Griswald. In the late morning hours while steeping salt beef in great pots set upon the cooking stove, Griswald mentioned that, like the meaning of my last name, he had been a mason prior to his being pressed into the Navy.

I replied that my father was a master mason, and member of the Old Dundee Lodge on the Thames which impressed him not a little.

"Stands to reason," Griswald said. "I supposed there to be a mason in your line, you havin' the name. There was a time I had me hopes o' going back to the trade."

Supporting his legless hip against the spice cabinet so that he might free his flour-coated hand, he wiped the sweat from his sad, droopy eyes. Reaching down with a heavily tattooed arm, he massaged his stump while saying, "Them hopes was dashed the day the Frogs shot this off. That was 'fore your time, back in the Seven Years War, it was. After they discharged me from the hospital, I tried to go back to work only I can't get me arse onto no scaffold without me havin' two legs. I come back to the Navy 'cause here's the only place what'll have me now." He shook his long face causing his loose, sagging cheeks to waddle as he met my gaze. His eyes were the colour of dull jade that seemed to speak of years of inner pain. He caught me glancing at his legless hip and, at length, said, "You still got your limbs, lad. You could make your daddy proud by going back to the trade the minute your feet hit the docks o' England. Don't end up as I have; and for the bleedin' Christ, keep an eye out for the press gangs. Else, someday you'll be sending your poor wife and babies the paltry scraps they shell out as wages." His voice had risen to an angry pitch as he withdrew an iron spoon from the cabinet and slapped it against the stove, rending a loud clang. "And them babies nearly starving and you not being able to do nothin' about it." Turning away, he wiped his cheek with his forearm.

From similar stories I had heard since aboard, I knew his pain was shared by many and I considered myself most fortunate to have left my family in good stead. "My father is dead," I said.

The pale spark in his eyes dimmed even further as he shook his head while speaking in a gravelly tone, "Sorry to hear of it."

I opened the door to the fire box below the stove, covering my mouth and nose with my shirt to keep from inhaling the thick smoke as it filled the space, and threw a few chunks of wood into the fire. The pots were boiling heartily now, throwing off a beefy odor that mixed with the steam and wood smoke. "Very kind of you, I'm sure," I said. "He was a good man and I hope to be like him someday."

Griswald pushed himself away from the cabinet and hobbled over to stir one of the pots. "You've got some growin' to do but if you hold up your end you just might make somethin' o' yourself, either in the Royal Navy or back home as a mason. The way I sees' it, a man can't go wrong as a mason. Yes, sir, that's where I'd put my stock if I was you."

"I worked with my father as his tender for a while," I said.

Griswald shot a sideways glance and said, "Like it, did ya?"

A memory of my father came to mind. He was smiling with satisfaction while standing with trowel in hand and laying on mortar I had just prepared and I said, "I've yet to enjoy anything more."

A smile creased his leathery features and, after some contemplation, sported a long stemmed fork in my face as though to emphasize his words. "Ya know, I may not be in the trade but I'll be a mason till the day I die. Bein' a mason ain't only a trade, hell, it's a way o' life. There's an understandin' to the order o' things most people don't know. And there's the master masons like your daddy who rightly knowd' things most masons never come to understand. He'd o' gone through a good many degrees and come to know some o' the mysteries of life. If I knowd half o' what your father knowd, I suppose I wouldn't o' lost me leg. Hell, it's more like I wouldn't have even been pressed into the Navy. What I mean to say is, there are things you'll learn as a Mason, that is, if you make it back—things you'll be much better for the knowin'."

"Such as the Seven Principles?" I asked.

Griswald's long chin dropped, stretching tight the sagging skin of his cheeks. At first he said nothing, as though trying to compose a sentence and, having nothing for it, dropped and slowly shook his head.

"How'd ya' hear o' the Seven, you bein' just a tender?" Without awaiting my reply, he went on, "The reason I'm askin' is I worked as a mason for a good many year 'fore I come to hear o' the Seven. I knowd they is well guarded secrets 'cause I ain't never got far enough along in the order to be given the meanin' of the Principles."

Turning to face me, a dull spark within his eyes grew and I wondered if I detected a hint of jealousy in his voice? After a brief pause, he nudged my ribs with his finger and asked in a low voice, "So, how?"

I suddenly felt as though I had already said too much. But he was a mason, I reasoned. Surely it would not be taboo to speak of the Seven to him. "Well, I heard it spoke of."

"To you, lad?" Griswald prodded.

"Well, no, not directly to me." I said cautiously. I started to explain that it was in a dream yet I suddenly felt my blood flushing through my veins.

"So you listened in on yer father without him knowin'?" he said disapprovingly. "You shouldn't o' done that, lad." His demeanor became cordial as he said, "Anyways, what did he say about the Seven Principles? Did he say what the first one was?"

The First Principle is the Principle of Mentalism. The universe is mental, existing within the mind of the ALL, I thought. Nothing is truly solid even though it appears to be so. Everything is composed of the thoughts within the mind of the ALL. However, as I tried to answer, I could only stammer, "The, the, the, the Key…"

"You know about the Key?" he said, incredulously. "Does your daddy have the Key? Come on, lad. Out with it."

I could not say it. Why could I not say it? "No, I already told you my father is dead."

"Aye! That you did. Then who has it?" he barked, before making an obvious effort to restrain himself. Then, asking with disingenuous concern, he said, "Did he give it to ya, boy? Why, you ain't even full growed." Leaning close, his foul breath hot on my ear, he said, "Tell me boy, where is it now?"

Recalling the words of Mrs. St. Clair as she said, "Tell no one of this, but use the knowledge to teach only those who are ready to receive it," I said, "I don't know. You see, I only heard it mentioned by someone at one of the mason contests."

"And who might that a' been, son?" Griswald pressed.

"I never got a look at him. I only overheard it."

With that, Griswald threw up his hands. "So you don't know any more o' the Seven than do I, other than they's Principles?"

"Seven Hermetic Principles, yes, that is all that I know."

He shot a glance at me and, as he stirred another pot, said with a note of suspicion, "You do know they's Hermetic, then?"

"Yes! Although, for the life of me, I haven't a clue who this fellow Hermes actually was," I lied.

With a nod, he was about to speak, but stopped himself and I suspected he knew more than he let on. At length, he seemed to be considering something before he said, "Well, you should be safe. If you don't know what the Key is, much less where it is, you should be quite safe."

"I don't understand," I said, quite puzzled. "Why should I not be safe if I were to know the Key's location?"

With sweat running down his forehead to form a droplet on the tip of his long beak-shaped nose, he turned and, leaning close, gave me a very serious stare and whispered, "Because men have been killed for it. Some just 'cause someone thought they had it, some 'cause they was thought to know its location. There have been many copies made but only the original has the power."

"Why should one desire to kill for it?" I asked, not a little shaken by this bit of intelligence.

"Because the cove what has it can shape his own life, as well as the things about him—shape 'em to his own gain, and I can't see no cove what wouldn't fancy havin' that power at his disposal."

"What things about him? How does he change the things about him?" I asked.

"Well, somehow he learns to change things from one thing to 'nother, such as lead into gold. O' course, I don't rightly know if it's true, but then if it weren't, why would anyone kill for it?"

"Who has been killed for it?" I asked.

"Well, for one, over a thousand Templars."

"A thousand Templars? When?" I asked in disbelief.

"You ain't heard of Black Friday?"

"No, I haven't." I said.

"Friday the thirteenth? Certainly you've heard of that."

"I have, but what has superstition to do with the Templars?" I asked.

"Why, it ain't got nothin' to do with superstition. It's history I'm talkin' about."

"I don't understand," I said, my interest sparked.

"Well, I ain't sure of the facts, ya' understand, but I'll give you the gist of it."

Scratching his stubbly chin, he stared into the brown liquid of the steeping pot and said, "In times past, the Templars was once many and very powerful," he said, opening his arms wide. "They was rich like kings and 'ad land in France to boot—a lot o' land. The Frog king was rich too, but he wanted to know how they come by their riches 'cause he wanted everythin' the Templars had. It weren't long 'fore he caught wind o' the Key.

Word is that Hermes was a sorcerer who lived in Egypt. Most say he had great magical powers and before he died, he forged a Key out o' gold. Then he sent his ghost into the Key after he died. 'Course, it's just a legend but word was the Key come to be buried under Solomon's Temple where the Templars dug it up durin' the Crusades."

"Was there anything else under the Temple?" I asked.

"Gold and the like, sure, but it was the Key what made 'em rich. And it was on account 'o the Key that the Frog king throw'd the Templars into the dungeons. After that he spent years torturin' 'em so's they'd tell 'im where it was."

Griswald paused and, pulling up his greasy apron, wiped the sweat from his brow with it before continuing. "They would o' told 'em, sure, 'cause there ain't no cove what can stand up to years of horrible pain. Fact is, only one man knowd where it was. And he bein' a salt who had his own ship got word o' the king's dealins' and sailed 'fore they could take him. Ha! Sailed clean away to Scotland is what I 'eard." Leaning close, he whispered in my ear, his rancid breath burning my nose as he said, "And the word is the Key went with 'im. And Scotland is where the Templars come to call themselves Masons so's they wouldn't be tracked down by the king's spies!"

"Who was the Knight who escaped by sea?" I asked.

"Well, there weren't just one, lad. You see, a lot o' Templars was merchant seamen. But the leader o' the men who sailed to Scotland, I heard, was a man named…" He scratched his head for a moment and, with resignation, said, "I 'eard the name but I…" His lips parted, exposing a rotten toothed smile and he exclaimed, "Payen! That's it. The man's name was Payen. Married a woman there in Scotland named St. Clair. The leader of the Templars was burnt at the stake in France after they couldn't get him to tell of where the Key was. He cursed all what done it to im' 'fore they killed him. That was on Friday the Thirteenth. Them what done it to him all died within the year is what I heard."

Taken aback by the name, St. Clair, I could see the old woman's eyes staring into my soul, and had an odd sensation that she was there in the galley with me.

Griswald's smile vanished and, with a solemn expression, he said, "Do ya realize the power o' such a thing? Do ya understand what can happen to ya if someone even thinks yer privy to the whereabouts of the Key?"

"I quite take your point," I said. "I imagine having the Key would be like having the power of Merlin himself, as well as all the devils of the world wishing to kill you in order to possess it. As I spoke, I recalled the dream of the bent nails, and it became crystal clear why Hendricks had murdered my father.

Gripping the table before me, I felt as though my fingers were compressing the wood beneath my hands as I saw everything falling into place. Hendricks came by after the funeral wishing to buy our home, thinking, with the loss of Father's income, we would be in such a poor state of affairs that we would have been happy to sell the house.

If he had been successful he would have had all the time he needed to take it apart, piece by piece, until he had the Key.

It must have been he who uttered, "He's the Keeper, ya know!" the day of the *crusher* contest. Perhaps he had recently discovered through some intelligence that Father had the Key and simply waited for an opportunity. I only served to hinder his murderous plot by hammering those nails into the scaffold planking. Only he did manage to pull them out, the cold hearted bastard. Yet, in spite of his diabolical efforts, it is I who have the Key. I wonder if he knows that I have it. I hope, for Mother and Lilly's sake, that he does. For, if not, he will be scheming for another way to get at it.

"Something botherin' ya boy?" Griswald asked after observing that I was quite caught up in thought.

"No, not at all," I said, trying to regain my composure. "I was just considering old Merlin."

Griswald puckered his lips and gave out a whistle before saying, "Merlin indeed. Well, enough of that. I'll say it again, return to the trade the minute your feet land in London." Then, pointing a ladle in my face, "And unless you don't care to survive this voyage, I wouldn't be speaking o' no Key to no one on this ship or off."

"Then if I could only manage the continual crying out of my stomach from meal to meal for more food, perhaps I may survive just fine," I said. Turning to face him, I posed the question that had been brewing since I first reported to the kitchen for duty that morning.

"Would it be putting you out, sir, if I were to beg you to inquire of the captain a permanent position as your assistant?"

"Feeling poorly all the time, are ya?" he said with a knowing smile.

"Always!" I replied.

"When I was young like you, I had me the same situation. Some eats more, some less, but you is like I was. You ain't getting enough food to do yer work, is ya?"

"No, sir! I am continually famished."

"The captain won't approve of you working down here permanently, 'specially since he just promoted you to Ordinary, but I'll see what I can do."

From then on, I was much indebted to Griswald for my added weight and strength, for each time we were piped to breakfast, dinner, or supper, he heaved extra portions onto my plate while handing me the occasional piece of toast for my pocket. Had it not been for his help, I would certainly have withered away and become too weak to keep up with the other seamen, ultimately disappointing the captain and losing my newly acquired rating.

This position gave me no armor against the antagonistic Midshipman Lewis, for my new status only served to add fuel to the flames of his hatred of me. With the common knowledge of his being saved from certain death by me, I wondered how long he could bear the knowing glances from the crew. I strongly suspected that he had plans to bring about either my humiliation or demise. If I were to place a wager, my money would be on the latter, for as long as I remained alive, I stood as a daily testament to his failings. As life continued aboard the *Deception* with its monotonous routine of deck scrubbing, sail tending, gunnery exercise, and catching what little rest I could find within my hammock, Lewis eyed me closely and silently smoldered.

One day during the afternoon watch, the July sun beat down so heavily upon the exposed deck planking that the oakum oozed up from the seams, filling our nostrils with the heavy odor of tar before a slight breeze wafted it to leeward.

All about the deck was a scene of madness as men set off against one another swinging swords, cutlasses, and boarding axes while engaged in small arms practice. Set off in pairs, we would charge our opponents, then they us, beating each other back and forth until our arms could no longer hold our weapons. I had worked up a sweat, my arms and shoulders near exhausted from fending off the endless blows of Schultz's battle axe when, above the din, I heard Lewis calling out in his breaking adolescent voice, "Mason, avast your playing and come over here. I shall show you how a real fight is done."

Schultz and I ceased our pretended hostilities and I left him. Stepping through the throng while ducking to avoid the swing of blades and axes amidst the odor of men's armpits, I approached Lewis who stood with his cutlass at the ready. My chest was heaving from the recent exertion, and though my vision was blurred from the sweat running into my eyes, it was obvious by his freshly washed face that he had, thus far, yet to engage in battle with anyone. He had stood by, observing my strengths and weaknesses until he was sure that I was fairly fagged out. His smug expression told me that he planned on using my exhausted state to do me serious harm.

He had me at a serious disadvantage. If I refused his order, he would have the satisfaction of calling me the coward before informing the lieutenant, which would result in even more humiliation. The punishment for disobeying an order could be as severe as a flogging and as light as being caned, which is to have your backside exposed while being beaten with a wooden cane. I was, as he had said while upon the mainmast, "fucked," and could find no way out of the situation. He would have my blood, either from his sword or by a beating from the cane. I quickly reasoned that the cane would be the worse of the two for, if I were to be cut by his sword or, perhaps even killed, at least I would not be the coward.

My only chance was to take the offensive so, without hesitation, I raised my cutlass, placing him on guard before he could utter any of the usual insults. Not unlike a bull, however, he seemed unperturbed and drew his lips back to reveal his snarling jagged teeth.

During my career as a thief, I had learned to look for telltale signs of a cully's intended actions, thereby saving myself from being taken up and bound to await the constable. The key to all these signs were the eyes. Locking onto Lewis' deep-set, baboon-like eyes told me ever so clearly not only what his next move would be, but what he was thinking. And at that moment he was thinking, I have him. Yes, I've got the little bastard now. Unfortunately, I believed he was right. His thrusts were throwing me off balance and his swings were coming down hard with a ringing clang, sending vibrations up my blade and nearly driving it from my hand. With each blow, I could feel my already fatigued arms losing their ability to fend off.

In his eyes, I could see that he had planned this for days. He was going to make it appear as simply a slip of the sword. It would be recorded in the ship's log as an accident. Seaman Mason, discharged dead. After all, he was an officer and I only an ordinary seaman. What could I do? While he was pounding me down to a point where I was onto one knee, I could see he was taking great pleasure in beating me. My rage began to build for, knowing that I had dealt with much more than the likes of him, I felt ashamed of the way I was handling the situation. I had completely forgotten that I carried the Mason Key and that I was the only one who had access to the secret knowledge and power that it embodied. That power, however, was something of which I knew very little, much less how to exercise or manage it. There were the tenets, the Principles, the first of which must be the most important of all seven.

While deflecting the blows, I struggled to remember the mechanisms of the First Principle. A mental universe could be altered simply by imagining it to be so; the important factor being that I must believe completely and harbor absolutely no doubt in my ability to do it. Could I do it? Then, I remembered that I had done it with the help of Mrs. St. Clair when imprisoned in the cask within the ship's hold. Can I do it alone? I asked myself as Lewis' blade hammered down onto my cutlass. I can do it and I will do it!

With a conviction that seemed to be rooted in the depths of my soul, I envisioned my body refreshed and full of that morning drive that takes you through the entire day. I felt my arm become as rigid as the steel of the cutlass it held. In a flash, my heart pounded new energy into my extremities and I became filled with renewed strength.

Lewis swung down hard and I deflected the blow off to my side while stepping in close, thereby swinging my blade up to within an inch of his face. His smug expression transformed to the look of a spooked horse as he realized he had misjudged me. Even worse for him was that I had put the sword to his face in front of many witnesses, one of which was Third Lieutenant Tarlington then observing us from the passageway above.

In a glance, I could see Tarlington's thick lips puckering, a thing he did while contemplating a decision. Perhaps he was considering putting a stop to our melee.

Lewis' blood filled his face, turning it cherry red as he stepped back to avoid my next thrust. Then, in a millisecond he recovered and, in a fury, came at me with all the force of his weight bringing his blade down toward my head.

Only this time I was ready for him. Rather than block, I sidestepped not nearly as quick as I had wished for his blade sliced the sleeve of my shirt before hitting the deck.

Thrown off balance, he fell toward his sword and, before he could recover, I held my cutlass once again to his undefended throat, the blade lightly touching his skin.

I dearly wished to run it through his neck, but as our eyes met, I saw his mortification in having lost to me. Payment enough, I thought.

Even so, with the blood drained from his face, he seemed to be weighing the risks of an attempted counter thrust. I held my blade to his acne scarred neck, maintaining a slight pressure on his pimpled skin while he stood motionless as a granite statue, no doubt, very much aware of my mental thrust.

Then, slowly, very slowly, he pulled himself away from my blade.

"I believe you are dead, sir!" I said, with my chest heaving and my throat constricted, and it took all of my restraint to withdraw the blade.

"You ga…got lucky," he stammered, while using his shirtsleeve to wipe the sweat from his brow. "I only tripped."

Schultz had been standing off to the side of our little encounter and Lewis suddenly turned on him, saying, "What are you looking at? Get back to your practice, you goddamn Hessian."

Shouldering his axe, Shultz turned and stepped over to rejoin the other men in small weapons practice.

Lewis glared at the faces around him and barked, "Damn yer eyes! That means all of you!"

As though we were puppets on an invisible string, we quickly resumed our mock combat rather than be subjected to the wrath of his mortification. As I swung my cutlass, I caught a glimpse of Lieutenant Tarlington, his hand covering his mouth, while his barrel chest and rounded shoulders quivered involuntarily.

Until then, I had had my doubts about the Mason Key. Now, in light of recent events, I realized with absolute certainty that the teachings were valid. The First Principle is true, and if not for my belief in it, I might have been dead in those past few minutes. I resolved from that point forward to trust and believe completely the nightly teachings that I received in my dreams and to remember them to the best of my ability. The universe is indeed "Mind" and anyone who possesses a mind may influence the universe. Perhaps Moses knew this, perhaps even Christ knew this, but to attempt to explain it to the masses would be futile. As Mrs. St. Clair said, "Teach only those who are ready to learn," but before all else, I must teach myself.

After supper, when we had slung our hammocks, Schultz, pipe in hand, came over to me and, before going up the ladder to take a smoke, said, "You learn another ting today. Der werk *mit der* cutlass… you dun *gut*. An you din't kill der little *sheiza*. You dun *gut*."

"Do you really mean that, Schultz?" I said with surprise at receiving a compliment from, excluding the captain, the most stoic man aboard.

"*Ja*, I do," he chuckled, before sticking his pipe between his teeth and climbing the ladder to the main deck.

The day had been both sweltering and long, and the night didn't fare much better. I had stripped to the waist before climbing into my hammock, yet the stifling air beneath the deck planking, still hot from the day's sun, was suffocating. With no breeze from the open gun ports on either side of the deck, I couldn't find from the stifling heat. My sweat-soaked trousers clung to me and aggravated the salt sores on my backside and, when I could bear it no more, I threw on my shirt and went up on deck for some fresh air. Apparently not alone, I encountered much of the crew lying about over hatchways and along any board that would support them. With no room on deck, I scaled the shrouds to the mizzen topgallant yard and lashed myself to the furled topgallant sail. It was not long before I fell into a light slumber as the ship rose, swayed, and fell into each successive swell. From time to time I could hear distant bits of a conversation as it drifted up to me from the poop deck. At first, I ignored it but, at length, the words grew nearer. I turned my focus onto the snaps, squeaks, and groan of the ship's rigging and was close to sleep when I recognized the restrained retort of Lewis who was speaking to Midshipmen Tomkins.

Having climbed the mizzen shrouds some time after me, they had stopped at the topsail yard in an attempt to gain privacy. In the darkness above them, I knew they couldn't see me, so I remained still and listened. As they spoke, the breeze steadily increased. Only a gentle gust at first, yet it continued to grow in succession. With wind now in my ears, I could only catch a few words every now and again.

"I am senior and…will do…I say," said Lewis.

"You can't order…" returned Tomkins.

"Oh yes…can! You will…I say or I will…you…like a sow's …"

At this point, I turned to look down. Although there was only starlight, I could make out their dim forms. Tomkins, half the size of Lewis, was in Lewis' grasp and it appeared Lewis had his hands around Tomkins' throat. Then Lewis released Tomkins just as Lieutenant Bengs came on deck to escape the heat below.

So the bullying did not end with the crew, I thought. He had his way with his fellow "mid's" as well.

With Bengs on deck, Lewis and Tomkins descended the shrouds and, as I drifted back to sleep, wondered what Lewis might be up to.

At 4:00am, eight bells struck and the bosun stood at the hatchway piping all hands with the cry of, "Larboard watch, ahoy!" Shortly thereafter, he descended the ladder sounding out the usual, "Rouse out there, you sleepers!"

Untying my lashings, I could see the ebony sky still showed no sign of the dawn and the air felt warm as a slight breeze made the topsails luff and crack. As I slid down a backstay, I could see the helmsmen, backlit from the light of the binnacle, doing their best to rein in the continual starboard to larboard drift.

Within minutes, men were filing out of the hatchways to muster at their duty stations. Harvey and I were assigned to heave the log and soon reported the ship's speed at a weak three knots. At five o'clock, the wash deck pump was rigged and I was down on my knees alongside Harvey working up the first sweat of the day.

I could never get used to the chafing of my skin from my salt-stiff clothing, and though the fabric would soften when drenched by the wash-deck pump, it would stiffen even more once it had dried.

During the last rain, I had dashed below decks to bring up all my clothing so as to rinse them out. During a heavy downpour, we beat shirts, trousers, blankets, and hats upon the hammock netting to work out the white salt grains that had settled into the creases and folds. So encrusted were our clothes that their rinsing created a milky saline drip that trickled onto the deck into a stream that joined with the streams from the other men's clothes before running out through the scuppers.

The days that followed were spent in the continual routine of navy life aboard a Man o' War. Each knew his duty and I, now one of the conditioned seamen, carried out my work in a seamanlike fashion.

To be sure, the challenge was always there, whether at gunnery practice, furling sail, bending on, which is to install a new or fresh sail onto the yard, or stepping masts, and we were continually in competition with one another. As such, we did foolish things, and from time to time, those things caused serious injury to the crew, whether a crushed foot, broken arm, or broken neck. Such is what happened to Seaman Adams.

Adams was a fine sailor having had the experience of many years at sea, yet it took only one stiff gust of wind to do him in. He had just released his hold on the topgallant yard in order to pull the gasket under while tying off a reef knot. The man only uttered a cough when he struck the topsail yard with his back, throwing him forward and face down. There was only a muffled groan as his shoulder grazed the mainsail yard. The snap of his neck, not unlike the sound of a brittle tree branch, was the last sound heard from him as he took the lower mast backstay across his face, spinning him onto his back before his lifeless body hit the deck with a bounce.

One would think that after witnessing such an accident, the prospect of going aloft would be accompanied by the feeling of dread. But this was not the case with me for in spite of having seen both my father and this man fall to their deaths, I loved it up there. It was the only time on the ship that I felt truly alive. I could feel the full force of the wind in my face, watch the sails billowing out as the sun broke the surface of the horizon, and feel the dull thud transcending up the mast as the hull cut through the crest of the waves. Even with the constant threat of danger, I could not deny myself the experience of such splendor.

As the weeks passed, I was soon handling sail as well as the best of them. As for sliding down a backstay, a feat that used to destroy my hands, my thick growth of calluses made it a thrilling ride. Some of my mates jokingly called me the "monkey," a name of which I was quite proud, for I had earned it by climbing faster than any of them.

With a sideward glance at the tattooed men working with me, I felt an increasing sense of belonging. Although I missed my home, my memories of London were an odd combination of both good and terrible. I often wondered how Mother and Lilly fared with the loss of the income I had provided them, but I took comfort in knowing Mother had access to my bank account and could stretch a farthing further than the most frugal women of our manor. I found it increasingly easy to accept the fact that I should not return home for a long, long time. Looking ahead, I wondered what awaited me in the American Colonies, a place I had only read of, and found a degree of pleasure in the anticipation of seeing it firsthand.

At six bells, the sky was cloudless as the sun had climbed to a point of about ten degrees above the horizon. We had just finished holystoning the deck when the lookout hailed, "On deck there! Sail, hull-down, three points off the starboard quarter."

Newcomb slung his glass over his shoulder and scrambled up the shrouds with a speed that nearly matched my own. Soon he was at the main topgallant crosstrees scanning the area pointed out by Simmons, captain of the maintop. After studying the strange sail, Newcomb slid down the backstay, wiped his hands on his kerchief, and sent one of the hands to notify Captain Cole.

This was the first sail I had seen on this voyage and realized I would soon have the opportunity of seeing the signal flags flying.

Soon, the captain appeared on deck, pulling on his trousers and stuffing in his shirt before ordering the signal.

Harvey informed me we would first hoist our colours and see if the other ship responded in kind. For if she turned tail and ran, it was likely to be a Colonial smuggler or an enemy French vessel.

Tomkins now had the glass and had placed himself in Newcomb's previous position in the maintop while studying the other ship for the responding signal. After careful study, he announced, "British colours!"

I strained my eyes in the direction pointed out but the ship was too far off to be visible from the deck.

"Can you make out her rig?" Captain Cole asked.

All ears were turned skyward, awaiting Tomkins' reply.

"Cutter, sir! She's signaling." The crew remained silent.

"Packet, *Sky Queen,* Captain Riggs commanding. Urgent matters."

"Invite her captain aboard," Cole said, while on the way back to his cabin.

The order was given to "heave to" and we went to work hauling in the courses and bracing the fore and main topsails—a maneuver completely new to me. Once completed, I could easily understand the reasoning. Both topsails in this "V" configuration served to work against one another spilling as much wind as they caught, causing the ship to gather no headway while giving little to no leeway. Within minutes the little packet was "hull up," a term used to describe the distance of a ship that has its hull visible above the horizon, and a very short time later she lay hove to within half a cable's length. Her gig was soon hoisted over the side while our marines made up a side party at our entry port. When the gig pulled alongside, the seas were tossing it about so much that, although the captain managed a good grip upon the boarding ladder, he lost his footing and hung momentarily by one hand while the sea washed him from shoes to waistcoat. His curses filtered up the side while the marines did their best to restrain the chuckles that forced through their gritted teeth.

The bosun blew his fife, announcing the *Sky Queen* captain's arrival at the entry port. Of medium height, he was a large-framed man with thin curly brown hair tied back in the customary club fashion. While Captain Riggs stood before the marines, his wide-set jaw and thick pursed lips pronounced his indignation while a stream of seawater spilled from his trousers and shoes.

I was surprised to see the pristine new broad turn-back white lapels that ran from the collarbone to the *Sky Queen* captain's soaked waist, making him, in fact, a lieutenant. I later learned that his title of Master and Commander was generally given to a lieutenant rising in rank and given command of a sloop or cutter. The address of "captain" was merely a courtesy until he could achieve the rank of Post Captain. The marines stood at attention while Newcomb escorted him to the captain's cabin.

It was only a short while before Captain Riggs emerged from the cabin and quickly went down the entry ladder to his gig. No sooner had he reached the *Sky Queen's* entry port than the packet let fly her square topsail and large main staysail, hauled her wind and was making six knots before her gig was hauled up into the stern davits.

As the little ship left us like a racehorse in full gallop, Harvey muttered,

"Where do ya suppose she's in such a hurry to get to?"

I had no idea and was about to state as much when the call came for "All hands."

Expecting the usual orders to prepare for getting underway, I was surprised when we were called to assemble in the waist just forward of the poop deck. Soon thereafter, the captain came on deck.

With a solemn expression, his thick furrowed brows fixed upon the deck beneath him and, for a long moment, he looked at no one. Then, taking hold of the banister with both hands, he pulled himself up the ladder to the Poop Deck where he turned to address the crew. Before speaking, he took time to look each of us in the eye and I realized, though we were many, he recognized each and every one of us. At length, he folded his hands behind his back and spoke.

"Men, other than crossing the Atlantic, most of you know our destination, but few know our mission. I am sure that, with our ballast of field ordnance and our hold stacked with crates of musketry, some of you have figured it out. Well, we are indeed bound for New York. Our mission is to deliver these arms to General Howe's troops. Though our mission is a relatively simple one, many lives depend upon it, for these weapons will be crucial in getting the colonial rebellion under control.

The reason I have called you here today is that I just have received news concerning our mission. As I have stated, our mission was to deliver ordnance to New York, however, now it has become much more than that. The service I will ask you to perform is the most demanding any captain can ask of his men. I am asking of you something I can only force you to do under the threat of death by the Articles of War. I, however, do not desire your obedience under this threat. Instead, I would prefer that you do your duty voluntarily. We are, as you well know, at war with France. I have just received word that a fleet of Frogs are on their way to OUR COLONIES to assist the TRAITORS." At this, he paused to allow his words to sink in. Then, continuing, he said, "The only way we can stop them is to destroy them at sea. Will you do your duty? Will you fight alongside me for your King, for your country?"

All around me a cry rose to an almost deafening roar, "Huzzah for the captain!" Spittle flew from their mouths as they cheered, "Huzzah for England!"

Covering my face, I wondered what war could mean for us. We were to fight the French? I pretended to cheer with the men but my heart wasn't in it. I only wished to sail with the crew to wherever we might go, but a battle with the French had never occurred to me. Having practiced running out and firing the guns obviously had this purpose in mind but, until now, it had been just that—practice. To actually fire upon other ships where return fire would be expected was quite another matter. We could all be killed. Why did they seem so happy about this? They seem to have all gone mad. One would think they had just been offered wealth beyond their dreams. Other than dismemberment or death, what did they expect for their services, redemption from their sins? Or could they be thinking of an end to a miserable life of poverty? Did they so love their England that they would die protecting her? Could I be patriotic to a country that would have me hung if I returned?

It was my home, I reminded myself, and I am serving in her Navy. With a sigh, I conceded the fact that, hangman waiting or no, it is my England. Although the excitement was contagious, I couldn't help wondering what lay ahead. Suddenly, the image of the Mason Key came to mind and I wished to believe it would protect me. Then I realized that, if it hadn't saved Father from his deadly fall, it was foolishness to expect any better.

CHAPTER FIFTEEN

Sunday morning, the fifth week of the voyage, brought hazy azure skies with occasional dirty bottomed cumulus whose upper portions billowed to majestic heights as they lazily drifted back toward England. The frosty air coming in through the gun ports did little to cool our sweat-soaked bodies as we scurried about like rabbits in a warren, each racing the hourglass to get into his Sunday best. Struggling through the throng, I quickly ferreted out my sea chest from beneath one of the tables. These tables, generally used for meals, consisted of large wooden panels and were normally stored on the underside of the deck and above our heads. Now they were being used to hold various assortments of razors, combs, shirts and trousers. Once past the flying elbows and knees, I managed to secure enough room between the housed guns to rummage through the chest and extract my most presentable attire. Setting these aside, I carefully refolded my shirts and trousers before arranging them beneath my mess kit so as to make the whole of it presentable for Divisions Inspection. While immersed in this task, my ears were bombarded with a barrage of frantic disconnected conversations taking place throughout the gun deck.

"Where's me bloody shirt?"

"Who's wearin' my goddamn shoes?"

"Hey mate, could you give my hair a lookin' over. Jones ain't so good at tyin 'is an I sure as hell don't want it lookin' like 'is."

"What's so fuckin' wrong with the way I ties me hair?"

"Nothin', if you don't mind the back of yer 'ead lookin' like a cat o' nine."

"There's gonna be hell to pay, the lieutenant's going to..."

"That ain't the way to shine those buckles. Step aside and let me show ya how it's done."

"Even if he has to search every man jack on the ship, mark my words."

"Hey Schultz, go easy on them shoes man, you're gonna' polish the leather right off."

"We got a lot of dumb ones aboard but I don't know no one dumb enough to nab the lieutenants'..."

"Hey light along there with that chest, go easy with it now."

And so on it went until, at last, every one stood proud as a saint while wearing their Sunday best.

My seldom worn canvas trousers billowed out like miniature sails, as though ready to catch a good wind and increase the ship's speed. Fortunately, during the latest rain, I had managed to wash my duck shirt giving the white stripes a bright luster and fresh clean smell, a quality seldom present aboard the ship.

I felt a sense of pride as I pulled on my wool stockings and slid my feet into my black leather shoes with the brass buckles, a recent purchase from the locker of Mr. Sawyer. Within the hour of their purchase, I had the buckles polished to perfection and now inspected my appearance in the reflection of Maxwell's mirror. Except for my size, I carried the appearance of a genuine tarpaulin. When my mates stepped in line beside me, however, I appeared to be more like a miniature sailor. But then, if I raised myself onto the balls of my feet, I found that I was not much shorter than the shortest of them. Soon, I thought, I will be tall enough to be a short sailor and thereafter, if I take after my father, I shall be taller than the whole lot of them.

Having finished with my sea chest, I was imagining myself

towering well above the other seamen while they all looked to me for advice and favor when my daydream was interrupted by the familiar call of the bosun's fife as we were summoned up to the ship's waist.

Generally, on Sunday afternoon we gathered to stand in formation for the chaplain's services. Once this had been accomplished, we were brought in mind that this was the fourth Sunday of the month and it was required that the Articles of War be read aloud to the entire ship's company. This being my first time to hear them read, I was curious as to what they were about. My curiosity, however, soon turned to boredom for there were, in fact, thirty-six of these Articles to be read out, during which time we must stand erect and feign interest.

Although Lieutenant Bengs' voice carried the piercing ring of a sword striking an opposing blade, it took a good deal of effort to keep my mind from drifting away. Particular emphasis had been placed on Article Ten, which speaks that a, "captain who fails to get his men to fight in an action may suffer death." Then there was Article Twelve which goes on to condemn, "any person who, through cowardice, negligence, or disaffection, withdraws or stays back in time of action, or who does not do his utmost to take or destroy every ship that is his duty to engage," and, "'Anyone of the crew or officers who, failing to fight courageously or pleads for quarter shall suffer the penalty of death."

After hearing this, I understood why the men so heartily gave their approbation of fighting the enemy. Courage or loyalty seemed to have nothing to do with it, for though one might die in the fighting, he surely must die if he does not fight.

The gist of those words resonated in my mind long after the reading; for it became quite apparent these articles were devised to make the point that everyone on the ship was subject to punishment at any time and at the whim of any officer. In order to drive the point home, there was Article Thirty-six which is the last article. It states, "All other crimes not capital committed by any person in the fleet, which are not mentioned in this act, or for which no punishment is hereby directed to be inflicted, shall be punished according to the laws and customs in such cases used at sea."

Well, that pretty much sums it all up, I supposed. Just keep your nose clean and you will do all right. And if you get into an action, I swallowed hard on this thought, fight to the death if necessary. From what I had seen thus far, the Atlantic is extremely vast and it stands to reason the odds of running into an enemy vessel must be close to nonexistent. And to support my theory, there was the packet. It had been the first ship to which we spoke since leaving the North Channel of the Irish Sea. Perhaps it is just as well that I put it out of my mind. After all, if the Frogs don't arrive there ahead of us, Maxwell says, weather permitting, we shall be in New York within a fortnight and, with any luck, I may be afforded the opportunity of going ashore.

On the freshly scrubbed gun deck awaiting the captains' divisions Inspection, but for Maxwell and Harvey, we all stood at the ready. It seemed Harvey hadn't managed to tie Maxwell's hair into a respectable shape befitting a Jack Tar. Maxwell's amber mane lay upon the nape of his leathered neck, the strands spread out like the quills of a porcupine while Harvey's thick callused fingers worked feverishly to braid them into a perfectly rounded club shaped configuration.

"God's my life, man, hurry. I told you to leave well enough alone but nooo, you had to go and make it just so," Maxwell admonished, as beads of sweat ran down his forehead.

Harvey whispered, "I nearly have it, I tell you, just hold still."

"My, what a pretty job you've done of it, Harvey. You've made Maxwell proud, I'm sure."

We all turned in unison to find Lewis, seeming to have appeared out of thin air, standing nearby with Midshipman Tomkins at his side.

"I am sure you will have it together in time for the captain's inspection," he said with a smile.

Maxwell's face turned as red as his own hair and, not trusting his tongue, he clenched his jaw shut.

I couldn't ascertain whether his redness was due to anger at Harvey or mortification from being caught in an awkward situation by Lewis.

Stopping at our station, Lewis peered over my shoulder and spoke in a most uncharacteristically cordial voice, "Well, you men seem to have placed yourselves in good order. Tomkins, do take a run through their sea chests and see that they have everything in its proper place."

While I attempted to make sense of Lewis' friendly tone, a small part of me wished to believe that manger duty had done him some good. Perhaps he had acquired a better attitude toward the men, but his smug expression told me otherwise.

Once Tomkins had finished going through our chests, he said, "Everything appears to be in good order here, Mister Lewis."

Lewis raised an eyebrow and, with a complacent smile said, "Very well then, perhaps we should continue on so that we may assure the captain will find nothing out of order. He is in such spirits and it would be a pity to get his blood up over someone failing to have their kit together."

Due to the poor lighting of the gun deck, I couldn't be quite certain but thought Tomkins' complexion had grown a few shades pale with Lewis' comment. Saying nothing in response to Lewis' suggestion, he only nodded. From there they continued their stroll down the row of guns, stopping periodically to inspect another sea chest before ascending the ladder to the quarterdeck.

"Well, what d'ya make of that?" Maxwell said from the corner of his mouth.

"I don't quite know what to make of it," I replied.

Then Harvey cut in, "Well, I got a feeling that litter bugger is up to something. Did you see little Tomkins poking through yer sea chest?"

"No, I didn't. Why?" I asked with surprise.

"Course not, yer back was to him. You better take a look and make sure everything's Bristol or you might find yourself working watch n' watch," Maxwell warned.

"I suppose I had better then," I said, quickly dropping to my knees and pulling up the lid of my chest. A quick glance showed nothing amiss: my shirts folded neatly, my stockings set neatly to the side, my worn shoes, though torn, yet clean as I could get them. Then, I spotted it, a slight glint of something shiny near the edge of one of my folded shirts. I owned nothing shiny except for the buckles of the shoes that I presently wore, and then there were my shillings that Jim Bridges had handed me the day I escaped the noose. As for the shillings, I kept them in a small canvas sack in the bottom of my chest. Did Tomkins steal from me? I wondered. Just then, the bosun piped the hands to attention. Slipping my hands beneath the fold of my shirt, I retrieved a silver button with the engraved fouled anchor commonly worn by high-ranking officers.

Tucked beneath my pile of shirts, I found ten more of the same just as Maxwell whispered, "You'd better get to attention, the lieutenant's comin' with that little shite, Lewis along with his lick-arse, Tomkins."

Being caught while not at attention carried the consequences of a dozen lashes. Yet, I could not leave those buttons where they lay. Lewis had attempted a put up job on me and I wasn't about to be done with like some unsuspecting cully. Being caught with those buttons in my possession, however, would gain me a great deal more than a dozen lashes. Reaching down past the edge of my things, I withdrew the pouch that held my shillings. Placing two shillings beneath my shirt, I replaced the pouch and, scooping the buttons into the palm of my hand; I closed the lid and sprang to my feet a split second before they came into view. Had I been as tall as I had previously wished, they would have seen me. I breathed a sigh of relief. My height, or lack thereof, had given me that split second.

The three came to an abrupt halt directly in front of me. The air was tense about us while the puzzled expressions of the men bespoke the question, why hadn't they started the inspection at the forward end of the deck as was the general procedure? And where might the captain be? I wondered, while staring into Lieutenant Bengs' cold, unforgiving eyes.

"This is the thieving scum!" Lewis said, pointing his dirk at my face while barely concealing a triumphant smirk.

Lieutenant Bengs' shot a raised brow at Lewis and, but for a second, his jaw dropped ever so slightly, leaving a visible gap between his thin lips.

He didn't believe me capable, I thought.

Then, he stiffened and turned his icy countenance upon me.

"WHERE?" he demanded.

"Sir, I..."

Before I could finish my sentence, Lewis cut me off, saying, "Sir, Tomkins discovered them in his chest when we were going over the men's things."

"Over the men's things? I gave you no such order," Bengs said, coldly.

"I only thought our time might be put to good use. That is, to make certain their kits were acceptable for the captain. Didn't you agree Tomkins? It was mere happenstance that we came across them, I suppose." Tomkins' chin trembled as he stuttered, "Aye."

"Enough! Bring them to me now!" Bengs ordered.

Lewis' disappointment was apparent, for until now, he had been thoroughly enjoying the telling of his lie. Why was Bengs so angry with him? After all, he did find his stolen buttons.

As he brushed past me, I pretended to lose my balance and steadied myself with a hand on Lewis' waistcoat. Shoving me aside, he stooped to bend over my trunk and said, "I believe you said they were in here somewhere, didn't you, Tomkins? Oh, what have we here?" he said, gleefully. Withdrawing his hand, he spun around and, as a magician might do, turned his palm upwards and opened it to reveal a shiny shilling.

"It is my money, sir," I said.

"I know it is money, damn you," he hissed. Then, in a quavering voice, "Where are they?"

"Excuse me, sir but, where are—what?" I replied.

Saying nothing and digging in with both hands, Lewis tore through the chest.

Bengs tapped his sword on the deck and said, "My patience is growing thin, Lewis. You have but two seconds to explain yourself," and, as he spoke, a small glimmering object fell from Lewis' hand before striking the deck with a ring.

"Ah-Hah!" Lewis jubilantly barked, only to realize he had spoken too soon as he bent over to retrieve yet another shilling.

"Did you find more of my money, sir?" I asked, with feigned concern.

Lewis did not respond and continued rifling through my chest. With his backside presented to us, his upper body was bent below his waist making the tails of his coat point upward and giving the appearance of an odd looking bird. Then, with his head nearly inside my sea chest, he held out another shilling between the tips of his fingers and out to one side, as though he had found some piece of evidence. It was at that moment that the buttons rolled, one by one, out of his waistcoat pocket, bouncing as they hit the deck and, like returning prodigal sons, came to rest in a small pile at the toe of the lieutenant's shoes, one bouncing to lie flat and shiny, fouled anchor up on his instep.

Lewis hadn't moved, though his eyes had followed the buttons in their departure from his waistcoat pocket. Straightening slowly, he turned to face the lieutenant. His complexion had changed to a pink luster, giving his pimples a white spotted pronouncement. The seriousness of his predicament, however, must have been too much for his quick tongue to function properly and all he could mutter was, "Thaaah, thaaahh," before pointing at me and, finally able to speak, said, "Hee, he-he put them in my pocket!"

For a moment we all appeared like wax statues, no one uttering a sound, while the only thing that moved was a loose lock of Lewis' hair as a cool refreshing breeze swept across the deck.

While the steady swish of the sea ran past the hull, the ridges that had risen in Lieutenant Bengs' forehead slowly transformed back into smooth ivory. With a deep sigh, he said evenly, "Give him his money!"

"But, he did it!" Lewis protested, his upper lip now puffed out and sweating.

"He did it, SIR! Is that not what you meant to say Mister Lewis?" Bengs shot an accusatory glance at Tomkins, who stood silently, tears welling in his half closed eyes, while a clear stream of snot traced down the trough of his short upper lip.

The charade was over and there would be hell to pay for these two. Yet I knew full well, had they succeeded, the hell they will pay would be nothing in comparison to my own.

"GIVE MASON—his money," Bengs said, his voice trailing off as he struggled to control his anger, for it was not good manners to berate even a junior officer in front of the crew. Lewis started to pick up the buttons when Bengs withdrew his hanger and stuck the blade into the deck at the edge of the tiny pile and ordered, "LEAVE—those."

Lewis froze, his eyes upon the blade which was less than an inch from his fingers.

The buttons poured from his grip onto the rolling deck and a few wheeled on end where they halted under the shoes of the men standing opposite us. A drop of sweat fell from the chubby lump of Lewis' nose onto the deck as he carefully picked up my shilling. Turning to face me, his eyes carried an almost palpable threat of death as he dropped the shilling into my open palm.

Closing my fingers on it, I could feel that it was oily and wet. "Thank you, sir!" I said, with my best innocent face.

They left as quickly as they had arrived, Lewis, slump-shouldered and head down like a whipped puppy, his hanger swayed awkwardly behind him as though it were his tail between his legs.

"Well, how do ya like dat?" Schultz commented. "He done caught himself stealing da lieutenant's buttons." His voice, cracking on the word 'buttons,' sent us all into an uncontrollable fit of laughter.

Soon the fife blew and Captain Cole appeared at the forward end of the gunroom near the manger to begin his inspection. Stopping briefly at our station, he furrowed his brow and glanced about while not looking any of us in the eye as was his usual practice. As we stood at attention with eyes still watery and red, he appeared to take no notice and continued down the line of washed and clean shaven men.

"Why he not say nutting bout our red faces?" Schultz asked.

"Aw, he probably thinks we're overdue for the privy is all," Maxwell reasoned. Then, turning to me, said under his breath, "Well, I gotta know. How? How did you do it?"

Suppressing my satisfaction, I put up the most lethargic expression I could muster and said, "Do what? Did you not hear Schultz say that he did it to himself?"

The next time I saw Lewis was while witnessing his punishment. In all my days aboard, I had always feared the dreaded punishment of having to "kiss the gunner's daughter," and felt utterly triumphant that the one receiving it was Lewis and not me. Actually, the only thing being kissed was his arse with the knotted end of a rope. The gunner was not involved, however his daughter was deemed the long eighteen-pound gun he had been bent over and there, lashed to. I was most surprised to see he no longer wore the midshipman's uniform but instead wore the common seaman's attire of checked shirt with red-and-white striped canvas trousers. With incredulous amusement, I realized he had been sent before the mast and was now no better than the rest of us. I thought he should have been hanged for what he did. In London, I knew firsthand that that would have been the punishment. Even still, I was immensely satisfied with his new circumstance.

If they had hung him, I would have been cheated of seeing him, day after day, holystoning the deck and hauling on halyards and braces.

Lewis seemed to take the pain well for the first six strokes, but then he gave way, breaking into a series of wailing screams. When the punishment was over, twenty-four strokes in all, the skin of his buttocks had taken on a cherry red luster that rose to small ridges from the rising whelps. The captain seemed satisfied before ordering the bosun to take him below so the doctor might see to his flaming cheeks. As he stiffly hobbled by us, I saw again, the same hatred in his tear-soaked eyes. I knew he still had plans for me. It was not over and I resigned myself to be continually on the lookout for this unrelenting bastard.

On the following Thursday, the captain of the maintop nudged me out of a deep sleep for the evening watch. This was one of those times when, after getting into our hammocks at 0830 hours, one only had three and a half hours to sleep before reporting for duty to work the next four hours. The evening watch ends just in time to hear the bosun yelling down the hatchway, "Rouse out there you sleepers!" and though you are then off watch, you will not rest in a hammock until the following evening.

When my dangling feet touched the deck, I found that the ship was heeling heavily while gyrating in a most violent manner. I remained hanging from the hammock rail for nearly a half minute before finding a lull in the motion that afforded me time to get my feet down and gain balance so as not to be catapulted into one of the unforgiving iron guns. Having been on this watch, one quickly learns to sleep fully dressed for, getting to one's chest and rummaging through it in the dark is not practical. When I reached the top of the ladder and took hold of the knotted rope's end, a hard salty stream of ocean spray struck me full in the face. In the next second, the salt water was washed away by large splattering droplets of driving rain that plunged into my nostrils and mouth nearly choking me.

Before I could gain my bearings, I was shoved out onto the heaving slippery deck by the rest of the men on my watch as they rushed up from below. I quickly groped for a handhold and, finding none, lost my footing and fell onto my back sliding feet first down the sloping deck into blackness. Reaching out for anything to take hold of, a jolt of pain shot up my arm as my wrist took a blow from the wheels of a gun truck. I managed a hold on the gun's training tackle. This arrested my slide not a moment too soon for my legs were then dangling out over the ship's side through one of the scuppers.

The deck was still hard over and all the water that the ship had taken on from the last wave was making its way past me through the scupper and felt as though it would either drown me or drive me into the sea with it. My hold upon the training tackle was all that I could manage for my other arm was pinned beneath me, and as though the water coming through the scuppers was not enough to deal with, the crest of a passing wave caught hold of my feet and did its best to take me with it. The strain on my arm was nearly unbearable but I had no other recourse but to hold out as long as possible, knowing full well that if I lost my grip, I was a dead man. At length, the ship began its slow rise while the deck rolled the other way and, before it heeled back toward me, I managed to get my other arm from beneath me. Taking hold of a ring bolt, I fought my way back onto the deck. No sooner had I groped my way out of the scupper than a pair of feet hit me in the back and careened down the length of my body. Desperate hands tore past my shirt before getting a hold around my waist.

"Is that you, young Mason?" Maxwell gasped.

"What's left of me," I said, while holding onto the training tackle with a vise-like grip.

"Sorry about that, mate," he said apologetically, before using me as a rope to pull himself back onto the deck. Climbing to his feet, he offered me his hand and said, "I am most beholdin'. I believe you just saved my life."

"I hope that doesn't mean you must kill me now," I said, while regaining my footing.

"Well, if I was a snot-nosed pimple-faced little shite of a mid,' I suppose I might, at the very least, have a go at it," Maxwell joked.

My eyes had adjusted to the dark and now I could make out the low black hulks of the guns which stood ready to knock your shins bloody if you happened to walk into them. Beyond the guns, Billings, captain of the mainmast, stood thin and lean while his narrow eyes peered out from above the other men as he barked out orders, "Take care not to lose your arse up there," he cautioned.

We were to take in the topgallant and double reef the topsail. We all knew that going aloft in this wind would be extremely dangerous. The mist and spray was so thick that the main shrouds appeared to vanish and reappear every few seconds. Groping my way up from the main chains was tough going. The shrouds felt slimy in my grip and I was never sure of a good handhold. The wind tore at my body as though it were a raging river and I a shallow rooted tree on the bank of it. My shirt billowed and flapped as though it were a sail about to part while, at the same time, catching gusts that threatened to tear me from the ratlines.

I had never gone aloft in wind such as this. While making my way to the topmast, I noticed a strange singing vibration in the shrouds. Being the smallest and lightest, I was given the task of going all the way up to the topgallant where I must wait for the helmsman to luff up before hauling in the sail. When I had managed the topgallant yard, I found that there were only two of us up there. With the wind and spray in my face, I felt my way out onto the yard while the other man sidestepped the footropes behind me. Unable to make out his face, it was impossible to say anything to him with the wind howling in our ears.

Once the helmsman luffed to windward, we hauled the sail in with all of our strength. Even with the wind eased, the canvas tore the skin of my fingertips and beat my hands raw before we managed a decent furl and lashed it secure with the gaskets. The man beside me seemed to be having difficulty, his hands repeatedly losing their hold, and I wondered if he was as much in fear of being blown into the sea as was I. Once we had the sail secured, we stepped to the mast to wait for the helmsman to cause the leeward sail to luff. With the wind tearing at our clothing, we held onto the shrouds for dear life until, at last, we saw the windward side of the sail luff.

Without waiting for orders to do so as we would not have been able to hear them, we lay out onto the yard. Once we had the sail furled in, we made our way back to the crosstrees. As we were ready to descend the shrouds, the other man politely motioned for me to go first. Stepping onto the ratlines, the wind struck me with such force that I was driven back away from the mast and, had it not been for a good hold and the instinct to spread my feet outward within the space between the ratlines, I would have been thrown out to sea. Before I could pull myself back toward the shrouds, however, cold hard steel grated across my ribs and I stared in disbelief as the man on the yard withdrew a foot long blade from the hole it had made in my shirt.

Lightning flashed, illuminating Lewis' pimpled face and, in that instant, I could see his deep-set eyes studying my stomach for evidence that his dirk had run me through.

Placing my feet on the outward sides of the shrouds, I loosed my grip, allowing my hands to slide down the wet pitch of the singing cables as another thrust from the dirk cut the air above my scalp. I knew that my decision to slide bordered upon insanity, but I would rather die from the fall than let the bastard have another go at me. If I could make it to the topsail yard, I was sure I could get help, but could I stop my slide in time? Even with the cold rain on the shrouds, my hands were heating up and I dared not put my feet between the ratlines, for to do so would surely break a leg. Placing my instep against the shrouds for balance and added drag, I squeezed the shrouds as hard as I could. For several feet my speed continued without check before slowing. Then, the ship heeled to such an angle that I was brought nearly horizontal, bringing me to a full stop at the topmast crosstrees. By this time, however, the topsail had been reefed and everyone had already gone down to the deck. Glancing up, I could see Lewis sliding down the topgallant halyard and, before I could get to the backstay which would be my only quick escape to the deck, he came to a halt directly in front of me, effectively blocking my way. With a smug grin, he thrust his blade hard at my stomach again. To avoid the deadly steel, I was forced to throw myself sideways and fell into oblivion. My arms, however, swinging like a cartwheel, caught hold of an upper backstay that led up to the mizzens topmast. With a desperate hold upon the stay, I hung, suspended above the pitching deck while Lewis studied my predicament.

Dropping down to the main course with blade in teeth, he crawled out onto the backstay in pursuit. Methodically slashing at me, he forced me backward until I had no choice but to go up the backstay toward the mizzenmast. Hand over hand, feet locked around the rigid hemp hawser, I pulled myself upward like an upside down inchworm. A sharp pain jolted me as his blade cut deep into my calf, just below the knee. Pulling hard, I fought to keep him at bay. The wind rocked me like a cradle, threatening to tear me free, but I held firm and, keeping my feet locked over the cable, made my way up the incline. I could feel the tension on the stay as Lewis made his way after me. I knew that if I were to slide down a backstay to the deck, my only chance to do so lay in my ability to get to the mizzen well enough ahead of him. My ribs burned where my flesh had parted and, even though my shirt and trousers were soaked from the driving rain, I could still feel the warm touch of my blood as it traced its way down from my ribs to pool in the backside of my trousers.

Although I reached the mizzen top crosstrees first, Lewis was close behind. In fact, so close that, had I gone for the backstay, he could have easily cut my throat within the space of time it would have taken for me to get onto it. I limped instead to the topmast shrouds for, with the swelling in my calf, I could not use the ball of my foot and was forced to hobble on my heel at each step down the ratlines. As the ship violently rose and twisted, I took hold of a halyard and slid the remaining distance to the fighting top with my hands. The friction burnt into my calloused hands like a torch and I could smell singed flesh before I hit the platform hard on my heels. Fortunately, my calluses were thick.

The fighting platform gave me no surcease, for no sooner had I reached it than Lewis had dropped, not unlike a spider, down a topsail bunt line. A madman risking death, he miraculously landed feet first onto the wooden planking opposite me. Instantly, he leaped around the mast, slicing the air about me. To avoid his blade, I was forced to fall backwards.

Reaching behind me, I found nothing but space and fell over the after side of the platform. This time, my fall was broken as I slammed into the mizzen gaff, a spar that runs diagonally and holds a sail known as the driver. It felt like a mortar exploding in my brain and my spine was jolted so that for a moment, I could not move. The pine spar ran up the length of me while my legs hung on either side of the triangular sail, and I lay precariously balanced while directly above me, I could make out the dark silhouette of Lewis.

Lightning flashed in the distance and I could see him glaring towards the deck below. Not finding my mangled body where he was sure I would have struck, he remained at the edge of the platform and searched the area below.

The ship heeled to larboard and I slid off the gaff, barely managing a handhold on the middle brail, a line used to haul in the sail. Hanging by only one hand, I tried in vain to get hold of something with the other while, at the same time, Lewis had spotted me.

He was edging his way onto the gaff and I could see that he was closing fast.

I shouted for help but my voice was completely muffled by the howling wind.

As the ship heeled to starboard, throwing me against one of the mizzen vang lines, I managed a hold with my free hand. I was too far out and down for Lewis to get at me with his blade should he risk the loss of his grip on the gaff.

For a second, he paused to study the surrounding rigging. Then he realized he could get at me by cutting away the line securing the vang block and went to work. The vang block is a pulley used to control the port and starboard motion of a sail known as the driver, a large triangular sail running fore and aft near the stern of the ship which, at times, works as a kind of steering mechanism for the sails and, unfortunately, was the very sail to which I clung.

With the driver vang severed, the wind whipped me around like a flag and, in spite of the thrashing, I managed a better hold upon the middle brail of the driver just as the vang line in my other hand went slack. The force of my own weight tore my grip from the brail and I fell helplessly down the leech of the driver. Desperately clutching at the boltrope to slow my fall, I felt a tug on my shirt as the heavy wooden vang block grazed past me in its fall to the deck. With the parting of the vang, the driver shook so violently that it tore from my grip and I fell farther, taking the mizzen sheet under my arm, the friction building until my momentum slowed. With a jolt that knocked my breath from me, my fall was stopped, leaving me dangerously suspended above the taffrail, a rail which stands at the back of the ship. A shape whipped past me from above and turning, I saw Lewis strike the taffrail within an arm's reach of me. In cutting away the vang, he had been thrown about as had I, only he hadn't found a handhold. Even above the howling wind, I heard the cracking sound of his neck as it snapped and, like a broken doll, his head twisted to one side in an unnatural puppet-like position. The lightning flashed, and, for an instant, I could see his scowling expression before he went over the rail into the raging sea. The lightning flashed again and I saw him for the last time, his hair spread about him in the water, his face now devoid of expression as he sank beneath the crest of a following sea.

Just as the lightning faded, something else caught my eye. In a blur, I could make out a sou'wester jacket as the man wearing it wavered off balance and leaned over the taffrail as if he were about to fall in after Lewis.

I suppose it was more a reflex than stupidity when I released the grip of one of my hands on the mizzen sheet block and took hold of the man's sou'wester just at the shoulder. In the space above the waves, we hung together, suspended over the stern of the ship. I didn't know how long I would be able to hold him. The driver shook and shivered, threatening to throw us both off the sheet and I could feel the blood from my wounds flowing down my stomach to my hips. I thought I must surely have a better chance if I released him but my fingers would not release. The rope of the driver sheet cut deep into my other arm before tearing from my armpit to catch in the bend of my elbow. Pain burned in deep and my arm felt as if it would give way. The lightning flashed as a wave washed over us before picking us up and, for a brief few seconds, took some of the tension off my arm.

When the wave left us in the air again, it felt as though the combined weight of our bodies would cause the rope to tear clean through my arm. I attempted to cry out but the wind blew down my throat, cutting off all sound. Intense pain surged with each pulsing beat of my heart and I was certain my hand would soon lose its grip. Each time I felt I must give way, however, a wave would pick us up, allowing me to secure a better hold. Then, as another wave dropped beneath the stern, the wrenching pain in my arm ceased and numbness slowly spread toward my hand. Soon after, I felt nothing and drifted into blackness.

I don't know how long it was before I found an edge to the darkness and could see that we were still there, the man's dead weight beneath me, the rope cutting into my arm; my fingers numb and locked.

As I observed the scene, seemingly from outside myself, Mother appeared in her purple velvet gown with the burgundy trimmed collar that was her favorite social attire. She was bending over me, her gold chandelier earrings dangling from those delicate ears, and smiling with eyes that were spring fed pools of love as she said, "Son, you shall not die. Hurt a great deal, yes, but your soul and power is forever," and just as quickly as she appeared, she vanished.

Then my father stood over me, his smile showed great pride and he winked, giving me that look, the one which means, "I shouldn't have to tell you because you already know what you're supposed to do." Leaning close, he whispered into my ear, "The universe is mental."

The twisting tearing pain in my shoulder and elbow returned and I said, "Father, the universe is tearing my arm from its socket. This man's weight is too great for my body to hold. I must let go."

Then Father gave me that look again. "The universe is mental, son. Imagine your arm as strong as the shrouds of this ship and it will become just that. If you believe it to be so, then it shall be. Everything is in the mind of the ALL, as well as in your own mind. Believe it and know it, Son."

"If that is true," I replied, "then why couldn't you save yourself from death? Why didn't you stop yourself from falling? We were left alone with no means to support ourselves." The pain in my shoulder increased and felt as though it was being viciously stabbed yet, I had to know. "If you had that power, then how could you allow that to happen?

"The one thing we do not have power over is our mortal death," he said solemnly. "We cannot know how or when it is time, we have no power to stop it, son. I know that you pulled through for the family in the only way you could, and it has brought you here. And here you shall find your power. If you believe, you will do as I have told you."

"I believe you, Father. I believe you." As he suggested, I pictured my arm with the twisted tarred hemp fibers of the shroud binding it together. No sooner had I done this than I felt secure that my arm would not tear away.

Placing his heavy hand upon my face, his fingers were rough and calloused, scoring the skin on my cheek as they brushed by. Then another hand took hold of my shirt as a rope slid around my waist before pulling up painfully snug under my arms and squeezing the air from my lungs.

"Get some purchase on it now. Dear God! Captain." The knifing pain stabbed through vibrating layers in my head and, as it penetrated each layer, increased until it became a horrible noise that grew into a deafening roar. I seemed to be buried in pain and incapable of thought with exception to one, a despairing desire for the pain to end before it drove me mad. Then, suddenly, it did end. I was lying on the deck and my arm felt as though it no longer belonged to me. Someone was holding me down while someone else worked at my hand. I could see a marlin spike prying my fingers apart not unlike a knotted rope, then everything faded back into the painless blackness.

The next thing I knew, I was lying in a hammock down in the sick berth. The familiar odor of the bilge, mixed with garlic and scotch, filled my nostrils. Familiar, because it was the scotch embedded essence of Doctor Hoffman's breath.

A tingling sensation had returned to my shoulder and arm and, along with it, an unceasing throb that became more intense with each second. When attempting to shift my position in the hammock, I discovered my arm had been bandaged in thick gauze. The deck beam above suddenly came down so close that it thumped against my padded arm and stayed there for a good many seconds before pulling away. The storm must have grown to something very powerful. I shouldn't be here, I thought. I am needed up on deck.

With a start, I recalled holding a man from falling into the sea. The scene appeared clouded and I vaguely recalled thinking that I should let go. "Dear God! Did I drop him?" I shouted.

"You most certainly did not, young Mason," said a familiar raspy voice from somewhere nearby.

"Who's there?" I asked.

"How does the arm do?"

Immediately following the voice, I heard the sound of a cork plunging into a bottle as Doctor Hoffman magically appeared beside me. I peered over the side of my hammock to see an old ladderback chair nailed to the deck planking beneath me where he had been sitting.

"Can you move your fingers?" he asked, taking hold of my bandaged arm while he manipulated the fingers in my hand.

Straightening my fingers, I made a fist and felt a dull ache throughout my bruised and stiffened forearm.

The wide bridged nose flattened and his tobacco stained teeth produced a smile as he said, "Well, that's more than I had hoped for, a good deal more."

The deck beam above me was now more to the side of my hammock and I could see that the doctor had shored himself up from the slanting deck by resting his foot against a deck support post.

"Should I not be on deck, sir?" I said. "My watch is out there in that storm and they need all the help they can get."

"I'll be the judge of that. Now see if you can straighten your arm."

"That should be no trouble at all, sir," I said, and proceeded to straighten my arm. I could only manage to straighten it half way before it seized up like a knotted rope and rendered a deep burning ache. "OWW!" I yelped, and quickly folded it back to its previous position.

"Well, that hurts like the blazes, don't it?" the doctor observed.

I winced with complete agreement.

"For the now," he said, "I wish you to keep it as it is, however, I should like to see you move your toes."

I did as he requested with little difficulty, however, when he had me bend my ankle, it felt like a rope had snapped in the back of my leg.

"That will do. Fortunately, you should suffer no permanent

effects from these wounds provided they don't putrefy. As for the ribs, you were extremely fortunate. Only two dozen stitches were required."

"Did he cut through?" I asked. I must know, for a punctured lung was always fatal.

"The ribs did their work as God had intended and protected your lungs. On the morrow I shall ask you to attempt straightening your arm again. And as for returning to your duty, put it out of your mind. You would be a liability to your crew in this storm." Placing his hand on my shoulder, he smiled and said, "And I should think that saving the captain's life is duty enough for one day."

"The captain? I saved the captain?" I said, quite surprised.

"You most certainly did. However, with a brain injury…"

"Brain injury?" I said. "Will he die?"

"Hard to say at this juncture. That driver block gave him a nasty blow to the back of the head and until he regains consciousness we shall not be sure of anything. In the meantime, I have him secured comfortably in his quarters." As he spoke, he turned a concerned eye towards his pale-faced assistant, Mr. Tims, who had just finished seeing to two other men with bandaged extremities.

Tims stumbled and coughed his way towards us, his frail frame almost ghostlike as he approached.

"Tims!" the doctor said. "I shall have to put you down soon if that cough persists."

Tims held onto the deck support beam while trying to catch his breath. His wheezing sounded not unlike tormented souls crying out from hell.

"I'll be all right, sir," he said, before another series of coughs overtook him. After a break, he said, "Just let me get my breath. Besides, there is no one else available to assist you."

The doctor frowned and said, "If that is what is keeping you on your feet, then let me assure you, I can find someone to fill in on a temporary basis until your strength returns."

Tims shook his drooping head sending sweat from his pointed jaw onto the deck. Turning to make his way back to his chair, he said between raspy coughs, "You need me."

After two days, I was allowed out of my hammock. With help, I managed to get to the deck and, once I had a firm footing, found that my leg, though quite tender, was able to take my full weight. As I looked about, I noticed with relief that the storm had abated, for the deck beneath me was no longer heeled hard over. A short time later, after I had gained my bearings, Griswald had sent a man down with a box of biscuits along with a tankard of hot tea. Sitting on a chest, I sipped and chewed with the rest of the injured.

Lewis had tried to kill me, I remembered. Now he was dead. I wondered how the crew had taken this. There would most certainly be questions. The captain had nearly been killed by Lewis' actions. Did they know what really happened? I decided it best to say nothing on it until asked.

During the previous day, there had been several new additions to our company as yards and cargo had shifted, crushing bones beneath them. During that time, I slept not a wink for I was continually awakened by agonizing moans and cries from men whose injuries made mine pale in comparison.

Burned into my mind had been the night's most disturbing event where I was part of a captive audience during the amputation of a man's leg just above his shattered ankle. Prior to this operation, the doctor had one of the man's mates pour a pint of uncut rum down his throat. After some minutes, the rum seemed to calm him. The doctor, however, then twisted a screwing device that clamped off his leg just above the knee to stem the flow of blood. As the pressure was applied, the man bit down upon a piece of leather, grinding his teeth into it. As the doctor took out a small knife, he quickly sliced away skin, tendon, and muscle above the mangled shins and foot while his mates held him down, he writhing and moaning in a voice that cut to the soul of us all. The flesh, now cut away, exposed two bones, one being the larger of the two, and the doctor picked up a saw. The grating of steel upon bone permeated the air while his mates turned their contorted faces away from the work. Within a few seconds, God was kind and granted the poor fellow unconsciousness. I gritted my teeth as I saw the doctor skillfully pull the excess skin over the freshly severed bone, tendons, and blood vessels before he quickly sutured it into a rounded stump.

"This should provide ample padding over his bones, giving him a fine stump. Fortunately, I was able to save the knee and, barring infection, your friend will, with the help of a proper wooden leg, live to walk again."

The man came to and, seeing what had been done to him, cried out for God to take him. His mates gave him another swallow of rum while the doctor bandaged the stump. Soon after, they laid him into a hammock. This was done while the ship was bucking and heeling heavily like a crazed horse, yet the doctor carried on as though he were working on a level table in a London hospital.

The following morning he woke me with cheerful words.

"Good news!" the doctor said, while descending the ladder into our stuffy quarters. "The captain has regained consciousness."

"Bravo!" we all chimed, as the news was a great relief to us all. To lose the captain would be terribly bad luck and we were most grateful to have him safe.

"How does he do, sir?" I asked.

"Well, he is resting and needs a good deal of sleep before we can expect his complete recovery. I did, however, request of the captain that you fill in as my interim assistant so that Mister Tims may have time to recover his strength. The night's work has taken its toll upon him and he shall not be of any use to me in that state," he said, using his bottle of scotch to point out Tims who lay wheezing in his sleep. "It's consumption, you know. He'll not be around for another voyage. I am going to miss him. He is both skillful assistant and friend."

"Are you certain, doctor? You really desire me to take his place?" I didn't relish the thought of working down in these stuffy quarters; for to do so would be like existing within the confines of a coffin all the while aching with every fiber to catch a breath fresh air.

The doctor appeared to be smitten by my response and, turning a shade of crimson, berated me, saying, "Oh, I am quite sure, young Mason. And if you don't cease with that scowl, I'm liable to believe you don't appreciate the good favor the captain has bestowed upon you for saving his life. Shall I tell him when next he regains consciousness that you refuse his kindness?"

Taken aback by this admonition, I was speechless and struggled to find my tongue.

The doctor, taking my silence to be pig-headed indifference, went on to berate me even further. "Shall I say, captain, sir, Seaman Mason says for you to bugger off, sir!"

If he must put it that way, I thought, I suppose it is set in stone. Squaring my shoulders, I put on my best smile and said, "Sir, I would be forever in the captain's debt for the honourable privilege of being your assistant."

CHAPTER SIXTEEN

"How do you like the sling?" Doctor Hoffman asked, once he had made a final adjustment.

"I like it just fine, doctor," I said, testing its support as I moved my arm back and forth. A good deal of swelling remained around my elbow while an ugly bruise ran down the entire length of my arm. My shoulder, however, gave me no discomfort, which truly amazed the doctor. Still, there was a good deal of injury done to the tendons around my elbow, making it impossible to straighten my arm.

The doctor said that, "Since there appears to be no sign of any severed tendons, your arm should heal with no permanent disability."

Then there was the cut along my ribs and another below my knee where Lewis had penetrated clear to the bone with his dirk. Although the stitches appeared healthy where the blade had sliced the thin layer of skin over my ribs, the doctor had not spoken of my leg which caused me to fear the worst. I decided I must know and, gathering my courage, asked, "What of my leg, doctor? As yet, I am unable to straighten it." I took in a deep breath, and whispered, "Have I been hobbled?"

Giving me a whimsical glance, he said, "I was just about to come to that. You were most fortunate in that the dirk went into the calf muscle, cutting with the grain, instead of across. Had it cut across... Well, you see, the muscle fibers are like the shrouds of the ship. If one were to cut across with an axe, you sever the cables and risk losing the mast. If one cuts down between the shrouds along their length, however, you merely sever the ratlines which are easily repaired while having done no injury to the shrouds." Turning, he went to his chair and sat down heavily and, with a troubled expression, reached behind the chair and withdrew a bottle of Aguardiente. Popping the cork, he took a heavy swallow, let out a sigh and said, "There is no sign of pus and I will remove the stitches next week. If you continue along this course, I have no doubt you shall regain full use of your leg. Still..." he broke off, seemingly searching for the right words. "Still, there is the most puzzling thing I have seen in all my years as a ship's surgeon."

Here it comes, I thought. There must be something he doesn't wish to tell me, something terribly wrong with me. "Pray tell, doctor, what is so puzzling?" I asked.

"Your wounds are healing perfectly and at a most uncommon rate," he said, his thick brows furrowing. "Your shoulder—I cannot fathom how your arm did not tear from the body. The captain is perhaps eighteen stone and you are no more than nine. Yet you held him, all the while the ship rising, falling, heeling, and for how long, no one is certain." Waving his hand in a gesture of resignation, he said, "Mind you, I am not a religious man, but it is most puzzling to me how you didn't drop him into the sea and lose the use of your arm in the process."

Once the storm had abated and the gun ports were able to be opened without shipping water, the doctor had ordered the men to set in place the canvas chutes which funneled fresh air into the sick berth. I must confess, had I spent another day without the fresh air, I believe we might all have succumbed, for the foul air had grown so diminished that the light in the glims were reduced.

Ready for my first day as a doctor's assistant, I took in deep breaths near the chute in an attempt to clear the fog from my head. I knew that when the weather turned foul, the gunports and hatchways would, again, be secured, causing the air in the spaces below deck to return to its former state. I hoped I would heal quickly and be returned to my watch station before that happened.

"Well, what do you think?" Hoffman asked, seeing my flaring nostrils.

"Nothing like clean fresh air, doctor," I said with a smile.

"Good. Now let us get to work."

The days passed in a completely different way, for I was no longer on the larboard watch, now having the same sleeping and working hours as a warrant officer. The work was, to say the least, never difficult, for there were no decks to holystone, no lines to haul upon, no rigging to scamper up at a second's notice; not that I was capable of doing so with my arm in a sling and my leg bent to a shape resembling that of a dog's hind leg.

As for the captain, his health improved daily, as did my arm and leg. He could be seen on deck for short periods of time wearing the heavy bandage wrapped about his head just above his ears. From time to time he would take hold of the taffrail or some officer's arm as he seemed to have lost his sea legs.

The doctor said his stitches were healing nicely and that he would soon remove all seventy five of them. I had not been given the opportunity to examine the wound myself, for the captain was the doctor's personally attended patient, but was informed that the spanker vang block had laid his scalp open from his occipital bone to his temple. The doctor said that before raking the scalp and tearing it back, the force of block had left a slight depression in the back of his skull.

While we were on the quarterdeck taking in the sun and crisp air, Doctor Hoffman took me aside and, looking about to assure no ears were close, said, "For the captain to recover after such a severe blow was testament of a very thick skull. And as for you, your shoulder not having been torn from the socket, as well as your elbow staying intact suggests you have an uncommonly strong skeleton." Then, with a chuckle, he said, "If you and the captain were the same person, you would be near upon invincible."

Captain Cole was not invincible however, and Lieutenant Bengs appeared a different man. The responsibility of running the ship had always belonged to Bengs as he was the ship's first officer, yet now he had temporarily placed that burden onto Lieutenant Newcomb while enjoying his newfound power as acting captain. Several of the men had experienced a good deal of this power and were now under my care in sick berth with their backsides flayed open. Bengs' generous use of the cat had, in short order, sent waves of hatred throughout the ship with no one escaping the effect. If not for the omnipresent knowledge of the captain's steady recovery, I had no doubt there would have been an attempt on Bengs' life. As it were, his continuing brutality severely tested the bonds of that restraint to the point that it had grown frayed and threadbare and I wondered if it would soon part.

By the end of my first week under the doctor's tutelage, I had gleaned a great deal of medical knowledge. My duties charged me with the care of all the men in sick berth. This was comprised of changing the dressings of the six injured men, and applying a poultice to the backs of the men who had been severely flogged. My other duties included serving the patients their three square meals and hauling out their chamber pots. In my spare time, I would peruse through the doctor's books. He kept such titles as *"The English Herbals"* by Nicholas Culpepper, or *"The English Physician Enlarged,"* which contained much advice upon the treatment of patients, as well as the treatment of various medicines and herbs. Then there was John Woodall's *"The Surgeon's Mate,"* a book the doctor cherished most of all along with his copy of James Lind's *"Treatise on the Scurvy,"* both of which led to much discussion wherein he informed me of his standing membership in the Royal Society. Seeing that this had impressed me a great deal, he went on to say that he was present at one of the society's meetings when the great explorer Captain James Cook read his paper on the subject of scurvy and how he had, with complete success, made use of Lind's and Woodall's recommendations. Fortunately, none of the crew had this dreaded malady due to the diet suggested by the doctor where every man was, each day, obliged to consume a portion of sauerkraut as well as a diluted portion of lime extract.

As for the patients in the sick berth, they all were mending quite well except for McNiel, the man who had had his lower leg amputated. His stump had attained the odor of dead flesh and the doctor feared he would have to amputate it at a higher elevation on his thigh. As the hours passed, however, his condition continued to deteriorate to such an extent that the doctor no longer thought he would survive such an operation. All that could be done was to keep him as comfortable as possible and dose him with an occasional tincture of laudanum. Laudanum seemed to me to be the most amazing drug in the doctor's medicine chest for it took the agonizing pain from a man in minutes. I asked the doctor if it might be best to risk amputating Hasting's upper leg. If we dosed him heavily with laudanum, perhaps the pain might not weaken his condition further. But he informed me that neither the leg nor the pain would be the thing that would kill him.

"His condition is so poor that his body will not recover," the doctor said. "The gangrene has already entered his blood and an amputation would only serve to bring his end at an earlier time. No, we must keep him as comfortable as possible and let him pass without any more aggravation from the likes of us."

Then there was Tims. His consumption treatment consisted of bleeding once a day where the doctor would lance a vein in his arm and I would hold a container with measurements etched in the side and let the doctor know when it had reached two ounces. Then a potion, of which I do not know the contents, was administered for a few days before beginning the diaphoretic called, "James' Powder." This kept him from sweating and the doctor informed me that it was used to strengthen his blood vessels that supplied the sweat glands in the skin. After the first week of this treatment, Tims showed signs of improvement whereupon the doctor discontinued the bleeding and diaphoretic, and assigned him to simple bed rest.

On Monday of my second week as doctor's assistant, Maxwell came down to visit McNiel whose condition was now known throughout the ship. Maxwell was saying his goodbye to McNiel just as the doctor had gone to see to the captain. Before Maxwell left the sick berth, he came to where I stood so that he might have a word with me. I served him a cup of tea while he sat in one of the pine chairs and I noticed that he was fidgeting with his shirtsleeve. I could see he had some distress which I attributed to McNiel's condition, they being close friends. Sitting in the chair opposite, I waited for him to speak.

At length, he seemed to be struggling to find the words before breaking the silence and asked, "How's that arm holdin' up?"

"Very fine," I said. "The doctor says it will be as good as new in a few more days and that I shall remove the sling on the morrow." I pulled back the cloth and showed him my bruise, which had now taken on a blackish-blue hue with a yellow ring around the edges. Maxwell eyed it with some interest, then, with a quick glance at the men sleeping in their hammocks, motioned for me to come closer.

"It was I who pried your fingers from the captain's coat, do ya know?"

I said nothing and he went on.

"I didn't think you would 'cause you didn't seem to have your wits about ya. Had to use a marlinspike, I did, yer fingers bein' so tight bent on holdin' him."

I leaned across the space between us and he put his mouth to my ear, saying, "There's trouble brewin'." Pausing, he looked around to see if any of the men had taken an interest before proceeding. "There's some what question how Lewis got overboard and how the captain got knocked on the head."

The hairs on my arm stiffened. "What do you mean?" I asked,

as a chill seeped into my entrails, reminiscent of the feeling I had had that dark day before they had taken me off to prison.

"Bengs is fillin' the captain's ears about maybe you cut that brace and sent Lewis to Davy Jones. That it was you what nearly got the captain killed."

"Why would he think that?" I said. "Everyone knows Lewis had it in for me."

Maxwell winced. "That's just it. The word is that ya took advantage of that fact to make yerself look innocent. At least that's what one of the boys in the mizzen crew overheard through the skylight."

"Does the captain believe this?"

"No one knows what the captain believes. But with Bengs pressin' him while his head ain't quite right, I wouldn't be surprised if ya wasn't charged… Or…" he pulled his hat off to wipe his brow.

"Or HANGED?" I finished his sentence, unable to keep my voice down.

"I'm sorry, lad. I just thought ya should know what might be in store for ya."

My skin crawled and, once again, I felt the noose of Tiburn Tree awaiting me. "I am innocent. He tried to kill me. Don't my wounds prove that?" I opened my shirt and pulled back the bandage to show the stitches where Lewis' dirk had cut my ribs to the bone.

Maxwell looked at my chest and shook his head. "Looks like the doctor did a good job of patchin' ya back together. Anyways, he's been pullin' fer ya. Tellin' the captain there ain't no such way you could have been the one what cut the vang. Well, yer gonna get outta this'n. No one else believes ya done it. Leastways, no one who will say it to my face." Maxwell glanced over at three of the men snoring in their hammock. "Those poor buggers ain't done nothin' to deserve the floggin' they got. Just bad luck they was in plain sight of Bengs when their hands slipped on a brace. He's a sick bastard, ya know! He was smilin' when the cat ripped their backs open."

Maxwell stood up and, giving me a pat on the back, showed a sympathetic smile before pulling his hat over his curly, red locks and stepping up the ladder.

For some time, I sat in the chair, frozen in thought and hadn't even noticed when the doctor returned.

"What's amiss, my young assistant?" Doctor Hoffman inquired, a look of concern in his wooly brows.

"Oh, it was simply good to see Maxwell again," I said, attempting to shrug off the old familiar feeling of doom.

"Well, it appears you will be working with your friend soon," he said, pointing to Mr. Tims who had been up all morning with much colour returning to his face.

"I suppose the captain will put you to work as soon as I inform him of Tims' returning health. It was most pleasurable to have you assist me young Mason," he said, offering his hand.

I took it and smiled, saying, "The pleasure was mine, sir. I have learned a great deal here. Perhaps someday you shall again require assistance."

"Well, if ever I do, you shall be the first I call upon," he said with a heartening smile.

The sun's heat stung our necks while we stood at attention. It was Thursday, noon, a time when the officers, by means of a device called a sextant, detect the sun at its zenith to determine our latitude and the beginning of a new day, a procedure called the "noon observation." The captain appeared on deck in uniform for the first time since the accident. Most of the men, myself included, couldn't resist glancing his way to reassure ourselves that he was back in charge. Life under Bengs had been a dog's life for most of them. There had been continuous starting with the ropes end, as well as five floggings in twice as many days. The ship's morale had dipped to its lowest during this time and if not for the captain's progress, round shot would have been rolling at the officer's feet long before this day.

It was in the afternoon watch that I was called to the captain's cabin. I stepped aft, my gait, now improved to a slight limp, though my knees trembled from apprehension of what lie ahead.

"Wait here till you are called for," commanded the marine sentry who stood watch at the captain's door.

I did as he said and stood silently for near on two bells before the door opened.

Tomkins stumbled out and his saliva-covered chin trembled while a rain of tears ran from his squinting eyes.

If I hadn't known better, I would have believed he had been kissing the gunners daughter. I couldn't help thinking, what in God's love did they do to you? I've been standing here all this time and didn't even hear his screams. You poor little blighter, I thought. But then, what do they have in store for me? Surely nothing as severe as that, no, they'll probably just hang me from the yardarm at sunset before feeding my corpse to the sharks.

"Enter!" commanded Captain Cole.

I stood motionless as waves of fear washed through me. I wanted to run but there is no such escape on a ship. Startled by the sentry slamming the butt of his musket into the deck, I stepped shakily through the door.

The familiar sweet odor of pipe tobacco hung in the air while the captain sat behind his intricately carved desk of seasoned mahogany. The bandage was now reduced to a long strip of one-inch white cotton tightly wrapped about his head. With his gaze intent upon the page of one of many ledgers before him, he placed the brown-stained ivory pipe to his lips and I wondered what words he would use to condemn me. Would they be similar to those used by the magistrate in my trial at Newgate? I wondered how a man could condemn one who saved his life, but then recalled that Lewis was one that would have done so with extreme pleasure. The captain couldn't be like Lewis, could he?

The sunlight streaming in through the gallery windows glanced off the gold buttons that ran in lines of three down his chest. Their significance was important and I recalled Harvey instructing me that the three rows of engraved fouled anchors signified a post captain of more than three years seniority. I had not seen the captain dress in this way unless there were some ceremony or order of business at hand, and I felt a glimmer of hope when I remembered that a sentencing was generally read aloud to the ship's company on Sunday. Perhaps this may only be an investigation. My hopes soon crumbled as I realized that such an investigation would be a mere formality prior to sentencing.

To my left was the first lieutenant who, also in full uniform, stood stiffly with his usual disapproving expression.

This is it; I am a dead man, I told myself, and flinched as the captain cut the air with his trumpeting baritone voice.

"Mason, do you know why I have asked you here?"

"Yes, I do, sir," I stammered, "and may I be candid, sir?" If I am to be hung, I thought, I shall not have another chance to state my case.

"Please do!" Bengs gestured with opened hands. The fact that Bengs had spoken out of turn visibly irritated the captain. Cole shot him a disapproving glance, after which, Bengs silently took a seat.

"I am innocent, sir," I pleaded. "I did not murder Lewis. It was he who tried to kill me. He cut me with…"

The captain broke in, "With the same knife he used to cut the spanker brace. Yes, we know this. Young Tomkins has, with some persuasion, come forward to tell us of Lewis' plan to do you in by way of the theft of Lieutenant Bengs' buttons." He paused to draw on the pipe and, as he continued, the smoke drifted out of his nose.

"Having failed at that, he vowed to kill you at the first opportunity, preferably aloft, and during a gale when most hands would be too occupied to have taken notice."

He blew out the last of the smoke from the side of his mouth in the direction of Bengs who, though feigning no notice of the insult, was betrayed by his indignant pursed lips.

"And he nearly pulled it off," continued Cole. "This morning Bartlow was caulking the deck seams that had loosened from the storm and, when he was betwixt the devil and the deep blue, he found Lewis' dirk stuck into the outboard side of the deck just beyond the taffrail. It must have slipped from his hand during his fall. The amazing thing is that in spite of the wind, rain, and heavy following seas, the dirk retained a stubborn patch of cloth beneath the hilt. This, at first inspection, appeared to be of no consequence; however, Maxwell noticed that upon that stitch of cloth was a portion of red embroidery. The letter 'M' was unmistakable as no one else on this ship saw fit to have their clothing stitched with identifiable letters," he leaned forward, "for most seamen understand that any theft cannot be taken further than the hammock netting. You, however, weren't a seaman when you allowed the purser to persuade you into having those letters sewn onto your clothing, were you?" Without waiting for my reply, and leaning back into his chair, a smile curled at the corner of his mouth as he said, "It would seem Mister Sawyer's, uh, persuasiveness has provided the means to clear you of a capital crime. You see, there can be no doubt the cloth was torn from your shirt, most probably when Lewis withdrew his dirk from your ribs. This irrefutable evidence has put us to questioning young Tomkins who disclosed Lewis' plot entire. Although he is complicit in Lewis' dealings, the fact that he did so under threat of death, and the fact that he is not near a man, much less a full grown boy, will weigh heavily in his favor when considering punishment."

A wave of intoxication swept over me. Once again, I had escaped the noose. Lewis' own knife had cleared me. Had it gone into the sea with him, there would always be doubt and I, most likely, would be following Lewis to Davy Jones while sewn into my hammock with a round shot at my feet and a stitch through my nose.

"Young Mason. I want to thank..." Captain Cole coughed, returned his gaze to the top of his desk, and shuffled some papers before his eyes met mine. "What you have shown in the days since you joined the Royal Navy has both surprised and impressed me. You learn quickly while, at the same time, behave as a gentleman. You must come from a good family for, although your first appearance aboard this ship told me otherwise, your kind of character does not spring from the gutter." He paused, waiting for a response but, seeing as I was at a loss for words, continued. "Therefore, in good conscience, I find it improper to allow you to remain as an ordinary seaman. It appears, of late, that we are one midshipman short of our full complement. I have decided to rectify that shortage." Pausing to let his words sink in, he gave Bengs a cold stare before continuing, "From this moment forward, and so long as you continue to deserve your station, you are to be addressed by your subordinates as 'sir', for I have promoted you to the rank of midshipman. Congratulations, Midshipman Mason," he said, rising to present his thick heavy hand, "and please accept my most sincere gratitude for saving my life."

—✈— EPILOGUE

Mister Sawyer, the purser, had delightedly sold me several midshipmen's uniforms which, after alterations, still hung about my frame with fabric to spare. Looking me over carefully, he shoved the two guineas I had paid him deep into the pocket of his bulging waistcoat and, with a jovial smile on his chubby jowl, said, "Never fear Mason, sir. You shall grow into them in no time at all—no time at all."

Standing near the bowsprit, I watched the seas cresting like points of obsidian beneath a setting sun while reflecting on my past.

I had traveled, in the course of a few years, from the despair of losing my beloved father, to a life of pure survival on the streets of London, to the prospect of dying a horrible death by the gallows of Tiburn Tree, to a filthy stowaway aboard this great ship – and finally, to becoming an honorable midshipman in her Majesty's Royal Navy. I had come from a place with no path and no hope to one of astounding legacy with a new life as a respected seaman.

The legacy my father and Mrs. St. Clair had bestowed upon me through the tragedy of his death felt undeniably powerful – but frightening as well. I felt drawn to explore the power of the Key; I felt sure that all of the events that brought me to this place, this time and in this moment were ordained and not powered by circumstance. I felt I had much to learn in the role of Keeper of the Key–now Keeper of the Mason Key.

Envisioning the Key with its ancient Egyptian writing, the tourmaline eye staring into my soul, and remembering that it resided within me, I wondered when I would be instructed upon the Second Principle. Would I ever fully understand them all? And if I did, what was I to do with that knowledge?

I gazed out over the endless watery expanse while the bow thundered as it thrust through the crests of heavy waves sending spray high into the rays of the sun. Following the rolling sea as it swept westward, I realized that this ship will soon be approaching the American Colonies and wondered what awaited me there.

While in New York, should I jump ship and begin a new life? Or should I take my chances and return to England as Midshipman John Mason?

With the thought of Mother, Lilly, Laura, and Pike I knew I would take my chances. And there was the unfinished business I had with Hendricks. I took in a deep breath and made a vow to be the last person he would see on this earth. Perhaps by then I will have grown a little taller, possibly even gaining a stone or two making it impossible for anyone to recognize me—perhaps not even Zack for I certainly could not afford to cross his path.

Optimistically, I reminded myself that London is the largest city in the world and avoiding the likes of him would not be an impossible thing. Still, after what I went through in Newgate, not to mention what Laura did to effect my escape, I durst chance returning any time soon. How I do miss them, I thought, and wondered what I could possibly do to assuage this ache that I shall carry until next we meet. My thoughts were interrupted when a call came from aloft, "On deck there! Six, make that seven sail, possibly more."

"Where away?" asked Lieutenant Bengs.

"Hull down, two points off the larboard bow!"

"Can you make out their rig?"

As I followed everyone's gaze, Captain Cole sprang onto the deck, and I could see Midshipman Tomkins in the topgallant cross trees with his glass trained on something beyond the eyes of anyone.

That is, anyone on deck, for it was well concealed beyond the curvature of the earth. Tomkins dropped the glass, allowing it to hang from a tether tied to his waistcoat and, cupping his hands around his mouth, called down, "Three are ship rigged. The others appear to be brigantines, sir."

"Can you make out their colours?" asked Bengs.

"FRENCH COLOURS, SIR!" Tomkins replied, with his maintop ear-piercing screech.

Within a few seconds, the drums were beating to colours and, running to my station, I felt prepared to face whatever the future may hold.

The End

Thank you for reading my book!

Dear Reader,

I hope you enjoyed *The Mason Key, Volume One*.

As an author, I love getting feedback. I would love to hear what your favorite part of the story was, and what you liked or disliked, please share your thoughts with me. You can write me at david@dfolz.com and visit me on the web at www.TheMasonKey.com.

Also, I'd like to ask a favor. If you are so inclined, I'd love a review of *The Mason Key* on Amazon and Goodreads. You, the reader, have the power to influence other readers to share your journey with a book you've read. In fact, most readers pick their next book because of a review or on the advice of a friend. So, please share! You can find all of my books on my author page here: http://bit.ly/DavidFolzAuthor.

Thank you so much for reading *The Mason Key, Volume One* and thanks for spending time with me and these amazing characters who adventured the high seas in the eighteenth century.

Best regards,

David Folz

GLOSSARY

aft. To the rear of the ship.

aloft. In the rigging above the quarterdeck, or any open deck.

alow. Below.

astern or abaft. Behind, or to the rear of the ship.

avast. Cease, stop.

boatswain, also bo'sun. A naval warrant officer in charge of the hull and all related equipment.

crosstrees. Two horizontal crosspieces of timber or metal supported by trestletrees at a masthead that spread the upper shrouds in order to support the mast.

fo'c'sle, or forecastle. (1) The forward part of the upper deck of a ship. (2) The crew's quarters usually in a ship's bow.

foreward. To or in the direction of the bow.

gunnel. Variant of gunwale; the upper edge of a ship's or boat's side.

larboard. The left side of the ship which is today known as the port side.

poop deck. A partial deck above a ship's main afterdeck.

quarter deck. (1) The stern area of a ship's upper deck. (2) A part of a deck on a naval vessel set aside by the captain for ceremonial and official use.

taffrail. (1) The upper part of the stern of a wooden ship. (2) A rail around the stern of a ship.

sheet. (1) A rope or chain that regulates the angle at which a sail is set in relation to the wind. (2) Plural or, sheets: the spaces at either end of an open boat not occupied by thwarts: foresheets and stern sheets together.

shrouds. Ropes leading usually in pairs, or multiples of pairs, from the ship's hull to the mastheads to give lateral support to the masts.

starboard. The right side of the ship.

stays. Ropes that support the masts from bow to stern.

stone. As referred to weight, one stone is equivalent to 14 pounds.

About the Author

An avid researcher, David Folz harbors a love of history with a preference for the eighteenth century. Having spent many years sailing, the author brings his experience and imagination to his stories.

Honing his writing skills through decades of study and research, Mr. Folz enjoys sharing his adventures with the reading public. He resides with his wife on the coast of Oregon.

Be sure to read these other books by David Folz

The Mason Key II
Aloft and Alow

Continuing in Volume II, John Mason struggles to grasp the Principles of the Mason Key. It's 1778, the American Revolution is raging, while in the Atlantic the British are in battle with the French. John Mason and his friend Schultz are stranded aboard the enemy French ship after it has been abandoned and are forced to sail the massive ship alone. Encountering a hurricane, the ship is destroyed upon a reef. Left to his own ingenuity, along with newly discovered Principles, young Mason struggles to survive on a deserted island in the Bahamas.

The Mason Key III
The Return

While working on a plantation, Mason is shanghaied aboard a slave ship bound for the west coast of Africa. Forced to work or die, Mason awaits the opportunity for escape. Mastering the Third and Fourth Principles of the Mason Key, Mason uses his newfound ability to escape his iron shackles and later, a volcanic eruption.